NEW STORIES
FROM THE SOUTH

The Year's Best, 1994

The editor is grateful to Lisa Poteet for her interest, her good taste, and her excellent organizational skills.

Edited by
Shannon Ravenel

NEW STORIES
FROM THE SOUTH

The Year's Best, 1994

Algonquin Books of Chapel Hill

Published by
Algonquin Books of Chapel Hill
Post Office Box 2225, Chapel Hill, North Carolina 27515-2225
a division of Workman Publishing Company, Inc.
708 Broadway, New York, New York 10003

ISSN 0897-9073
ISBN 1-56512-088-4

CONTENTS

PREFACE   VII

Barry Hannah, NICODEMUS BLUFF   I
From *Carolina Quarterly*

Melanie Sumner, MY OTHER LIFE   27
From *Story*

Robert Love Taylor, MY MOTHER'S SHOES   50
From *The Southern Review*

George Singleton, OUTLAW HEAD & TAIL   70
From *Playboy*

Nanci Kincaid, PRETENDING THE BED WAS A RAFT   84
From *Carolina Quarterly*

Frederick Barthelme, RETREAT   124
From *Epoch*

Robert Morgan, DARK CORNER   136
From *South Dakota Review*

Nancy Krusoe, LANDSCAPE AND DREAM   163
From *The Georgia Review*

Ethan Canin, THE PALACE THIEF   170
From *The Paris Review*

Leon Rooke, THE HEART MUST FROM ITS BREAKING   215
From *North Carolina Literary Review*

Reynolds Price, DEEDS OF LIGHT   223
From *TriQuarterly*

Kathleen Cushman, LUXURY   249
From *Ploughshares*

John Sayles, PEELING   264
From *The Atlantic Monthly*

Richard Bausch, AREN'T YOU HAPPY FOR ME?   279
From *Harper's Magazine*

Pamela Erbe, SWEET TOOTH   295
From *The Antioch Review*

Tony Earley, THE PROPHET FROM JUPITER   321
From *Harper's Magazine*

APPENDIX   341

PREVIOUS VOLUMES   349

PREFACE

That old woman has money, we know it, old withered dugs,
used to teach high school. They say she even taught me thirty
years ago but I'm not sure, I was mostly away on drugs.
                    —From "Nicodemus Bluff," by Barry Hannah

What would William Faulkner have thought of those opening lines of Barry Hannah's story set in Mississippi, a story
about a boy and his father hunting with his father's friends?

A lot has happened in America since Faulkner's young Quentin
Compson was asked to "tell about the South. What it's like there.
Tell what they do there." Faulkner's name is now synonymous with
Southern Literature, but since his death over thirty years ago, Mis-
sissippi and the rest of the South have undergone some changes.
What was once open landscape is dotted now with cinderblock
shopping centers housing Blockbuster Video, Radio Shack, Taco
Bell, Pizza Hut. Drugs are available to high schoolers. So are sub-
machine guns.

All of us, at one time or another, are nostalgic for a simpler, safer
time. Some days we wish for the five cent stamp rather than the
Fax machine, for stories told from the front porch swing rather

than from the CD-ROM. We'd like to think that somewhere in the American South quiet, set-apart life still exists. We'd like to believe that if we could just go deep enough into the South, we'd find a town where Eudora Welty's characters were still gossiping at the beauty parlor or a city where Peter Taylor's characters could still stave off scandal. We'd even be willing to settle for one of Flannery O'Connor's occasionally violent back roads.

But look what we're confronted with right on the first page of the first story in *New Stories from the South, 1994,* a story written from what is still known as the Deep South. In the very first line, the narrator guiltlessly admits he was on drugs in high school. Have mercy!? Couldn't Barry Hannah have just left that part out?

Not if he wanted to tell this particular narrator's own particular story, he couldn't. This Mississippi boy grew up in a Mississippi with drugs in its high schools. And Barry Hannah, having entrusted him with narrating the story, insists that he include everything that helps make its point. Still and all, "Nicodemus Bluff" is, at its heart, a story about a boy who wants to be proud of his father. Nothing new about that theme, Lord knows.

In another of the stories in this ninth annual edition of *New Stories from the South,* a character spending a weekend at an Alabama Gulf Coast convention motel links up her "little Toshiba with Compuserve for a quick scan of the AP and UPI wires" and finds "a piece about a woman who was out of work and who beheaded her three children while they slept, then told her neighbors she was offering them as a sacrifice for the Darlington 500, a stock car race. The woman's name was Lolita Portugesa." (From "Retreat," by Frederick Barthelme.)

Though Flannery O'Connor would have been momentarily unfamiliar with the technology that produced this story-inside-the-story, she would have applauded Barthelme's use of it to zero in on our age-old fascination with the urgency of violence.

I think she would also have liked "The woman's name was Lolita Portugesa." The job of fiction is to give the news names and faces— and souls.

Peter Taylor would immediately recognize the Assistant Head-master of St. Benedict's school in Virginia and the boys to whose education he has devoted his life, but perhaps neither Peter Taylor nor the Assistant Headmaster could have envisioned the living arrangements he makes at the end of his long unappreciated ser-vice to the school: "I found lodging in a splendid Victorian room-ing house run by a descendant of Nat Turner who joked, when I told her that I was a newly retired teacher, about how the house had always welcomed escaped slaves." (From "The Palace Thief," by Ethan Canin.)

In another story, a Tennessee belle working for the Peace Corps in Africa fantasizes about marrying her local beau: "Since Yousouf was the son of a man with three wives and twenty-one children, our engagement announcement would take up a full page of the *Stipple Star News*. Everyone would be horrified. . . . Two years ago at the Memphis airport, [Dad] had made me promise him that I would not come home with a Senegalese man." (From "My Other Life," by Melanie Sumner.)

In Tennessee Williams' day the idea that a Southern father might put his daughter on a plane to go alone to live in Africa would have seemed shocking, but Tennessee would not have been surprised by the fantasizing. Southern daughters—from Temple Drake in Faulkner's *Sanctuary* to Peyton Loftis in Styron's *Lie Down in Darkness*—have long dreamt of ways to shock their elders. It seems they still do. Even if the Sexual Revolution has made it a bit more of a challenge, that classic rebellious urge will find a way.

Popular culture has blurred the lines once so clearly drawn between races and classes. Tabloid TV has stirred our melting pot into froth. No topic is taboo today. But it is the writers, not the talk show hosts, who will take us deep into the regions inside those lines.

"Oh yeah?" you say. "And what makes Barry Hannah so differ-ent from Phil Donahue?" Hannah, Barthelme, Sumner, Canin, and the twelve other fine writers whose stories are gathered here this year are all after something beyond sensationalism, something having to do with human motivation, a vein that does not lie on the surface. Kafka called fiction "an ax for the frozen sea within."

It's clear that the great themes of literature are likely to hold for as long as human beings are around to write and read. It's the specifics from which those themes are built that change. The world we live in is evolving. And the South is not exempt from the evolution. If our writers have anything to tell us about our own condition, then the literary South of their stories must change to reflect the real South of their experience—the one that makes the South more than an abstract idea.

If William Faulkner and Flannery O'Connor and Tennessee Williams were young writers today, might they be writing about high schoolers' drug use, white girls sleeping with black boys, women attracted to violence, and African-Americans and white Americans joking together about slavery? You bet.

Shannon Ravenel
Chapel Hill, North Carolina
1994

PUBLISHER'S NOTE

The stories reprinted in *New Stories from the South: The Year's Best, 1994* were selected from American short stories published in magazines issued between January and December 1993. Shannon Ravenel annually consults a list of 95 nationally distributed American periodicals and makes her choices for this anthology based on criteria that include original publication first-serially in magazine form and publication as short stories. Direct submissions are not considered.

NEW STORIES
FROM THE SOUTH

The Year's Best, 1994

Barry Hannah

NICODEMUS BLUFF

(from *Carolina Quarterly*)

T hat old woman has money, we know it, old withered dugs, used to teach high school. They say she even taught me thirty years ago but I'm not sure, I was mostly away on drugs. One thing about my body or bloodflow or whatall, I'm twice as put away as anybody else on a drug, always have been. I declare that I stayed away from the world thirty years and more. So when I saw the old woman on her porch chair as we ran by—running out the drugs of three decades—I just saw a new crone, not somebody I'd ever known. She was sitting up there taking up space and money, the leaves of the tree limbs reaching over her head looking like money itself, green. Say she used to teach me. I wonder what.

They stood me up and walked me when I was on those 'ludes and reds. No man ever liked a 'lude or red better than this man. They walked me around the high school halls and set me in the benches and showed me food, I guess, in the cafeteria. It is amazing what I never knew, amazing. I accompanied people. I was a devoted accomplice, accompanier, associate, minion, stooge. The term *et al.* was made for me. But I can't remember how. We would be in church or jail. I would just look around and take stock of the ten or so feet of box—a cube, I guess—around me and see what was in it, my "space," yes really. My space ended at ten feet wide, deep and high. Couldn't tell you further what was out there. It could be bars or a stained glass picture of Saint John baptizing Jesus Christ in the Jordan River, boulders and olive trees hanging over the water.

What was going on I wanted to be away from I believe was my father and his friends years ago at the deer camp in Arkansas. Something happened when I was out there. My father died that next week but it's like not only is he not dead but he is hanging at the border—the bars, the church window—of my space, that ten-foot cube—bloody and broken-up and flattened in the nose, a black bruise on his cheekbone because of what happened to him with those others years ago down in the swamps.

We used to be better folks even though my father's people had nothing. My mother was a better sort, a secretary to a wealthy lawyer in town. There seemed to be hope of our rising in the community. It's vague how you get to be "somebody" but mainly it has to do with marrying the right woman, then they honor you. Acts of kindness or neighborliness do not really count. I have seen people do acts of kindness over and over and although people smile, looking at them in their yard and thanking them, "much obliged"—this circle of doing for folks and making them "much obliged" is funny, don't you think? the way payback must forever continue amongst world citizens, kind to kind—they'd not think the man of any esteem. What made esteem was not acts of kindness but money, clothes, car, house, posture, lawn. You knew where you belonged in that time, and we were on the edge of being respected "gentlefolk" of the town (not my term but Dr. Debord's, the preacher-friend and chairman of the sociology department at the Methodist college in town who helped me for a while. He wouldn't like my thoughts about the old crone as we ran by, the old crone with her nice lawn, expensive auto, elegant house). That old woman is like time and my dog, how awful. My dog had its whole lifetime in my youth. Time was tearing it to pieces. Once out of one of my early drug stupors I looked at it and it was suddenly dilapidated and ancient and I started crying. Said she was a looker and I had a crush on her. Tried to write stories to get her attention. Now look at her. I am looking at all my drug time, decrepit, sitting on the porch. My mother had an easy gracious manner and dressed well naturally although she was not of moneyed people. She was a person of "modest understated grace," Mr. Kervochian told me once, wanting me not to forget what a valuable woman she was, so I'd have something to get up in the morning for. I run around the block again and again, gasping "success, success."

Dr. Debord had certainly tried everything else. However, getting me to admit the story was tough and deep, the story about my father—Gomar, he was called—so as to get up and be about my work at the animal shelter; my father that week among those new acquaintances who were going to be his new and lasting crowd—up from the failed farmers, the beer-for-breakfast mechanics, loiterers, and petty-thieving personnel who were his people. Yay for him, some people were saying. To bring himself up into genteel society. I think most people approved of his rise. In the old days the whole county knew each other, don't doubt it, and you might have thought there was some god placed in an office with account books where he let out the word on the social worth of all citizens hereabouts, keeping tab on these as rose, fell, or simply trod down the rut that was left by the prior generations; the word went around and was known.

But at ten years old what did I know when my father and the rest of them were out at that lodge? I did not know my father had borrowed heavily from Mr. Pool and that was why we had a nice house, lawn, two cars, even a yard man who rode a riding mower, a Negro man named Whit who was nice to me. Whit cut himself chopping down a tree for us and I recall thinking that his blood might be bluer and was surprised. Why do people live here at all, I ask? They must know this is a filthy, wrong, haunted place. Even the trees that are left look wrong or wronged, beat-up. The red dirt is hopeless. The squirrels are thin and there is much—you can't get around it—suicide on the part of possums, coons, armadillos, and deer who tried to exist in the puny scratch but leap out on the highway. Also there are no stories of any merit to come out of this place. The only good woods are near the base of the little mountain. (Let me tell you something about all the drug pushers around here. They are no mystery to me. They are just country sorry, like my father's people. They aren't a new wave of punk. Country sorry.) Someone had a house and land and saved the woods at the west base of the little mountain (805 ft.). This person would shoot trespassers, hunters, and fishermen. (There was a deep black pond in the middle.) Nobody went in. The woods were saved. They were thick and dark with very high great oaks and ashes and wild magnolias, even bamboo, like nothing else around. Thicker, much, even than the woods over at the deer camp near the Mississippi River in Arkansas, with sloughs and irrigation ditches where the ducks come down too. Also you could catch winter crappie in the oxbow lakes if you could sit still in the cold. (Allow me to express myself about those woods near the mountain here. They were owned by a doctor who was an enormous dealer in drugs. Well I know.) In Arkansas it was sportsman's paradise. The only thing better I would see would be (later) the marijuana plantation at the state university where they grew it legal for government experimentation. I saw that once driving by with somebody when I was seventeen and almost came out of my cube of space to get them to stop the car. (No, I could never drive; didn't learn to drive until I was twenty and that is when I finished high school too. All of this delay, I believe, is because of what they did to my father.)

My father then had these acquaintances: a banker, an insurance man, a clothing store owner, a lawyer (employer of my mother), an owner of a small company that made oil pumps for aircraft engines, a medical doctor. Then there was Mr. Kervochian, a druggist, who turned out to be the kindest and the one who told me the whole story years later when he was dying of pancreatic cancer. My father—we had the lawn, the porch, the two cars, the nice fishing boat, the membership in the country club—I say again was lent heavily some money by three of these men. They told him it was a new kind of loan they were practicing with, a way to help really deserving men from the country who wanted to better themselves. It was agricultural rates interest, very low. It was "special" money on collateral of his personality and promise; and it entailed his being close by to aid these men at some business schemes; close by like at beck and call, said Mr. Kervochian. My father would get nice things immediately and pay it off so that he could enjoy the good life and pay along for it, not waiting until he was old like many men did, left only a few years to enjoy their station and bounty after a lifetime of work. They liked my mother and they thought my father was admirable the way he tried to sell real estate out in the country where the dead farms were. He knew them when they were dying and could be had.

He managed to get Mr. Pool and Mr. Hester a piece of land from a crazy man for almost nothing. The man went down to Whitfield, the asylum at Jackson. The land they used for turkey houses. That's where I came in: at age ten I went out there twice a day on my bicycle to feed and water the turkeys. I had a job, I was a little man. I was worthy of an invitation to the deer hunt. Everything was fitting together. My father had some prestige. He was arriving and I was well on the way to becoming a man of parts myself.

I can't remember why I was the only boy out at the deer camp in Arkansas. But I went along with my father, Gomar, and had my own gun, a little .410 single shot, for the delta squirrels, very fat, if I saw them, which I did but could not hit them much, at age ten. Something would happen when a live squirrel showed up in the bead at the end of the barrel. The squirrel would blur out and I'd snap the gun to the side, missing all of it. I think I embarrassed my father. A boy around here should be able to shoot at ten. The rest of them weren't hunting yet. They were in the lodge drinking and playing cards. I could hear the laughter getting louder and how it changed—louder and meaner, I guess—while I was out in those short stumps and wood chips on the edge of the forest. I remember seeing that cold oily looking water in a pool in one stump and felt odd because of the rotten smell. They didn't know why I was frowning and missing squirrels out there and had gone back in to laugh harder, drinking. I could smell the whiskey from where I was and liked it. It smelled like a hospital, where I was once to have a hernia repaired.

The large thing I didn't know was that my father owed all this money to the three men, and he was not repaying it on time. I thought there were just his new friends, having them in this sort of club at the lodge, which was as good as a house inside or better with polished knotty pine walls and deer heads and an entire bob-cat on a ledge. Also a joke stuffed squirrel with its head blown off, as I couldn't do out there smelling that rotten water, standing in the wet leaves in rubber boots made for a man, not my own, which I was saving for dry big hunting. I remember in December every-thing was wet and black. They said flash floods were around, water over the highway, and we were trapped in until the water went down. Then it began to get very cold. I went inside, without much to do. I came back outside with a box of white-head kitchen matches and started licking them on the head, striking them, and sailing them out so they made a trail like rockets, then hit and flamed up before the wet took care of them. I thought the future belonged to rockets—this had been said around—and I was very excited to get into the future. My father was providing a proud place for me to grow and play on our esteemed yard. One night I was watching television, an old movie with June Allyson. Her moist voice reached into me and I began crying I was so happy— she favored my mother some. But my father owed all this money, many years of money. It seemed the other two, Mr. Hester and Colonel Wren, weren't that anxious about it. But the banker, Mr. Pool, who owned the lodge, was a different kind.

The trouble was, Mr. Kervochian told me, as he died of pancre-atic cancer, that my father thought he had considerably reduced the debt by getting that piece of land from that insane man for almost nothing. This provided grounds for a prosperous turkey farm for the men. Twenty or more houses of turkeys it would be. My father supposed that he had done them a real turn, a very handy favor, and he felt easy about his lateness of payment. He assumed they had taken off several thousand dollars from it and were easy themselves. He thought things had been indicated more than "much obliged." It was riling somebody, though. Just the money—considerable—wasn't all of it. Something else very terrible was mixed in.

I didn't catch on to much except their voices grew louder and here and there a bad word came out. My father asked me to go back to my bunk in another room. There wasn't anything to do back there but read an R encyclopedia. I could read well. Almost nothing stopped me. My father could read but it was like he learned the wrong way. He took forever and the words seemed to fly off on him like spooked game. He held his finger on the page and ran it along like fastening down the sounds. My mother taught me and I could not see the trouble. I was always ahead of the teacher. I felt for my dad when I saw him reading. I knew this feeling wasn't right, but I wanted to hold his hand and read for him. It almost made me cry. Because it made me afraid, is what it did. He wasn't us.

The terrible thing mixed in it was that my dad was good at the game of chess and vain about it. He had no degree at all—I don't believe he had finished high school, really, unlike Mr. Pool, who had college and a law degree. He had never played Mr. Pool but he had whipped some other college men and he was apt to brag about it. He would even call himself "country trash," winking, when he boasted around the house, until Mother asked him to quit, please, gloating was not character. But Mother did not know that my father, when he played chess, became the personality of a woman, a lady of the court born in the eighteenth century (said Mr. Kervochian). The woman would "invest" Dad and he would win at chess with her character, not his own man's person at all. Mr. Kervochian took a long time explaining this. The chess game, as it went on, changed him more and more into a woman, a crafty woman. He began sitting there like a plain man, but at the end of the game he couldn't help it, the signs came out, his voice went up, and his arms and hands were set out in a sissy way. He was all female as the climax of his victory neared. He would rock back and forth nervously and sputter in little giggles, always pursing his lips. It wasn't something you wanted to look at and those he defeated didn't want to remember it. It unnerved them and made them feel eerie and nervous to have been privy to it, not to be talked about. I didn't know what was going on, with the noise out there in the great "den" of the lodge. Mr. Hester and Colonel Wren, the doctor (Dr. Harvard) and the oil pump company owner (Ralph Lovett), with Mr. Kervochian just leaning near them, drinking, were playing poker that night. Only two of them had gone out to hunt a little in the rain and vicious cold but come back. My father and Mr. Pool were at the other end playing chess very seriously. My father's feet became light, tapping on the floor as with princess slippers. All through the other quiet I heard them.

Mr. Kervochian, dying of cancer, told me it was not clear how my father's change came about or even where he learned to play chess, which was a surprise—his chessmanship—unto itself. He was not from chessly people. They were uneducated trash and sorry—even my grandmother Meemaw, a loud hypochondriac, a screamer—had failed on the farm and in town both and lived between them, looking both ways and hating both of what they saw. But Gomar, my dad, knew chess, maybe from one month in the army at the time of the Korean conflict, after which he came back unacceptable because of something in his shoulders (is what he said when I asked him once). My mother looked at the floor. She hated war and was glad he'd never been in one. But I wanted him to have been in the war. Mr. Kervochian believed somebody in the service taught him, but where he came in contact with the "woman" he does not precisely know. But early on he was playing chess with the circuit-church riding minister at the church near Meemaw's home. Some time somewhere the woman in him appeared. It was a crafty, clever, "treacherous" woman; a "scheming, snooty, snarling" woman, rougher than a man somehow in spitefulness. She knew the court and its movements and chess was a breeze for her. She'd take him over about mid-game or when things got tough. It would lurch into him, this creature, and nobody could beat him. He beat a college professor, a hippie who was a lifetime chess bum that lived at a bohemian café; a brilliant Negro from New Orleans; two other town men who thought they were really good. Something was wrong, terrible about it. He wasn't supposed to be that good.

He might have picked up the woman who inhabited him from somebody in the army, or from that preacher, whose religion had its strange parts, its "dark enthusiasms," Mr. Kervochian said, weakly speaking from his cancer. We don't know, but it led to that long rain of four days at the deer camp, the matter of the owed money, and Mr. Pool, the banker, who professed himself a superior, very superior chess player.

Voices were short but loud and I heard cursing from the "den" where the men were. They were drunk and angry about the rain. When I peeped out I saw the banker looking angrily into my father's face. My father's face was red, too. He saw me at the door and told me to go back in the room.

I said, Daddy, there's nothing to do. He brought our guns over to me and said, Clean them, without looking at me. Then he shut the door. It was only me, the R encyclopedia, and the guns with their oil kit. I went on reading at something, I think Rhode Island, which was known for potatoes. The doctor, Dr. Harvard, I could hear complaining and very concerned about the rain cutting us off, although we had plenty of food. I recall he wasn't drinking and was chubby with spectacles, like an owl, looking frightened, which wasn't right. I didn't like a doctor acting frightened about the weather. My father and Mr. Pool were in a trance over the board of pieces. Mr. Kervochian was drinking a lot, but he wasn't acting odd or loud. This I saw when I cracked the door and peeked again. Mr. Kervochian had a long darkish foreign face with heavy cheek whiskers. He stared out the window at the white cold rain like a philosopher, sad. He liked Big Band music—there was some he had brought on his tape machine—and I learned later that he wrote some poetry and might be a drug addict. He seemed to be a kind man, soft, and would talk with you (me), a kid, straight ahead. He never made jokes or bragged about killing game like the others, my father too. I remembered he had given me a box of polished hickory nuts. They were under the bed and I got them out and started playing with them.

The thing was, Mr. Pool did not believe any of my father's chess victories. Something was wrong, or fluked, he thought. It couldn't be that a man from my father's circumstances could come forth with much of a chess game, to Mr. Pool, who, with his law degree and bankership, hunting, golf, and chess, thought of himself as a "peer of the realm," Mr. Kervochian said later. "A Renaissance man, a Leonardo of the backwater." There was a creature in Mr. Pool, too, Mr. Kervochian said, hoarse and small because of his cancer. Mr. Pool owned the lodge and midway (*"media res,"* said Mr. Kervochian) in his affairs he began thinking to own people too. He had a "dormant serfdom" in his head. His eyes would grow big, his tongue would move around on his teeth, and he would start demanding things, "like an old czar." Thing was, there was nobody to "quell" him when he had these fits. He did pretty much "own" several people, and this was his delight. People were "much obliged" to him left and right. Then he would have a riot of remembering this. He would leer "like Rasputin leching on a maid-in-waiting." Mr. Kervochian knew history. Pool was "beside himself" as the term had it: "himself outside the confines of his own psyche." Like he was calling in all his money and the soul attached to it. I could hear they had been talking about money and Mr. Pool was talking over all the conversation. My father's point was that the purchase transfer from the old loony man was worth a great deal as a piece of work and should make some favorable patience about the loan on Mr. Pool's part. But I didn't know all that, what their voices were saying. I knew hardly anything except for the strange loudness of their voices with the whiskey in them which was an awful thing I'd never heard.

I knew my father wasn't used to drinking and did not do it well.

Once the last summer when he was coming up in the world, he had bought a bag and some clubs, some bright maroon over white saddle oxford golf shoes, a cart, and took me with him to try out the country club. I remember he had an all green outfit on. This was the club where those men who were his new group played; but this was a weekday, a workday, and he wanted to come out alone (only with me) because he'd never played. So he rolled his cart into the clubhouse and we sat in a place with a bar. He began ordering glasses of whiskey almost one after the other. I went around here and there in the chairs and came back and sat, with him looking straight at me, his ears getting red and his eyes narrowing. I didn't know what was happening but the man behind the bar made me think everything was all right, saying "sure" and "certainly" when Daddy wanted another glass of whiskey. But then he, my father, wouldn't answer me at all when I asked wasn't it time to play golf. I wanted to chase the balls and had several on the floor, playing.

"You know, really. You're not supposed to bring your bag in here," said the barman, kindly.

My father looked like he didn't know what the man was talking about. I pointed at the golf bag and said, He means your club bag, Daddy.

"What?" He looked at me, whining-like at me.

Then he drank another whole glass and something happened. I watched my father fall to the side off the chair, knock over the golf cart and bag, and hit the floor, with his golf hat falling off. I got up and saw he was really down, asleep, at the other end of his saddle oxfords maroon and white. He had passed out.

My mother came from the office of the lawyer to pick him up after the barman called. I sat in the chair and waited for him to wake up while other people came in, not helping, just shutting their eyes and looking away. I was awfully scared, crying some. It wasn't until a long time later I learned (from Mother) that he was afraid to start playing golf and embarrass himself, although there were just a few people at the course. He wasn't sure about the sticks or the count. My mother whispered this to me but I never understood why he'd go out there at all. My father, I say, had no whiskey problem, he just couldn't drink it very well and hardly ever did. My mother I don't think had any problems at all and she had high literacy and beauty.

At the deer camp the weather would not quit. I can't recall that kind of cold with that much rain. One or the other usually stops but on top of the roof the roar of water kept up and my window outside was laid on by a curtain of white, like frost alive. They were quiet in the "den" for a long, long time. I imagined they were all asleep from drinking the whiskey. I liked imagining that because what was out there was not nice, I'd seen it, even if they were only playing chess, a game I knew nothing about, but it looked expensive and serious, those pieces out there, made of marble, a mysterious thing I knew my father was very good at.

Mr. Kervochian knew the game and had watched Mr. Pool (Garrand, his first name) defeat many good ones around the town and in big cities. Mr. Pool wore a gray mustache and looked something like an old hefty soldier "of a Prussian sort," said Mr. Kervochian. You could picture him ordering people around. You could feel him staring at you, bossing. He'd hardly looked at me, though. I was not sure, again, why I was the only child out there.

It got late at night but the lights were still on out there. I had gone to sleep for a while, dreaming about those polished hickory nuts and squirrels up to your hips. When I peeped out I saw all the others asleep, but Garrand Pool and my father, Gomar, were staring at the board without a sound. They had quit drinking but were angry in the eyes and resolved on some mean victory, seemed to me. It was fearsome. The others in the chairs snoring, the rain outside. Nothing seemed right in the human world I knew. Then Mr. Pool began whispering something, more hissing maybe, as grown men I knew of never did. Pool was saying "Stop it, Stop that. Stop that, damn you!" This made my father's body rise up and he put his hand down and moved a piece. He stiffened to a proper upright posture with shoulders spread back, and then this light queer voice came from him. I didn't know, but it was the woman overcoming him. Even in his wrist—thinking back you could see a womanly draped thing. His fingers seemed to have become longer. Now this was another evil: Mr. Pool knew nothing about the woman and thought my father was mimicking him. He seemed to be getting even angrier and I shut the door. Let me tell you, it was odd but *not* like a nightmare. Another kind of dream maybe even more wicked and curious, a quality of dream where the world was changed and there was a haze to it, and you couldn't get out by opening your eyes. It made you weird and excited, my father's voice and posture and hands.

"Now hunt, old toad," he had said actually to Mr. Pool, jangling high-voiced like a woman in a church choir.

So I had to open the door a crack again.

Mr. Pool stood up and cursed him and told him something about "deadbeat white trash." But my father said something back shrilly and Mr. Pool I thought was coming out of his skin.

"Don't you mock me with that white trash homo voice! I won't stand for it!"

The other men woke up and wanted to know what was happening. Nobody had had any supper. They ate some crackers and cheese, commented on the steady rain, then went back to their rooms to sleep. My father and Mr. Pool had never halted the chess and paid no attention to anybody else. I was very sleepy and lost-feeling (in this big lodge, like something in a state park made for tourists). I lay there in the bunk for hours and heard the female voice very faintly and was sick in my stomach through the early morning hours. Ice was on the inside of the window. I could feel the cold gripping the wall and a gloomy voice started talking in the rain, waving back and forth. It wasn't any nightmare and it was very long, the cold wet dark woods talking to me, the woman's voice curling to the room under the doorjamb.

Another whole person was out there playing chess, somebody I never knew. A woman and I thought, somehow, sin, were in the lodge. Without a dream I was out of the regular world and had prickly sparking feelings like they had put you in a tub of ice and then run you through a wind tunnel.

At daybreak they were still at the game. Garrand Pool had started drinking again. He was up looking out a kitchen window and my father was leaned over studying the board, cooing and chirping. Mr. Pool was going to say something, turning around, but then he saw me in the doorway and stopped, coughing. When my father turned in the chair, I didn't recognize his face. It was longer and his mouth was bigger. His eyes were lost behind his nose. I was very glad he didn't say anything to me. He hurled back then as if my eyes hurt him. I shut the door again. Soon there was a knock on the door. I felt cold and withered.

But it was Mr. Kervochian. He told me to dress up, it was cold out, had quit raining, and he was going to take me out, bring my gun. In a few minutes the two of us walked by Mr. Pool and Daddy, frozen at the board, not looking up. Mr. Kervochian brought me some breakfast out on the porch—some coffee (my first), a banana, and some jerky. It was hurtfully cold while we sat there on the step. I could smell whiskey on Mr. Kervochian, but he had showered and combed his hair and had on fresh clothes. My boots were new and I liked them, bright brown with brass eyelets. I felt manly. I think Mr. Kervochian was having whiskey in his coffee.

"Let's go about our way and see what we can see, little Harris," he said.

"Don't you want your gun?" I asked him.

"No. Your big shooter's all we need."

I picked up the .410 single, which was heavy. He told me how to carry it safely. We walked a long time into the muddy woods, down truck tracks and then into deep slimy leaves with brown vines eye-high. I tripped once, went down gun and all with shells scattered out of my coat pocket. Mr. Kervochian didn't say anything but "That happens." We went on very deep in there, toward the river, I guess. How could cobwebs have lived through that rain? They were in my face. Mr. Kervochian, high up there with his Thermos, could float on the leaves and go along with no danger, but I was all webby. He began talking, just a slight muddiness in his voice because of the drink.

"He used to have a colored man out here with us, like successful Southern white men have at a deer camp. A happy coon, laughing and grinning, step and fetch it. Named Nicodemus, you know. Factotum luxury-maker. Owing so much to Pool Abe Lincoln's proclamation didn't even touch him. Measureless debt of generations. Even his pa owed Pool when he died."

"Mr. Kervochian, what's happening with my daddy and Mr. Pool back in the lodge?"

"Old Pool's calling in his debts. He always does, especially with some whiskey in him. He's that kind, perfect for a banker, gives so gladly and free, then when you don't know when, angry about the deal and set on revenge. Gives and then hates it. One of those kind that despises the borrower come any legal time to collect."

"Are they playing for money? Is that why they're so mad?"

"They could be, a lot of money if I heard right, whatall through their whispering. I don't know for sure. It's a private thing and you can be sure Pool's not going to let it go."

"It's like nobody else's in the lodge."

"Let's hunt. Tell you what: there's got to be big game down by the river."

We walked on and on. Cold and tired, stitch in the side, sleepy, was I.

We were on a little bluff and then there was just air. He caught me before I walked out into the Mississippi River. It was like a sea and I'd almost gone asleep into it, that deep muddy running water. "Watch ho, son!" he said. Then I was pulled back, watching our home state across the big water.

"You've got to watch it around here. Something's in that bluff under us. It's haunted here. This would be a very bad place to fall off."

The river was huge like a sea and angry, waves of water running. "Why is it haunted?"

"Nicodemus is under the bluff, son."

"That colored man? Why?"

"Old Pool and Colonel Wren."

"Are you drunk now, Mr. Kervochian?"

"Yes, son, I am."

"Please don't scare me."

"I'm sorry. Pay no attention to me. I can get sober in just three minutes, though, boy."

We walked back toward the lodge very slowly, the Nicodemus place behind me and the chess game going on, I guessed, ahead. We saw two squirrels, but again, I missed them. I didn't care. Mr. Kervochian said I was all right, he wasn't much of a hunter either.

"You know, all under our feet are frozen snakes, moccasins and rattlers, sleeping. All these holes in the ground around us. Snakes are cold-blooded and they freeze up asleep in the cold winter."

I didn't like to think of that at all.

Then it began raining all of a sudden, very hard, as if it had just yawned awhile to come back where it was. We were already stepping around ditches full of running water.

"Little Harris, there is a certain kind of woman," he all at once said, for what? "a woman with her blond hair pulled back straight from her forehead, a high and winsome forehead, that has forever been in fashion and lovely, through the ages. And that is your mother. Like basic black. Always in fashion. Blond against basic black and the exquisite forehead, for centuries."

I said nothing. We stopped and saw through the forest where Mr. Hester and Colonel Wren went across a cut with their guns, out trying to hunt but now caught by the rain, heading back to the lodge. We didn't say anything to them, like we were animals watching them.

"She used to come in the drugstore for her headaches. A woman like that in this town, I predicted, would always have some kind of trouble. That nice natural carriage, big trusting gray eyes."

"It's raining hard, Mr. Kervochian."

When we at last returned to the lodge my eyes were hanging

down out of their holes I was so tired. There were empty plates on the bar of the kitchen and nobody in the chess seats, just empty glasses and cups on the table. Dr. Harvard said they had left off the game and finally gone to bed, thank God. He peered at the rain past us beyond the doorway and commenced fretting, almost whining about the weather and the thunder and when were we ever going to get out of here, the way the roads were flooded over. There was no telephone, and so on. To see a grown medical doctor going on like this, well, was amiss. It changed me uglily. I went right on to bed and was out a long time.

When I woke it was late into the day and going out I saw Mr. Pool and my father were sitting there again, at it after their nap. They looked neither left nor right. My father suddenly gave a yelp, shrill, and I thought Garrand Pool had done something to him. But he was only making a move with a chess piece that must have been a good and mean one, because Mr. Pool cursed and drank half a glass of whiskey.

Mr. Kervochian took his place at the window with a new glass. He looked out into the weather as if he could see a number of people, all making him melancholy. Colonel Wren and Mr. Hester were all wet. They threw more logs on the fire and got it really blazing. They talked about more poker. Nobody knew quite what to do with all their big grownup bodies and eyes and ears trapped in by the rain these days. Dr. Harvard nagged himself asleep again. The insurance man, Mr. Ott, came tumbling in the door holding his hand. He had cut it on an ax out there chopping wood. The blood was all over it and when he put his hand in the sink it dripped down in splotches around the drain. They woke up Dr. Harvard and he was in the kitchen with Mr. Ott a long time. Then he went out in the rain to get his bag. Mr. Ott needed stitches. I was fascinated by this, sewing up a man. Dr. Harvard worked over Mr. Ott for a long time. Every now and then Mr. Ott would cry out, but in a man's way, just a deep *uff*! I looked over at my father and Mr. Pool. They had never even looked up during the whole hour.

Then Colonel Wren said he was going to have something, damn it all, and went outside with his gun, where in late evening it was just sprinkling rain. Everybody had read all the magazines. I found an old Reader's Digest Condensed Books and went back to read something by Somerset Maugham.

It put me to sleep although I liked the story. I guess it was after midnight when I heard them making more sound than usual out there. I went out in my pajamas. The men at the poker table were high on beer, maybe, but they were very concerned about Colonel Wren. It was raining, thundering and lightning, and he hadn't returned. One of them called him a crazy Davy Crockett kind of fool. Mr. Kervochian, sipping at the fireplace, put in,

"Closer to it, Kaiser Wilhelm the Second. Shot ten thousand stags, most of them near-tame. Had a feeble arm he was trying to make up for."

Then who comes in all bloody and drenched, with a knife in one hand and a spotlight in the other, but Colonel Wren. He was tracking mud in and shouting.

"There's breakfast out on the hook, by God!"

We went to the door past Mr. Pool and my father, frozen there, and saw a cleaned deer carcass hanging on the board between two trees. It showed up sparkling in the spotlight beam in all the rain.

"That's just a little doe, isn't it?" said Mr. Kervochian.

"That's all the woods gave up, help of this spotlight," said Colonel Wren, very loudly. "It'll eat fine. Come that liver and eggs in the morning, partners, we'll have an attitude change here!"

I won't say any more that my father and Mr. Pool paid no attention to any of this, and didn't do anything but play and take little naps for the next two days straight.

After breakfast around eleven that day, I drove out with Mr. Kervochian and Dr. Harvard to check the roads. We looked out of the truck cab and saw wide water much bigger than it used to be, the current of the creek rushing along limbs and bushes. It was frightening, not a hint of the road. Dr. Harvard was white when I looked at him. Later Mr. Kervochian explained that every man has a deathly fear and that Harvard's just happened to be water.

There was more poker and Big Band music on Mr. Kervochian's tape player, now and then a piece of radio music or weather announcement. But the next two days they argued mainly about Kilarney Island. Colonel Wren said he knew the deer were all gathered there from all the flooding. And that there was an old boat, they could go out in the Mississippi and shoot all the deer they wanted. The rain shouldn't stop them. This wasn't a god damned retirement lodge, they were all hung over and bitchy from cabin fever. He wanted to start the expedition.

"Our old boat should be right under Nicodemus Bluff," he said. There would be nothing to rowing out there.

I looked over at Mr. Kervochian. The others were arguing about whether that old boat was any good anymore, the river would be raging, it was stupid and dangerous. Mr. Kervochian, looking with meaning at me, said that was hardly any hunting at all. The deer on that island, which was only fifty yards square, would just be standing around and it would be nothing but a slaughter.

"You couldn't shoot your own foot anyway, Cavort-shun," said Colonel Wren meanly. "You're an old thought-fucked man." Then Wren looked down at me. "Sorry," he said.

But early the next morning we were all ready to get out of the place. Except for you know who, at it, in another world. Mr. Pool suddenly won a game, but he just got tight-lipped and red in the face to celebrate. I didn't want to look at my father's face. When Mr. Pool said "Checkmate, Gomar!" it sounded like a foreign name in the house.

I went along with them, taking my gun. Mr. Kervochian took a gun and his Thermos. The rain was very light now in the early morning. The plan was, when they got to the island, Colonel Wren was going to scare a deer off the island just for me. It couldn't swim anywhere but almost right to me on the shore and I could blow it down. I wanted to do this. A deer was larger than the squirrels and I wasn't likely to miss. So there I was at ten all bloody in my thoughts, almost crazy from staying in that lodge around that chess tournament that who knows when it would end, both of them looking sick when I could stand to look at them.

We tracked that long way out to the bluff. They went down and found the boat and set out with the paddles, three of them. Mr. Kervochian stayed with me. He seemed to either care for me or wanted a level place to drink. With all these people the bluff didn't seem that fearsome, so I asked him what about Nicodemus, what happened?

"You can't tell this around, little Harris."

"I wouldn't."

We watched them flapping and plowing the water, heading left and north to the island, just a hump out there a half mile away.

"Looking at it several ways, it's still a wretched thing. The man was full of cancer. Owed Pool a lifetime's money. Couldn't afford a hospital. He asked Pool to shoot him and so they did. I don't know which one."

"He'd been with them—"

"His whole life. You could blame Pool for the cancer too. The way he gave, then hounded. Nicodemus, that man, still, wanted 'to keep it in the family.'"

They were hollering now out in the tan water, paddles up in the air. Something was wrong with the boat. They turned it around and headed back in. You could see the boat was getting lower in the water. The going was very slow and there was a great deal of grief shouted out. They must've been up to their knees. But my sense of humor was not attuned correctly. I heard Mr. Kervochian laughing. The river to me, though, looked like the worst fiercest place to drown. They came back under the bluff, their guns underwater and their throats stuffed with rage.

Then of course the rain came on, half-strong but mocking, and you could feel the sleet in it. The wet men said almost nothing flapping back through the woods. It took forever.

There was a shout ahead, a cackling. Down the cut I could see some motion in those stumps in the edge of the lodge clearing.

The cackling and now a yipping called at us through the last yards, a stand of walnuts where on the ground you crunched the ball husks of the nuts with your boots.

Mr. Pool was beating my father on the neck with a pistol. It was a long gun. He kept whacking it down. But my father, holding his hands over his head and trying to dodge, kept cackling and yipping. Thing was, he was laughing, down on his knees, fingers on the top of his head, kneewalking and sloshing through the pools. It was there where the water lay rotten-smelling in the tops of the stumps, putrid and deep back in your nostrils.

"It's all mine, free and clear. I won it! I won it!" my father was shrieking, in that woman's voice.

He couldn't know we were standing all around him. He was shrieking at the ground. Mr. Pool didn't know we were there either. He hit my father, Gomar, again. The gun made an awful fleshy thunk on him.

"You trash scoundrel. Stop it, stop it!"

Then Mr. Pool drew around and saw us all, then me especially. He hauled my father around facing me, on his knees. Garrand Pool was a big man and my father had gone all limp. His face was cut, his nose was smashed down. He looked horrible, the rain all over his face, and his face long, his mouth hung down gaping like frozen in a holler.

"Show him. Talk for your son. Let him see who you are."

I went up close to stop Mr. Pool. I was right in front of my father. He came up with his face, and you could tell he didn't want to, but couldn't help it. He spilled out in that cracking cackling female voice.

"I won! I won!"

Then Mr. Pool just thrust him off and he fell on his face out there in that stinking water.

What Garrand Pool had done seemed awful, but my father almost cancelled it out. Nobody could make a direction toward either one. I know how they felt.

The next morning we left. Dr. Harvard was terrified, but the water had receded some and the tall trucks whipped right out through it and to the highway.

He couldn't even look at me for days when we got home. He was all bandaged up and sore. I never saw my father full in the face again. His face would start to turn my way, then he'd shake it back forward.

Nobody, I heard from Mother, ever bothered us about payments of any sort ever again while she was a widow. We had the house, the nice lawn, the two cars, a standing membership in the country club, which I only used to get loaded at and fall in the pool over and over again, swimming underwater long distances full of narcotics until my wrungout lungs drove me to the surface.

My father never got it right at the country club either, you see. The next week after the deer lodge he was walking at twilight down the road next to the golf course. The driver of the car says he swerved out of a sudden right into the nose of his car. They didn't find any alcohol in his blood, and none of it made much sense unless you had seen his eyes trying to call back that terrible woman's voice, pleading right at me.

The extra money my mother had, her legal secretary's salary free and clear, was in a way my downfall. She did not know how not to spoil me, and I always had plenty of money, more money than anybody. And Mr. Kervochian felt for me deeply, truly, I will never blame him. He was of that certain druggist's habit of thought that drugs are made to help people through hurtful times. You wouldn't call him a pusher because he meant only the kindly thing, he saw I was numbed, shocked and injured, so he provided plenty of medicine for me. He gave some to my mother too. She wouldn't take hers. So I got hers and took it. I went back and he was always a cheerful giver.

Later, he even came down to the jail and brought me out after I'd be taken in, accompanying somebody, some group, somehow an accomplice, just lugging there and near keeling over in that racing little sleep I loved. Never did I fight or even complain much. My mother never remarried. Her looks, her high brightness and carriage, you would have thought she could have a number of prominent handsome men, but she was a woman, I found out— maybe there are a few of them—who don't want but just the one marriage. They are quite all right going along alone. I was shocked, I believe when I was eighteen or thereabouts, only slightly Nembied in the kitchen, when she told me she actually had loved my father very much. Then I was confused even a bit more when she said,

"Your father was a good man, Harris."

"He *was?*"

This confused me, as I say. I'd hated him for being on his knees with that voice at the lodge, I'd hated him for being killed, and I was angry at him through his brother, his own country trash brother, when I saw him at Dad's funeral in a longsleeved black silky shirt with a gold chain on his chest. His own brother in not even a suit.

Soon I needed some more drugs and went by Kervochian's.

"My mother said my father was a good man. Is that how you saw him, Gomar Greeves?"

" Gomar? . . . Well, Harris. Frankly, I just don't know. I hadn't known him that well. But he was probably a good man."

Later, but before he got sick, Mr. Kervochian, sharing a 'lude with me, began trying to have a theory, like so: "This state is very proud of its men's men. Its football-playing, tough rough, whiskey-drinking men. But I tell you, you calculate those boys at the Methodist college who come by the store here. At least *half* of them are what you call epicene—leaning toward the womanly too. The new Southern man is about half girl in many cases, Harris. Now that means their mothers raised them. Their fathers didn't get into it at all. So these men, maybe Gomar was a country ver- sion, the woman came—"

"I don't want to hear that, any of that." I was thinking of that awful Meemaw.

"But it was—I watched and heard closely, closely—a brilliant courtly woman invested him, a spirit—"

I just walked off from him.

Of course I returned for drugs. He told me two things about Mr. Pool and one about Colonel Wren, but I hate to repeat them because here my testimony gets pushy toward life's revenge, but I'll say the real fact is, Kervochian didn't have to tell me, I saw Pool plain enough around town. The man began losing his face. It just fell down and he got gruesomer and gruesomer and at last just almost unbearably ugly. He went and had galvanized electric facial therapy—$500—at the beauticians, but nothing would save him. The last time I saw him in a car windshield he was driving with nought but two deep eyeholes hanging on to a slab of red wrinkled tissue. He had got strange too. He had women out to the deer lodge. His wife found out about it and went over and burned it down. Then Colonel Wren, whom I never saw again, did a thing that got him "roundly mocked," said Mr. Kervochian. Wren was a veteran of Wake Island, where the U.S. soldiers had bravely held off a horde of Japanese before they were beaten down, the survivors going to a prison in China until the end of the war. Wren wrote a long article for an American history magazine, telling the true story, in which he figured modestly and with "much self-deprecation." Then in the next issue in the letter section of that magazine there was a long letter from a man who was a private at Wake with the others. He went on to say how modest the then Captain Wren was, too modest. He had exposed himself to danger over and over, carrying wounded in one arm and firing his .45 with the other, etc. The letter was signed Pvt. Martin Lewis, Portland, Oregon. All was fine until somebody found out Wren had written the letter himself.

"In his seventies, old Wren. Pathetic," smacked Mr. Kervochian.

None of these happenings raised my spirits and I am putting them in only in memory of Mr. Kervochian, who died such a long painful death, but had explained nearly the whole town to me before he passed on.

When we lap that old woman's house and see her sitting there, on her porch, grand car to the side, safe and nestled in, blasted dry with age, I still say over and over "success, success" to my running buddy. Forever on—maybe I'll get over it—I hate a good house, a lawn, the right trees, I despise that smart gloating Mercedes in the drive, all of it. Early on, I moved out of our house, way back there, thirteen or fifteen or something like that. I believe I moved into a shack, maybe even I lived once in a chicken shack. I have missed a great deal, but as the drugs run out with each kick and step, I am beginning to see the crone, once my teacher, go back in time. My legs are pushing her back to a smoother face, a standing position, an elegant stride, a happy smile, instructing the young cheerfully and with great love.

Now there is something for tomorrow. What are women like? What is time like? Most people, you might notice, walk around as if they are needed somewhere, like the animals out at the shelter need me. I want to look into this.

Barry Hannah is a writer-in-residence at the University of Mississippi in Oxford. The Mississippi Institute of Arts and Letters recently awarded him their 1994 fiction prize for his short story collection, *Bats Out of Hell*. In past years he has been likewise honored by the editors of *Esquire* and The American Academy of Arts and Letters. He enjoys teaching, fishing, tennis, and his splendid friends in his small town.

Quite simply it's always a voice inside that starts my stories, and when the voice feels finished, the story is over. There are plenty of thoughts and "concepts" running about in my head, to be sure, but they are nothing until the voice starts. I couldn't shake this hopeful, very careful voice of a man declaring himself after a long life on drugs, caught between age ten and age forty. As for the father and his humiliation, I have noticed throughout my life that it is not uncommon for athletes or intellectuals to change personalities entirely under the severe stress of highstakes games. Witness, for instance, the psychosis of John McEnroe—the helpless squalling of a mean brat. I do not see why a certain kind of man might not even change sex during the riot of math in the head required by chess. When you are tenuous in all things, as is the father, something's got to give.

Melanie Sumner

MY OTHER LIFE

(from *Story*)

In Africa, I often imagined that my parents were dead. Although my mother sent me long letters and my father wrote on the backs of her pages, signing his name beside a martian face that he colored in with his highlighter, Jesse Ray and Dean had receded so far back into my mind that I pictured them as midgets. They had the bluish white skin of zombies, and like the people in my dreams, they spoke with their mouths closed. When I pretended they were dead, I got drunk and cried for hours. Then, lying on the cool black-and-white tiles of my living room floor with the batiks and wooden masks spinning slowly around me, I fantasized about my wedding with Yousouf Ibrahima Diop.

We would be married at the First Baptist Church in Stipple, Tennessee. Since Yousouf was the son of a man with three wives and twenty-one children, our engagement announcement would take up a full page of the *Stipple Star News*. Everyone would be horrified. They would flock to the wedding and crane their necks to see Darren Parkman say, "I do," and kiss a man as black as Satan.

His beauty would outrage them. He was slender, long-limbed, and high-gloss black all over except for his palms and the soles of his feet, which were pink. His lips were a deeper pink, cut into a wet, exquisite curve. He had a straight nose, flaring delicately at the nostrils, and enormous eyes so thickly lashed that they appeared to be lined with kohl. I pictured him walking down the aisle—smooth, catlike—and hoped someone would faint.

Even in my wildest moments, I could not imagine my parents at this ceremony. Two years ago at the Memphis airport, Dean had made me promise him that I would not come home with a Senegalese man.

"I haven't asked you for many things in your life," he said, "but promise me this. Promise your Dad that you won't marry a black man."

"Peace Corps volunteers aren't allowed to fraternize with the natives," I said, but he looked all the way into me with those blue eyes, and I promised.

I don't remember how I met Yousouf, but when I realized that I loved him, I stopped answering my door. He came to my apartment at different times of the day and night, trying to catch me at home. I always waited until I heard his footsteps growing faint on the stairs before I bent down to pick up his note. Then one day I opened the door. It had never been locked.

Although he kept a room on the outskirts of Dakar, where rent was cheaper, Yousouf spent most of his time at my apartment. I made it clear to him that I would never give him a key, and it took him three months to get one off of me. After a year, we began to talk about marriage.

"The reason I won't marry you," I told him, "is that I would hate your second wife." He was sitting on a Moroccan cushion, one skinny leg crossed over the other one, clipping his toenails into the palm of his hand. He was naked except for a pair of black bikini briefs and the string of leather talismans he wore around his waist.

"*Mais, non,*" he said, lifting his head so that I could see the strong, clean line of his jaw. "*Quelle deuxième femme?*" He flashed his white teeth and assured me that it was entirely too expensive to keep more than one wife on a banker's salary in Dakar.

Once I showed him a newspaper photo of the Ku Klux Klan marching down Main Street in Stipple. "*Bilaay!*" he exclaimed in Wolof. "*Xoolal góór-ni!*" I leaned over his shoulder to look at the

men. Their white robes and pointed hoods resembled the cos-
tumes that nine-year-old Senegalese boys wore after their circum-
cisions, when they paraded through the streets. "Will these men
kill me?" asked Yousouf. "Will they come to our wedding and
shoot me with pistols like the American cowboys?" He rolled his
eyes to the ceiling, pretending to be afraid, and then wrapped his
sinewy arms around me and buried his head in my neck. "But my
Boy will save me," he said in my ear. "My *Boy* will say, I love one
African man. Let him live!" He kissed me on the ear and whispered, *"N'est-ce pas?"*

Then one day I received a letter from Jesse Ray informing me
that she and Dean were coming to Dakar to spend Christmas with
me. Enclosed with this letter was a package of letters written by
ten-year-old girls in the First Baptist Church, commending me for
my work as a missionary in Africa.

I read the letters on my windowsill, with one leg dangling over
the side of the building, and a fifth of Four Roses bourbon beside
me. In the parking lot, seven stories down, the guardian turned his
wrinkled face up and squinted. To Muslims, bare legs are more
provocative than bare breasts. I waved and poured more bourbon
into my Coke. I unfolded the letter again and imagined that it
read:

"It is with great sadness that I inform you that your mother and
father were not among the survivors of this plane crash. . . ."

I had not told my parents that I had a Senegalese lover, and I
had not told Yousouf that I had parents. *"Merde!"* I said to the
empty room. Then I staggered to my feet, took a mask off the wall,
and fitted it over my face. I stood in front of the mirror and prac-
ticed explaining to Yousouf, in French, the sudden appearance of
a woman and a man I called Mom and Dad.

The right moment to give this speech never arrived. I ended up
blurting out my confession in bed, two days before my parents'
arrival.

"Tu rêves," Yousouf mumbled, pulling the blanket back over his

head. Since I insisted on keeping the windows open, and he shivered in the seventy-degree winters, this is how he slept.

"I'm not dreaming." I pulled the cover away from his face. His hair was cut short, and his ears were small and round, fitted close to his head. I traced them with my finger. "My parents are coming on Christmas Eve. You have to move your clothes out of my closet."

He sat up, crossed his arms over his chest, and shivered. *"On ne t'a pas trouvé dans une poubelle?"*

I winced. "No, I wasn't found in a trash can. I lied."

"Donc, tu n'es pas orpheline?" I would miss the sound of that word. Who could help but love someone called *"orpheline"*?

I took a gulp from the wine glass on my nightstand and said, "No. I'm not an orphan. I'm just an asshole."

"What's an asshole?"

I pointed to my rear end. He raised his eyebrows and carefully repeated the word. When I stood up to refill my glass, he said, "Bring a mango juice. Asshole."

When I got back into bed, Yousouf said, "You know, Darren, in Africa we say that if there are two paths, and on the shorter path there is a man who waits to kill you, then it is faster to take the longer path. I am surprised that now you tell me you are not an *orpheline*, but I am not angry. To Americans, words seem very important, but in Senegal the words are not the meaning."

Then, apparently remembering that I had told him he is supposed to hug me when I cry, he put one arm awkwardly around me and patted me on the head. "You drink too much," he said. "You are young and pretty and intelligent. You have a man who doesn't drink, and now you have parents. Why are you wanting to die?"

"I want to live," I said. "I just have too many lives."

"You are too complicated, Darren. I know you do not like my advices, but listen to me this one thing. When your parents come here, show them our African hospitality. Show them *Teranga*." I stared out the window. *"Boy. Ss, boy-bi."* He caught my chin in his hand and turned my face toward him. Then he rapped his knuckles lightly on my head, as though testing its hardness, and said, *"Têtue."* Our child, he had told me, would be beautiful and stubborn.

The next night Yousouf packed up his toothbrush, razor, and shaving cream and took all of his suits out of my closet. "My mother is not concerned about your color," he told me as he examined my pink Polo shirt and then added it to his suitcase. "But she asks me not to live with you, and she says I should not marry you except on the condition that you convert to Islam. I answer her that the American girl is too independent. *N'est-ce pas?"*

"That's my shirt," I said.

"Our shirt. Why do you put your parents to a hotel? They should sleep here in your bed. You can sleep on the floor. You should not drink all the time alone in your apartment. It is Jesse Ray and Dean who are the orphans." He paused in front of the mirror to pat his hair smooth. "Hello, Mr. Parkman," he said, holding his hand out to the glass and smiling. "Hello, Papa."

On Christmas Eve, he drove me to the airport and waited in the car while I went inside to find my parents. I am half the size of the average gazelle-legged Senegalese, and I used this to my advantage. I bent low as I sped through the crowd, clasping my purse to my belly and sticking my elbows out.

"Mademoiselle!" hissed a boy. He sidled up beside me and spread his long black fingers across my arm. *"Mademoiselle, attends!"* I ducked and turned, slick as a greased ball in water.

I spotted Dean and Jesse Ray before they got through the gates. They were wearing London Fog trenchcoats and stood next to a pile of matching leather luggage. Their cheeks were pink with excitement, and like all Americans in foreign countries, they looked absurdly friendly. I waved. They looked right through me.

Dean walked away from Jesse Ray and stared intently into the crowd of black bodies around me. He wore a tweed cap. Beneath his open trenchcoat he wore starched, creased khaki pants, a V-neck sweater the color of corn silk, and a blue button-down shirt. He had replaced his gold watch with a plastic one, as I had instructed in my last letter, but neither he nor Jesse Ray had followed my suggestion to remove their wedding rings.

"Dad!" I called, waving my arm. "Dad, I'm here!" He looked frantically all around me.

When he saw me, his eyes glowed, and his arm shot into the air and stayed there, waving. "Darren!" he cried. "Hi, Darren!" There was a huge, silly grin on his face, and he kept waving. Tears rolled out of my eyes, and I tried to squeeze them back. Still waving, he called out, "Jesse Ray!" The Tennessee accent reverberated through the airport, and people stared at him. "She's over here! I found her! Here she is!"

Jesse Ray spun around. For a moment she tossed her head this way and that, and then she threw her arm up in a wave. She had once held the title of Miss Western Tennessee, and she still walked as though she wore a banner across her chest. She had never learned how to smile, but her eyes shone with soft lights. They were sea green, shadowed with an intelligence that would have been unnerving if one could stare into them longer than the second she permitted.

"Now hold onto your bags," I said as I led them outside. "Watch your rings. These guys will pull them right off your fingers."

"Baayileen suma yaay," I yelled to the two boys leaning in close to Jesse Ray.

In greasy English, one of them was saying, "Madame! Hello, Madame. Are you from Los Angeles, California?"

"Hello," she said. "No, we're from Stipple—" One of the boys was already untying her shoelace so she would look down while the other one went for her pocket.

"Thief!" I shouted. "Get lost." A man pulled on Dean's suitcase, crying, *"Taxi! Venez monsieur!"* Dean pulled back on the handle, smiling all around with his Rotary Club smile. "This is the welcoming committee," he said. A leper planted himself in front of him and rattled a coffee can of coins.

"*Aycaleen,*" I yelled. As I looked for Yousouf's car, I waved my hands at the tightening circle around us.

"Why are they hissing?" asked Jesse Ray. "I don't know why I minored in French. I don't remember a word of it." To the delight of the crowd, she hissed back. "They sure are black," she said, as a man pushed an African mask in her face. "And tall."

Suddenly, a boy scooted into our circle on a homemade skateboard. He had no legs and rode the board on his belly, propelling himself with both hands, on which he wore flip-flops. He wheeled right up to Jesse Ray, raised himself off the board with his hands, and said, "*Bonjour, Madame.*" He smiled. "*Donnes-moi cent francs.*"

"Lord a mercy," said Jesse Ray. "Dean, look at this one."

"*Babeneenyoon,*" I said to the boy. "Tomorrow." He paddled around with his hands and turned his sly face up to me. "Oh, you speak Wolof," he said. "*Mayma xaalis.*" His voice was unctuous, wheedling, and hard as the cement beneath his hands. When I didn't give him the money, he demanded it in French.

"I told you to go away." I turned my back to him and looked for Yousouf.

"You told me to go away?" he repeated, as though amazed by my rudeness. "I beg your pardon, Mademoiselle. I'm not talking to you anyway."

When he wheeled around to Dean, I jumped between them. "*Aycaleen, Demuleen,*" I shouted. "*Baay u suma Pàpp! Baay u suma Mama!*" I yelled this so harshly that my voice broke. I waved my arms at all of them, rasping, "You're rude! You're not normal!"

"*Nous sommes corrects!*" the legless boy yelled back. "You're the one who is rude!" The smooth mask of charm had dropped from his face. He laughed in a long hiss and called me a whore.

"Go to hell!" I screamed. I wanted to kick his head and send him flopping off the sidewalk.

My parents were watching me with wide eyes. "Why Darren," said Jesse Ray, "I believe you're acting uglier than they are."

Then Yousouf hopped out of his car, parting the crowd as he walked up to greet us. Dean gave him the same noncommittal smile he was giving all the black men around him and pulled back on the suitcase. "Dad!" I said in a low voice. "This is my friend. This is Yousouf. He wants to put your suitcase in the car."

Yousouf smiled. He looked sharp in his suit, a navy blue one that he wore with my pink Polo shirt and the tie I had given him last Christmas.

"Excuse me," said Dean. He let go of the suitcase to shake Yousouf's hand. He had told me once that he judged a man by his fingernails. As I watched the white hand clasp the black one, I checked Yousouf's manicure; it was perfect. *"Don Jour,"* Dean said.

Without a second's hesitation, Yousouf replied, *"Bonjour, Monsieur."* In English he said, "You have only been in Senegal for half an hour, and you are already speaking French."

"Just one word of it," said Dean, following him to the car.

"It's *Bond Jour,* Dean," said Jesse Ray, "Not *Don Jour. B* as in Boy."

"You sit in the backseat with your parents," said Yousouf. In the car, Dean patted my knee and beamed at me. "It's been seven hundred and nineteen days since I last saw you," he said. "I counted each one."

"What beautiful weather," said Jesse Ray. "It's just like Hawaii." On Avenue Pompidou, they laughed at the giant Santa Claus revolving on a rooftop.

"I guess the Africans would think Santa Claus is black," said Dean. "I never thought of that."

"We didn't think the Muslims celebrated Christmas," Jesse Ray said. "We brought you a tape of Christmas carols and a Christmas tree, a miniature one with miniature lights and ornaments and even miniature tinsel."

"I plugged the lights in to make sure they work," said Dean. Each time he spoke to me, he touched me, as though he feared I wasn't really there. They thanked Yousouf for carrying the luggage up to the apartment but barely noticed when he left.

Still wearing her trenchcoat, Jesse Ray stood in the center of my living room and said, "Darren, I have missed you. You may not think so." Her nose turned red, the way it did when she was going to cry.

"Hug your mother's neck," said Dean. "She loves you." I gave her a bear hug.

"Your Dad missed you," said Jesse Ray, digging in her black pocketbook for a Kleenex. "Went through a depression. Just sat in that chair every night. Moped. Sometimes he'd go in your room and just stand there. I got to where I had to leave the house."

When we both looked at him, Dean smiled bashfully. He was sitting on the vinyl couch where no one ever sat. "This couch must have a loose screw in it somewhere," he said. He bounced twice in his seat and then got down on his knees to look beneath the frame.

Dean's hair was completely white, and his pink scalp showed through the strands he combed over his bald spot. Jesse Ray's hair was a color she called bronze. She wore a red dress covered with lions and zebras and a chunky necklace of wooden beads she had bought in Memphis. Both of them looked so white.

"Here," said Jesse Ray. "I brought some of my work to show you. I'm doing African art now." She rummaged through a suitcase and handed me a sheaf of prints she had made with cut potatoes and ink. As I flipped through the primitive images of lions, tigers, and turtles, she said, "My art teacher thinks I should change my name. Jesse Ray doesn't sound like an artist's name. She suggested I use my maiden name, Darren, but I told her that was your name now. You wouldn't like that, would you?" When I didn't raise my head, she said, "I didn't think so. Do you want one of these prints? They're not very good. The potatoes were a little soft." I took the turtle and studied her signature in the corner.

"I like your name," I said.

"It's country. Everybody had a double name back then. We didn't have much, but we got two names."

Through the open windows, the sound of drums beat in the room.

"The natives are rising," said Dean.

"It's probably a wrestling match," I said.

"Your apartment sure is clean." He gave the couch two shakes, dusted the wooden frame off with his handkerchief, and then walked to the window.

"It's bare," said Jesse Ray, "But she likes it that way. Spartan."

Yousouf and I had recently redecorated the apartment. After we hung the black curtains figured with white fish skeletons, he had stepped back to admire them and said, "This is our home." Then he pulled out his key, winking at me before he slipped it back into his pocket.

"So this is your color scheme," said Jesse Ray. "Black and white."

"Is Use-off one of your students at the university?" asked Dean.

"He said he works at a bank," said Jesse Ray. "You don't listen."

"He's a real good-natured fellow."

"He's a good-looking boy," said Jesse Ray. "Cute personality."

Dean tested the window on its hinge until he was satisfied that it didn't need oiling. Then he looked out. "You've got an ocean-side view," he said. "This is good real estate property. I thought you'd be living like a pauper over here in Africa. Does the Peace Corps pay the rent?"

"The Senegalese government stole it for me."

"We've got to get that sunset," said Jesse Ray. She set up the Camcorder, but the light wouldn't come on, and long after the sun had dropped into the sea, she and Dean were still arguing about it.

"Well, dad-blame it then, you read the directions yourself," she said. She handed him her owl-eyed glasses, which he set firmly on his face. Then he opened the instruction booklet and snapped the pages between his fingers.

"It's all in Japanese," he said.

I suspected that the print was just too small for him to read, but I said, "How silly of them to write in their own language."

"She's getting crabby," said Jesse Ray. "We should go to our hotel and let her rest." As we walked out the door, she glanced at the pack of Marlboros in my hand and said, "Still smoking, I see. I brought you a picture of a black lung."

"That was thoughtful of you," I said. Then I felt mean. I put my arms around her rigid back and dropped my head on her shoulder. She gave me a quick hug and pushed me away saying, "I just don't want to go to your funeral. Children should outlive their parents."

"I don't guess this place would burn down to the quick," said Dean, "with all this cement." He watched me lock the door and waited until I had stepped away from it before he tried the handle to make sure it was locked.

"There's no fire escape," said Jesse Ray. "Don't take the elevator if there's a fire."

Dean stopped. "Goodness gracious, no!" He looked hard at me. I was trying to untie my goatskin bag to get some matches.

"I can never untie your knots, Dad. Why did you tie my bag?"

"I was trying to help you. I didn't want everything to fall out. Here, I'll get it. Don't ever get in the elevator if there's a fire."

"I know that."

"She knows that," said Jesse Ray.

"She's a smart girl." He patted me on the back. "I guess she'd get out pretty quick." When the gray walls of the elevator closed around us, he said, "I guess they don't have fire drills in Africa."

As I walked them down the street to their hotel, I held their hands. "Don't go outside," I said. "Don't talk to anyone. I'll be here in the morning to get you."

"Now you know what we went through when you were a kid," said Jesse Ray. "Every time I turned my back, you had wandered off somewhere." I had already decided that if they showed up at my apartment during the night, Yousouf would have to crawl out the window and stand on the ledge. Since he was afraid of heights, I didn't know how I would get him out there, but I intended to try.

When I got back to my apartment, I found Yousouf in bed with the Ziploc bag of brownies Jesse Ray had brought me. He was trying to sing along with "Frosty the Snowman." The lights of the Christmas tree scattered like sequins over his black arms. *"C'est cool ça,"* he said, examining the zipper of the bag. "These clever Americans."

I stretched out beside him with a glass of bourbon. "Do white people look funny to you?"

"Toubab." He drew out the word, the way children did on street corners and tossed my hair in his hands, saying, *"Toubab* hair! Ha, ha." Then he was serious. "Your family is handsome. Dean and Jesse Ray seem wise. *Ils sont* 'nice' *quoi."* As he ran his hand along my thigh, I watched the colored lights of the Christmas tree slide over our skins. *"Eh, orpheline?"* I pressed my face in his shoulder, and he took the glass out of my hand, saying softly, *"Suma Boy, kooku daal,"* which was a phrase from a song about a woman leaving a man.

On Christmas Day, at nine A.M. sharp, I sat Jesse Ray and Dean on the rickety wooden bench beside the parking lot of my building. This gave Yousouf some extra time to get out of the apartment.

"Now make sure you don't leave your pick on the sink," I had told him, "or a sock on the floor, or your . . ." I stopped. I sounded exactly like Dean and Jesse Ray.

"I am going to lean out the window and yell, 'Hello, Papa Dean; hello, Mama Jesse Ray,'" Yousouf said. He took my chin in his hand and kissed me.

After dark, the whores did their business in this thin strip of trees along the edge of the street, but in the morning it belonged to a bent little man in a red stocking cap who sold coffee and bread.

"They served a breakfast buffet at the hotel," said Jesse Ray, narrowing her eyes as the man rinsed out a dirty plastic cup and began stirring Nescafé and hot water into it. "Are we drinking after people?"

We opened gifts in my apartment. Islamic chants screamed out of the mosque's loudspeakers in a static roar, drowning out Handel's "Messiah." As Dean unwrapped the grinning wooden mask rolled in one of my old curtains—yellow *legos* printed with violet squiggly creatures—he said, "This will be yours someday. You'll inherit all of the African things."

"She won't inherit everything," said Jesse Ray. "The other children will get their share, too."

"She'll inherit all the African things. These are hers."

"Stop talking about dying," I said. I checked my watch to see if it was too early for a drink. It was midmorning.

"Open another present," said Dean. He had a smile on his face, and with his eyes he was telling me to smile now. I tore the red paper from the package and removed the Polo shirts I planned to rewrap and give to Yousouf after my parents went home.

"These are going to swallow you whole," said Jesse Ray, "But I got the size you wanted. I guess you like them big." As I gently set the shirts on top of the heap of other gifts they had given me, I considered telling them the truth, but Dean was still trying to make me smile, and Jesse Ray had taken out her camera.

I wanted to take my parents to a Catholic monastery where bongo drums were played in the service, but Jesse Ray insisted on going to the Baptist mission. She had contacted the missionaries from Tennessee.

"Most of the Senegalese are devout Muslims," I said. "The rest are devout Catholics or devout Animists. Do you know how many converts the Baptists have snatched up in the last five years?"

"I don't care for your language," said Jesse Ray.

"Two," I said. "And those were Methodists from Sierra Leone."

"Ha, ha," said Dean. "Everybody get along."

The service was terrible. It was centered around a duet given by the missionary couple's two daughters—lanky girls with stringy blond hair and pink combs sticking out of their back pockets. Neither of them could sing a note. One of them forgot the words. I rolled my eyes at Jesse Ray, who stared straight ahead and pretended not to notice.

Afterward, she cornered the preacher and made a big deal about how we were all Americans here in Senegal and all Baptist to the bone. "How many people in your fellowship are Senegalese?" she asked, glancing at me to make sure I was listening.

"Well," he drawled, "I don't know. They all look alike to me."

"Darren can tell them apart," said Jesse Ray.

When we were back in the taxi she said, "You're right. He was a dumbbell." Then she leaned out of the window with the Camcorder and shot everything on the street, something I had asked her not to do. Someone threw a rock at the taxi.

Later that night when I heard Yousouf's knock on my door: two long raps, and then a short one, I stayed in the window. I wanted to know if he would use his key. When I heard his footsteps moving away, I ran to the door and opened it.

He stood very straight in the doorway and kept his arms by his sides. *"Qu'est-ce qu' il y a, Darren?"*

"Don't leave me, Yousouf. Please don't leave me."

"My *Boy*. You feel solitary." Then he saw the bottle in the window. He frowned. Loosening his tie, he walked to the bedroom, saying, "Really, you are difficult sometimes. I want to use the key, because I am thinking, maybe she is sitting in the window drinking bourbon and will fall. Then I am thinking, maybe Dean and Jesse Ray are here. They will ask, why does this boy have a key?" He sat down on the edge of our bed and removed his socks and shoes. Without looking at me, he shined each shoe with a sock and set the pair neatly against the wall. "You see, Darren, the pains you give me."

"Why do I have to pretend that you are just my friend? The man I love is none of my parents' business. They can't run my life."

He was silent as he undressed and hung his clothes in my closet. When he was lying naked on the bed, he folded his arms behind his head. "You must respect your parents. I notice that you do not do this enough." As I climbed in beside him, he pressed me against his chest and pulled the sheet over our heads. His smooth, supple skin smelled of indigo. I tightened my arms around him and licked the silky hollow in his neck.

"What afraids you, Darren?"

"Nothing."

"But there are many things to be afraid of in Africa. Three o'clock in the morning is the worst time. Then you can see a white horse, or even a woman. You know, if you see a white woman at this hour, she is the devil. She will make you make love to her, and then you will be schizophrenic."

Long ago I had stopped trying to convince Yousouf that there is no such thing as magic. Like most black Muslims in Senegal, he ranked witch doctors with religious men and insisted that genies are mentioned throughout the Koran.

"What scares you?" I asked, expecting another horror story about the *kangkurang,* a spirit dressed up as a tree that chases newly circumcised boys, or the genies that come through open windows at night and jump inside of your chest to eat your heart.

"I am afraid that you will go back to the United States and forget me here." When he kissed me, his face was wet.

In the middle of the night, I woke up to the crack of bone against bone. Outside, under the low curse of a man, a whore wailed. Yousouf was leaning out of the window. The faint light from the streetlamps exposed the delicate ribs moving beneath his skin and cast a purple sheen on his smooth, round buttocks. Somewhere in the trees, the whore laughed, then sobbed, then laughed again—high and wild. Again, the man hit her, and again she screamed.

"Stop him," I said, sitting up in bed. "Do something!" When he didn't answer, I thought he might have walked in his sleep. I ran to the window and screamed, "Leave her alone, you black son of a bitch."

"Viens-toi!" Yousouf pulled me away from the window.

"Why is she here? Why doesn't she leave him?"

"She's a whore," he said, holding my wrists. "She has no mother. Where would she go?"

"I'm sorry. Yousouf, I'm sorry I said that."

"You have stress. This is very obvious." For a moment, it was so quiet outside that we could hear the ocean washing up on the sand. Beyond the streetlamps, all around the city, drums beat in and out like the heart of a beast holding Dakar against his chest.

The next morning Jesse Ray came to my apartment. Yousouf had left ten minutes earlier to hire a taxi to take us to his mother's village. When I saw my mother standing at the door my heart jumped, and then my head began to hurt. "What's wrong?" I demanded.

"Nothing is wrong. You look tired. Did you stay up late? Dean is coming. He wanted to take the stairs. He's all in a dither because there's not a fire escape in your building."

"I told y'all not to leave the hotel without me." I glanced around the room to make sure Yousouf hadn't left anything lying about. To me, the whole apartment smelled like sex. "Last week a seventy-year-old Peace Corps volunteer was beaten up and mugged in broad daylight. I don't know why you won't listen to me."

"We're not seventy yet," she said. "Two fellows did follow us real close, trying to sell us some watches, but I told them we weren't interested. They snickered about it but didn't bother us after that. I'd like some coffee."

I followed her into the kitchen where she put a pan of water on the stove and found the Nescafe. I leaned against the sink, blocking her view, but Yousouf had already washed and dried our two coffee cups and put them away.

"I don't know how you live without hot water," she said. "I guess you've got some things to look forward to when you come back home." She made a face as she sipped her instant coffee and then said, "So you want a white house with a picket fence and a German shepherd. No husband?" I had written about the house and dog in a letter. "No grandchildren?"

"You'll have grandpups."

"Thank you." She wet the corner of a dish towel and rubbed a spot off of her vest. "I got this out of your closet at home," she said. "I hope you don't mind. You left it."

"It looks nice on you." It was a fringed suede vest, embroidered with cowgirls; I had worn it when I was sixteen.

"I can still wear young clothes," she said. "Whenever I show my senior citizen discount card at the grocery store, the cashier can't believe that I'm sixty-one." As she twisted the towel in her veined hand, I watched the diamond glint on her finger. Dean had given her the ring when she was twenty, and she had never removed it.

Now she looked around my kitchen as if she might find a machine gun leaning against the wall, or a black man peering out from a cabinet. I knew that she had made this unannounced visit to see what I was really doing in Senegal, and in a way I admired her for that. Jesse Ray was tough.

"More coffee?" I asked.

She cleared her throat and said, "You aren't planning to marry Yousouf, I hope."

"He's just a friend."

"You better make that clear to him. He sure does seem to like you."

"I'll keep us white."

"It's not that. Yousouf is a good-looking man, and just as nice as he can be, but there are cultural differences that you should be aware of. Religious differences. A man is so different from a woman to begin with that you don't want to start out with somebody as different as a . . . martian."

I brushed past her, took a beer out of the refrigerator, opened it with my army knife, and drank. She stared. "I have a headache," I said.

"Louise Darren Parkman." When she pressed her lips together, the wrinkles around her mouth cut into deep lines. The rest of her face seemed to sag. "Why do you need alcohol at eight o'clock in the morning?"

"My head hurts." For a split second, she looked me in the eye. Then she turned away. I finished the beer in silence while she looked for an aspirin.

In the parking lot, as the driver tied our luggage on the roof of his taxi, Dean explained our change of plans to Jesse Ray. "Yousouf's father is spending the holidays with his third wife here in Dakar, so Yousouf is lending his car to them." He spoke as though he had been dealing with the nuisances of polygamy all of his life. "We're going to take a taxi to the village. Yousouf's mother is the first wife." If Yousouf drove his Peugeot into the village, he would be hounded for money the rest of his life.

"Where's the taxi?" asked Jesse Ray.

"This is it," said Dean, pointing to the blue-and-yellow van painted with pictures of African women carrying bowls of fruit on their heads, African men dancing around them, palm trees, and big yellow suns. One window was covered with cardboard, and the front window appeared to have been put back in with tape. Across the back of the van, in heavy black letters, there were supplications to Allah.

The driver was arguing with Yousouf about the price. He had apparently thought Yousouf would be traveling with Africans, and now that he saw the leather luggage and the cameras, he insisted that we all pay the *Toubab* price.

"*Déédéét!*" said Yousouf. He pressed his hand to his breast and flapped his arm like a chicken wing, twice, to emphasize his refusal. Each time the driver pulled a bag off the roof, Yousouf returned it.

"Board," he told me. I jerked open the door, which almost came off the hinges, and held it for Jesse Ray.

"Put the camera away and get in the car," I said. "Please, Mom. Don't take the driver's picture. It's not polite. He isn't an animal in a zoo."

"Yousouf lets us take his picture," she said. She climbed in the car and made a face through the cracked window. "What I can't understand is how you can tell us that we are being impolite when you are so rude to your parents."

After we were all in the van, the driver cursed, jumped in his seat, and jammed a piece of wire into the ignition. The prayer beads and the blond Kewpie doll hanging from his rearview mirror swung against each other as we bounced down the road. He drove like Evel Knievel, slamming around cars that stopped for lights, bearing down on goats crossing the road, skidding to stops in front of children. Once, for no apparent reason, he drove down a street in reverse.

"I'm just not going to look," said Jesse Ray, widening her eyes as another van, top-heavy with rams, careened toward us. We were out of the city, and the desert stretched out on both sides of the road, vast and empty.

The taxi dropped us off at a *marché* where we piled onto a donkey cart driven by a gaunt man with dust in his hair. He lashed a whip across the donkey's ribs, and we bumped down a rutted path into the dry millet fields. The millet was just stubble poking up through the sand. There was nothing else on the ground but enormous anthills.

"We've got to get pictures of these," said Dean. Yousouf told the driver to stop, and Dean and Jesse Ray got out with the Camcorder and two handheld cameras, one for slides and one for prints, to photograph the anthills. While the donkey nosed around in the sand for something to eat, the driver cleaned his teeth with a chew stick.

"Why are they looking at those?" he asked Yousouf. It was as odd as if an African had been riding along in a taxi through New York City and asked to stop so that he could photograph the fire hydrants.

As the sun rose higher in the sky, my eyes began to hurt behind my sunglasses. There was nothing between us and the sun—no building, no tree, no cloud. The sky was a white glow. It was easy to see pools of blue water in the distance, but there were none. There was nothing around us but dirt and light. "Imagine living way out here without a car," said Dean. "What if you needed a doctor?"

An hour later, we came to a circle of mud huts that looked like forts children might build. The tin roofs shimmered like water. A woman with a baby strapped to her back stood over the well rapidly throwing one hand over the other as she drew up a leaking bag of water. Nearby, a girl pounded millet with a pestle as long as an oar. She sang, threw the pestle up in the air, and clapped her hands twice before she caught it. Her arms were beautifully toned.

The children had seen us coming and were running toward us. They wore ragged Goodwill clothes, and their bellies were swollen up like balloons.

"*Jërëjëf waay,*" I said to the driver as I reached into my purse for the fare.

"I'll pay for it," said Dean.

"Don't open your wallet. You have more C.F.A. in your pocket than the average Senegalese man makes in a year."

He put his arm around my shoulder and said, "You're going to make it." The love in his eyes embarrassed me. I reworked the latch on my purse. "I was worried about leaving you alone when I die. I can't leave this earth without knowing that you're all situated. You've grown up out here, though. I think you can fend for yourself now. That gives me peace of mind."

"All she needs is money," said Jesse Ray. Before we were even out of the cart, she had the camera rolling. The children halted a short distance away from us and bunched together, giggling and falling against each other as they called out, "*Toubab! Toubab! Toubab!*"

"What are they saying?" asked Dean.

"Honkey."

"Play ball!" cried Jesse Ray. She hastily tore the Christmas paper from a red ball and threw it to them. Shrieking, they began to fight for it. In a robotic voice, she said into the Camcorder, "We are now in Yousouf's village. Yousouf is Darren's friend in Senegal, West Africa. He is working on his Ph.D. in economics and works for the present time at a bank. These are the village children." Then she handed the camera to Dean and ran into the crowd, clapping her hands and crying, "Ball! Throw the ball!"

The men, who had risen from their mats to greet us, didn't know what to make of this spectacle. "Please, Mom," I said with my teeth clenched. "Please put the camera down. We're supposed to greet the village elders. This is rude. You're embarrassing me."

"Oh, hush," said Jesse Ray. She threw the ball back into the crowd of screaming children, crying, "Whee! Whee! Play ball!" An old man wearing a ragged brown robe and a fake leopardskin cape looked at my mother in amazement. *"Kii borom ker le,"* said Yousouf, and he went to greet the head of the village.

"Dad," I said. "The chief is staring at Mom. Make her behave." He put his arm around me. "She's just excited," he said. "We've never been in a village before. Show me what you want me to do."

We shook hands, first with the men, then with the women who stood behind them retying the *pagnes* around their waists, and finally with the children rounded up by a woman who switched their ankles with a stick. They edged shyly toward us and held out their limp hands.

I studied all of the women's faces, looking for Yousouf's mother, whom I had never met. At last, she emerged from a dark doorway in a billowing white cloud of gauze. Instantly, I recognized Yousouf's face. On her, the jawbone was softened, and the cheekbones were not quite as sharp, but those were his eyes.

Her upper lip was painted a deep red, and her gums were dyed blue. Gold earrings glinted from her ears. She was a big woman, but she curtsied nimbly before Dean. When he curtsied back, the other women laughed.

Dean enjoyed the attention. He glanced away from the buxom young woman in the black bra, who couldn't stop giggling, and held his hand out to Yousouf's mother. "Dean Parkman," he said loudly. *"Don Jour."*

She looked just to the side of his head, which was level with her own, and said, *"Bonjour, Monsieur."* This was the extent of her French. Yousouf translated our greetings.

When he introduced her to me, she looked me dead in the eye. I had asked Yousouf once how she felt when his father married a second wife.

"My mother is a good Muslim," he said. "She turned to the education of the children. She gave to us all of her love."

"Did she love your father?" I asked.

"Very much. I used to hear them laughing in bed. They were in love. But she got old. She had her children, and we still needed her."

Now she looked about forty. Her face was smooth and glossy, but I could see the years in her eyes.

She spoke in Mandinka, a soft language from the jungles of the Casamance, as indecipherable as the sound of rain. As she talked, she continued to look me in the eye. The sun burned down on us, and flies gathered around my eyes and mouth and nose. I let them land on my face without trying to brush them away—she stood so still. I tried to show my respect by glancing away now and then, but I wanted to see everything in her eyes. She was the most serene person I had ever met. Finally, she finished speaking and was silent.

Yousouf turned his head to look at Jesse Ray, who had picked up a naked baby with talismans tied around its neck and belly. Then he looked down at Dean's white loafers and translated, "My mother says that since she does not speak French or Wolof, and you do not speak Mandinka, you cannot talk to each other." She smiled at me. There was nothing coy or malicious in it. It was a beautiful, kind, wise smile, and I understood that she would never give me her son.

"I'm her mother," said Jesse Ray, stepping in front of me to shake her hand. "Mo-ther," she said loudly, stretching her lips to exaggerate each syllable. The fringe on her vest swung as she turned to point at me and back to herself. The sun bore down on us with the hot white intensity of a spotlight. When I began to see red, I closed my eyes.

With my nostrils full of the smell of sweat and milk and dung, I looked past the shifting red dots behind my eyelids and saw myself in America, laying flowers on my parents' graves and walking back to a white picket fence, through the gate, past a German shepherd, and into my house.

"Darren," said Yousouf. "*Ça va?*"

"*Ça va,*" I replied, opening my eyes.

Melanie Sumner grew up in Georgia and now lives on the island of Chappaquiddick. Her first book of fiction, *Polite Society,* will be published by Seymour Lawrence/Houghton Mifflin in the spring of 1995. Her stories have appeared in *The New Yorker, Story, Boulevard,* and other magazines. Her story "The Monster" will appear in the anthology *Voices of the Exiled* in the fall of 1994. She earned her degrees from Boston University and the University of North Carolina at Chapel Hill and has been awarded fellowships at The Fine Arts Work Center and Yaddo.

I'm a little embarrassed to confess that "My Other Life" is pure autobiography. Here and there, for the sake of brevity and structure, I altered a few details, but for the most part, the dialogues could be recordings and the scenes, to the best of my memory, actually occurred. I've often worried that since so much of my writing is autobiographical, I lack imagination and am not really writing fiction; however, I recently told a therapist what had gone on in my life in the last three days and she said, "Oh, that would make a great play."

"But that's my life," I said. "Why is everything a story?"

"Because you're a writer." She explained that as a writer, my unconscious is constantly selecting the elements of a story from reality. This is why it seems that when I'm going about my business or someone else's, plots unfold.

On the other hand, I wonder if anything is not a story.

Robert Love Taylor

MY MOTHER'S SHOES

(from *The Southern Review*)

A boy of twelve, the year my father was dying, I used to go out to the garage during the summer evenings, just after dusk, and put on a pair of my mother's high heels. I found them in a grocery sack of my sisters' and my outgrown clothes to be given to the Salvation Army. Black leather sling pumps of the style fashionable in the previous decade, the forties, they did not seem badly worn, and they were not so large on me that they would slip off when I walked in them, not with the strap buckled to the last notch. I walked out of the garage in them, and when I reached the street, I could see the cars whizzing past on Robinson Avenue, a half-block away. In the other direction, at the end of a two-block–long row of bungalows, lay a dark blankness.

This blankness was in fact a park, Edgemere Park, where in the daytime I might have gone to climb trees or wade in the warm water of a shallow creek. But at night the park looked faraway and menacing, a shimmering deep pool of darkness. And so I went no farther than the end of the driveway, standing as long as I dared, breathing in the sweet night air. It was a strange, eerie time. Neither a gifted nor a dull child, I craved getting by, preferably unnoticed, but there I stood, risking discovery and certain ridicule—and for what? For the pleasure of it. It pleased me. I don't know why.

Sometime during that autumn the shoes disappeared. The Salvation Army must have picked them up while I was in school. I was sorry to see them go. We never seemed to have enough money, and now that my father had stopped working, there would be even more stringent economies. Mother wasn't likely to throw away another pair of shoes soon. I regretted the loss, but by this time my father's illness had become severe and I imagined that my deprivation might have been ordained as a way of making me pay attention to him and take up the role, as directed by my mother, of man of the family.

Mother worked full-time at Kerr's Department Store and served as our father's nurse all the months of his decline. We children did little to help her. After all, she did not tell us, not for the longest time, that he was dying. He worked too hard, she always said, and when he came home from his office at Oklahoma Gas & Electric one hot July afternoon and said he didn't feel so well, she said he just needed to catch up on his rest. We—my two sisters and I— believed her. But he never went back to work at all. By the end of the summer he seldom left the back bedroom. Some months later we were told he had cancer. I do not know if there was ever any pain. He was a silent, grim man, then as before. At Christmas he went to the hospital and after a few weeks was operated on, and we thought that would be the end of the trouble. We have to hope and pray for the best, Mother said. After the operation, he stayed in the hospital another three weeks before coming home. His body afire with secret wanton rot, he survived the remainder of the winter, lasted through the spring, and died on June 21, 1954, two days after his fortieth birthday, in his bed. Now at last he would rest, my mother said.

The Edgemere section of Oklahoma City where we lived was nowhere near the edge of any mere, which an elementary schoolteacher had told us was an old-fashioned word from England that meant sea. The park two blocks from our house, with its trickle of red water, was bordered by pleasant, quiet neighborhoods of modest but comfortable homes, most of them one-story, built during the boom years of the twenties, made of red or buff brick, their roofs pitched and pointed to resemble, though surely not intentionally, the little houses that cuckoo clocks inhabited. A few of the buff brick houses had wrought iron trim around the windows and along the front steps. Ours was one of these.

The garage sat apart from the house, in the far corner of a small backyard. This garage was filled with my father's things, his electric saw and worktable with its assortment of hammers, nails, screwdrivers, hacksaws, handsaws, drills, and odd tools I never knew the names for. There was no space left for the car. A black Ford, kept shiny and clean by my father, it sat in the driveway alongside my mother's well-trimmed forsythia.

During the warm months, my father labored Saturdays in the yard, mowing and trimming and raking and seeding and fertilizing constantly—so it seemed to me—and our grass was thicker and greener than all our neighbors'. In the cooler months, he went to the garage, kept the jigsaw whining, the sawdust thick in the air. He was skillful, I'm sure, and the solitary labor must have appealed to some deep, long-standing need to quarantine himself. For a time he made little cut-out figures, caricatures he had painstakingly traced from books and transferred to plywood—Dutch boys, hillbillies, cowboys, Old Black Joes, and Aunt Jemimas, which he then sanded, painted at last with brilliant colors, and attached to wrought iron spikes so that they could be stuck in the ground as decoration for gardens and yards. A gardening supply store where my father bought his fertilizer took some of them on consignment, and a few actually sold, but one day—this would have been a summer several years before his illness—we saw him unloading them from the trunk of the car. There must have been a hundred of them. He installed a few in our yard and rested the others neatly in a corner of the garage.

From the age of ten, I was a paperboy, throwing the *Daily Oklahoman* in the mornings and the *Oklahoma City Times* in the afternoons. My route consisted of an area about fifteen blocks to the south of Edgemere, an older section of the city where graceful old mansions faced tree-lined streets. The trees, mostly sycamores and elms, were the tallest in the city, their intertwined branches making bowers pleasant to pass beneath in the early morning, the light just beginning to flicker through the fat, shiny leaves. Best of all, however, was the depth of the winter before daylight, the tall windows in the mansions still dark, the inhabitants warm in their big beds. I felt as if I owned the streets and the houses, and the life in them could not begin until I had thrown the last newspaper.

The residents of those fifty-year-old mansions I rarely saw. When I called for my monthly payment, servants dressed in black-and-white uniforms came to the door. I seldom saw a car at any of these houses, though they had broad asphalt driveways, brick-columned porticoes alongside the house for rainless, snowless departures and arrivals, and large garages in back, some with apartments above the stalls. Servants lived in these garage apartments, I imagined, or poor relations.

In my family's bungalow in Edgemere, my sisters shared one bedroom, and, after my father took to his bed, I shared the bunk beds in my bedroom with my mother. The small back room, the master bedroom, was scarcely big enough for a double bed. All the rooms had a decidedly cramped feel to them. My father did not, we were constantly reminded, make a lot of money working for OG&E. Mother sold curtains and draperies at the uptown branch of Kerr's, about a dozen blocks from our house. Until my father no longer needed the car, she walked to work every day. There must have been some disability insurance, sick pay from OG&E, but this was not spoken of. My *Oklahoman* money, minus a small weekly allowance, went into my mother's purse.

As I began my route on one of the coldest of winter mornings that year of my father's dying, I saw a figure coming in my direction on the sidewalk about a block away. I stopped dead in my tracks. It was a woman, walking slowly in her high heels, as if afraid of slipping on a patch of ice. There was no ice, though a dusting of snow lay on the frozen lawns of the mansions. The woman wore a long coat with a fur collar. She didn't wear a hat, and her hair was whipped back and forth across her face by the wind. I took her to be my mother's age, or a little younger. At the corner she looked up. That must have been when she saw me for the first time. She stopped abruptly, on the verge of stepping down from the curb into the street. I looked away and began to move again, taking the next folded paper from my bag. I was about a half-block from the corner. After throwing the paper onto the next porch, I looked again for the woman and saw her walking away from me, rapidly, almost running. By the time I came to the corner she was nowhere to be seen.

In the days that followed, I thought little of this near-meeting. I was in the eighth grade, in junior high school, and one of the first boys in my class to persuade a girl to wear his identification bracelet as a sign of love. I had plenty of distractions. In the evenings that we did not go to the hospital to visit my father, I worked hard to complete my assigned chore before my older sister Lila had done hers so that I could beat her to the phone and, in the half-hour allotted to me, listen to my girlfriend, a fast and furious talker, tell me about the day we had experienced more or less together. After that, I joined my younger sister Sandra in our small living room and sat with her before the television set, doing my homework during the commercials and low points in the programs.

Mother went to the hospital every evening, leaving just after supper and returning in time to tell us to brush our teeth and get ready for bed. My sisters and I visited on Tuesday and Thursday evenings, and on Sunday afternoons. Because we had talked so little to him when he was in good health, conversation now seemed unnatural. Usually he was asleep, and we worked on our homework while our mother, with her chair pulled up close to his bed, read the latest *Look* or *Life*.

On some of the evenings when Mother went alone to the hospital, instead of calling my girlfriend or watching television I went back to my room, happy for the time alone there. I liked to read books that I had been given to understand were classics, *The Count of Monte Cristo*, *20,000 Leagues Under the Sea*, *The Call of the Wild*, *Riders of the Purple Sage*. Now and then I was distracted from my reading by the sight of something of my mother's that she'd left hanging on the railing of the bunk bed or on top of the chest of drawers, a pair of nylon stockings or a blouse or underwear. I thought wistfully of the hot summer nights I'd put on her shoes and walked to the end of the driveway and back. And I remembered the woman I'd seen on my paper route, the way she'd walked slowly in the high heels, the fur collar of her coat fluttering in the wind. It was almost as if I believed her to be the self I'd left behind in the summer, the night-walker in my mother's shoes. I hoped that I would see her again.

One evening I found a strange book on my desk. It was hardbound, black, and at first I thought it was a Bible. But when I picked it up I saw that its title was *Cancer: A Guide*. I sat down and read of a mystery in the blood, a secret born with birth itself, hidden in the dark reaches of gut and bone. I looked at illustrations that might have been of caverns, clouds, tunnels. Then, hearing the door of my father's room open, I knew Mother was coming and so I quickly closed up the book, turned out the light, and bounded up onto the top bunk. I heard her go into the bathroom, and then, my eyes adjusted to the dark, I watched her come into my room, the curves of her body pressing against her flowing nightgown. She believed I was asleep and settled herself quietly in the lower bunk. It was a strange feeling, hearing her breathing. There was a little whimpering sound she made, almost as if she were crying, but it wasn't the same and it never lasted long.

I rose well before her, sliding down from the bunk quietly. I liked seeing my mother sleeping. She slept on her side, facing the wall. It was comforting somehow, seeing her there, sleeping so soundly.

The book *Cancer: A Guide* appeared only that one evening and then disappeared. I guessed my mother must have left it there accidentally and had reclaimed it.

A few days after this, I saw the mysterious woman on my paper route as she walked down the driveway from the garage apartment in back of a gray granite mansion. It was cold and clear, the sky still dark, and stars glimmered through the bare branches of the trees. I stepped behind an evergreen hedge and listened to the sound of her high heels tapping on the concrete. When she came to the end of the hedge she turned in my direction and I decided it best to start moving again.

We almost collided.

She towered over me. Light from the streetlamp made her face very white. I had surely misjudged her age. She must have been closer in years to my older sister than my mother, though certainly no teenager. There was anger in her eyes, but she looked at me for only an instant before spinning around and stepping quickly back towards the garage. Unaccountably, I stayed there watching her. She wore the fur-collared coat, black patent-leather high heels, and carried a large black purse strapped over her shoulder. The coat looked gray in that dim light, the fur collar a dull yellow. When she came to the staircase that led up to the garage apartment, she looked back, though only for an instant, before hurriedly ascending. Now I saw something other than anger in her quick look. I imagined it was a sense of longing, of complicity, and I felt a powerful desire to follow her. But she was gone, and no lights shone from the apartment's windows.

I began to dream of her all day, picturing her as she paused at the foot of the stairs. In my mind I followed her, rose with her into a room dark like the caverns I'd seen in my mother's secret book of cancer.

What's wrong with you, my girlfriend asked during lunch in the cafeteria. Is your father . . . worse?

He was not worse, I said with some vehemence, believing I spoke the truth, for hadn't he always had this sickness in his blood?

She picked up her tray and left. At the end of the day she pressed into my palm my identification bracelet.

I began to live for my mornings among the dark mansions, the thick trunks of the sycamores, the webbed branches, and the last of the winter night sky. The woman I stalked was not, I told myself, my secret sickness, my birthright, not the mystery that lay ready to devour me, body and soul. She was a mystery, yes, a riddle, but restorative, luxuriant, lavishly life-giving.

Mercy Hospital was a three-story white stucco building shaped like a U. The Sisters of Mercy, in their old-fashioned black habits, their strange white hats with the upswept, pointed brims, stood behind the reception desk and patrolled the hallways. Watching one of them drift past in the hallway, I imagined her as a young girl, packing away dozens of dresses to be sent to the Salvation Army, then cutting off all her beautiful long hair, shaving her head smooth. It was a peculiarly romantic notion.

We were not Catholics. Mercy Hospital was less expensive than others and closer to our home. Mother took my sisters and me to the first Baptist Church for Christmas and Easter services, but we belonged to no church.

One evening when we entered my father's hospital room, we saw a nun standing alongside his bed, hovering over him. She was tall, and the way she leaned forward you could see her thin ankles and the backs of her well-worn mannish shoes.

Mother motioned for my sisters and me to wait outside.

They're converting him, Lila said as we waited in the hallway. That's why they let him in here in the first place, so they can take advantage of him and make him a Catholic.

Mother won't let them do that, Sandra said.

I agreed with Sandra.

Maybe something's wrong, I said.

Brilliant, Einstein, Lila said.

A chubby, red-faced nun came up to us and asked if she might help us find somebody.

He's in there, Lila said harshly.

The nun smiled sweetly and glided away. She had a pretty face, her large eyes clear and blue, and she had looked at me, I thought, with interest.

Mother appeared, gestured for us to come back into the room. The tall nun stood alongside our father's bed, pale and still in her black shoes.

I'm Sister Luke, she said with a pleasant smile. Please come over here.

We had advanced to the center of the room. Mother hung back at the doorway. On the other side of the room, by the windows, my father's roommate lay on his side with the sheets pulled over his head. My father was propped up in bed, but his eyes were closed. No one had shaved him, and the bristles on his cheeks were white and shimmery.

Your father wants to say something to you, Sister Luke said. You'll have to come closer, though.

My sisters, always less ready to obey, stayed where they were, but I did as the nun said. She took hold of my wrist and then with her other hand grasped my father's hand and placed it in mine. His hand was cold. It felt light as a feather. He looked at the nun and then at me.

Son? he said.

It's your son, Mr. Smalley, the nun said. Do you want your glasses on?

He began to pull on my hand, as if to raise himself up.

He wants to hug you, the nun said to me.

I love you, Larry, my father said as I leaned down to receive his embrace. He held me tight, pressing his bristly cheek against mine. When he let go, the nun called for my sisters, who approached him together, as if afraid to go alone. After pulling each of them down into his embrace and professing his love, he sighed heavily and looked at the nun.

There, now, she said, that didn't hurt at all, did it.

*   *   *

The morning after that visit a whiter light shone from one of the windows of the garage apartment. The curtains were pulled back, and I could see the blank gray of the ceiling. In a little while I saw the woman herself. Staring out into darkness from inside a lighted room, she could not have seen me, but I jumped back behind the hedge that had hidden us from each other the day before and waited a few seconds before daring to peek around it.

The light in the window had gone out and she was coming down the stairs. At least I thought I saw her. It was dark, and I did not wait around. I heard the tapping of her heels, but kept my eyes trained on the darkness ahead.

I began to get up earlier and ride my bike straight to the mansion before picking up the morning papers. I stood the bike behind the hedge and crept along the driveway towards the garage apartment. Sometimes the light in the window was on, sometimes not, but even through the darkened panes I imagined I saw movement, deeper shades of darkness that took human form, became a woman, possibly more than one woman. Once she came to the window in a white dress, stood there for what seemed a long time. Another time she appeared in bright red.

Days grew longer, warmer. By the time I came to the end of my paper route, the morning darkness was a faint, rosy grayness. Buds began to swell and glisten at the extremities of the sycamore branches. My father was home again, again in his bed in the corner bedroom. At last we were told he had cancer. But we must never lose hope. Mother bought him a new pair of pajamas made of a lustrous royal blue material that she must have thought cheerful, but its brilliancy made him look paler than ever. We visited him in the evenings just as when he was in the hospital, entering his room one at a time, Lila first, then me, then Sandra, and sat out our time in a metal folding chair by the side of the bed. He did not speak of his love again, nor pull me to him for a hug. Most of the time he was sleeping, even when propped up, his head hanging to one side and his mouth open.

When it came time to collect at the mansion belonging to the garage apartment, I stood in the bright and broad hallway and gazed at a grand blue carpeted staircase with white banisters. At the staircase landing a pair of tall, deep-set windows rose up, their white curtains held in place along the sides by a thick golden rope. The air smelled clean and dry.

A few times while waiting, I walked softly and swiftly to the staircase, clasped the smooth banister, and took several steps up, my heart beating wildly, my breath quickening. How easy to continue, climb first to the landing, turn, then ascend the remaining steps to the upper rooms. But, only slightly out of breath, I was back in position near the front door by the time the servant, none the wiser, returned with my money.

School days passed in a blur. I did enough schoolwork to get by, neither failing nor excelling, and I was friendly enough only to keep from being considered odd, without inviting confidence. My teachers remembered Lila, a poor student, frequently in trouble for passing notes or talking in class, and they must have found my mild and quiet diligence a relief.

My father lay in his bed, thin and pale in his blue pajamas. I studied his nose, the blunt tip, the dark hairs extending from his nostrils. Mother didn't have time to shave him daily, and I could see the silver bristles on his cheeks. His fingernails had grown as long as a woman's.

His life was a mystery to me. I knew his birthday, June 19, 1914. I knew he had been born in Stillwater, where his father once owned a small grocery store near the college. He did not attend college. He was twenty-four years old when he married my mother, who was eighteen, just out of high school. This would have been in Oklahoma City. They met, I always understood, on a blind date. There was an older half-brother, Uncle Ferris, in insurance out in the Texas Panhandle, who sent a Christmas card every year. My father's father died of natural causes a few years after my birth, and his mother, my grandmother, lived with a sister in Tulsa. I had been only a few times to the office where my father worked. I remembered it as a large gray room with dozens of desks, a big black typewriter on each desk, fluorescent lights hung from chains all along the ceiling. My father's desk looked like all the others.

I told my mother I did not want to visit my father again. It was a waste of time, since for all I could tell he neither knew nor cared whether I was there or not. I would go again when he was awake, when he recognized me.

If he did not sleep, she said, then he would likely be in great pain.

If I did as I wanted, she said, I would regret it the rest of my life.

One early spring morning as I reached for my shoes in the dark closet, my hand happened to fall upon something silky. It was one of my mother's slips, and, on an impulse that I did not stop to question, I held it up before me. It would fit me, I thought. Just as her shoes fit me so well last summer, this slip would fit me now.

She was breathing deeply, sound asleep in my bottom bunk. It was still dark outside, dark in the room. There was no rush to get ready. I had been rising a good hour and a half earlier than I needed to in order to put in my time at the apartment window. In a jiffy, I took off my shirt and jeans and, after a moment's hesitation, my underwear too. I then tiptoed back into the room, found the panties she'd left on the railing at the foot of the bunk bed, and returned with them to the closet. Listening closely for signs of a change in her breathing and hearing only the same steady rhythm as before, I stepped quickly into the panties, thrilled by the strange smoothness, and then pulled the slip up until I could get my hands through the straps. I rolled up a pair of my socks and tucked them in the spaces for breasts. The fit was fine, as I had hoped. If only I had her shoes, the pretty sling pumps I'd worn last summer. And a dress. Why shouldn't I wear a dress?

I tiptoed back into the room. Sometimes she left her shoes under the bed, but this time she hadn't. Nor had she left her dress on the doorknob. I might find a dress, or a skirt and blouse, in the bathroom dirty clothes hamper, but of course there would be no shoes in there. I had no choice but to go to the back bedroom.

I thought of my father, saw in my mind's eye the blunt nose, the wiry hair in his nostrils, the long fingernails, his open mouth sucking in the air. What if he woke at night, what if these were his waking hours, and I found him wide-eyed, lucid in his wonderful blue pajamas, staring at me? It could not be so, I decided. He was sick. Medicine would keep him in a deep, deep sleep.

I stepped out into the hallway. My sisters' bedroom was directly across from mine, the door open. I heard deep breathing, a small whimpering sound like the one my mother made sometimes. I might have gone in their room after one of Lila's dresses, but it seemed more likely that Sandra or Lila would wake up than our father.

I had no more than an hour, I figured, until the darkness would begin to give way to morning light. Quickly then, I approached the closed door of the back bedroom. It opened quietly and I shut it behind me, stood dead still, one hand on the doorknob. I could hear my father's breathing and the ticking of the clock on his nightstand. The air smelled stale, almost sour.

His bed was in the corner of the room, placed so that he slept facing the door, with the windows behind him. Just inside the door, to my right, was the chest of drawers, and on my left, no more than six feet from my father's bed, the closet. I knew all this by memory, but I could see well enough, after a few seconds, to take it all in. How was it that this darkness was so transparent? His blinds were pulled up, he never wanted them down. That might have accounted for it. Would the moon still have shone at that early hour of the morning? Light from a street-lamp? I saw him clearly, clearer than I wanted to. His head was turned towards me, his mouth closed, and he was staring right at me.

But I saw no sign of recognition in his eyes. Could he be asleep with his eyes open? His face, even with the mouth closed, looked as expressionless as when he slept. I held my breath, froze, not taking my eyes off him. Something suddenly flashed forth from his eyes. I never saw anything like it. It must have been pain, it might have been terror. It lasted only a second. Then his eyes squeezed shut.

I prayed that they might stay shut, even if it meant he was dead. God have mercy, I wanted that dress, those shoes.

The eyes did stay shut, the mouth dropped open, the blue pajamas shimmered in the filmy dark. He began to snore softly.

At the closet I took the first dress I touched, then leaned down and found my mother's high heels. In the bathroom I stepped into the dress. It went on smooth over the slip, it felt fine, there was the faint scent of my mother, and I smoothed the bodice, the skirt, looked at the dark image of myself in the mirror, the breasts rising the way they were supposed to, the dainty collar trimmed with lace. Then I eased my feet into the high-heeled shoes and when I stood up I had my balance.

I had to watch my step. There were no carpets in our halls and in spots the floor was likely to creak. I kept to one side, on tiptoe, glad of my last summer's practice in wearing high heels. Once in the kitchen, I crossed directly to the back door, unlocked it, opened it as quietly as I could. Then I stepped out into the last of the darkness.

Such a strange, fearsome elation! The leaves on the frail mimosa tree in our backyard looked burnished and lush, the grass glistened, the black Ford sat in the driveway, gleaming and terrible and monumental. I stayed on the grass, the high and narrow heels of my mother's shoes sinking ever so slightly into the ground, the tapered skirt brushing against my shins, the smooth slip cool across my knees, but even as I stepped around the Ford, letting my fingers graze the cold steel, I knew that I was not going to stop when I came to the end of the yard. This was different from last summer. A lovely, dangerous world lay before me, a universe secret and dark and forever. Edgemere! The whirring cicadas might have been the rustling wings of angels—I did not stop to think whether fallen or not. There must have been a chill in the air, but I did not feel cold.

The little houses sat hunched and still, the street curved gently down to the park, and every step took me deeper into the mystery of myself. The high heels resounded on the concrete. I let them sing out. I didn't look back. Ahead of me the trees of the park swayed and shook, as if sweeping the sky of the last of its stars. Resplendent, I was going down into that beautiful darkness.

And that is where I went. That is where I wanted to stay.

When the school year ended, my sisters and I were shamed into helping with the care for my father. Sandra and Lila shaved him and I helped Mother bathe him. She showed me the tube that curled from his penis into a bag beneath the bed, and how to empty the bag and change it. During this last phase, Mother grew more lively and cheerful, a change I attributed to our aid, but it may simply have been relief in knowing that the end was near. At any rate, I felt good about helping my mother, and, unlike my sisters, was not disgusted by my father. He seemed to me more like a great raggedy doll than the grim and distant father I'd known, who in my mind was already dead, might have died the moment he'd seen me coming into his room in search of my mother's dress and shoes. After that, he'd lost the power to frighten me. I grew fond of him.

At the funeral, a Baptist minister obtained by the funeral home spoke of God's love and the sacrifice of His only begotten son. He went on and on. My father, dressed in his gray business suit, lay in front of the altar in a copper-colored coffin with beige satin lining. I had gone with my mother to choose it, an economy model more sturdy than beautiful. My grandmother and her sister, white-haired ladies with canes, and Uncle Ferris, the half-brother from the Texas Panhandle, accompanied by a woman whose platinum-blond hair fairly glowed from beneath a tiny black pillbox hat and veil, sat alongside us in the family mourning area, a booth hidden from the other viewers by shaded glass. In the chapel proper a few people sat scattered about, a neighbor or two, some fellow workers at OG&E, I supposed.

Way out on the far north side of the city, the cemetery had almost no trees. The hot wind blew hard. My grandmother and great aunt wore black stiff-looking dresses. My mother wore navy blue, not the dress I'd worn, but the shoes were the same. She had tied a black scarf around her hair and bought black scarves for my sisters, a black clip-on bow tie for me. I heard Uncle Ferris tell Mother that it was a shame the way lives drift apart. He was holding the blond woman's hand, and she pressed her other hand down on top of her little pillbox hat while the wind kept lifting its black net veil.

The woman in the window never undressed before me, understand. This was no striptease. Nor did I hope for one. If it was myself I looked for, saw, desired, then it was enough to see her in full regalia, just like me, in my own way, when I circled Edgemere Park in my mother's shoes, a soft spring breeze pressing the skirt against my legs.

After my father's death, when I took up my position near the hedge and looked upward into the woman's window, I began to feel afraid—not of being discovered, it was more as if I feared *not* being discovered. Even when this modest fear became purer, more general, more intense, as it shortly did, I kept up the ritual. It became a test of my courage.

Then one morning a man appeared in the window. I drew back, thinking him my father. He was thin, stark naked, his body very white, hairless, the penis thick and risen. Turning away from the window, I saw him leaving the apartment, dressed now in a gray suit like the one my father was buried in, his black shoes shining. I ran to the station house, certain that he followed me, but he did not.

In a dream, my father wanted to tell me something, something important, but he could not say it, and I woke with tears flooding my eyes, with the keen sense that he had been here, here in my room, close.

I woke possessed by restlessness. It was only two o'clock, but I rose, made my way through the dark house to the back bedroom. I had no illusion that my father would be there. At first I thought my mother might not be asleep, and I waited behind the door, listening for sounds. But it was very quiet in there. When at last I thought it safe enough to peek around the door, I could see nothing at all. I stepped inside, stark naked, silent in my bare feet on the smooth planks of the floor, and made my way to the closet by touch. Then I stood very still until my eyes adjusted to the dark. My mother slept to one side of the bed, facing the wall. A breeze blew through the open window and the air smelled clean and fresh. She had scrubbed the room top to bottom and put up lacy curtains.

I dressed in the garage. When I was halfway to the park, a car came towards me and I jumped behind the nearest shrubbery. The car drove past without slowing down. It was not a police car, but I was badly frightened. I had certainly been seen, and wouldn't I be reported now as a prowler, a peeping Tom? I took off the heels and began to run back to the house, hitching up the tight skirt above my knees.

A light was on in the kitchen window. I crept up to it and peeked in. My mother sat at the kitchen table in her robe. She smoked a cigarette and sipped from a coffee cup.

I slipped back to the garage, took off the skirt, the blouse, and hung them carefully on my bicycle handlebars. It would have been smart, I realized, to have brought a change of clothes with me to the garage. Mother might not have missed me. Something else had awakened her. She would not have thought to check my room. Restored to jeans and T-shirt, I could wait until daybreak, throw my papers as usual, then appear at breakfast as if nothing out of the ordinary had happened. She would not miss the clothes, she had other skirts, other shoes, and there would be plenty of time after she had gone to work for me to return what I'd taken.

Then I saw the row of paper sacks and remembered: my father's clothes. She had set the sacks out in the hall and asked me to carry them to the garage, six of them altogether. I had leaned them against the closed door alongside the unsold yard ornaments, and now I went to them and found a shirt, a pair of slacks, a belt. Nothing fit, but I rolled up the trouser cuffs, the sleeves of the white shirt, pulled the belt in as tight as I could. It was not the same as wearing my mother's clothes. There was no transformation. I felt foolish.

But I could ride my bicycle in them, and that is what I did, placing my mother's clothes in the basket attached to the handlebars and slowly walking the bike to the edge of the driveway before jumping onto it and pumping as though my life depended on it. The loose-fitting trousers flapped in the wind like flags. I rode without thought of destination, whipping around the park and onto dark side streets. I wanted only to be far away from that house, far from the light of that window, that kitchen where my mother sat in a haze of cigarette smoke, making her way back from the dream that had awakened her, a dream like my own, I imagined, a dream of my father.

Then I came to the streets lined with tall trees and dark mansions. Out of breath, my legs aching, I stopped, dismounted at the driveway that led to the garage apartment. There was no light in that window, but I waited, sitting on my knees in the grass beside the hedge. After a while, rested, I took my mother's clothes from the bike basket and put them on again. As I folded my father's clothes, tears came to my eyes. I had an image of my mother doing the same thing, folding one shirt after another, the white shirts he'd worn to work, the useless socks, the absurd ties, the boxer shorts. Still the sacks filled up, six of them. And then there was no more and she stopped, she looked into the closet, she closed and opened the empty drawers. What was I looking for? What did I imagine I would find there? The sadness of these questions overwhelmed me. I sobbed furiously. Then I stopped.

He is not here, I told myself, my father is dead and I am not my mother.

I stepped away from the hedge, took a deep breath, walked up to the front door of the mansion. The bell rang out so loud I was sure that all the world heard it. But nobody answered. I rang it again and again but nobody answered. I tried the door. Locked, naturally.

And so I walked boldly to the side of the house, passed through the brick-columned portico, my mother's shoes clicking on the asphalt driveway, and then I stood poised at the steps that led up to the entrance of the garage apartment, my hand on the cool wrought iron railing. I hesitated only a moment before ascending. The night air was warm and sweet. The trees seemed to whisper, every breeze-touched leaf a tongue. I understood that secret language. It spoke of my beauty. Each step I took seemed further proof of it, a beauty born of my own grief, of a sorrowfully personal mortality. To live was no more than a fatal birthright. The miracle lay curled in the blood alongside the calamity.

I reached the door, knocked loudly, waited, knocked again. No light, no sound. I tried opening the door. Like the other, it was firmly locked. No one would open it, no one was inside. The realization seemed final, absolute.

I turned away and knew that I would go there no more. Day was breaking by the time I stepped back inside my parents' house, but everyone was sound asleep. I had plenty of time to change into my own clothes, ride again to the mansions and deliver the morning newspapers.

What else is there, after all, but to go back to the small, safe houses of our mothers and fathers, rest ourselves as long as we can in that sad clarity, that somber, subduing light? We live on the edge of a fathomless dark sea. No mansion on earth can contain us.

All the rest of that long summer of my fourteenth year, day broke in our house as naturally as sin. In the garage, awaiting the Salvation Army, the row of paper bags filled with my father's clothes sat next to the stacks of his toothless hillbillies, his grinning Aunt Jemimas. Inside the house, my mother rested nightly in the bedroom my father had occupied, and my sisters, dead to the world, afloat in their own dark dreams, their cagey sicknesses, slept on and on. Son and brother, I vowed to stay with them. You're the man of the house now, my mother kept saying, and so I was.

Robert Love Taylor, born and reared in Oklahoma City, now divides his time between Union County, Pennsylvania, and Grayson County, Virginia. He teaches at Bucknell University. *Lady of Spain* is his most recent book.

I *was probably a couple of years younger than my narrator when, like him, I found a pair of my mother's shoes in our garage, but the experience was, apparently, memorable. I came to wonder if a story might be made out of this slight but haunting memory. The rest of the story I made up.*

Although I never had a newspaper route, a number of my friends did, and I was always struck by the idea of a job that required you to be out in the early morning dark, that strange, dreamy time before the waking lives of most people begin. And what if there were another walker, someone with no obvious purpose for being out at such an hour? What would my fourteen-year-old paper boy—with an imaginative, even slightly disturbed, state of mind—make of such a ghostly figure? The possibilities intrigued me.

The story didn't get off the ground, though, until it occurred to me to yoke the boy's semi-hallucinatory adventures with the solid reality of his father's dying. My own father died quite suddenly at the age of sixty-nine. I was forty-one and living far away. For this story, then, I drew on memories of my two grandfathers' painfully drawn-out deaths, the rooms they lay in for so long and the downright heroic care of my grandmothers. The character of Larry's father, a remote man made even more remote by his long accommodation to death, exaggerates that of my father's father.

An odd mix of memory, displacement, and invention, then, ended by engaging an order of mysteries that made me feel I was getting at something important, writing fiction.

George Singleton

OUTLAW HEAD & TAIL

(from *Playboy*)

Normally I couldn't have made the tape that Saturday. Right there during the job interview a few weeks before, Frank, my soon-to-be boss, had said, "Rickey, is there anything about this job that you have a problem with?"

I didn't say, "I can't work for a man who ends sentences with prepositions." I couldn't. It was a job bouncing, or at least talking. I was going to be something called a pre-bouncer. If some guy came into the Treehouse and looked like he meant trouble, I was supposed to go up to him and start a little conversation, let him know this wasn't the kind of place to throw a punch without inelegant and indubitable consequences.

I have a way with words. I'm synonymous with rapport.

I said to Frank, "Well, I'd rather not work Saturday days because my wife has to go to temple and I have to drive her over there. I don't go to temple. Hell, I don't even go to church," I said. "I don't mind working Sundays, but I'd really like it if you could get someone to work afternoons on Saturdays for me. Night—Saturday night—I'll be here. The only thing I ask of you is that I don't work Saturday afternoons, say, until six o'clock."

Frank said, "You know, you talked me into it. Man, what a way with words. It's a deal. You're a godsend, Rick. I lucked out getting you as a pre-bouncer."

Frank had opened the Treehouse just outside Darlington, South Carolina a year earlier but didn't hire a bouncer or pre-bouncer right away. About the same time his insurance agent told him his payments would soon double, though, he hired me and a guy named Sparky Voyles to keep things down. During the first year Frank had put in claims for a whole new set of glasses, from shot and snifter to the special two-foot beer glasses he ordered, plus twelve tables, sixteen chairs and another tree stump to replace the one that caught on fire, causing smoke damage to the ceiling and forty-two stitches to his own head one night after a fearful brawl erupted over whether Chevys or Fords would dominate the circuit in the upcoming season.

Frank bought the Treehouse because of insurance, ironically. He'd worked in the pulpwood trade and a load of logs had slipped off a truck he was standing behind, came rolling right off like a giant wave and clipped him on the knees so hard they said he could run as fast backward as forward for a few days.

Of course, he couldn't run at all and had to get fake knees installed. His lawyer also got him another quarter million dollars or so because of a life-time's worth of pain and consequent night-mares. Frank took most of that money and made the Treehouse, a regular small warehouse building he furnished with tree trunks from floor to ceiling. If you blindfolded someone and took him inside the bar, then took off the mask and showed him around, he'd have the feeling that the entire building was set above the ground, built into the forest.

During the first year there were fights and insurance claims, but the second year started right with me and Sparky to quiet things down. Frank didn't want us to be too heavy-handed, though. He didn't want the Treehouse to end up so quiet it looked like a flock of mute birds had built their nests there. He asked only for stability.

Sparky had gone the same route as Frank—he worked at the rail-road before becoming a bouncer, getting paid under the table because he took in disability checks after his thumbs got cut off between two boxcars that had clanged together. They weren't supposed to collide and he thought he could prevent it from happening. He couldn't. Sparky had been a brakeman originally, out of Lexington.

Anyway, I worked hard pre-bouncing and kept up with what I had to know, which was mainly words. This is how I get back to the tape and that Saturday. What I'm saying is, because I'm so conscientious about my job, it could've killed my marriage.

Last Thursday, Jessie went into her doctor's office to finally have him go ahead and do that sonogram thing. She couldn't wait to know what our first baby was going to be, building her argument around the fact that we didn't make all that much money, so if it were a boy we needed to pinch even harder to save up for his circumcision.

Jessie works as a freelance interior decorator. She got her degree in art history and felt like it gave her the right to design living rooms.

I had to take Jessie to the doctor's office. But she couldn't get an appointment before four o'clock in the afternoon. I got clearance from Frank to get off work on Thursday, but that meant I had to come in Saturday morning at eleven, because the guy who normally worked Saturdays needed to go to a wedding. It was a simple and clean swap. There didn't seem to be that much of a problem.

So I took my wife to the doctor and she did what she had to do, but the doctor still couldn't even take a stab at the baby's sex, because the baby kept its back to us the whole time. I was hoping it'd be a girl. I have never seen myself as being the father of a shy son.

Two days later I drove Jessie to the synagogue. I drove back home in time to throw in a tape and set the VCR so I wouldn't miss *Bonanza*, which showed in syndication every Saturday on one of the cable channels. I set the station and time to record, then left for the bar.

I watch *Bonanza* every week. That's where I get my ways. That's where I get my ability to talk people out of starting fights. One time this burly truck-driver type seemed upset that a white guy came into the Treehouse with an African–American woman. There'd been a similar episode on *Bonanza* one time when Hoss piped up to a stranger, "Well, would you rather be blind and not have to see the ways of the world?" He said it to a redneck, of course. Words of wisdom, I thought right then and there. I've thought "words of wisdom" on more than one occasion while watching Ben Cartwright bringing up his boys the best he could. I remember watching *Bonanza* when I was a boy, too, and how I admired the way Little Joe and Hoss and even Adam handled themselves in town. My father, though, used to throw beer cans at the television set and say, "What them boys need to use a little more often is their trigger fingers, not their tongues."

It's that kind of thinking that makes it almost amazing that I became a pre-bouncer. If I had taken my father seriously back in the Sixties, I'd have ended up being something more secluded and self-centered, like a bookkeeper or a jockey.

I said to the burly guy, "Hey, there's two things that can happen here: Either you can learn to understand that love is blind, or I can get Sparky to come over here with his eight remaining fingers and blind you himself so you don't have to live with seeing inter-racial dating in your midst. *¿Comprende, amigo?*"

I pointed at Sparky. Without his thumbs, it looks like he could use his fists as skewers. The truck driver looked over at Sparky, back to me, then to the white guy and the black woman. He said, "Well, OK then," just like that. I stood my ground and tried not to shake. The little voice in my head kept thanking the Cartwrights over and over.

So I put the tape in the VCR, set the station and time, and drove off to the Treehouse. The bar doesn't open until noon, but I got there at eleven to help Frank clean up from the night before and set out our specials in the plastic stand-up signs on each table. Frank said, "How goes it, Rickey?"

I said, "Good."

He said, "Uh-huh. You know, we didn't really get to talk yesterday. I mean, I heard you say that you still didn't know if you'll have a little boy or a girl, but what else did the doctor say?"

I wiped off a table. Friday night had been pretty slow at the Treehouse. Down the road there had been a yearly festival with a battle of bands and a tractor pull. I said, "He didn't say much. He asked if she'd been taking care of herself, whether she'd quit drinking and smoking. She said she had, which is true, and goddamn, it ain't fun around the house, by the way. Then he said he thought her delivery date might need to be changed to about a week earlier. Not much else went on. He dabbed some goo on her big stomach and we saw this little crooked Vienna sausage–looking thing on the TV screen. Then he gave us the tape."

Well, no. I said, "The tape!"

I didn't say good-bye to Frank. I didn't tell him I'd be right back. I just left the Treehouse, got into my car and drove fifteen minutes back to my house.

It was too late. Right over the image of my as-yet-sexless child, the floating little thumb-sucking thing inside Jessie's body, Hoss now talked to Little Joe about how skittish the horses seemed to be all of a sudden.

Sparky said, "Well, it could be worse. At least she still has the baby. One time when I was working Amtrak, this woman came screaming out of the bathroom saying she'd miscarried into the toilet. We were flying down the track at about sixty miles an hour, you know. I was on my break and was eating an egg-salad sandwich in the dining car. I remember all this because I had a mouthful of egg in my mouth when the woman made the announcement."

I nodded my head and shoulders quickly, trying to get Sparky to finish the story. I needed to make some phone calls or talk to some customers.

Sparky said, "She came running out of that bathroom saying she thought the thing came out of her but she wasn't sure. On a train, you know, it goes straight down to the track. At sixty miles an hour you don't exactly have time to check what came out in the bowl underneath you. One time I had a kidney stone and I was supposed to be pissing into a strainer, but I kept forgetting. So I have a stone on the tracks somewhere between Lexington and Danville."

I nodded hard, waved my right hand like a paddle wheel for Sparky to finish up. A group of four women came into the Treehouse, all of them in their thirties. I needed to find a way to talk to them.

"This woman on the train—her name ended up being Brenda—had a nervous breakdown right there and then. She fainted. Two men who were afraid of airplanes and traveled on business trips to New York all the time got up and grabbed her, checked her heartbeat and breathing and put a pillow behind her head. I said, 'Damn, you don't see this every day on Amtrak, do you?' Well, as it ended up, we took her off the train at the next stop and sent her to the local hospital. That would be in Gaffney—we were doing the run down to New Orleans—and then, on our way back up, she waited there at the station for us. She got on board and said, 'I want you to tell me where we were when I miscarried. I want you to take me to the spot so I can give my baby a proper burial.' I told her that by this time—a couple of days had gone by—surely the miscarriage was gone. But she got on board the train and took it to Charlotte, and then we got out and started walking back south on the tracks. My boss said I had to do it and that I'd probably get a raise for the whole thing."

Two more women walked into the bar. I waved my arm faster for Sparky to get to the moral of his story.

"We found about twenty turtle shells," said Sparky. "You wouldn't believe how many turtles get stuck in between the tracks, especially snapping turtles when you're near a lake or in the swamp. We found turtle shells, and that was it. I wasn't even sure what I was supposed to be looking for. And if I did run across anything that looked like a baby, I didn't want to see it, or point it out to Brenda. So, as it ended up, after I finally convinced her that we'd gone past the spot where she miscarried, she walked over into the woods and got some sticks. She borrowed my shoelaces and made a small wooden cross, stuck it a few feet from the track and said she felt better. And an hour later this gandy dancer came from the station to pick us up. I wonder whatever happened to old Brenda," Sparky said, like I'd know.

He walked off with his hands straight down in his pockets, like trowels were attached to the ends of his arms.

I lost all pride and any bashfulness whatsoever and started asking women if they had any of their sonogram videotapes around their houses. I offered $100 to buy one of them.

Teresa Smiley said she'd be right back. Teresa Smiley said she kept her sonogram on a bookshelf stuck between a 12-step–program book and a Stephen King novel. Since her husband had custody of their little boy, she got depressed thinking about it but said, "A hundred dollars? Hell, I won't sell for less than three hundred."

It was one of those occasions when I didn't have time to check out the going rate for sonograms on the black market. So I said, "One fifty." I said, "Lookit, unless you had your sonogram on Thursday, there's going to be a different date down there on the screen. I mean, I'm going to have to go to great lengths to find a way to forge the video."

Teresa Smiley stared hard at me, then sat back down at her table, a table filled with women who worked third shift at the mill. Teresa said, "The memory of a child is worth more than a hundred and fifty dollars, Rickey. And your wife won't even notice the wrong date down there. We're interested in the baby, not the time of day. I'm insulted and you should be ashamed."

"A minute ago," I said, "you were saying how you got depressed even knowing the tape was around. Come on, Teresa, you don't know how much I need this tape." I told her my story but didn't explain about taping *Bonanza* over the image of my baby. I told her it was professional wrestling, so she would understand why I might be a little distraught about having to work on Saturday in the first place.

Teresa said, "Two fifty." I said, "Two," and she left to get the tape. I didn't even ask her if her child, too, was turned away from the camera, and if it wasn't turned away, if it was real obvious as to the sex of the child. When I saw ours, I wasn't even sure which was the head and which was the tail. To me, Jessie's sonogram looked like a picture of an ulcer or something on her stomach wall.

Sparky came over to me a few minutes after Teresa left and said, "You might have some trouble coming at you, but I'll be there."

I said, "What do you mean?" The worst thing that could happen, I thought, was that Jessie's service would be canceled and she'd come to the Treehouse to spend the day.

Sparky said, "Well, don't turn around immediately, but there's a guy down at the end of the bar staring a hole through you. It's Teresa's ex."

I didn't turn at all. I could feel the guy staring straight into my brain. The Treehouse had its regulars who came in every day—housepainters, self-employed body-shop men, the disabled, people who really worked only on Wednesday mornings over at the flea market—but there were people who came in haphazardly, maybe once a month, to sit by themselves and get over whatever it was that stuck in their craw. I never had to pre-bounce any of those people. First, it wouldn't matter—if they wanted to fight, they'd fight regardless of what I had to say. Second, most of them were so consumed with whatever bothered them they didn't have the energy to get off the bar stool and start a fight, though they'd probably like to see one.

I said to Sparky, "The one who got custody?"

He said, "That's the one. Name's Ted, but everybody calls him Slam. He won the state wrist-wrestling championship four years in a row, and the Southeast tournament twice."

I said, "Goddamn it." I thought, If only I'd taken the time to look at the videotape. I thought, If only the baby had turned around so we'd know the sex of it. I thought, If only Jessie hadn't gotten the appointment on Thursday. And almost caught myself thinking, If only I'd put on a rubber that night.

Sparky said, "I arm-wrestled him one time, but it's hard for me to get a grip, what without a thumb. Hell it was hard for him, too. I kept sliding right through his hand."

"Shut up, Sparky," I said and walked over to Slam. I said, "Your ex-wife's about to save my life, man. I screwed up and taped over the videotape of my child-to-be inside the womb, and Teresa's going to get y'all's so I can make a tape of it." I said, "My name's Rickey."

Slam said, "Wife."

I said, "Excuse me?" He didn't look at me. He seemed to keep staring at where I had stood talking to Sparky.

"Not ex-wife. Wife. Just like a piece of paper can't make a marriage, a piece of paper can't end one neither," said Slam.

I said, "Are you Catholic?"

This is no lie. Slam said, "I'm an American and it's the American way."

I said, "Oh. Well, then your wife is about to save my skin."

Tape the tape, I thought. I thought, I should've asked her to tape the tape. I mean, there wasn't a reason why Teresa shouldn't keep her own tape and there wasn't a reason for me to pay so much to more or less swipe hers. I tried to think of a way of getting to her before she even got back inside the Treehouse, so we could at least renegotiate.

Slam said, "What?" He held his beer in a way I'd not seen before, a half inch from his face and a quarter inch to the right. I thought he was using the can as a mirror to check out anyone who walked up behind him. Being a pre-bouncer, I notice things like that.

I said, "Your wife's saving my ass."

There's this look that only certain people can give. There's this look some people can give that's somewhere between smoke in their eyes and hand grenades in their pockets. Slam had that look. I turned my head toward Sparky, but he'd already started punching a guy named Cull who came in drunk and wanted a piece of a guy named Tinker for not painting his house evenly.

Slam said, "Well, I guess that's better than humping your ass, Bo." He said, "Glad to hear it," grabbed his beer and left the bar with it, either unaware of the law or unconcerned about the police who regularly parked across the street.

Sparky came over and said, "You got a way with words, Rickey. Whatever it is you said, you did it, man."

I sat down on the bar stool next to Slam's and concentrated so as not to pee in my pants like in the cartoons.

As soon as Jessie had taken that one-minute-and-you-know-if-you've-really-missed-your-period test in the bathroom, she pulled a Walkman out of the bedroom closet, put in new batteries and slipped in a tape of Mahler's *Fourth Symphony*. She pulled the earpieces of the headset as far apart as possible, strapped them around her sides and put the volume on full blast. Jessie said, "Rickey, we're going to have a baby."

I'd been watching her from the other side of the room. I didn't even know about the bathroom test. I had been sitting there on one side of the room reading my thesaurus. "A baby?" I said. "Are you sure?"

She said, "I have this theory. I believe that if you play music inside the womb, the fetus absorbs it, and when the baby comes out, instead of crying and screaming, it'll make noises similar to an orchestra."

I said, "What?"

She said, "The reason a baby always wails is that it absorbs the noises of the outside world for nine months. In the city it hears horns honking, people screaming, the conglomeration of people's conversations all going into one big drone, dogs barking, cats crying out in the night, the hiss of a teapot." She had a list of every possible noise, it seemed. She finally finished her dictum with, "So if I keep playing classical music, when the baby's in pain or wants its bottle, we'll be serenaded with French horns and oboes, the violin. Bassoons." She said, "Bassoons! And piccolos and flutes and cellos."

Hell, to me it didn't sound like all that bad a theory. I mean, it's logically possible. I said, "Why don't you order some of those books on tape, and then at night the baby can tell us stories."

Jessie put another Walkman on her own ears and left the room. She left the room a lot during her pregnancy. I'm not sure why and I've never asked—I've always tried to be sensitive to her needs.

Ted, or Slam, whatever, kept standing outside the Treehouse. He was waiting for his ex-wife, Teresa, I knew. Just about the time I started to go outside to tell him I wouldn't make a tape of his pre-born child, Teresa tapped me on the shoulder with the videotape. Like every intelligent woman with a lunatic ex-husband in her life, she had sensed danger. She had parked her Buick a few blocks away and come in the back entrance. I said, "Ted's here."

She looked around the place. She said, "Ted was in here earlier, but I don't see him now."

I said, "Out front."

"Oh. Well. Good," she said. "That'll be two hundred dollars, no check."

I only had a check. I said, "Hey, look, I got a better idea. Why don't we find another VCR and do a tape-to-tape so you don't have to lose yours totally? I mean, someday you might want it back." I kind of saw a big confrontation ahead, like when birth mothers arrange for adoptive parents, then change their minds in the delivery room.

Teresa said, "I won't change my mind, believe me. I've had it. I want a new life, bubba. As a matter of fact, I've already contacted the paper to advertise a yard sale for next weekend. I'm getting rid of my old high school yearbooks, too."

I said, "Well, OK." It was nearly three o'clock and I couldn't take the chance of Jessie's getting a ride home from the synagogue with one of her friends, slipping in her tape, and fainting when she saw that her baby had suddenly gained a clear and distinct shape that looked like Hoss. I said, "Hold on a second."

I bought Teresa a drink on my monthly tab and walked over to where Sparky stood in the corner of the bar, scanning the slim crowd. "Look, Sparky," I said, "do you have one of those twenty-four-hour bank-teller cards by any chance? I lost mine in the machine—not because I didn't have any money but because the back strip got dirty or something—and it's Saturday and the bank's closed and I need two hundred bucks right now to buy off the tape. I can give you a check today, or if you wait until Monday morning I can go over to the bank and get cash for you."

Sparky said, "I hope you remember this when you go and name your child."

I said, "I can't name my kid Sparky."

Sparky said, "I wouldn't expect you to." He reached into the wallet he kept chained to his belt loop and pulled out 200 one-dollar bills. He said, "My given name's Earl. Earl for a boy, Earline for a girl."

I don't know why I said OK, but I did. I figured if I could get Sparky drunk later on in the evening maybe he'd forget the promise.

"Here you go," I said to Teresa. She handed me the tape. She handed me her own personal sonogram videotape of the only child she'd ever had and said, "I hope I picked up the right one. Slam and me did some amateur strip stuff one night, but we never sent it off to any of those programs on cable."

I asked Sparky to cover for me, to use the word discretionary or castigatory should a fight seem imminent, and left through the back door.

There is a Supreme Being. Someone powerful exists, or at least existed for me that afternoon. I pulled out my tape filled with *Bonanza*, plus a half-hour special on the NASCAR season at the halfway point, and pushed Teresa's baby's video into my machine. It didn't need rewinding. I wondered if she'd ever really watched it.

It wasn't her strip show. Right there on the screen, in brilliant shades of gray, was a form. I couldn't make out eyes or genitals. There was no way possible Jessie could see the difference between her womb and that of a woman who grew up and lived in a mobile home.

I felt good about living in America.

The Supreme Being stayed on my side, because while the tape was playing, in walked Jessie, home from a committee meeting of a group called Sisters of Bashemath, Ishmael's Daughter. She said, "I thought you had to work."

I moved closer to the television screen down on the carpet, and held my forearm parallel to the date and time logo at the bottom. I said, "I went and got things going, but I started feeling a little nauseated."

Jessie came up to me, all smiles, and put her hand on the back of my neck. She said, "That's so sweet. You're having sympathy pains."

I knelt on the floor in front of the TV screen. I could hear Mahler's *First Symphony* playing out of the cassette attached to Jessie's stretched sash. I said, "Well, yeah, I had some pains all right, but I'm feeling much better now."

Jessie asked me to rewind the sonogram. I clenched my teeth, rewound it, prayed to all the superior beings ever invented for her not to notice the difference. And she didn't. While we watched Teresa's child float around in her belly, Jessie lowered the volume on her Walkman and pushed her chin in toward her stomach. She said, "We're watching you right now, honey."

I didn't say anything about any kind of name recognition, like, "We're looking at you, Earl or Earline."

I sat and watched. And I thought to myself, Certainly I want my own child to grow up to be happy and famous and healthy and intelligent. I thought, I want to be able to spend time with my kid, go to games, teach him or her how to communicate, take long trips across the country to see how different people live.

And deep down, oddly, I kind of wanted the kid I watched on the television screen to end up a bandit and a folk hero. I wanted that obscure head and tail I saw on the screen to grow up to be an outlaw of sorts, a fugitive. At that very moment I knew that I'd always keep up with Ted and Teresa's boy and help him out whenever it seemed necessary and possible. I'd tell him to keep moving—always—in order to stay content, to talk to strangers no matter how scary it might seem.

George Singleton was raised in Greenwood, South Carolina, and educated at Furman University and UNC-Greensboro. He teaches at the Greenville Fine Arts Center and the South Carolina Governor's School for the Arts. His stories have appeared in *The Georgia Review, Fiction International, Playboy, Kansas Quarterly, The Chattahoochee Review, The Crescent Review, South Carolina Review, The Cimarron Review,* and *American Literary Review,* among others.

W *hen I lived in Darlington I listened more than anything else, for people there had stories. One time my bartender friend George Standish was getting off work and he asked if I'd like to go see his baby-to-be on videotape. I said I didn't really care to do so—but that I would later— and then he said something to the effect of, "I just hope I don't tape Sunday's race over it."*

That image of some poor new husband taping a car race over his first child's first picture stuck with me, of course. A few months later "Outlaw Head & Tail" started. I sent it to Playboy. *Chris Napolitano asked me to add some tension to the Rickey/Slam confrontation, and to bring the ending back into the home. I did.*

At least that's how I remember things.

Nanci Kincaid

PRETENDING THE BED WAS A RAFT

(from *Carolina Quarterly*)

"Take off everything but your shoes—in there." The nurse handed her a green hospital gown.

Belinda passed an old man standing in his cowboy boots, his green gown tied at the neck and hanging open so his backside was exposed. Luckily he'd kept his underpants on. If they make some people take them off they should make everybody, Belinda thought. She was so small that the gown wrapped around her nearly twice. She tied the strings into bows.

"Put all your clothes and belongings in this sack," the nurse said when she came back, "and have a seat along the wall."

There were seven folding chairs in a row. Old men took up six of them. Belinda sat in the empty chair. I am twenty-three years old, she said to herself, and they've got me in here on goddamn senior citizens' day.

"You having trouble with your bowels?" a pink-faced man asked the black man beside him.

"Stomach. All it does is whine and rumble all day."

"Me, it's my bowels. Bowel trouble."

Belinda didn't want to sit with these old men, so feeble not even half of them had their gowns tied on right. She was stark naked underneath her gown too. They shouldn't have the right to know that.

She sat looking at her fingernails. They'd always been paper thin and so soft they broke right off if she just scratched a mosquito bite too hard. She had been meaning to get the fingernail clipper out and trim them good, but like half the things she was planning to do, she hadn't got around to it yet. It made her sick sometimes thinking about all the things she hadn't gotten around to. These men are old enough to die, she thought—but I'm only twenty-three. She began to bite the edges of her fingernails and tear them off with her teeth.

She wondered if the x-ray would hurt. 'Like making a movie out of an enema' was the way the doctor had described it. Did he think she was some kind of fool? Belinda's feet were sweating inside her leather-look shoes. When she got inside the x-ray room and took her shoes off her feet would smell to high heaven. Belinda looked down the row at the bare-legged men. The black man had on unlaced shoes with no socks. One man wore slippers. The little pink man next to her didn't have twelve hairs per leg and those he did have were an inch long and poked out like bent antenna wires.

"I hope to goodness I don't look as foolish as the rest of you," the man in cowboy boots said. "Not you, ma'am," he nodded to Belinda. "But don't none of us do a dress justice."

"If they'd a told me we was gon be sitting out here in these nightgowns I'd of thought twice . . ." the black man said.

"I'd of worn better socks," said the man on the end sticking his legs out in the air to show that he was wearing mismatched socks, both white, but one with a red ring and the other with a green one.

"I ain't done nothing but sit since I got here," the black man said.

"How long you been waiting?" Belinda asked.

"Past long enough. Ain't ate a bite since Saturday."

"Naw, they don't let you eat nothing," the pink man said. "Hollow you out like a drum."

The nurse called, "Mr. Ward, Mr. Miller, Mr. Faulk, Mrs. Bedlow. Follow me to x-ray." The group obeyed, single file, Mr. Faulk leading the line in his underpants and boots, which the others pretended not to notice.

All it was was a little blood, Belinda thought. She had quit worrying about blood a long time ago, three big-headed babies ago. Their heads like cannonballs the way they had blasted out of her belly, leaving her torn wide open and bleeding like rain all three times. And the doctor, a different one every delivery, just sewed her back up each time, like her body was some made-in-Japan outfit that had this one particular seam that would not hold and had to be reinforced every time she turned around.

"You're a mighty little girl to be having such a big-headed baby," the doctor had said after her first baby, as he stitched between her legs with his needle and thread.

"Big heads run in my husband's family." That was a lie because she wasn't but seventeen at the time and didn't have a husband.

"This'll fix you."

But afterwards Belinda was not what she called fixed. Virgil said after the baby, Penny, was born that Belinda was about like making love to the Grand Canyon. He had nearly ripped her stitches loose because he couldn't wait much better than a dog. Wouldn't hardly give her time to catch her breath nevermind heal her stitches.

She had cried until he finally quit bothering her. Until he took up asking her every day or two, "Belinda, how them stitches doing? Them stitches heal yet?"

"Certain things take time, Virgil." Most nights she lay wide awake, trying not to cry, because she was afraid she would never again be the same as she was before.

Then once in broad daylight, mid-afternoon, when Penny was sleeping good and Belinda laid down on the sofa to get a nap too, Virgil asked her as serious as a preacher to let him see those stitches.

"Please, Belinda. I never seen stitches. I want to see how they do it is all."

"Virgil Bedlow, keep your nastiness to yourself."

"You act like it's unnatural. I'm practically your husband."

"Practically? That dog don't hunt, Virgil. Practically don't put a ring on my finger, or give my Mama a minute's peace. And 'practically' sure don't qualify you to look at my stitches."

Virgil married her not two weeks afterwards. And now, two more babies later, here she was letting another doctor get his face right up between her legs and investigate the place she wouldn't even let Virgil investigate, and she called herself loving Virgil but never had met a doctor she liked much. And now in just a little while another complete stranger would be looking at her better than she had ever looked at herself. It gave her the creeps.

It made her think of the time she took that pocket mirror and locked herself in the bathroom to see if she could find out where the blood was coming from, but she had disgusted herself and quit it. Some things just have to be left to nature, she thought. But then she started hurting so bad—really bad—and she let Virgil drive her to the emergency room again. It was the third time in two months she had had an attack like this, but it was worse this time. She hurt so bad she was crying and Virgil carried her inside the hospital because she couldn't walk. That was when the doctors set up these x-rays. They didn't want to since Virgil was out of work and without any insurance. But they wrote on her chart, 'unexplained bleeding,' and told her to come back for special x-rays.

Belinda thought about that a lot, the doctors writing 'unexplained' as the problem. The problem was the bleeding hurt. When something hurts, you try to make it stop hurting. That's all. Explained or unexplained was beside the point. The truth was Belinda didn't know of much in this world that was explained to her satisfaction.

"Please have a seat along this wall," the nurse said. The group obeyed silently. When Mr. Faulk in cowboy boots sat in the cold chair he jumped at the touch of it against his skin. The nurse noticed this, reached over and said, "Let me tie that gown for you, Mr. Faulk."

The old man pulled back from her. "Naw," he said. "I don't like to be tied into nothing."

Belinda eyed Mr. Faulk with embarrassment. He's acting like he's at the insane asylum and his gown is a straitjacket, she thought. Maybe he thinks they're going to tie him to the x-ray table and give him shocks. Maybe he'd be better off if they did.

"Them machines can look right through clothes," pink-faced Mr. Ward said. "Isn't no need to make us undress like this because if the x-ray machine can see through skin then it can see through your clothes."

"If I'd a known that," Mr. Miller, the black man said, "I'd of thought twice . . ."

"I'm thinking twice now," Mr. Faulk said. "All that's got me here is my doctor saying these tests might stand between me and cancer."

"If cancer don't scare you, you a fool," Mr. Miller said.

"I lost my wife to cancer two years ago," Mr. Faulk said. "I quit tobacco the day she died. I smoked and chewed for fifty-eight years, then just quit cold."

"I reckon you miss it," said Mr. Miller.

"I could of picked a worse habit," said Mr. Faulk. "My wife always said she'd rather me have a mouth full of tobacco than a mouth full of lies. She said as long as I had my lips all over a cigarette butt then maybe I wouldn't have them on no other kind of . . ." The men laughed at Mr. Faulk who grinned exposing his brown tobacco-stained teeth and nodded that 'excuse my language' look toward Belinda. It was that fake politeness men do when they are secretly pleased with something nasty they have just got away with saying. It made Belinda sick when men acted polite like that.

Her own daddy had taught her every dirty joke he knew and never had made any kind of 'excuse me' at the end. She had sat on the back porch, nights, with her daddy so drunk he couldn't tell if Belinda was herself or her mother or some woman named Rosemary. He had spent many a drunken hour trying to teach Hopeful, their spotted hound, how to two-step to "Amazing Grace." More than once Hopeful seemed to get the hang of it at which point Belinda's daddy went crazy thinking about how rich they could get off a dancing dog like that. He got it in his mind that it was a story that should be covered by Walter Cronkite up in New York. Nevermind that Belinda's mother kept telling him Walter Cronkite had gone off TV a good ten years ago and might even be dead by now. More than once he ran up a long distance bill so bad that the phone company came out and disconnected the phone just to make a point. Belinda had always admired her daddy's enthusiasm once he got an idea in his head. She hadn't known back then that his enthusiasm was compliments of Johnny Walker Red—and that she was watching him drink himself straight into the grave.

"I ain't ate since Saturday," Mr. Miller said.

Belinda eyed Mr. Miller, who was cold Alabama black with tiny little cotton balls of hair over his ears and around the back of his head. He was the skinniest man Belinda had ever seen.

"What x-ray are you having?" Belinda asked.

"Top and bottom," he said. "They're going to look at them pictures and see what makes my stomach whine so."

"Well," Mr. Faulk said, "if it don't kill you it might do you some good."

"You ever been tested for tapeworm?" pink Mr. Ward asked. "Could be tapeworm that's keeping you from putting on weight."

"I used to be skinny," Belinda said, "before I had kids."

"You look like a kid your own self," Mr. Faulk said, "except I see that wedding ring on your finger."

"You look too little to have kids," said Mr. Miller.

"I'm twenty-three."

"How many kids you got?"

"Three."

"Three? Looks like you ain't had time to have three kids," said Mr. Miller.

"I got one six, one four, and one almost two." Belinda reached into her plastic bag and got her billfold out and showed the old men pictures of her kids, Penny, Patsy, and Lamar.

Mr. Miller looked at the round faced, big eyed children, the girls brown haired and the boy blond—like Virgil. "Woooo. They sure do smile," he said.

The x-ray itself didn't hurt Belinda a bit. It was all the probing and situating that came before that hurt. Once on the x-ray table Belinda kept her eyes shut the whole time even when the doctor tried to get her to watch the TV screen hanging overhead and see for herself what he was doing. She had never in her life wanted to see her insides, much less now with all the tubes and dyes shot up inside her and twisting and swirling around. Especially not since she knew there was something wrong.

"There it is. That's what we're looking for. See it?" The doctor said to his nurse.

The nurse snapped a bunch of electronic buttons and Belinda heard the whirr of machines all around her. Then she heard the doctor saying the word biopsy, and the nurse scurried all over the place grabbing up metal instruments and making a squeaking sound in her rubber shoes. Belinda was trying to pray even though she couldn't remember a single time in her life when praying had ever helped anything—but still, lack of results had never stopped her from trying. All she could think of at the exact moment was "make a joyful noise unto the Lord" so she just kept saying it over and over to herself, "make a joyful noise, make a joyful noise."

Virgil was waiting out in the car with the kids when Belinda came out after her x-ray. He didn't have any better sense than to let the kids eat Dairy Queen dillies while they waited, so when Belinda got in the car she sat in a glob of cherry dilly that Lamar had spilt. Virgil started the car. Belinda kissed Lamar and handed him over the seat to his sisters.

"So," Virgil said, "what'd they say this time?"

"Mama, we're thirsty," Penny said. "Can we stop and get a Dr Pepper?"

"Y'all just had ice cream." Virgil backed the car out of the parking lot. "Lamar, you sit still, you hear me?" He swatted at the boy, who started to cry.

"See what you done?" Belinda said to Virgil.

"Stop it!" Patsy shrieked, pushing Lamar over onto Penny's lap. "He stepped on my leg, Mama! Make him move over."

"I don't want him on me," Penny shoved Lamar back onto Patsy, so Patsy and him both screamed twice as loud.

Virgil slammed on the car brakes and leaned over the seat, "Do you want me to stop this car and wear your butts out?" he shouted, red-faced. The children quieted and sat in their places, pouting.

"Patsy won't stop touching me," Penny said.

"If I hear another word I'm going to touch all three of you—with my belt," Virgil shouted. "You hear me?" The children nodded and sat wilted but quiet on the hot plastic upholstery. The truth was Virgil had never used a belt on the children. His threats always seemed to work well enough.

Virgil ran his hand through his wet hair and eased the car out into traffic. It was hot for April. They drove several blocks, Belinda holding her hand out the window, opening and closing her fist. Her fingernails were bitten to the quick and pink with soreness. She had to tell Virgil. He had every right to know. "Virgil . . ." she said, but he wasn't listening.

Two screaming fire trucks appeared in the rearview mirror. "Look out, Daddy," the children shrieked. Virgil tried frantically to maneuver the car out of their path. "Shit!" he gunned the motor and shot across two lanes of traffic. The sirens, startling and deafening, came from out of nowhere almost sideswiping him as they roared past. Virgil ran a red light and swerved completely off the road nearly hitting a sign that said CAUTION SOFT SHOULDER. "Damn." Virgil slammed on the brakes, sliding to a stop, slinging the children hard against the front seat. "Sonsabitches going to kill somebody." He looked at the children, stunned but unhurt, as they climbed back onto the seat and put their faces to the window to watch the fire trucks race on. Virgil flung his head back against the seat and ran his hands over his face. "Damn."

Belinda touched Virgil on the arm, and said very quietly, "They found a spot on my womb, Virgil."

They lived in a rental trailer behind Belinda's mother's house. They had gotten a little behind on the rent—two and a half years behind to be exact—since Virgil had been out of work and just able to pick up odd jobs now and then. So in exchange for free rent Belinda and Virgil listened to Grace's endless talk of Satan. Every bad thing that happened from the earthquake in Mexico to Lamar wetting his pants Grace called a Satan attack.

"A spot on your womb?" Grace said. "A malignant spot? My God, Satan has outdone himself now!" She hugged Belinda fiercely, crushing her. "I rebuke you, Satan, in the name of Jesus Christ our Lord and Savior! Do you hear me down there?" She waved her arms above her head and began to cry, "Satan has given my baby girl cancer!" She shrieked upward to God and downward to the Devil, a frantic translator, her body undulating and contorting wildly for several minutes. Then she was still.

"You got to get baptized now, baby," she said grabbing Belinda by the shoulders and squeezing. "You got to." She looked right into Belinda's eyes. "Promise me."

"I've been baptized, Mama. That time at Gulf Shores."

"That don't count. Nearly drowning yourself in the ocean is a completely different thing. Getting baptized can't be an accident. It didn't take, baby. You know that. You're a backslider like your daddy, so you got to keep on until it takes. You got to get baptized for real."

"Maybe." Belinda looked away from her mother.

"Maybe?" Grace shrieked. "God hates maybe! He hates it worse than a flat out no! " She circled the room with her arms raised, "Satan, I rebuke you for making my baby say maybe when anybody worth a damn can see it's time for her to be saying yes. Yes! Yes! Yes!"

Patsy and Penny ran from the room, and little Lamar climbed up under the coffee table and lay dead still, sucking his thumb.

"Don't start this, Mama," Belinda said, "Please."

"If you die unsaved, I'll never forgive you, baby," Grace said. "If you die without inviting Jesus into your heart . . ."

"Shut up, Grace," Virgil shrieked. Belinda and Grace both turned to look at Virgil who had never before raised his voice at Grace, his mother-in-law, his landlady, primary authority on salvation. Virgil cleared his throat, and said, "Belinda is not going to die. And that's final."

There are things that take a little while to get used to. Your own death is one of them. The news hit Belinda the same way it had when she was five and her daddy, who was a preacher then—way back before he switched his allegiance from Jesus to liquor—predicted the end of the world, on March 4, 1972. Belinda had agonized for four long months until then, listening daily to her daddy's rendition of 'the fiery end' and what would happen to all who were not good enough or forgiven enough to fly up to heaven with the angels. She swore it was the fear of hell that had stunted her growth. And then, March fourth comes and . . . NOTHING.

Late that night, seeing that God had let him down and that his family was alive and well whether they deserved to be or not, Belinda's daddy had sat out on the porch, finished off a whole bottle of whiskey, and cried. "A man can't count on nothing in this life," he said, "except disappointment."

"Maybe things will go better next time," she said, patting him. Belinda realized then that her daddy didn't remember that March 4 was her birthday. She had lived to be six years old and the world had not ended. God hadn't declared her birthday the worst day in the history of the world, which she appreciated. But God's failure to do so broke her daddy's heart.

So maybe the end of the world would not come this time either. The doctors had said they needed to study the x-rays. They said the word biopsy so many times Belinda wanted to slap their faces. They said it might be possible to go in and cut away that spot, but Belinda knew better. What did they think, that people were like bananas and you could just cut off the rotten spots and everything would be fine? No. If there was a rotten spot in Belinda it was floating all through her and would not sit still long enough to be cut out. She understood that completely.

Three nights in a row when she and Virgil got into bed he did not even try to make love with her. Instead he wrapped himself around her, laid his head on her bare breasts—which suddenly felt to both of them like hard knots under her skin, all the softness gone from them—and he wept pathetically. Belinda held his head in her arms as though it were detached from the rest of him. "You haven't cried since your daddy's funeral," Virgil said to Belinda, as he sat up and wiped his eyes with the backs of his hands. "You're the one that ought to be crying."

"I'm saving it up," she said.

"It's not normal, holding things in like that."

"If I start crying, I'll never stop, Virgil. I'll flood this trailer and drown us all."

"You're going to bust wide open if you don't."

That night she dreamed Virgil's head was a football and it was her job to get it across the goal line without fumbling. She kept running in the dream, gasping for breath and gripping Virgil's head tight, pressing it against her breasts. Huge fat men were chasing her, grunting. Just one more step and she would score! Then—suddenly—the goal line disappeared. And a whole stadium full of people roared with laughter at the way she had been fooled.

She woke up because Virgil was slapping at her in his sleep, trying to get his head loose from her grip. "It's too hot to cuddle," he said, and rolled over on his side of the bed. Belinda cried most of the night, because in the dream she was humiliated in front of thousands of people.

"I always wanted to do things with my life. You know, Virgil? Something people would notice."

Virgil didn't answer.

The third night, after Virgil began to snore, Belinda got up and went to the kitchen where she rummaged through the potholder drawer looking for a pack of cigarettes that her mother had left. She had never smoked, but now that she was dying she figured she might as well. She lit a cigarette on the gas stove, singeing her hair in the process. Then she climbed up on the counter and reached into the small cabinet above the refrigerator where Virgil kept his liquor. She pulled out a bottle of gin and poured herself a glass. She tore paper out of one of Penny's school notebooks, got a pencil from the rack over the telephone, and sat down at the table and spent most of the night writing a list.

THINGS TO DO BEFORE I DIE.

1. get baptized one more time
2. get my picture made the next time the photographer comes to Sears (give copies to everybody)
3. make love to at least three other men (just to see what it's like)
4. find Virgil a girlfriend (who likes kids)
5. tape record birthday messages for my kids up until they turn 21. Tell them I love you everyday.
6. smoke and drink all I want to
7. cuss all I want to
8. tell the truth if I feel like it
9. lose ten pounds and get a better hairstyle.

The next morning Belinda called Virgil's sister, Delores, to see if she would cut her hair and give her a body wave. She agreed and threw in free 'sun streaking' which Belinda did not even ask for and which made her hair sort of golden around her face, almost angel-like. It took almost four hours altogether, because Delores had to work Belinda in between her regular customers. Belinda spent the extra time asking Delores about the girls Virgil used to go with before he met her. And Delores backtracked through Virgil's flimsy lovelife all the way to when Virgil was in the sixth grade and liked a girl named Candy, who Delores remembered as 'very developed for her age.'

"What ever happened to her?" Belinda asked.

"I don't know. Probably everything. Here." She handed Belinda a mirror and swung her around in the swivel chair. "See if you like your hair in the back."

Belinda studied the back of her head. She was thinking, 'I've gone all through my life just fixing the front of my hair, and the sides—because that's the only part I could see. I've never worried about the back of my hair—only other people see that.' The thought seemed to prove a selfishness in her that she had always suspected was at her core.

"I like it." She handed the mirror back to Delores. Delores told Belinda that if she wanted to come back the following Thursday she would glue on some false fingernails too. And she wouldn't charge her a dime to do it either.

"Look at Mama!" Patsy shouted when Belinda came home. "She's beautiful." Virgil looked up from the newspaper and whistled.

"I want Aunt Delores to do my hair like that," Penny said.

Belinda smiled, not just because her family thought she was pretty, but because Virgil had been circling phone numbers in the jobs section of the classified ads and she had not had to say a single word to make him do it.

That night while the family slept, Belinda smoked another cigarette and sipped another glass of gin and wrote a second list.

Virgil,
This is what I need for the funeral.
1. new dress (can put on layaway)
2. matching shoes (size 5 narrow) (see if they have any real leather ones on sale)

3. new bra (30-A, fiberfill)
4. new bikini panties (size 4)
5. new lace slip (size 30, girl's dept.)
6. panty hose (petite, Nearly Nude)
7. tasteful earrings (let Delores pick them out)
8. outfits for kids
9. new suit and tie (for you)
(Delores promised to fix my hair)
(Do not let Mama talk about Satan at my funeral. It scares the kids.)

When Belinda went to bed she dreamed that the old black man from the hospital died. All the men waiting for x-ray were at his funeral in their green hospital gowns, underpants, cowboy boots, and mismatched socks. They said he died of tapeworm. No, they said, he died of starvation waiting his turn to get x-rayed. When Belinda looked into the casket that the doctors were rolling up and down the hospital hall he looked like he was asleep with his skinny hands folded over his chest. He looked peaceful until Belinda noticed his feet and saw that they were burying him in those same unlaced shoes with no socks. She screamed for them to stop! She screamed that Mr. Miller wasn't ready yet . . . but nobody could hear her, not the doctors in their masks or the old men in their green gowns, which flapped in the wind like angel wings lifting them up off the ground. Belinda woke up gasping for air. She sat upright in the bed and looked over at Virgil sleeping with his mouth open.

The next morning she gave Virgil the list. "I don't want to be buried in any old stuff, Virgil. Promise me."

He looked at the list and went completely pale. He had to sit in a chair to read it all. When he finished he looked up in silence at Belinda who was scrambling eggs for the kids' breakfast.

"I'll pick out my own dress, put it on layaway. The rest we can get little by little, but if I go before we've got it all you'll have to get the rest yourself. I wrote down all the sizes."

Virgil folded the list and put it in his shirt pocket. He ran his hand through his uncombed hair.

"Put Lamar in his high chair," Belinda said.

Virgil began stuffing the boy absentmindedly into the chair, hurting his legs. Lamar began to cry. Virgil slid back the tray and tried it again. Belinda put a plate of food in front of Lamar and he stopped crying.

As Virgil walked out the door Belinda called, "Wait, Virgil!" She was washing Lamar's face with a washcloth. "The panties and bra and slip, you know, I want them to match. Make sure. I always wanted a complete set of matching underwear."

The hospital called that afternoon because Belinda had missed another appointment. She apologized and let them reschedule her in two weeks, knowing full well she was not ever going to that hospital again unless they took her dead body there to do an autopsy.

That night Belinda told Virgil she was going over to her sister's house in Moulton and instead she drove out highway 64 to the Bare Facts Lounge. It was her sister, Lily, who had told her about the place. Belinda made sure it was a Tuesday because that was ladies' night and the drinks were free. The whole evening shouldn't cost her a penny.

On her way she stopped at the Texaco station and went in the bathroom to put on extra lipstick and tease her hair up a little bit and unbutton her blouse two buttons. She couldn't let herself die wondering whatall she had missed.

Virgil hated to dance. Belinda had not danced a single dance since she married Virgil. But inside the Bare Facts the music was so good she felt something stir inside her just listening to it. It was happy moaning. And it was dark inside the lounge too and she didn't know exactly what to do once she walked in, but it didn't matter because right away a man came over to her and said, "You want to dance, Sugar?" and she said yes.

He was twenty-eight, his hair was black and his name was Gable. His mama named him after she saw *Gone With the Wind*. He was a good dancer and pretty cute if you looked at him right. He had come to Alabama to work on the new interstate, was from just outside New Orleans, and liked to drink beer in longneck bottles, which Belinda thought was classy. He told Belinda she had pretty hair and acted real interested when she showed him the pictures of her kids.

"Looks like you got a real tiger on your hands." He was looking at Penny. "And a sweet pussycat," looking at Patsy. "And a linebacker," looking at Lamar. "I sure hope your husband is not a linebacker?" he smiled.

Belinda laughed. "No, he played shortstop."

Gable howled, and twirled Belinda out onto the dance floor. By their third or fourth dance Belinda was not a bit nervous. When any other man asked her to dance, she smiled and said no thank you, then smiled at Gable, who winked at her. She drank three gin and tonics and by ten thirty was thinking of some way she could get Gable to kiss her. It wasn't hard to do. When they slow danced she looked him right in the eye and smiled. Then she slid her hand down his chest and rested it lightly on his belt. (Touching Virgil's belt like this used to work with him—even if she did it accidentally.)

"Let's get some air," Gable said. And they walked outside and he started kissing her and kissing her and kissing her. Her heart was pounding just the same as it would if she loved him.

They couldn't go to Gable's place because his wife and little boy were there, and he didn't suggest a motel, which was fine with Belinda because she wouldn't go to one anyway. They drove out to the interstate construction site, a quiet dirt road that Gable knew about and he rolled out a piece of tarp in the truck bed and they lay down together in the moonlight. Belinda had never dreamed that getting made love to would be as easy as this. She had expected to have to try harder.

"We can pretend this is the Hilton Hotel down at Daytona

Beach, overlooking the ocean," Gable said. "Or the Fairmont Hotel in downtown New Orleans."

"Have you been those places?"

"Actually, no. I never have. But I been to Paradise Motor Lodge just outside Mobile." This struck them both as hysterically funny and they lay in the truck hooting with laughter.

"It's okay," Belinda said. "I'm real good at pretending."

"Good," Gable wrapped his arms around Belinda, "I like a woman with imagination."

Gable was a good kisser. She would have been happy to lie there for hours and let him just kiss her. Virgil had forgotten all about kissing he was always in such a hurry to get to the other. But Gable went slow, which Belinda thought was nice. It gave her time to enjoy each individual aspect of things.

When Gable was naked Belinda stared at him. She asked him to stand up so she could see him better and he laughed at her, but he did it. She looked him over in a way she had never looked at Virgil and he didn't seem to mind. She was suddenly so brave. She looked at him in pure amazement. "You're beautiful," she said.

What she couldn't believe was that his, you know, penis was not at all like Virgil's. Virgil's penis was pink, so pink that it sometimes glowed in the dark. But Gable's was dark and bluish, and besides that he had lots of hair on his chest that ran down his belly pointing like an arrow. It took Belinda's breath away. She had never known men's penises came in different colors.

"My husband is the only man I've ever made love to," Belinda whispered.

Gable smiled, looking at her hair which went a little frizzy in the damp night air. He probably thought she had naturally curly hair. And he was smart enough to know which questions not to ask. "Listen," he said quietly, "I don't want to do anything you don't want—"

"We have to!" Belinda said, louder than she meant to. Then she said softly, "I want to."

*   *   *

That night Gable trailed Belinda all the way home to make sure she got back safe. She could hardly keep her car on the road because her mind was still in Gable's truck bed where she had gotten so deliciously dizzy and couldn't seem to undizzy herself afterwards. She had never heard a man say so many sweet things in her life. Now that she knew what words could do for making sex seem like so much more than sex she would not be the same anymore and she knew it.

She had been lying there thinking she knew why Gable's wife married him, because of all the things he could think of to say between kisses—and right in the middle of lovemaking—right in the middle of it!—when Gable said, "Your husband is one lucky man, Belinda. I hope to God he knows it." After that she could not undizzy herself.

When she got home she went straight to the kitchen and got out her list from the bottom of the potholder drawer where she had hidden it. So far she had only checked off 'Get a better hairstyle.' Now she checked off 'Smoke and drink all I want to.' Then she crossed out the line that said 'Make love to at least three other men' and wrote above it 'Make love with Gable three times.'

When she got into bed she looked at Virgil, asleep and clutching her pillow in such a way that she could not bear to pull it loose from him. She kissed him lightly and lay down beside him in the dark.

Weeks later Belinda was in line with Penny, Patsy, and Lamar in the Sears children's department. She was wearing a borrowed dress and her new hot pink fingernails. Delores had fixed her hair and done her makeup for the picture. She was having the kids' picture made too, because she thought it might be nice to be buried with a picture of them in her hand the way some people get buried holding little Bibles or plastic lilies.

The trouble was keeping the three of them still and quiet in the borrowed Food World buggy while they waited in line. She had already gone through one pack of breath mints trying to keep them quiet and was pulling out the sugarless gum when she heard someone behind her say, "Hey there, Candy. I heard you moved back. Sorry to hear about you and Cliff breaking up."

"Well, don't be sorry," the woman said, "I'm not."

Belinda turned to look at the woman in line behind her. She was a pretty blond woman with a huge bosom. She was wearing shorts and her legs were birdlegs, but very tan. She had no waist, but it didn't matter because her chest was what you mostly noticed. Belinda said to the woman, "I don't guess you're the same Candy that used to know Virgil Bedlow in the sixth grade?"

The woman smiled. "Sure, I knew Virgil. Skinny boy with blond hair."

"Right. He's my husband now."

"Oh, that's nice."

"I couldn't help overhearing that you're divorced."

"Yes." Candy rolled her eyes and took a cigarette out of her purse, "Thank god."

"Smoking is bad for you," Penny said.

"Hush, Penny," Belinda put her hand over the child's mouth. "I was thinking," Belinda said, "Virgil would love to see you again. Why don't you come by the house sometime."

The woman stared at Belinda suspiciously. "I haven't seen Virgil in ten years. I wouldn't know him if I saw him."

"He looks good. He hasn't got fat."

"Why do you want me to see Virgil so bad? You don't even know me."

"I've heard Virgil mention you," Belinda lied, but she could see Candy didn't believe her.

"You do like kids, don't you?"

"Sure."

"You got any kids?"

"One. Toby. He's five. He's living with his daddy right now."

"I see," Belinda said.

Candy sucked hard on her cigarette, her hand shaking a bit.

Belinda could see that Toby was the subject that could unravel Candy and she was touched to know it. And Virgil would go crazy over a huge set of bosoms like Candy had underneath her mint green stretch top. Belinda could forgive another woman huge breasts if she had reason to believe there was a heart of gold underneath them.

"So you'll come by and see Virgil?"

"No, I don't think so."

"Next!" the photographer said, motioning to Belinda and her kids.

"Look," Belinda said to Candy as she lifted the kids from the grocery cart and herded them over to the carpeted box in front of the camera. "You want to know the truth? I've got a spot on my womb. I could die anytime and when I do Virgil will be real lonely. And from the sounds of it, you're pretty lonely right now too . . . and I just thought . . . well . . . the two of you might—"

"Our turn, Mama!" Penny pulled Belinda away. Belinda posed for her own picture while the kids stood beside the photographer saying, "Smile, Mama. Say cheese." Belinda licked her lips til they shone and grinned showing her teeth.

Afterwards, as Candy took her own turn in front of the camera, she said, "You tell Virgil I said long time no see." So Belinda wrote their address on the back of a two for the price of one Safeguard soap coupon. "In case you want to come by sometime," she said. Candy took the address, folded it, and stuck it inside her knit top. Belinda imagined Virgil's home address resting in Candy's cleavage. She herded the kids through the Sears store and out into the afternoon heat.

On the way to the car she spotted old Mr. Faulk walking along with a lady friend, a short fat woman. Belinda almost didn't recognize him with his clothes on, a snap up cowboy shirt and a pair of black polyester jeans. And he was wearing a cowboy hat and sunglasses and chewing on a toothpick. It was his boots that gave him away.

"Hey," Belinda said. "You remember me from the hospital? How did your x-rays come out?"

Mr. Faulk recognized Belinda, looked at the grocery cart full of kids, and smiled. "Diverticulitis is all. You know, when your intestines balloon out and you get these little pockets of waste that you can't pass, and—"

"I don't want you to tell me about it."

"They got me eating oats three times a day. I feel like a horse, all the oats I eat."

"It could of been worse," the fat woman said.

"How about you?" Mr. Faulk watched Belinda move away, the cart rattling on the gravel.

"I got bad news," Belinda shouted.

When Belinda got home Virgil was furious. His red face sent the kids scurrying to the back of the trailer. "What the hell do you think you're doing?" Virgil grabbed Belinda and shook her as he spoke.

At first she thought he must have found out about Gable, but she didn't see how. They had been really careful, only seeing each other at the Bare Facts Lounge the last five Tuesday nights and a couple of afternoons at her sister's house when they thought Lily would not be home. Once she had walked in on them. They had already made love and were making cheese and pineapple sandwiches in the kitchen. Lily had stared at them a full minute before thinking of what to say. "Belinda Bedlow, Virgil is going to kill you!" Belinda smiled and sat on Gable's lap. He was wearing nothing but his underpants and was very embarrassed. "I'm going to die someday anyway," she answered.

"The hospital called!" Virgil shrieked. "And your doctor called! They want to know what's wrong with you!"

"I thought it was their job to know."

"They say you haven't been showing up for your appointments. They say you don't return their calls." Virgil's face was anguished.

"That's right."

"Shit, Belinda, don't worry about paying for it if that's it. I'll get—"

"It's not the money," Belinda slung a Sears bag into the closet. "What then?"

"I don't want any treatments."

"You don't want them?" Virgil slapped his hands against his head. "They said you might die without the treatments, Belinda."

"They never said these 'treatments' could keep me from dying. It'll kill me faster, Virgil. Don't ask me how I know, but I do. Besides, all my hair will fall out and—"

"Your hair?" Virgil sank into a chair and looked at Belinda like she was a total stranger.

"It'll kill me faster, Virgil. I can feel it."

"So," Virgil stood up, began pacing around the room, "my wife has cancer and that's just fine with her, right?" He picked up a pack of cigarettes from the kitchen table where Belinda had left them the night before and slung them at her, hitting her in the chest. "You know what I think? I think you want to die, damn you."

Virgil grabbed the car keys and two beers, hung together in their plastic noose.

"Where are you going?" Belinda said.

"I'm getting out of this insane asylum."

"I'm the one dying," Belinda shouted. "Or have you forgotten?"

"Well, I don't have to hang around here and watch you enjoy it." Virgil walked out the door.

Belinda picked up the closest thing, an open jar of strawberry jelly sitting on the kitchen counter, and threw it at Virgil just as he shut the door. The jar hit the door and broke. Sticky, red goo splattered everywhere. "I hate you," she said.

Sometime after midnight Virgil came home drunk. The kids were asleep. Belinda was sitting at the kitchen table reading the instructions for the new tape recorder she had charged at Sears on her mother's credit card. Virgil stumbled over to her and she stood up to help keep him from falling. He put his arm around her and she walked him back to the bedroom where she pulled off his boots and helped him into bed.

"Virgil," she said, "I didn't really mean it when I said I hate you."

"I know that. You married me, didn't you?" He rolled over on his back and crossed his arms over his forehead.

"I'm just so tired, Virgil, you know? And if I have to die I want to do it right. That's all. I want to do dying better—Virgil, are you listening?"

Virgil was sound asleep with a smile on his face.

Belinda sat up most of the night talking into her new tape recorder. She made each of her children four years' worth of birthday messages that first night, and kept it up over the next few weeks until she had them all legally grown.

Penny,
I bet you're real pretty now. You'll have to ask your Daddy to explain things. He won't want to talk about it, but keep asking him. He knows even if he acts like he doesn't. If your Daddy has a new wife, then ask her instead. Women always know more about the facts of life because most of the facts happen to women. I love you.

Patsy,
When I was eight it seemed like Lily had a better time of things than I did. Her being the oldest sort of smashed me down. So don't let that happen to you. Sometimes your Daddy might try to speed you up to Penny's age and sometimes he might try to slow you down to Lamar's age, but it's just because you're in the middle which gets him confused. Mama loves you.

Lamar,
If it seems like you get yelled at more than anybody and blamed for everything, it's just because you're the youngest. One day you'll probably be bigger than everybody in the house, even

your Daddy, maybe. If you have a new Mama now I hope you like her. It won't hurt my feelings. Love, Mama.

Then Belinda made Virgil a couple of Christmas messages.

Hello there.
Just be careful, Virgil, picking out a new wife if you haven't done it already. You have to pay close attention to what you're doing the second time around.

Virgil,
This is the last Christmas message I'll make since you're surely remarried by now to a woman who probably won't want to hear your dead wife's voice wishing you a Merry Christmas on a tape recorder. I bet you've forgot all about me by now. But don't admit it, if you have. Do you ever think about that night at Elk River?

And she even made her Mama a couple of Christmas messages, too.

Mama,
Guess what? I'm up in heaven and—I know you won't believe this—but Daddy is up here too. God is so much better than you ever thought. He forgives people.

Mama,
Merry Christmas again! Me and Daddy are having a great time flying around up here. You can see everything from heaven. Sometimes for fun we fly over New York City and hover around watching all the Yankees and foreigners. You are right about New York City, Mama. It is every bit like you imagined and me and Daddy think it's probably the best thing that you live in Alabama.
Happy New Year!

Making the messages was exhausting, but Belinda went about it in a very organized manner. As soon as she got them all finished she was going to give them to a lawyer that Dolores's husband, Kicker, told her about who could dole them out one message at a time on the proper dates. She had handwritten all the instructions and dates for the lawyer so nothing could go wrong. She couldn't leave the tapes with Virgil. He would listen to all of them the first night and after that he might lose them altogether. Same with her mama and Lily. So a lawyer was best. She had never met any lawyers, but she loved the idea of having a professional handle things in her absence.

Gable was on Belinda's mind twenty-three hours a day now leaving only one hour to cram everything else into. The only way in the world I can give him up is to die, Belinda thought. He was like medicine—that tasted good. A painkiller she was addicted to.

Belinda thought heaven must be a place full of men like Gable. Enough to go around. One for every woman. Men with lips like a bed you lie down in. Men who know the things to say that Gable knew. His mouth. It kissed her, it spoke to her, and it could do other amazing things that caused her to come out of her skin and rise glimmering and fluttering like some powdered moth toward a hot light overhead. He could make her moan and scream and afterwards he could make her laugh. It was worth dying young for.

Gable didn't know Belinda was dying and she never wanted him to. She liked how it was between them and didn't want to mess it up with sympathy. One night they were wrapped around each other, naked, late, late at night, the rain falling warm and sweet and before she knew it Belinda was saying, 'Gable, I love you. I love you.' The words came out of her in abrupt uncontrollable leaps, like burps, burps she felt rise up from deep inside her, slide up through her chest, puffing as they went, until finally, they surfaced and blurted out. 'I love you,' she kept saying and Gable hugged her so hard she thought she would break in half.

"Baby," he said, "Sweet, sweet baby."

Belinda burst into tears and clung to him, wrapping her bare legs around his, her arms tight around his neck. She buried her face in his chest and cried the way a car moves with its tires flat, a slow, powerless thumping, a lopsidedness, that must run its course before the brakes can be applied. Gable rocked her back and forth. But she couldn't stop crying. "You cry all you want to, baby," he said. And she did. She cried like she was breaking and crumbling into tiny parts inside and crying herself out in lumps. He kissed the top of her head and kept rocking her and rocking her. "I'll help you, baby," he whispered. "Whatever it is, I'll help you."

When she awoke the wet tarp was pulled over them and the rain had stopped. She thought at first that Gable was asleep too, but when she lifted her head she saw that he was watching her. As soon as she stirred, he reached for her, tucked her hair behind her ears with his warm hands, pulled her close, and whispered sweet things.

Afterwards she went home to limp-limbed Virgil, sprawled half on and half off the bed, exhausted from his half-hearted job search, asleep with the TV on. She looked at him as though he was one more of her children, a sweet boy someone must take care of. She brushed the hair out of his eyes and turned off the TV and turned off the lights and climbed in bed beside him, thinking their bed had the hardest mattress in the world, amazed that a tarp covered metal truck bed could seem so much softer and warmer, even in the pouring rain. Everything was cried out of her. For the first time in a long time she felt completely empty—and clean.

The next night, unexpectedly, Candy stopped by for a beer on her way home from work. Belinda took it as a sign, God speaking to her indirectly. She hadn't believed she would ever see Candy again—but, like Grace always said, God works in mysterious ways—and here was Candy. It was like Belinda's replacement stepping in early to learn the ins and outs of the job. And Virgil was smiling like a fool.

At first Virgil didn't recognize Candy, but after Belinda nudged his memory he was smiling and saying, "What ever happened to . . . ," and little Lamar was sitting in Candy's lap, and Penny and Patsy had remembered her from Sears and were drawing her some pictures to take home with her, and all in all things went pretty well. Penny traced a yellow haired angel from the *New Testament Coloring Book* Grace had given her for her birthday and wrote Candy across the angel's chest. Belinda knew this was no coincidence. She nearly wept when Penny presented Candy with the drawing because she knew it was the work of God—setting her free. It made her mad. She could die now, and for the first time since her diagnosis—she was afraid.

When Candy left, promising to come to supper one Friday night soon, Virgil stood at the door watching her get in her car and drive off. Afterwards, partly bewildered, partly amazed, he had turned to Belinda and said, "What a pair of bazookas!"—a comment Belinda considered a religious experience.

"You feel okay?" Virgil asked Belinda regularly as the weeks passed. She usually said she was fine. But she had started taking lots of naps, sometimes putting all three kids in the bed with her and reading them stories out of her mother's old *Ladies' Home Journal* magazines. Everybody's favorite stories were from "Can This Marriage Be Saved?" Belinda would read both sides of it then take a vote on whose fault it was. Most of the time it seemed to Belinda that it was the wife's fault, and Lamar always voted the same way Belinda did. Penny insisted it was the husband's fault every time. And Patsy refused to vote because she didn't want to take sides.

"Don't be reading those kids that mess," Belinda's mother said. "They ought to be listening to Bible stories or fairy tales at their age. Not marriage," she said.

"Marriage is as farfetched as any fairy tale," Belinda said. Sometimes they watched *Donahue*, Belinda and all three kids sprawled on the sofa, eating mayonnaise and lettuce sandwiches. Whenever Phil had a panel of medical experts for his guests, then Belinda changed the channel and they watched *Andy Griffith* reruns and laughed like crazy at Barney Fife making a complete fool of himself.

Belinda had small episodes of bleeding. Sometimes painful. Sleep seemed to be the best medicine. The children enjoyed Belinda's new laziness, lying around the trailer in her pajamas until noon. Taking long afternoon naps pretending the bed was a raft and the floor was an ocean full of sharks. Playing cards for hours. Lamar was already learning his numbers.

Belinda spent some of this time telling the kids about heaven. All the same things her daddy had told her. That you can eat and drink anything you want to in heaven, because there's plenty, and it won't make you sick or fat. Food is joy—you can just gobble it up. Everybody has naturally curly hair there, you never need a comb. Nobody's skin breaks out. Nobody has crooked teeth. You get a good singing voice and automatically know the words to all the songs. And they have rock and roll in heaven—not just hymns. You can fly, stay up late, sleep on the clouds, and do anything you want to. And all the animals are tame and they have wings too, so the ponies in heaven fly. So do the big dogs and they'll let you ride them if you want to. The kids loved to hear Belinda tell about heaven—and she hoped that after she died, when Virgil said, "Your mama is in heaven," they would think about it and be glad.

But secretly Belinda was suspicious of God. She had become suspicious early on—partly because Grace had stayed so furious on His behalf for most of her life. If God was even half as angry as Grace, it would be too much to bear. For several Easters after Belinda's near drowning her mother had dressed her in crinoline, flowered hat, and white gloves, to take her to church and get her baptized. "Everytime I think that you might have drowned without ever committing your life to Jesus . . ." Grace said with tears in her eyes. But each time Belinda had panicked and started crying uncontrollably—which woke her daddy up. Hung over, he staggered into the kitchen to save Belinda from Grace who was attempting to drag her out to the car.

Righteous and outraged, Grace and Lily went off to the Easter services while Belinda and her daddy got in the truck and drove to Greenbriar to eat barbecue. Belinda had ruined many a Sunday dress dribbling red barbecue sauce down the front of them. "You look like you been shot in the heart," her daddy said, dipping his napkin in his sweetened iced tea and smearing the stain over her chest trying to remove it. She had come home in the afternoon only to have Grace strip the new dress off her and throw it in the trash.

So it was easy for Belinda to believe God was a father and not a mother like some modern people were saying. Even so she didn't entirely trust him and had only known he was real on two occasions—when her babies had sucked her breasts and milk came out—and when she made love to Gable. Sometimes with Gable still inside her—knowing full well her daddy was watching them from above—she would look up and say thank you.

Belinda noticed that Virgil tried to stay gone as much as he could. "Be back later," he'd say on his way out the door. And Belinda and the kids had long stopped asking where he was going. When he was home Virgil watched everything Belinda ate. "You had any vegetables today?" he'd ask. "You need to eat vegetables every day." It never occurred to him to go to the store and buy any, or bring them home and cook them.

Belinda understood Virgil. He was an easy man to understand, which is what she had loved about him in the beginning. Now sometimes she wished she didn't understand him so well. She wished she didn't know what he was thinking and how he was feeling all the time. It wore her out, but at this point it was impossible to stop understanding him. He hadn't made love to Belinda in months, not since the first mention of her spot, and it wasn't because he hadn't tried. He just couldn't seem to get his equipment going anymore no matter how Belinda tried to help him, and after a few failures he had quit trying altogether. "It's not catching," Belinda had whispered to Virgil.

"I know that."

"Then what?"

"I got too much on my mind. I can't concentrate anymore."

Belinda knew what was on Virgil's mind. It was more than the sad details of their lives, a dying wife and three kids who were going to keep on and on needing things for a long time. No job and no money. What bothered Virgil most was that he had no say in anything that happened. Nothing minded him. Maybe the kids were still young enough to think he was in charge of things. They still ran from the room when he began to shout, but they would outgrow that soon, start talking back, start asking him for big, expensive things he would be unable to get. He knew it already. Nothing minded Virgil. Not Belinda, his own wife, who refused to go to the doctor. Now, not even his body which had practically quit on him. Once Belinda died—there wouldn't be anyone around to pretend he WAS in charge.

That's why, for the time being, when Belinda and Virgil went to bed at night sometimes she wrapped herself around him and said sweet things to him. "I'm sorry I don't feel like making love anymore."

"That's okay." Virgil lay on his back, staring at the ceiling.

"Remember that time I first saw you at the Dairy Queen, Virgil? You were the best looking thing, eating that pineapple sundae. I said to myself, I have got to get that boy to notice me. I said that's the only boy in the world who will do."

Virgil pulled Belinda to him and hugged her tight.

Virgil had not got a job yet, but even without a job he had managed to get a few of the things on Belinda's funeral list, which he carried with him at all times. He had already bought her Nearly Nude panty hose and was pleased with himself over it. And he had got her two sets of fake pearl earrings since they had been on special two for a dollar. She had tried to make him take them back because they were not at all what she had in mind. But he had kept them. He had cleared all the kids' toys out of the cedar chest and put the panty hose and the earrings in there, thinking that each item he got, he would put in the cedar chest and pretty soon Belinda would have everything she needed ready and set aside. A hope chest for the afterlife. In fact, she thought it would suit her just fine if they buried her in the cedar chest and saved the money for the casket.

On Friday morning Belinda drove to Huntsville to meet Gable at Madison Mall. He took off from work to help her pick out a dress. She didn't tell him it was the dress she would be buried in. Belinda had lost weight without realizing it, and after trying on a few dresses in the junior department had been sent down to the pre-teen department where she fit perfectly into a girl's size twelve.

She settled on a pretty lavender dress with a lace collar and cuffs and a tiny bunch of fake violets at the neck. It had millions of little buttons down the back and a deep purple sash at the waist. It was as pretty as some wedding dresses Belinda had seen and since Belinda had never had a wedding dress she especially liked it. The saleslady said a bride had recently chosen that exact dress for her flower girl to wear. It cost fifty-eight dollars and Gable tried to pay for it, but Belinda wouldn't let him. She put it on layaway the way she had promised Virgil, thinking that it would probably take him the rest of his life to get it paid for, but knowing that in a pinch her mother or Lily would help pay it off.

Afterwards Gable took Belinda to eat at Morrison's Cafeteria. It was her favorite restaurant and she got the fried shrimp and tartar sauce, but she couldn't eat. Gable didn't notice at first. He was telling Belinda that his wife and little boy had gone back to New Orleans—maybe for good and he didn't blame them. Gable was twenty-eight years old and had been married for what he called the ten longest years of his life. But still, he had cried when they left and promised to send his wife some money every month until she could get herself going. She was registered in a dental hygienist course in Baton Rouge. And he promised his boy, Buddy, that he would send for him in December and take him to Gatlinburg for Christmas. So now his house was empty. He lived alone and that meant he and Belinda could skip the Bare Facts and go straight to his place when they wanted to be together.

Belinda was uneasy about this news because it was something she had prayed for, but she certainly never expected God to answer her prayer. He never had in the past so she had become careless in her asking. She had been asking Him for Gable pretty regularly though and thanking Him for Gable too, never dreaming God would respond by sending Gable's wife off to Baton Rouge and clearing the way for them to be together like two regular people in a regular bed in a regular house.

Gable also told her that he had put in a word for Virgil at the construction company and thought there was a good chance he would get hired. This news made Belinda teary. She picked up her napkin and blew her nose.

"I want you well taken care of," Gable whispered. "That's all."

"He'll do a good job," Belinda said. "I promise. If somebody tells Virgil just exactly what to do he'll do it the best he can."

"You're not eating," Gable said, looking at the nine fried shrimp, untouched.

The truth was Belinda couldn't eat. She was feeling sick. Really sick and had been fighting it all morning because this was supposed to be such a happy occasion—all day at the mall with Gable. And tonight Candy was coming to eat supper with her and Virgil and the kids. Belinda tried to push the sickness out of her mind, but it kept coming back like ocean waves that come and go, come and go.

The waves of sickness scared her as much as the ocean that time at Gulf Shores when she was a little girl and the tide had sucked her way out over her head. The waves slapped her under again and again. She couldn't find the sky. Her daddy had swum out, grabbed her leg, and pulled her to safety. He cried and cussed while he pumped the Gulf of Mexico out of Belinda's lungs.

Her mother had stood apart from them with her eyes closed, quoting the twenty-third psalm. She remembered her daddy holding her up by the feet and shaking her until she vomited gallons of ocean. He pounded on her with his fists, screaming, "Breathe." Lily had run in circles around them, shrieking.

Belinda couldn't bear to waste nine Morrison's fried shrimp, partly because she didn't know if she would ever have a chance to eat them again, and partly because her daddy had raised her to eat every single bite and say it's good, whether it is or not. She had tried her best to live by that for twenty-three years.

"I can't eat it, Gable." Her face went pale. A sudden pain splashed through her. She moaned and slid low in her chair dropping her fork which clanked against the plate.

"You okay?" Gable jumped up from his chair. She was whiter than the tablecloth and her eyes were closed. "I have to go home."

She wouldn't let Gable drive her. He wanted to take her to the emergency room but the idea upset her so much he dropped it. He literally carried her to a pay phone and held her up while she called Virgil to come get her.

"Huntsville?" Virgil shouted into the phone. "What the hell are you doing in Huntsville?"

Holding Belinda's fried shrimp in a doggy bag Gable carried Belinda out to the car as she instructed him. He bet she didn't weigh ninety pounds. He lay her down on the front seat where she tossed her head and gripped her belly, making short, breathy shrieks. She was scaring hell out of Gable.

"Baby, what's wrong? Let me get somebody."

But Belinda refused. She lay still one minute then jerked her knees up and pressed them against her chest each time a pain hit. She made terrifying noises. Gable was wild. He turned on the motor and got the air-conditioning going for her. He put the radio on the softest music he could find. He circled the car like a madman, checked the tires for flats. Opened the hood of the car and checked the oil, memorized the tag number. And in between he climbed in and out of the back seat, reached over where Belinda lay and touched her hair, touched her face, and whispered, "Sweet, sweet baby." Sometimes she gripped his hand pressing her fingernails into it, but her fingernails were so soft they just bent. There was no stab to them.

It took Virgil forty-five minutes to get to Huntsville. Kicker drove him. Only minutes before they arrived Belinda had insisted that Gable leave. "Virgil can't find you here," she whispered. "He'll get all upset."

Because he would do anything for Belinda, seeing her so tiny and pale, Gable obeyed her, but just long enough to pull his truck up and park it right beside her car. "I'm right here," he told her. "I'm not going to take my eyes off you until Virgil comes."

Virgil and Kicker came through the parking lot like an ambulance. Virgil was shouting Belinda's name as he ran from the truck to her parked car.

"It's pitiful when you're invited to supper and you get here and have to cook it yourself," Belinda said to Candy. She was feeling better and was propped up in her bed sipping 7UP. Virgil had been frantic all afternoon. By the time Candy arrived he had finished an entire bottle of gin waiting for her. Belinda heard Virgil tell Candy what a close call they had had that day. She heard him take Candy over to the cedar chest and show her its contents. She heard his choked voice and the mention of 'Belinda's funeral list.'

Now Candy was frying pork chops and letting Penny peel potatoes for French fries. Patsy was setting the table, asking which side the forks go on. Lamar was on his rocking horse that Belinda's mother had got at a yard sale, its springs squeaking as he bounced. Virgil was lying in his battered Naugahyde La-Z-Boy. It was folded back into the rest position, and he was drinking beer from a glass, since company was there. "Wheel of Fortune" was on. They were all playing along with Vanna and Pat. "A stretch of time," Virgil shouted. Belinda could hear them laughing. "No," Penny corrected, "too many letters."

Belinda lay in the dark bedroom at the back of the trailer. It was cool. She had a floating feeling listening to her family in the other room. They will keep on just fine, she thought. "A stitch in time saves nine!" Virgil shouted. "Daddy wins!," yelled Patsy. "Shhhh-hhh," Candy said, "let Belinda sleep." Her voice had a certain music to it, mingled with the television applause and the shrieks of a woman who had a chance to win a pop-up camper if she could solve the puzzle.

Belinda leaned against the pile of pillows her family had brought to her bed. She was circled by every pillow in the house. Penny and Patsy and Lamar dragging their pillows to Belinda like three wise men bearing gifts. There were those tiny moments when Belinda would not trade her small life for any other, longer, or better life. There were those tiny moments when she felt sure.

Virgil had arranged Belinda on the pillows, arms here, legs there, head this way. Then he had turned out the light and let her sleep. She awoke to the happy noises of the children squealing as Candy pulled up in the driveway, blowing her car horn, bringing each of them a surprise, 'for after supper' she said.

So this is it, Belinda thought. This is how my life will be without me. She was grateful for the sounds coming from the other room. Lamar riding his little horse nowhere. Patsy clanking dishes. Penny shouting out alphabet letters. Candy saying, "Virgil, you and the kids wash up. Supper's ready."

"Damn, fuck, shit, hell," Belinda said quietly. She had long ago checked 'Cuss all I want to' off her list. She often muttered every vile word she could think of—but never in front of the children—just to exercise the right to do so. Just to use up her share of cussing, to make up for all the holding back she had done all her life.

The only thing remaining on Belinda's list of 'Things to Do Before I Die' was to get baptized one more time. Since that time at Gulf Shores she had been afraid to go underwater. Her mother had cried over her refusal to be baptized, saying, "Belinda, if you ever want a minute's peace you are going to have to drown yourself in the love of God."

If Belinda had to drown in somebody's love, she wished it could be Gable's. She wondered what he would do if he knew how sick she was. She wondered what he would do when she died. Who would call him? Who would explain things to him?

Virgil came stumbling down the hall to the bedroom bringing

with him the warm smell of food frying. He paused in the doorway. Belinda was pale and thin, lying in her white cotton nightgown, lost in the swirl of white sheets and pillows, smudges of mascara under each eye. She smiled at him.

Virgil was awkward, afraid to enter the room. He didn't look a day over sixteen, Belinda thought. He was unusually red-faced from the gin and his hair was short and boyish. It occurred to Belinda that he had gotten a haircut in honor of Candy coming to supper. Ordinarily Belinda cut his hair with the kitchen scissors.

"You okay?" Virgil asked.

"Better."

"You scared the hell out of me."

"Me too."

"No sense in trying to talk to you about the hospital I guess."

"No."

Virgil was drunk. He propped himself against the door frame, but kept slipping away from it as if a door frame were something you could fall off of. "I feel so damn helpless," he said. He ran his hand through his hair, but his hair was too short for it to be an effective gesture. He tried to look Belinda in the eye, but it was as hard for him as it is for some people to stare straight into the sun. He squinted as though Belinda was a glare. "I wanted to be a good husband to you, I swear to God, I did. I wanted to buy you things and take you places. I don't know what all went wrong. I thought I had more time, you know."

"You did just fine, Virgil." He made her think of her daddy the way he stood in the doorway, red-eyed, not coming or going either one, just swaying, undecided. Drinking always brought out the feelings in her daddy too. When Belinda and Virgil were seventeen Belinda realized that beer, lots of beer, made Virgil romantic. He couldn't seem to get himself going without it. But after a couple of six packs he could even say 'I love you.' Now beer didn't work, and it took gin to get Virgil to talk. Her daddy had been the exact same way. Sometimes Belinda felt sorry for certain kinds of men.

"There is one thing, Virgil."

"What?" Virgil tried to stand up straight. "You name it and you got it."

"Don't laugh."

"I swear I won't."

"I want to get baptized."

Virgil looked at her a moment, then saluted her, slapping his heels together, spilling the drink in his hand. "One baptizing coming up. I'll get your Mama to set it up at the church."

"No. Now. I want you to do it, Virgil. You and the kids. And Mama. And Candy."

"Candy?"

"You like her, don't you, Virgil?"

"Sure I do. I mean, she's all right."

"I think she likes you a lot."

"You do?"

"I know she likes you. I can tell."

Virgil's eyes filled with alcohol tears. "You deserved to be married to a doctor or a lawyer, Belinda. A man with a good credit rating. Don't think I didn't know that." Virgil shook his head to keep from getting emotional.

"Just don't hold me under too long, Virgil."

"What?"

"When you baptize me. I don't like for my head to go under."

"What am I supposed to say when I dunk you? I don't know anything religious?"

"Just read something out of the Bible."

"Penny!" Virgil yelled. He stepped into the hall as Penny came running to see what he wanted.

"Is Mama okay?" she asked.

"She's fine." Virgil put his hand on Penny's shoulder to steady himself. "You run get your grandmama to come over here. Tell her we're going to have a baptizing." Penny grinned and took off running.

Virgil stumbled over to where Belinda lay. He bent over her, kissing her forehead and her shoulder. Then he scooped her up in his arms and carried her down the hall to the kitchen.

"Virgil, be careful!" Candy said. "You might drop her."

"Patsy, go run your mama a tub," Virgil said. "Get it real full." Patsy skipped down the hall to the bathroom, followed by Lamar who ran after her dragging a pink stuffed rabbit at the end of a rope.

"What in the world?" Candy said.

"Virgil's going to baptize me," Belinda said. Virgil kept losing his balance so Belinda wrapped her arms around his neck and clung to him trying to keep him upright.

Candy stood with her arms outstretched, ready to catch them both if they tipped over. "Why don't you set her down, Virgil?" Candy said. "You're swaying."

"She ain't heavy," Virgil said. "She ain't heavy, she's my wife . . ." he sang, laughing at himself. Within minutes Penny came running into the trailer, followed by Belinda's mother who barrelled in the door, breathless. "I've waited all my life for this," she said.

"The tub's ready," Patsy shouted, pulling on Virgil's arm. "I made Mama a bubble bath."

Virgil carried Belinda down the hall to the tiny bathroom, followed by the kids and Candy and Belinda's mother, who was suddenly very quiet. Sure enough the tub was full of white suds. It looked like a tub full of cloud.

Virgil bent down on his knees. Candy rushed to his side, bracing him, helping him lower Belinda into the tub. Belinda's white nightgown billowed like a sail when it touched the water. Virgil poked at the air bubble, trying to deflate it.

"Look," Penny said. "Mama looks pregnant."

"Hush," Grace said, covering Penny's mouth with her hand.

Belinda sank into the warm, soapy water. She leaned against the edge of the white fiberglass womb and kicked her feet slightly.

"Turn off the lights," Virgil said. Candy reached over and flipped the light switch.

"Do you know what we're supposed to say, Mama?" Belinda asked.

"You ask for forgiveness, baby," Grace said, and she began shuffling through the Bible looking for a proper passage.

"Is the water too hot?" Virgil asked.

"It's fine," Belinda said.

"Then why are you crying?"

"She don't want her head to go under," Grace said. "She's always been scared of going under."

"Don't cry, Belinda," Candy said, her eyes full of tears too. She stood behind Virgil, who was squatting, leaning over the edge of the tub. Candy's knees pressed against either side of Virgil's rib cage, steadying him.

"I got you, Belinda," Virgil said. He took her face in his hands and turned her head to look at him. "I got you."

"It won't hurt, Mama," Patsy said.

Belinda closed her eyes and rested her head against Virgil's arm. The water was warm. She could smell the lemon Joy Patsy had used to make the bubbles. She heard her mother flipping the pages of the Bible. Lamar slung the stuffed rabbit into the tub and it sank. Belinda kicked her foot lightly and the water rippled in tiny waves. She tried to remember the happiest moments of her life.

"We're not going to do a thing until you say so," Virgil whispered. "Belinda, baby, you just tell me when you're ready to go under. You just say the word."

Nanci Kincaid, who claims as home states both Florida and Alabama, presently lives in North Carolina and teaches at UNC-Charlotte. She received her MFA from University of Alabama. Her first novel, *Crossing Blood*, was published by G. P. Putnam in 1992. She is presently at work on a second novel, untitled, and a collection of short stories, *Pretending the Bed Was a Raft*. She received a NEA grant in 1992. Her stories have appeared in literary magazines, including *Story*, *Ontario Review*, *Missouri*

Review, and *Carolina Quarterly* and have been anthologized in several collections including *New Stories from the South*.

I once knew a seven-year-old boy named Oscar, who, when asked what he would wish for if he could have a wish come true, thought a minute and said he'd wish for an orange and a pair of white socks. It made me think about the ways poverty infects the spirit, the way life whittles away at our ability to dream. I'm fascinated by the lives of the dreamers of small dreams —a woman who wishes for little more than a set of matching underwear, for example.

Like many Southerners, I've watched poverty try and defeat people and people refuse to let it. But I have also seen death come at people not as the enemy we are taught to believe it is, but more as an announcement of early release for good behavior. Sometimes certain impending death gives people permission—at last—to really live their lives, take their chances. In the small towns in the Bible Belt, poverty, disease, and death are still the great character builders. And pain and pleasure have managed to stay married despite the odds.

I don't know where the Belinda in this story came from exactly. I did see a tiny, exhausted Alabama girl in a hospital waiting room once juggling three squirming children in her lap, trying to entertain them with pictures from the Ladies' Home Journal. She looked more like an underpaid babysitter than a mother. Her hair was uncombed, her clothes were unwashed. It was clear she had been crying and might start up again any minute, but for the sake of her children and the people in the waiting room, she struggled valiantly to be cheerful. She nearly convinced me. She certainly impressed me. I knew that I would try to write about her at some point.

"Look," she pointed out an advertisement to her children. "Don't you wish you had you a big piece of cheesecake like that with all them cherries on top?"

Frederick Barthelme

RETREAT

(from *Epoch*)

The English department's first annual retreat was held at the Carlsbad Motel on the Gulf Coast of Alabama in late October. When Del and Jen arrived they met Del's brother Rudy and his assistant Mimi for dinner. It was the first time they'd seen Mimi, who was also Rudy's new girlfriend. Rudy had just taken over as chairman of the department and was having a bad time trying to be one of the guys. He wore a beaded buckskin jacket that didn't fit right, jeans, and motorcycle boots. He invited Jen and Del for an early dinner Friday in the motel restaurant, the Schipperke.

After they'd ordered drinks Rudy said, "What is that?" He was tapping the name on the restaurant menu.

Mimi said, "Who cares what it is? I'm so excited about this retreat—I'm dying to see all these professors in action. The Personal Makeover people say when you get people out of the office you see what they're made of."

"I don't know about that," Rudy said.

"It's a dog," Jen said. "On the menu."

"People *need* a chance to open up," Mimi said. "Show themselves. The PMI manual says they'll strip down for you, uncover their scars."

Del pretended to wave for a cab. "Cab!" he said.

"They send you all this stuff," Rudy said. "They have great graphs, really killer graphs in their brochures."

"Killer," Mimi said. She was young and looked like she was about to sizzle.

The waiter brought drinks, and after they'd been delivered around the table, Rudy said, "I'm glad Jen could come." He reached for Jen's hand. "I heard you were thinking of not coming—why was that?"

"Mammogram," she said. "I was scheduled for this afternoon. I moved it."

"You going to eat these crab claws, Rudy?" Del said, snapping four or five of the fried claws off Rudy's plate.

"PMI reps gross sixty to eighty thousand the first year," Mimi said. "I may moonlight for them."

"No kidding?" Del said.

"Even if it's stupid, there are worse ways to spend a weekend," Rudy said. "You see Pokey Willis brought that graduate student of his?"

"See, that's exactly what I'm talking about," Mimi said, her face brightening as she pointed a crab claw at Rudy. "People need a chance to go public with their stuff."

The Carlsbad Motel was six stories, as clean as beach places ever get, given the traffic. The staff was used to dealing with the small bore conference trade, so Del's job turned out easy—he did the set up, then stood around outside the meeting rooms taking care of people who couldn't find the public restrooms or the bar.

After dinner Friday he made sure the correct conference rooms were going to be available when they were supposed to be available, unpacked some handouts Rudy and Mimi had prepared, and went over the luau plan with the motel's Director of Conferences & Workshops. Then he set up the Projection Video System in the Matrix Room for the nine o'clock showing of a taped program Rudy had gotten off C-SPAN, a panel on the film *JFK*, which was back in the news for some reason. That was followed by a discussion period moderated by a regional assassination buff who had slides, and who went through the evidence again, including some of the new material released the previous year from Dallas police files, details about the detention of the "three tramps," and some CIA materials recently leaked to the press. He had a lot of slides of car crashes, too. Snapshots taken right after the crashes, with body parts strewn around, splashes of blood dripping down windshields, ripped up faces.

It was hard to know, since Del was in and out of the conference room, whether these deaths were related to the assassination, or a separate interest of the speaker.

Finally there was the two A.M. Late Sky Seminar. An astronomy guy took everybody to the beach. They stood in a circle holding hands and staring up while this guy told them what they were looking at. Jen stayed in the room, but Del was out there, squeezed between Mimi and some hefty woman. Mimi's hair was wolf-like.

Most of Saturday was free—the faculty people went into town, or sat on the beach, or slept. There was a late afternoon round-table discussion of departmental priorities. Del made sure there was coffee and the correct number of Style Three snack trays, but that was it. Saturday night was the luau.

All afternoon a pig had been roasting in one of the two fish ponds in the courtyard. The pond, which was twice the size of a Jacuzzi, had been filled in with dirt, then dug out again to make a pit to cook the pig. Mimi had Xeroxed "Pig Hawaiian" handouts that explained the long Hawaiian tradition of cooking a pig this particular way, buried in dirt, covered in palm leaves and pineapples. She had encountered this style years before in her travels for the Geiger Foundation, the handout said. The pig was her baby.

The luau was scheduled for the courtyard, but as soon as people got their first drinks it started storming, and everybody had to trail inside. At first they all stood there staring out the huge glass. Mimi had gone overboard on the decorations—dime-size glitter disks,

Christmas lights, tiny white paper flowers, sagging used-car-lot boas of twisted mirror-finish plastic. It was third-worldish when the rain hit.

The pig was hustled out of the courtyard strung between two six-foot Pier One bamboo poles carried on the shoulders of Ken and David Whitcomb, twin homosexuals who team-taught a class in rock video, baseball, and Madonna, and taken to the motel kitchen where it was cut up into oven-sized portions and rushed to completion.

Jen had dodged a lot of the weekend, so had agreed to attend the luau, but when the rain hit she caught Del in the lobby and said, "I'm going to the room. I'm bringing you bad luck."

He said, "I'll be there in a minute. Just as soon as I get these pig eaters squared up."

"I'll wait for you," she said.

Del moved everybody to ballroom two, the Blue Conquistador Room, which he had arranged to have available against just such a contingency. When he got it set up, he went and sat out in the courtyard for a minute. The rain was spotty by then, unnaturally large spurts of water that looked like there was somebody on the roof shooting a hose.

He sat on the lip of the still working pond and stared at fat goldfish circling in the alarming blue water. There were hidden lights in the pond, and when fish swam through them it was as if the fish themselves were strangely shaped bulbs. One fish was almost as big as one of Del's new cross training shoes. The shoes seemed much bigger and brighter than they'd seemed in the store—he'd been thinking about that all afternoon, wondering if he'd made another shoe mistake. He stared from fish to shoes, then back to fish. The fish was much smaller, he decided, about the size of a believe-it-or-not potato.

When Del got back to the room Jen said, "Thank God they roped it off." Jen was on the bed in her ribbed underpants and a kid's T-shirt. "I thought for a minute we'd be staring into the burning eyes of that thing as it was yanked out of the dirt. I thought we'd have to watch them burst."

"They take the eyes out," Del said.

"In Hawaii they probably suck them out," she said. "Like they do out of chickens in France."

"They're too big," Del said. He stood at the mirror pushing the tip of his nose to make it a pig nose.

"Your brother's new gal said it was the most beautiful pig she ever saw," Jen said.

"Let's go home," Del said. "Or leave here, anyway. I'm ready."

"What, tonight?"

"Let's tell them we're going home and then move to another motel—what about that? Just you and me on a high floor. Romance. Wind. Pounding rain."

"Sounds good," Jen said.

They were sprawled together on the satiny comforter that spread over the bed like simulated icing on a microwave cake. "I hoped it would," he said.

"But we're probably not going anywhere," she said. "Are we?"

She'd spent Saturday rooting through a few stories from the local newspaper, then she linked up her little Toshiba with Compuserve for a quick scan of the AP and UPI wires. She told Del she found a piece about a woman who was out of work and who beheaded her three children while they slept, then told her neighbors she was offering them as a sacrifice for the Darlington 500, a stock car race. The woman's name was Lolita Portugesa. She had gotten up at midnight in her trailer in a quiet fishing village north of Tampa, grabbed a Chicago Cutlery carving knife that had been a Christmas present from her ex-husband, Fernand, and slashed off the heads of her children Miniboy, 8, Squat, 6, and Junior, 3. All this was from the police report, Jen said. The woman then hacked at her own wrists in an unsuccessful suicide attempt. The Florida authorities said she would be given a psychiatric evaluation to determine if she was sane. A note Portugesa left in the kitchen for her ex-husband, Fernand, read, "I am leaving to you the heads of our children. This is what you have deserved."

There was a knock at the door as Jen finished telling him this story. "Jesus," she said, getting out of the bed and pulling on jeans. "What, now they catch us?"

Del put his hand over his eyes as if to hide.

Mimi was at the door. "Rudy wonders if you will join him in the garden," she said. She was wearing a swimsuit, one piece, way low in the front, with a long but open wrap-around skirt and backless heels.

"What's the Big Rudy want?" Jen said.

"He wants to thank you," she said. "Both. He's proud of the way things are turning out."

Del said, "I guess he's deaf, dumb, and blind?"

Jen frowned at him, and said, "It hasn't been so bad."

"You haven't been out of the room, how would you know?" Del said.

Mimi said, "Everybody downstairs loved the pig."

"Well, I didn't *love* the pig," Jen said.

"So I guess you're not in the preponderance, huh? You guys want to come down now?" Mimi said. "Or later? Like in a minute or two, when you have time to get straightened away?"

"You go," Jen said. "There's one other story I want to download. It's a guy who caught a fish with a human thumb in it. Six people disappeared in this lake recently, so they don't know whose thumb it is. It's a detective thing."

"Yeeech," Mimi said. "We have to talk, Jen."

"What other kind of thumb is there?" Del said.

Jen tapped Del's shoulder. "Go on. I'll find this, and then I'll change, get my makeup all straightened away, and then I'll be right down. Show Mimi your elevator moves."

"She likes me in elevators," Del said.

"I do not," Jen said, ushering them out the door. "I just said it was possible."

The elevator was lined in seat cover vinyl, dusty rose colored, with a thick, padded handrail all around the interior, something to prevent kids from hurting themselves when they bashed their heads against it while rampaging up and down in the building, as the designers apparently knew they would. Mimi leaned against the rail on the far side of the car, her head turned to stare at the clicking numbers over the door. Del studied her calf.

"I need to get away for a while," she said, not taking her eyes off the numbers. "Maybe I should go back early. Maybe tonight."

"Ah," Del said. He smiled and nodded, but felt that it was too much, too phony. "We were talking about leaving, too. Everything's done, really."

"Yeah. Maybe we'll go together," she said. "Why not?" She hit the Emergency Stop button.

"What's this?" Del said, pointing to the control panel. "What're you doing?"

"Let's rest a minute," she said. "OK? Let me just rest a minute here, Del. I don't ever get to just rest, you know? Since Rudy took this job I'm all over the place and I don't say a thing. I argue, smile and nod and wave and make my eyes twinkle and draw my lips back and do my nostrils—but I never rest. I'm not like most women."

"Mimi," he said.

"Have we ever talked, just you and me?"

"No," Del said. "But we will, we'll talk all the time."

"I like you, Del. From the moment I met you. I love Rudy, but that's not the same thing. I suppose you know what I'm talking about, don't you? One of those suddenly-out-of-whack things?"

"We did that, didn't we? Back when we were thirty?"

"Yeah, that was fun. Two years ago. Longer for you, huh? I miss it already."

Del caught himself nodding again in a silly way. He stopped.

"I used to want children," Mimi said. "I always figured I'd be good at that. I always think of the kinds of things I'd say to them. I'd tell them not to let anybody kid them, that people will say anything, they'll say they love you, but they really don't. They try, but no matter what they're after, they're not after what you're after. Not usually."

"That's kind of depressing, Mimi. I don't think we're supposed to tell kids that kind of thing," Del said. "It's OK to get depressed, and maybe it seems like it's that bad, sometimes, maybe it even is, but we're supposed to keep it to ourselves, I think." Del had his arm around her. They were slumped against the back wall of the elevator. The call bell was ringing.

"That's why I don't have any. I keep pointing to Rudy, talking to him about little Rudys," she said. "But he isn't buying."

"Well say good-bye to projectile vomiting."

She gave him a look and there wasn't any laughing in it. "I'm pretty forlorn tonight," she said. "Sorry."

"Never mind. It was stupid," he said, gently finger-combing her hair.

"Once I was at the store and this guy who looked like Rudy came in," Mimi said. "He held a stun gun on this checker. I'm standing right there. I couldn't get over it—Rudy's double. After all the TV shows, the cop shows, the movies, the mystery books, here was this guy in Pass Christian. Anyway, so I talked him down. Just like TV. We had a talk about stun guns. I told him the way he was holding his he was going to take big electricity."

"When was this?"

"Couple months ago."

"He was holding it wrong?"

"How do I know?" she said. "A guy talked somebody down on 'Cops,' so I tried it. I said he was going to burn his ass if he zapped her. He was thin, sick-thin like cancer, so I asked him if he'd been checked up recently. I pointed at this spot on his neck with my fingernail and asked him if anybody had looked at that. There wasn't anything there, a smudge, but I made it sound like there was something, trying to give him a little doubt. He said he thought he was holding the gun right, he'd read the instructions, he'd shot it off on a dog that way. I asked what happened to the dog. He said it spit up and then bit him, and I just shook my head. 'There you go,' I told him."

She was threading her fingers in and out between the buttons on Del's shirt.

"Rudy likes gun magazines. You don't, do you? He gets dozens of them but he never reads them. *Soldier of Fortune,* stuff like that. He's always decoding the mercenary ads in the backs of those magazines. Like, when it says 'rotunda OK' that means the guy does kidnapping. 'Wet work' used to be one. Stuff like that. And *Paintball*—have you seen that one? Rudy's dying to play paintball. The magazine's full of masks and paintball guns, crossbreeds of forties futurism and nineties street weaponry. Full head dressings, choice of ball colors. I look, too, but I'm afraid of guns. Aren't you?"

Del caught her hand, slowed it down, then held it for a minute. "Let's see, I shot a squirrel once, a long time ago. I felt bad afterwards—it was worse than after really ugly sex. Once I shot a bird out of a tree, one off a wire, and I killed a groundhog at my uncle's farm when I was ten. I think that's the complete catalog."

"I guess killing's not about manhood after all," Mimi said. "I'd be afraid to have a gun, though. How would you avoid it? How would you stop playing with it, pointing it out the window at passersby and stuff? Going over the line?"

"That'd be a problem," Del said. He eyed the panel with the floor numbers on it. "Bell's ringing," Del said.

"At least there'd be the risk," she said. "Don't we all go a little nuts and slam the hammer through the bathroom wall sometime? Crack up one of those hollow-core apartment doors? Wouldn't we use a gun then, if we had it? Or like when Rudy started to jump up and down on the mini-satellite dish because it wouldn't find G2-A? What we do in private is scary sometimes. Maybe that's a good reason not to have a gun."

Del started to slide out from behind her but didn't make it. She had him pinned. She had a bittersweet aroma, a new scent, dark and slightly overdone in a nasty way.

"I figure we can do anything we want, Del," she said. "Whenever we want to do it. Anytime. Anywhere. Just get right down and do what we want and nobody ever knows the difference, nobody ever knows what goes on."

"Rudy's waiting, isn't he?" Del said.

"I guess, but he's way down there and we're way up here."

"We're not that far," he said, sliding sideways on the rail, pressing out from behind her.

She backed away, holding up her hands like TV wrestlers do when they want to persuade the ref they're making a clean break. "Hey, if that's what you want," Mimi said. "I was thinking you might want to open up some, like PMI says, you know, show yourself, but if that's not the way you feel, OK. It's up to you, I'm just following the keys here—that's what these things are for, right? These retreats? To let you guys catch up?"

"You are lovely, Mimi," he said. "Really."

Then she stalked him playfully around the edge of the little elevator, and when she caught him they held each other for a few long seconds, then separated. Mimi smiled at him, traced his cheek with the backs of her nails. "I'm fine," she said. "I'm a lot better than I appear." She fingered the red Emergency Stop button for a minute, eyeing him, then shoved that button in, and hit the one that said Lobby.

Rudy was on the edge of the goldfish pond staring into the lighted water at the big things circling in the thickened sea grass. "I love these," he said to Del, pointing into the water. "If I had it to do over again, I'd be a fish, I swear to God. See how they move? Look at that, look at the white one there."

"Mimi said you wanted to talk?"

"Yes, sir." Rudy leaned to one side to look around him. "Where's your partner?"

"She's resting. Too much Hawaii, I think."

"Ah." Rudy shook his head and stared at the fish more. "I tell you, that Jen. She looks a little like Mimi, you know? She's just real nice and young. And so on."

"Thank you," Del said. "I'll pass along your compliments."

"How'd you like the weekend? No problems?" Rudy said. "You and Mimi get along OK? She's peculiar, like she seems one way at the college and completely different when she's not there."

Del took a minute, then shook his head. "I don't know what you mean."

Rudy reached out to shake his brother's hand. "Doesn't matter. I just wondered. We're going over to the beach. You and Jen can leave if you want to. Tomorrow's nothing."

"Probably not," Del said. "We'll probably stay."

"Up to you," Rudy said, noticing Mimi in the lobby. She was waving.

"I guess I *do* know what you mean," Del said. "About Mimi. She's so calm. We came down in the elevator. It was the only time we had to talk, you know—"

"Yeah," Rudy said, rocking his head back. He dropped a fingertip into the water and the potato-size fish swam up for a look.

Mimi came out the doors into the courtyard and strode toward them, her heels clicking on the paving stones.

"I gotta run," Del said, getting up.

Mimi did a little circle right next to him, brushed a hand across his shoulder. "You ready?" she said to Rudy.

"About," Rudy said.

"Boy, I like it out here," she said. "I used to be out all the time, at clubs and parties, I used to see people, I used to do stuff. I remember what it's like, what night smells like when you're out here on your own. Sometimes I watch MTV, those dance shows where the kids jerk at each other every way they can, so hard, and it just carries me away, you know? I feel every move they make."

———

Fred Barthelme's novels, *Second Marriage, Tracer, Two Against One, Natural Selection,* and *The Brothers,* have, along with his stories collected in *Moon Deluxe* and *Chroma,* brought him international recognition as a

chronicler of the suburban New South, particularly the Gulf Coasts of
Florida, Mississippi, and Texas. His fiction has appeared in *Esquire, The
New Yorker, Harper's Magazine, Epoch, Kansas Quarterly, Chicago Review,
TriQuarterly,* and elsewhere. He lives in Hattiesburg, Mississippi, where
he directs the Center for Writers, which is the creative writing program
at The University of Southern Mississippi, and edits *Mississippi Review,* a
national literary magazine.

*The story "Retreat" started with a photograph a friend showed me of a
luau he'd attended while vacationing in Hawaii with his parents. The
hotel cooked a whole pig, underground, covered in banana leaves and pineapples and so on, in what was said to be a traditional Hawaiian style. He
told me the pig was real tasty. I thought it was grotesque, stupid, vulgar, sad,
and charming, all at the same time—sort of classic America. Still, after the
Irony Wars we know that we make things real, so this phony baloney cookout
was a genuine experience for the participants, as good as any. That odd,
conflicted thought started the story (it was called "Pig Hawaiian" then). I
stirred in the self-actualization stuff because another friend got into some
intimacy trouble at a regional academic convention. I was interested in the
cliché that people "let themselves go" at those things, as if they're suddenly on a
new planet that won't come close to Earth for another million years, and how
easily we tell strangers our secrets, sure that the secrets won't come back to
haunt. It was intriguing to put that idea together with the two brothers,
where the intimacy certainly would come back to haunt. Against these back-
grounds the story moves along, commenting here, remarking there, always
leaning toward good faith and generosity, trying to laugh with and at each
other while not giving up on the hope of romance.*

Robert Morgan

DARK CORNER

(from *South Dakota Review*)

I'd die if anybody around here knowed I was one of the Branch
girls that walked through this country back then. I don't think
a soul here realizes that was me and my sisters. I sure haven't told
them. If people had any hint of such a story it would spread faster
than flu germs, narrated around in every baby shower and phone
call.

If people knowed I was one of that big family that stopped here
like beggars way back yonder, I couldn't have married and lived on
this creek. Not that these kind of people ever accept anybody that
ain't their kinfolks even if they marry kin and live here forty years.
I guess I was always meant to be a foreigner, but at least they wasn't
no scandal. Nobody had dirt on me. I was lucky that way.

You take the people at the church. Somebody will whisper a person stole something from the building fund, or so and so was stepping out on her husband while he worked at the Du Pont plant,
and next thing you know it's gone from one end of the valley to
the other as fact. It don't pay to trust nothing you hear, unless you
see it with your own eyes. And even then you can't always be sure.

We had got off the train at Greenville. I say got off, but it was
more like they throwed us off, Mama and Daddy and me and my
five sisters. Daddy had bought us tickets far as Atlanta, and we had
come all the way from Brownsville, Texas. I don't know where he

got the money for the tickets, except from selling what little we had. And maybe he sold some things we still owed money on. He had done it before.

Our tickets give out in Atlanta, and we was still two hundred miles from Uncle Dave's house west of Asheville. It was a great big train station and we stood around with our cardboard boxes tied up with string and Mama's trunk of clothes with a few pots and pans.

"Let's get on the train," Daddy said.

"We ain't got no tickets," I said.

"You hear what I say. Get on the train," Daddy said.

Crowds was pressing all around us, and my sisters was trying to look unconcerned, like tourists coming back from a month in Florida or a visit to St. Louis.

"They'll put us in jail," I said. I was always the one to argue with Daddy when he concocted his schemes. Not that it ever done any good except to get him riled. Nobody else would face up to him, and it just got me in trouble.

"We'll ride until they throw us off," Daddy said. "And then we'll have to walk."

"You mean they'll throw us off the train while it's moving?" I said.

"Do what your daddy says," Mama said. She was always telling me not to argue. The more she told me the worse I was for arguing. I feared something terrible was about to happen. We'd had hard times in Texas, but we never had been throwed off no train.

"Every mile we ride is one less we have to walk," Daddy said.

We got our things on that train just before it pulled out of the station. I was so worried I couldn't enjoy a minute of the ride. We had craved to get back from Texas to North Carolina. I was homesick to see the mountains, and our kinfolks at Asheville. But I didn't hardly notice the mountain we passed outside Atlanta and the hills and red clay fields. It was beginning to look like home, but all I could think of was what was going to happen.

Daddy told us what to do, and we got further than we ever hoped we would. I don't know if the conductor was just lazy, or we was lucky. It was a crowded train, and we moved around from one car to another. Once when we seen the conductor coming my sisters and me hid in the washroom till he had gone to the next car. Daddy and Mama slipped back into the baggage car once. Daddy had rode the railroads a lot, after the Confederate War, and he knowed all kinds of tricks.

I was sick with worry, and it seemed like the longest train ride I ever took. We made it past one stop in the Georgia hills, and then all the way across the Georgia line. My sisters and me held our boxes tight so we wouldn't lose them when we got caught and throwed off. The train rumbled and lurched along, and we moved from seat to seat and car to car. I felt like I was taking a headache and wanted to throw up.

We crossed a river into South Carolina, and though the hills was no higher the countryside seemed more familiar. The trees looked the way trees was supposed to, not like they did in Texas and Mississippi. It even seemed like the air was different. My hands was sweating so they stuck to the box I was carrying.

"Let's try to get to the back," I said to my oldest sister Katie. When we come out of the washroom the conductor was nowhere in sight. I was looking for Mama and Daddy. Daddy had said we should not stay all together, but I didn't want us to get thrown off the train at different places. I was trying to look down the length of the car when somebody tapped me on the shoulder. I jerked around so quick I dropped my box. It was the conductor. "Come with me," he said.

I felt my whole body go hot with embarrassment. When I bent over to pick up the box my face got even redder. As we followed the conductor through the cars to the front everybody watched us. Shirley, my littlest sister, begun to cry. I took her hand.

The conductor led us to the front of the first car. That surprised me, for I thought they would throw us off from the back, from the porch of the caboose. But Mama and Daddy was standing by the door of the first car. Daddy looked out the window at the passing fields. He did not look at me.

"The law allows us to put you off at the next stop," the conductor said. "That's all we can do to deadbeats and white trash."

Daddy turned to the conductor, then looked away.

"You low-down trash are lucky today," the conductor said. "The next stop is normally Anderson, but this train only slows down there to throw off the mail. You've got a free ride all the way to Greenville. Of course, when we get there I'll have the police arrest you."

Shirley started crying again, and I held her by the shoulders. We had had some bad times in Texas, but we had never been arrested. The sheriff did come to our house and carry all our things out into the road. They made us leave the house, and they dumped all our clothes and furniture out in the sand on the side of the road. That was painful, let me tell you.

And while we was standing there trying to decide what to do, and Daddy was talking about going to borrow a wagon, and to look for accommodations, to telegraph back to Asheville for money, the wind come up. The wind in Texas will hit like a pillow in your face and knock you back with surprise. It will come up out of nowhere and lift everything loose and snatch it away.

Before we knowed it our clothes and Mama's bolt of cloth, her box of patterns, and all our magazines and papers got jerked off the pile and flung away. We all grabbed something, but the rest got whipped away. It was like trying to stop a flood with a poker.

"Catch my hatbox," Mama said. But the hatbox tumbled off the pile and went rolling along the dusty road. It broke open and all Mama's scarves and handkerchiefs went flying over the weeds. The wind jerked things out of our hands and sent them swirling up in the air. It wasn't a twister exactly, but it was like a twister.

As our things scattered and went flying Daddy run around trying to catch this and that. But everything he touched got pulled away. Finally he stopped and started laughing. His hat got blowed away and he faced into the wind, his hair pushed back, and laughed. It was a bad laugh. It was a laugh like a curse. He looked at us holding our boxes and dresses like he expected us to laugh too.

And then when the wind died down a little he started stomping and kicking the furniture that was left. He kicked a chair until he broke one of the legs, and then he picked up the chair and beat the other chairs. Mama had a dark green vase she had brought from North Carolina and he banged that till it broke. Everything that was little he stomped on.

When he stopped laughing and kicking we didn't have nothing left except what we held in our hands. In the weeds along the edge of the road we picked up a few stockings and clothes. They was still Mama's trunk left, and one little table we could sell to a secondhand store.

The rest of the way to Greenville we stood up on the train. It was like we didn't have a right to a seat now that we was found out. The conductor didn't say we couldn't set down, but we didn't just the same. I guess we was afraid he would tell us to get back up. Mama stood looking at the floor and Daddy watched out the windows. Shirley quit crying, and then Ella Mae started. I held them both, one on each side of me. Callie and Katie and Rita didn't say nothing.

It must have took another hour to get to the station in Greenville. I didn't hardly notice the little shacks with the rows of collards behind them outside town. We rolled by warehouses and cotton gins, coalyards, and water towers. It was beginning to rain.

The conductor made us stand on the train until everybody else had got off. The other passengers looked at us as they went by and whispered.

"Are they going to put us in jail?" Ella Mae whispered.

"Hush up," Mama said.

Shirley begun to cry again.

"Look what you've brung us to," Mama said to Daddy.

"At least you didn't have to walk all the way from Atlanta to Greenville," Daddy said.

Finally the conductor led us into the station. He took us to this little office where a policeman was waiting. Daddy carried Mama's trunk on his shoulder and set it down by the door.

"These are the people," the conductor said.

"Is the railroad preferring charges?" the policeman said.

"They are thieves," the conductor said.

It was musty in the office. The rainy air made the smell more noticeable. It was raining hard outside now, and you could hear horses and wagons splashing in the street. The conductor left because the train was ready to pull out.

The policeman didn't say nothing to us for a long time. He looked at us like we was stray cats they had picked up. I seen he enjoyed lording it over us, making us feel worser.

"You're hoping I will arrest you," he said finally. "So you'll get to spend a night in jail and get a free meal."

"We just want to be," Mama said.

"Trash like you are hard to break," the policeman said. "To put you in jail would waste the taxpayers' money."

"We didn't hurt nobody," Daddy said. "The train would have come to Greenville anyway, where we was on it or not."

"Shut up," the policeman hollered. He leaned his face about three inches from Daddy's. "You should be horsewhipped."

He made us stand there feeling awful for about half an hour. He called us trash and scum and deadbeats, then told us to get out of his sight and out of town. He said he wouldn't waste a penny of the taxpayers' money feeding us.

We carried our boxes and Daddy carried the trunk to the door of the station. It was raining hard, and we stepped to the side of the entrance under the overhang. The policeman followed us to the door. "Get on away from here," he said.

We started walking out into the rain. We held the boxes over our heads to protect us a little. We didn't even have newspapers to use for umbrellas. It was raining harder than ever. Once Daddy stopped and looked back, but the policeman was still standing at the door and he hollered, "Go on now, get!" like we was stray dogs he was chasing away.

I didn't know what we was going to do. It was pouring cold rain and the wet was beginning to sink in under our arms. It had been spring in Texas, but it was late winter here. I just had a little old jacket, and it was already soaked.

Greenville was bigger than it seemed at first. At least it stretched out farther. I figured if we could get out in the country we could stand under a pine tree or maybe crawl into a hayloft. Maybe somebody would let us set on their porch until the rain slacked off.

They was nothing but stores along the street far as I could see. Puddles stood on the bricks, and in places the sidewalk was only mud. My teeth was chattering, and my feet squished inside my shoes.

"Where we going?" Rita said. "I got rain in my face."

"Hush up," Mama said.

People hurried past us on the street, stepping out of our way. Horse apples stained puddles.

"I'm stopping here," Daddy said. He had to set the trunk down to open the door. It was a dark little store with KALIN AND SON written on the window. Daddy carried the trunk inside and we followed him. It was so dark I couldn't see nothing at first, and it wasn't much warmer inside than it was out. But at least it was dry. A little man with glasses stood behind a counter, and they was a kind of cage around him. The place had a funny smell, like silver polish, and brass and bronze things.

"Don't touch anything," the little man said. He watched us crowding into the dark store, and dripping on the floor.

"I want to sell this," Daddy said, and pointed to the trunk. "What's inside?" the man said.

"Just some clothes, and pots and pans," Daddy said.

"You want to sell the clothes?"

"I'll sell anything you will take," Daddy said.

"Don't drip on the furniture," the man hollered at Katie. She was standing close to a stuffed chair. Maybe she had started to set down in it. Everything in the store was used. I realized it was a pawnshop. "Let's see what you've got," the man said.

Daddy took out the blouses and stockings, the extra pair of pants, a frying pan and a saucepan, and laid them on the counter.

He took out Mama's scissors and thimble, some knitting needles, and the family Bible.

"That's not for sale," Mama said.

"It's worth nothing to me," the man said. Daddy set the Bible aside. Then he lifted the leather trunk up on the counter, and the man looked inside.

"I'll give you two dollars," he said.

"For the trunk?" Daddy said.

"For all of it."

Daddy looked at Mama and back at the pawnbroker. "The scarves are worth five dollars," Mama said.

"Two dollars it is," the man said.

"I'll keep the pants," Daddy said.

"Keep the pants," the man said. "They're worn out anyway." The man give Daddy two silver dollars and a box to put the Bible and pants in.

It seemed to be raining even harder when we stepped back into the street. It was like the sky was tearing to pieces and falling on us. The rain seemed cold and greasy. We walked past the rest of the stores and we walked past rows of houses that didn't have no paint on them. Wagons went by and splashed us, and we tried to stand aside out of their way. My dress got splattered with mud.

It was such a relief to get out of town finally into the country where they wasn't somebody watching us every step. We stopped at a store the first crossroads we come to. They was men playing checkers by the stove inside and they looked around at us like we had come from the moon. But the warm air felt mighty good.

Daddy bought a box of soda crackers and a can of sardines for each of us. We hadn't had nothing to eat since before Atlanta.

"Where is you all from?" the man at the counter said, looking at our wet dresses and dripping hair. Our boxes was wet and soft.

"We're from Asheville," Daddy said. The men around the stove had quit talking. Daddy walked over and held out his hands to the stove door. They shifted their chairs around to make room for him, and the rest of us moved closer to the stove.

We stood in the dark store and ate our sardines. I tried not to get juice on my dress or spill none on the floor. But I was so hungry I didn't care too much. When I finished the sardines I wiped my hands on the soda crackers before I ate them.

"Where is you all going?" the man at the counter said.

"We're going back to Asheville," Daddy said. "We've done been to Texas."

When Daddy sold our house near Asheville he said he could buy a thousand acres in Texas with the money. He said we would raise cattle in the sunshine, and not have to do no more hardscrabble farming. He wanted to get away from the fussing and backbiting in the church. He wanted to live in open country, and not in the shadow of a mountain. We went to Brownsville because that is where Great-grandpappy had been give a square mile of land by the Republic of Texas for fighting in the war against Mexico. That was way back before the Confederate War even. Great-grandpappy had gone out there and fought against Santa Anna, but instead of taking his tract of land he come back to the mountains. The family had talked for years of going out there to Brownsville and claiming that land.

"I'll bet they's a thousand head of cattle on that property," Uncle Dave would say at Christmas dinner.

"They might be gold on it," Daddy would say. "It's close to Mexico and they's gold in Mexico."

But when we got to Texas, after riding on the train for almost a week, Daddy went to the courthouse in Brownsville and they said they didn't have no record of Great-grandpappy ever owning any land grant. They asked him if he had any receipt for taxes paid on the land. Daddy didn't have no records at all except what he had been told by Grandpappy. They asked if he had any deed, or any charter from the Lone Star Republic.

So Daddy give up trying to claim the square mile of land and tried to buy a place. We had spent some of the money going out to Texas, but he still had about eight hundred dollars. We lived in a boardinghouse, and every day we went out looking for property to buy. But he found all the good ranch land and all the farmland wasn't for sale. Most of the places for sale wasn't fit for nothing. It was the poorest soil you ever seen. Wasn't nothing but a little brush growing on it. And it was too dry, even by the river, to do any real farming. People growed little gardens, but they had to carry water to them in buckets.

The place Daddy finally bought wasn't neither a farm nor a ranch. It was about a hundred acres outside town. Somebody had tried to grow cotton on it at one time. Daddy was going to try to raise cotton and some wheat. He bought an old horse and he put all us girls to hoeing cotton and carrying water for the garden. The water there tasted awful. We drawed it from a well and carried it in buckets to sprinkle on the peas and corn and potatoes.

It was like that ground had no life in it. The soil was dead, and had no grease at all. It was flat and starved of water. In Carolina you put a seed in the ground and it springs right up. In the hot bare soil at Brownsville the seeds went to sleep, and when they did sprout they made the sorriest corn you ever seen. I doubt we got five bushels to the acre.

Daddy kept spending his money and couldn't get none back. Times got leaner and leaner. We lived on cornbread, and we lived on taters. We lived on whatever we had. We run plumb out of money. They wasn't no money in Brownsville except what the big cattlemen brought in, the people with big ranches. They wasn't no jobs, and what they was was took by Mexicans. Mama and me done sewing, but they wasn't much of that to take in.

Every week they was less to eat. Daddy sold off his shotgun, and he sold off his horse, and he sold off his tools. We lived on grits, and then one week we lived on tomatoes because we had a few bushes that come in. It was always hot and dusty, or cold and wet, in Brownsville. They wasn't no in-between times. Maybe we was so hungry and worried we didn't enjoy the pretty weather when it come. I just remember mud, and I remember dust.

When you fall off your dresses don't fit no more. They hang on you like sacks. You wonder how you ever filled up your clothes. And when you're worried you get weak and lazy. You sleep late in the morning and you go to bed early at night. You fall asleep in the afternoon. You want to sleep and forget how bad things is. If you close your eyes and fall asleep, maybe you will dream things is better. You get to where you don't want to go any place or do anything. It all winds down, like you want to stop living, to stop the worry of living. I dreamed the world was a breast from which we sucked, and sometimes the breast went dry.

Daddy tried to borrow money, and he tried to find work. He worked a few days for a blacksmith helping to shoe horses. But mostly they hired Mexicans because they didn't have to pay them nothing.

"The Lord is punishing us for leaving Asheville," Mama said.

Finally the sheriff come and throwed all our things out of the house.

When we left the store it was beginning to get dark. I felt some better after eating the sardines and soda crackers. But I hated to leave the warm stove and go back out in the rain. My box was so wet it was about to crumble.

"Where we going to sleep?" Katie said.

"Hush up," Mama said. "We'll find a place."

The road beyond the store was nothing but mud, and we walked along the edge in weeds and grass. The grass was getting green, but they wasn't nothing else putting out in upper South Carolina. We met a man in a wagon coming back from mill. He had several meal sacks in the bed behind the wagon seat. He looked at all us girls like we was something from a circus.

"How do," he said.

"How do," Daddy said.

They wasn't any houses that seemed friendly. Most was set way back from the road, and big dogs barked in the yards. You'd see a lantern or a lamp around some. Others was dark but had smoke coming out the chimney. I knowed Daddy was looking for an empty house. We was too many to stop and ask for hospitality. Or maybe we was too wet and discouraged to stop and ask anybody to take us in. If we'd had plenty of money, we'd have stopped at the biggest house and asked for room and board, and they would have took us in. And when we offered to pay like as not they wouldn't have took our money. It's all a matter of how you're feeling, and what people think of you. We was too wet and wore out to have any pride, or confidence.

Daddy had coughed in the store two or three times. I thought he must have got a cracker crumb caught in his throat, or the smoke from the stove was bothering him. But he coughed again several times while we was walking up the road.

It was almost dark when we seen the churchhouse ahead. They was tombstones in the yard, some of them leaning everywhich way like they was drunk. The church was just a little building, all dark and set back in the woods. They was a damp smell of wet leaves and oak trees all around.

"Let's stop here," Daddy said.

"This is a graveyard," Ella Mae said.

"Hush up," Mama said.

The meeting house door was unlocked, and we all climbed the board steps and slipped inside. It was so dark we couldn't see a thing.

"It smells musty," Rita said.

"It's colder than outside," Callie said, her teeth chattering. Daddy searched through his pockets and then struck a match. The churchhouse wasn't no bigger than a regular living room. It had benches and a platform up front for an altar. They was a barn lantern hanging from a rafter. The little stove at the side didn't look no bigger than a coal bucket with a pipe coming out of the top. They was a pile of cobs and kindling beside the stove.

"I'll start us a fire," Daddy said, and begun coughing again.

"I ain't sleeping in no church," Rita said. "Not with all the graves outside."

"Me neither," Shirley said.

"Hush up," Mama said.

"The Lord said he would provide," Daddy said. "And what he has provided is his own house."

"You can't sleep in a church," Callie said. "It would be a sin."

"Ain't no sin," Mama said.

The churchhouse was so cold we was all shivering and chattering our teeth. It seemed twice as cold inside as out in the rain. Daddy put some kindling and cobs in the stove and lit them. We crowded close to the light of the fire.

"Ain't we going to light the lantern?" Katie said.

"A light might attract attention," Daddy said. None of us argued, because none of us wanted anybody to see us in the church. We might not be doing anything wrong, but we didn't want anybody to catch us there either.

Daddy left the door on the little stove open, and as the fire caught it begun to throw out light and warmth. We moved two of the benches up to the stove and set down. We had been standing up and walking since Atlanta. It felt sweet in my bones to set down and hold my hands out to the fire.

Daddy started coughing again. I guess the dampness had sunk into his chest.

"You need something hot to drink," Mama said.

"Be awright," Daddy said. "Once I warm up."

Mama untied the box she had been carrying and tilted it toward the firelight. She looked through the combs and brushes and packets of needles and took out a crumpled paper sack. "This is the last of our coffee," she said. "I ground it before we left."

I could smell the coffee. It had been ground for three days, but still smelled good. Mama got up and started looking around the meeting house. She felt her way among the benches and around the edge of the church. Behind the altar she found a bucket and dipper. It was for the preacher to drink from when he got all hot and sweaty preaching. The bucket was about half full of water. Mama set the bucket on the stove and poured the coffee in.

"I hope that water's clean," Daddy said, and coughed again.

"It smells fresh," Mama said. "It was brought in on Sunday, I reckon."

As the water begun to simmer and the bucket rattled on the stove it filled the church house with the smell of coffee. The water started to boil and Mama stirred the coffee with the dipper. It was like the fumes theirselves made us feel better. My face begun to tingle from getting warmed up after being cold and wet so long. My fingers started itching as I held them out to the stove.

After the coffee had boiled about five minutes Mama set the bucket off the stove. We didn't have nothing to drink out of but the dipper. We'd have to drink the coffee scalding hot. Of course Daddy always drunk his coffee that way anyway. Mama dipped out about a third of a dipper full and handed it to Daddy. "Sorry I don't have any cream," she said.

"And no sugar neither," Daddy said.

"And no crumpets at all," Mama said. She laughed, and Daddy laughed. We all started laughing. It felt so good to get warm, and to be setting down in the privacy of the church, we all felt a little lightheaded.

"Would you like some coffee, ma'am?" Mama said to me, after Daddy had drunk from the dipper.

"After you, ma'am," I said and giggled. We all laughed again. That's the way we drunk the coffee, passing the dipper around with exaggerated politeness.

"Coffee, ma'am?" I said to Rita.

"Please," she said, and took the dipper.

The coffee made us feel happy and silly. It warmed the mud inside our bones, and the soil in our blood. We laughed and drunk coffee, and then Daddy started coughing again.

"You need some pneumony salve," Mama said.

"I just need some sleep, and a day in the sunshine," Daddy said. After we finished the coffee we pushed eight benches close as we could to the stove, and we laid down on them to sleep. I was so tired I must have dropped off, bang. As I slept I heard Daddy coughing, and I dreamed it was raining. I dreamed again the world was a great breast from which we sucked milk and coffee and time. Everybody sucked all they could, and sometimes the breast went dry. It was a long hard dream, like I was walking and working. When I woke the fire had died down in the stove and Daddy was still coughing.

We didn't have nothing to eat in the morning, and we didn't have no more coffee. And all the wood and cobs by the stove had been burned up too. We didn't even need to get dressed since we had slept in our clothes. Daddy said we had best get out of the church before it got completely light. "The Lord has shared his house with us," he said. "But some of the deacons may not be as kind."

Daddy was coughing bad, and his face was flushed like he had a fever.

"You ain't in no shape to walk," Mama said to him.

"I'm in better shape to walk than to set here and freeze to death," he said.

It had quit raining in the night, but it was wet outside, and they was a fog over everything. You couldn't even see the road from the church door. I was so stiff from sleeping on the bench, and so sore from walking the day before, it felt like I had to walk sideways. I needed to stretch and rest, and I needed to wash my face. But they wasn't nothing to do but start walking.

"I never thought I would sleep in a church," Rita said as we stepped onto the wet grass.

"It's bad luck to sleep near a graveyard," Callie said.

"Hush up," Mama said. "We've got a long way to walk and you might as well save your breath."

We walked through the fog up the muddy road. Daddy's coughing made dogs bark from houses we couldn't see. He would cough and we could hear echoes. We tried to surround the puddles and walk on the grass when we could. Men on horses passed us, and wagons passed us. But nobody offered us a ride. They was too many of us.

My feet was sore and my shoes was still wet from the day before.

My right shoe had broke open down where the lace started. I had to favor that foot or I'd get more mud in the shoe. It was the grit in the mud that hurt. The grains of sand cut into my toe, making a blister.

But we couldn't walk fast anyway. Daddy had always walked ahead and the rest of us had to keep up with him. But that morning he walked slow, and he took little steps. Sometimes he coughed so hard he had to bend over holding to his knees.

By the middle of the morning it begun to clear up. The fog opened in places and you could see the sun. And then the fog just seemed to melt into itself and disappear. It was a clear morning, with everything wet and shining. You could see the blue mountains ahead. At first I thought they was clouds, but they went all the way across the world to the north. The fields everywhere was plowed and red and the pastures and yards dark green. You could see buds on the maples and oak trees looking red and light green.

As we kept walking Daddy's cough got worser. We come over a long hill and down beside a branch where they was a line of sycamore trees. Daddy coughed until he was red in the face, and he leaned over holding to a sapling. It was like he couldn't hardly get his breath. They was a house about a hundred yards ahead.

"You run down there and get a dipper of water," Mama said to me. "Ask them for a dipper of water."

I told Katie to come with me. We hurried on, trying not to step in puddles. In some places the branch had washed right across the road, and we had to jump across the muddy water. They was a big cur dog in the yard and it come growling out at us.

"Anybody home?" I hollered from the road. "We just want a dipper of water." They was smoke over to the side of the house and I walked around the edge of the yard till I seen this old woman bent over a washpot.

"Could we borrow a dipper of water?" I hollered. The dog growled and come toward me. But the woman looked up and called the dog to be quiet. I walked over to her.

"My daddy's sick," I said, "and we need to borrow a cup of water."

"Where is your daddy?" the woman said. She had a snuff stick in her mouth and didn't take it out to talk.

"He's down at the road," I said.

"Why lord a mercy child," the woman said. "You bring him to the house. I don't want nobody sick out on the muddy road."

The woman called to the cur dog, and Katie and me went back to get Daddy and the rest of them. The old woman stood in the door watching us walk across her yard. The house was a big frame house, but it looked like it had never been painted.

"You all come right in and set down," the woman said. She had us set down around this big table in the kitchen. We must have been a sight in our wrinkled clothes. "Where you all from?" she said.

"We're going back to Asheville," Mama said. "We been to Texas."

"Lord a mercy, you mean you walked all the way from Texas?"

"We rode the train to Greenville," I said. I knowed we looked awful from being rained on and sleeping in our clothes. I wished I could wash my face and comb my hair.

The woman's name was Mrs. Lindsay. She said her man had gone to mill. He always went to mill when she done her washing. That way he didn't have to help carry water from the spring. She give Daddy a drink of water, and she made a pot of fresh coffee and served us biscuits with jelly. She give Daddy a spoon of sour-wood honey for his cough.

I drunk the hot coffee but I couldn't eat the biscuits. They must have been cooked for breakfast for they was cold and greasy and the jelly made them seem slimy. I must have been half sick myself. I set there trying to be polite and watching Mama and my sisters eating biscuits and jelly, and I thought my stomach was going to turn. But the coffee made me feel better. And the honey seemed to help Daddy's cough.

"The roads is terrible this time of year," Mrs. Lindsay said. "A wagon will sink almost up to its axles." I knowed she was hoping we'd tell her what we had done in Texas, and why we was out on the road with just the clothes on our backs and our little cardboard boxes. But they really wasn't no mystery to it. We was broke. Else why would a man and woman and half a dozen half-grown girls be out walking the muddy road? She was trying to be neighborly, but I could see she was curious.

After we drunk the coffee and they ate some biscuits it was time to start again. Mrs. Lindsay give us some sweet taters to take with us. Daddy was the quietest I'd ever seen him. He wheezed when he breathed, but he wasn't coughing so bad. "Much obliged," he said.

"It's turning off cold," Mrs. Lindsay said as we stepped out on the porch. And sure enough, the sky was bright and clear, and the wind had picked up a chill. It was coming from the north, right where we was headed.

Daddy used to tell us stories about way back yonder when he was a boy. He said they was a time, after the Texas war, when near about everybody wanted to go to Texas, because of all the free land. People that lived on little scratch-farms squeezing a living from rocks and trying to put in crops beside branches would just up and disappear. People left their little washed-out farms by the dozen. Sometimes they burned the barn and house down to get the nails. But most of the time they just left, took their horse and mule and wrote "GTT" on the doorpost, "Gone to Texas." Sometimes they might be going to Arkansas or even Indian Territory, but they still wrote "GTT" because Texas meant the West, which was a big place.

When Daddy got tired of farming his wore-out acres over in West Asheville, and after they had a big fuss and falling out at the church over who was to be the new preacher, and then when Grandma died and Mama and her sister Hettie got in this awful feud about who was to heir the silverware, he just up and sold his little dab of land on the creek and we headed out for the west. "Gone to Texas" he would say to hisself and smile, like he had a secret, like he had found an answer to his troubles. I just wish it hadn't been so different from the way he planned.

After the coffee and Mrs. Lindsay's hot kitchen the wind felt fresh and thrilling in my face. After about a mile we come across the top of a hill and the air hit me smack in the face. It was getting colder, and we didn't really have no winter clothes. The mountains rose ahead, black and far away.

I buttoned my little jacket tighter around my neck and we all walked closer together. The sun was still warm on our backs. If we stayed closer together, those in the middle and back could keep warm. But whoever walked in front had to take the cold wind.

"You walk in front," Mama said to me. I knowed she would say that cause I was younger than her and Daddy and older than the other girls. It was my job to take the brunt of the cold air. I wished then I'd ate some of the greasy biscuits. When you're out in the cold without much clothes on you have to think yourself warm. It's like you make extra heat with your will to push the cold back. You make your whole body tense and alert and you meet the cold air with the heat of determination.

I got out in front and walked like I was shoving the cold air ahead of me. I was breaking trail through drifts and shoals of sharp wind. The road was drying and the lips of ruts was firm enough to walk on in places. The wind was drying a crust on the clay. Daddy started coughing again.

"Don't hurry so," Mama said.

We had to slow down and stop while Daddy coughed. The honey that soothed his throat was wearing off. Daddy must have coughed for five minutes, and then throwed up the coffee and biscuits. When we started walking again he was slower. He still carried the box with the Bible and pants in it. But he let the box dangle on its string while he coughed.

"We ought to find a place to stop, where you can lay down," Mama said.

"No, I'll be awright," he said.

I didn't see no hope but to keep walking. If we didn't get to

Uncle Dave's soon it looked like we would all die on the road. I
didn't feel no pride anymore about going back to Uncle Dave's
with nothing. We was flat, and it didn't do no good to deny it.

The road was getting steeper, up and around hills. We crossed a
creek on a shackly footlog. I noticed Daddy's hands was trembling
as he held onto the rail. He had always been the strongest one of
us, but he had lost his get up and go. Seemed like every house and
cabin we passed had a woman doing her washing in the yard. Must
have been raining for weeks, and the first clear day they was trying
to catch up. You could smell the smoke from fires by the branch.
The smoke got knocked around by wind and smelled like ashes
and lye soap.

Finally the road went into a deep holler. They wasn't any more
hills, and it seemed the tracks disappeared into the side of the
mountain.

"This is Chestnut Springs," Mama said. And we all knowed what
she meant. Chestnut Springs was at the heart of Dark Corner,
where most of the blockaders, the whiskey men, lived and carried
on their business. What she meant was it was getting toward the
middle of the evening and we had to climb up the mountain and
cross into North Carolina before night come. We didn't want to
be caught in Dark Corner after dark.

"Girls ain't safe in this country," Mama said. "Ain't nobody safe
after dark."

I tried to walk as fast as I could but not get ahead of the others.
Daddy was wheezing and walking with a limp. His face had red
splotches on it, like people's with a fever does. He limped not like
he was crippled, but like he didn't have the strength to take regular steps.

The houses we passed looked like ordinary houses, except they
was little. Every place had a dog that run out to bark and sniff at
us. I knowed it was better to ignore dogs, or if one seemed mean
you could reach out your hand and it would wag its tail. People
come out on their porches and called their dogs back. They said
"Howdy" and they watched us walk up the holler like they'd never

seen such a big bunch of girls hoofing up the road. None of my sisters said nothing all evening. They was too tired, and too embarrassed.

The creek looked like it had red paint spilling into it from the patches behind the houses. It must have been raining for a long time for all the slant ground seemed full of wet weather springs bleeding muddy water.

We come to this place where the road went right up the side of the mountain, swinging back and forth. It was called the Winding Stairs and they must have been fifty switchbacks. I didn't see how a team with a wagon could make it around the sharp curves. It was more like climbing steps than a road.

Mama was helping Daddy to walk, and Katie started holding his arm too. They got on either side of him and held him up. There against the face of the mountain we was out of the worst wind. I begun to sweat a little. But Daddy was out of breath. We had to stop to let him rest. Nobody said nothing. We was all thinking the same thing, that we had to get up the mountain before nightfall.

When we finally reached the top of the Winding Stairs I seen it wasn't the top of the mountain at all, but just the lip of a valley floor. They was poplars growing along the branch and little houses set back on the sides of the ridge.

"Where is this?" I said to Mama.

"This is Chestnut Springs," she said.

They was several taverns clustered along the road at the place where spring water was piped down off the mountain into a trough. Horses was tied to rails and you could hear people laughing in all the places. In one house they was fiddle music. A woman that was only half dressed come to the door of a tavern and looked at us go by.

"Let's hurry on," Mama said. But she didn't need to say nothing. We was all afraid. I had always heard about the shooting and knife fights at Chestnut Springs. It was said somebody was killed about every week there.

A man wearing clean overalls and a fine gray hat stood on the porch of one of the houses. He tipped his hat to us and said, "How do."

I answered back, but not so as to seem too friendly. I didn't want to invite any attention to us. Just then Daddy started coughing again. He took the worst coughing fit he had yet, and Mama and Katie had to stop and hold him up. It was like every inch of his body heaved and shook with the coughs. He wasn't strong enough to take deep breaths anymore.

"Give him a drink of water," the man in overalls said. He brought a dipper from the spring. Mama waited a second, like she didn't want to have nothing to do with the strange man, and then she took the dipper. But Daddy was coughing so bad he almost choked when he took a sip from the dipper. He tried to swallow and coughed all the water out, spraying some of it on Katie's dress.

"Maybe he needs some medicine," the man said. He pulled a flat whiskey bottle from the pocket of his overalls. Other men had come to the door of the tavern and was watching us.

"He don't need none," Mama said.

"Might help him breathe," the man said. "It's the best medicine they is." The man's face was red, like he had had a lot of liquor hisself. But he didn't seem drunk. He was just calm and helpful. He held out the bottle and Daddy reached for it. Daddy took a little swallow and held it in his mouth, like he was holding his breath to keep from coughing. And then he took a longer swallow. He coughed. but only after the liquor had gone down. "Much obliged," he said, wheezing.

"You folks need to find a place to stay," the man said.

"We'll be on our way," Mama said. We started walking on up the road. It was getting late, and the valley was in shadow. The music had stopped in the tavern and everybody in Chestnut Springs seemed to be gathered on the porches watching us. The sun was still bright way up on the peaks, but it would be dark in another hour. They would be frost that night; you could feel it in the air.

"I could find you a room," the man said. "My name is Zander Gosnell. I don't believe your husband should be out in this wind."

"We'll be on our way," Mama said. "We have to get to the top of the mountain by dark."

We started walking again. The man stood by the side of the road watching us. He had on the cleanest overalls I had ever seen. They even had a crease ironed in each leg. His hat did not have a wide brim, but it looked finer than any hat I had seen in Texas.

When we got further up the road the fiddle music started again. I didn't look but guessed the men drifted back into the taverns. I wanted to hurry, but they was no way Daddy could walk faster. They was nothing ahead but the holler in deep shadows.

"Where are we going to stay tonight?" Rita said.

"Hush up," Mama said. "We'll find a place."

"Daddy still has a dollar," Callie said.

"He has a dollar and twenty cents," Ella Mae said.

"He don't neither," Shirley said. "It's only a dollar and fifteen cents."

"Hush up," Mama said.

Daddy wasn't coughing as bad, but he seemed even weaker. It was like the liquor made him slow and sleepy. His eyes shined with the fever. Part of the time he walked with his eyes closed. "Are we home?" he said. That was the first time I knowed he was out of his head.

"We ain't home," Mama said. "We still got to cross the mountain."

"I want to stop," he said.

"We can't stop yet," Mama said. "We've got to climb over the mountain."

The road ahead looked so dark I wondered if that was why this place was called Dark Corner, because the mountain was so black and the holler so deep. I could hear wind high up on the ridge, but by the creek they was spring peepers chirping. I shivered, and I knowed Daddy must be cold.

I took Katie's place on the other side of Daddy, but he was having trouble standing up, much less walking. They was a crackling in his throat, and his breath come in quick pants. The sun was gone now and the cove looked cold and shadowy.

We got Daddy about a mile up the road, to where they was a steep turn over a little branch. Mama said it wasn't much more than a mile to the state line. I don't know what we would have done if we had got to the state line, for we was still thirty miles from Asheville, but it seemed to us desperate to get to North Carolina and out of Dark Corner by nightfall.

But I seen Daddy wasn't able to go no further. We was almost carrying him. He was so sick and fevered he didn't know where he was no more. And I don't reckon he much cared either. He wasn't paying no attention, and he was hot as a stove. He would have fell down in the road if we hadn't held him up.

When the worst things happen to you it's like you know how bad they are, but you don't quite feel it. So many bad things had happened since we got to Brownsville that maybe I couldn't feel anything anymore. I was so worried I had quit shivering, for I knowed this was the worst we had seen. But it was like the Lord was protecting me by giving me something to do. Mama was wore out, and my sisters was tired and scared.

"You help hold Daddy," I said to Callie. She took him under his arm. He was leaning over now, breathing short and hard.

It was getting dark quick. I followed the branch from where it crossed the road. Laurel bushes growed almost in the water, and they was no clear place at all. We couldn't let Daddy lay down in the muddy road. I squeezed my eyes to see in the dark, and remembered you could see most at night by looking out of the corner of your eyes.

About fifty feet up the branch they was a little open place among the laurels. It was a kind of shelf of ground above the branch. I went back to the road and we almost carried Daddy up there through the bushes. It took all of us to help. Rita and Ella Mae brought the boxes, and they was crying. Mama didn't even tell them to hush up.

After we laid Daddy down in the leaves and put what scarves and clothes we had over him I looked in his pockets for the matches. He had a little box with not more than five or six matches in it. They was a hard wind on the ridge above, but by the branch we felt only gusts. I heaped up some leaves and little sticks, and after striking four of the matches finally got a fire going. Me and Callie felt around in the dark for more sticks, bigger sticks that wasn't too damp.

When the fire got brighter we could see Daddy had took even worser. He had the kind of pneumony that chokes you up and smothers you fast. His breath come in quicker and shorter pants, like his lungs was full of water. The fire lit his face and the laurel bushes like some terrible dream. Mama set by Daddy and held his hand. She didn't say nothing.

To keep from looking at Daddy smothering I went out in the dark to gather more sticks. It was going to be a long cold night. I built the fire higher to warm us. The flames crackled and the branch splashed below us. Up on the ridge the wind roared like a train in a tunnel. I lost track of time, but sometime during the night I heard this voice and woke up. There at the edge of the laurels was Zander Gosnell. He held a blanket and jug.

"I thought you might need these," he said.

We wrapped Daddy in the blanket and give him a drink from the jug. Zander helped me gather more sticks for the fire. My sisters was still asleep, and Mama just set by Daddy and wouldn't say nothing. Zander and me bent over Daddy, giving him drinks from the jug. I watched our shadows move on the laurel bushes. They stretched like some kind of puppets in a story you couldn't make any sense of.

Sometime before daylight Daddy quit breathing. He gasped harder and shorter, harder and shorter, and then he just stopped. I don't think he knowed a thing after it got dark. I don't think he knowed where he was. He kept talking all night about farming and planting corn. He said it was time to plant the corn.

After Daddy was dead and turning cold in the dawn we was all so washed out we didn't know what to do. I don't know what would have happened if it hadn't been for Zander Gosnell. I guess we would have buried Daddy with our own hands. But Zander got some of his friends from Chestnut Springs and they carried Daddy down to one of the taverns. They laid the body out and made a coffin for him. Mama said Daddy wanted to be buried in North Carolina.

Some of the women there at Chestnut Springs, some of the bad women, helped us clean our clothes and even give us some new things to wear. They was bright and silky things.

Then they put the coffin in a wagon and drove us to the top of the mountain, to the Double Springs Cemetery. And the liquor people had even got a preacher to preach the funeral by the grave. I don't know what we would have done without them.

We stood there in the cold wind while they funeraled Daddy. We must have looked like beggars and vagabonds in our odd pieces of clothes. The people of the community come out to see us. That's why I'm glad nobody knows I was one of that family. I didn't dream I would marry some day and come back here. I always wanted to thank those people in Chestnut Springs, but was afraid to give myself away. I've put flowers on Daddy's grave over at Double Springs many a time, but I'm glad people never knowed I was one of that family of girls. It was hard enough to live through that time, without having to live it down.

Robert Morgan is the author of nine books of poetry, most recently *Green River: New and Selected Poems*. He has published three books of fiction, including *The Mountains Won't Remember Us*. *The Hinterlands: A Mountain Tale in Three Parts* was published by Algonquin Books in 1994. A native of Henderson County, North Carolina, he has taught at Cornell University since 1971. His stories have been reprinted in *New Stories from the South* in 1991 and 1992.

"**D**ark Corner" *is one of those stories that grew out of a sliver of family rumor. The gossip was that one of my great-aunts by marriage had* *been taken to Texas as a girl. After her family lost everything there they returned to the mountains of North Carolina on foot. It was supposedly her husband who said, "I'm glad nobody here knows I married one of those girls that came walking through here from Texas." I barely knew the great-aunt and made up the story and her voice from that splinter of an idea. I tried to make the world of upper South Carolina as real as I could. Many of the boot-leggers in Dark Corner in those days were named Morgan, as well as Gosnell and Howard. My experience has been that the disreputable, and those living slightly beyond the law, are as apt to help you when you are in real trouble as the more respectable members of the community. I was happy to be able to show that in this story.*

Nancy Krusoe

LANDSCAPE AND DREAM

(from *The Georgia Review*)

Cows

A barn is a beautiful place where cows are milked together. Our barn has many windows facing east and west. These windows have no glass in them.

You get up early in the morning to milk cows. You pour warm white milk into heavy gray metal cans with matching metal tops that fit like a good hat, and these tops are very pretty, their shape a circle with a brim over the neck of the can.

Warm cow milk has a certain smell, a from-inside-the-body smell, the way your finger smells pulled out of your own vagina.

Women who are married to dairy farmers stand in their kitchens at their kitchen windows and stare longingly at their husbands' barns, but they don't go there. Barns are female places; they are forbidden places for women. These women stand at their kitchen windows staring at their husbands' barns because barns are beautiful female places, full of sweet-milked, happy, honey-faced cows being milked by men's hands or by machines with cups. Cows have rough-skinned teats, sometimes scraped and scratched, chapped and bleeding, which fit into these cups put on by men whose hands are not gentle.

So the wife I am talking about stands at her kitchen window facing east. She has no one to be with. Unlike the cows and the men in the barn (her husband and her son, who helps his father for a while), she is alone. I, the daughter, am in the barn, too—young enough to be there a little while longer. But I would like for the wife, my mother, to leave the farmer, to go away from the farm and the barn and this warm longing for cows.

Our barn is a cold place in winter with only the heat of cows to warm you. You stand very close to their large bodies so that you won't frost over like the windows of the kitchen where you stare, looking for your mother to see if she is watching you.

On the other side of the barn, the east side, are the hill and the lake at the bottom of the hill and the gray-brown grass that holds this hill in place in winter. Tiny slivers of ice float on the lake in winter, at dusk and during the night, and they melt each morning when the sun comes up. Our cows slide through mud to drink cold morning water, because even though they're full and ready to be milked, their mouths are saliva machines with licorice-colored tongues, thick and dark with cud and the need for water. I see them standing by the side of the lake, their knees bent a little, bracing themselves as they lean over the icy water, mud rising up their delicate sweet ankles. *Hurry, drink fast,* I say. *Hurry, hurry.*

Seeing them like this makes me want to be a cow, but which kind would I be? There are dainty, needle-brown Jerseys, big woolly Guernseys, and the large, black-and-white spotted, famous-for-milk Holsteins. There is also the plain black cow.

When cows come to the barn to be milked, it's a happy, sloppy time of day for them, and I am there waiting. They all push in at once, rushing toward me as I stand at the far end of the barn—in case one goes wild I will stop her—and running, some of them, because their favorite food is waiting there (that delicious grainy mixture of oats and wheat and barley and who knows what else that I, myself, eat along with them out of cupped hands). They are running toward me, looking at me, and then abruptly turning in, one by one, each into her own place, and someone will close the stanchions around their necks for milking, because you can't have them visiting—wandering around and disturbing each other during milking—of course not. Each one has her own place, her own stanchion, and she remembers it; out of fifty or sixty stalls, each cow knows her own. How: Smell? Number of footsteps from the door to the slippery spot at the entrance to her place? Or rhythm— how many sways of the heavy stomach, the bloated udder, back and forth to the stall that is hers?

I remember how it was to be inside the barn with all those steamy, full-of-milk, black-and-white cows, with their sweet, honey-barn faces and their clover-alfalfa breath. And their beautiful straight backbones that you could rub between your fingers across the length of their bodies, a delicate spine for all that weight underneath. And light falling through the windows. I washed their udders, washed them all with the same brown cloth soaked in disinfected water, their teats covered with dirt, and sometimes I didn't get it all off they were so swollen (of course, I didn't know how it felt, not for years did I know how that felt), but they didn't mind. No words were spoken there in the barn—or if they were, they weren't between me and the men. I didn't feel it so much then— well, maybe more than I thought—but I felt the bodies of cows, dozens of them, their big, sloppy, breathy faces and sighs in the barn with me.

In the kitchen, it isn't a happy time of day: cooking breakfast, half moon, half dark. My mother stands there waiting. Anyone could come, even cows could come to her flower bed outside the kitchen window, could lie down and wait with her for the farmer—and the daughter—to return. There is nothing to stop them from coming to her, coming to her window, nothing at all.

The Farmer

Sometimes men beat their dairy cows. Sometimes they hit them with lead pipes, and the cows fall down; they slide down in their cow shit on the floor of the barn, fall down on their bones into shit puddles while the daughter is standing at the barn door staring for a very long time at the floor, at the slick running cow pee that has soaked everything the cow was standing on and is now lying in, on her bones, and she is crying.

Is the cow crying? Heaving, trying to stand up on her feet (her feet are so pretty—little hooves like tiny irons), which slip again every time he hits her.

Her head's in the stanchion, her head's trapped, but she can stand up. *Please don't get up again,* I tell her, but it makes no difference: he hits her again. I hope cows don't feel pain; I hope they don't have brains. I hope they have fires in their hearts. If they had brains, I would have to hold them and kiss them and tell my mother at the window what has gone on—not just in her garden but here in her husband's barn. I would have to tell her I hope that the next time the tractor turns over, the farmer is under it.

When a man is beating a cow, a young cow, what is he thinking? Does he think how beautiful she is, struggling to stand? Does he think how she will never stand again unless he lets her, *unless he lets her?*

I am talking about cows that sometimes aren't so beautiful to look at. They love to bathe in slushy red mud, get covered in dirt. Their brains are made of salt licks and saliva so they won't feel pain, you see what I mean? What kind of puzzle could a cow solve? Not the kind a word would solve, a kind word. That's what I mean.

I am talking about women like my mother who watch barns, waiting, because they cannot stop watching with their eyes and hearts, as if smoke will arise, as if smoke will come out of that barn, as if the men and cows will be burned, as if she can stop her daughter from being there in the barn, in the fire, as if she can hold her daughter back, can close the barn door with the power of her eyes—but this will not be enough. The mother watches her daughter move in slowly toward the barn where she will become a cow, where nothing can stop her, where the cow she becomes is the cow her father beats with a metal pipe over and over on her back, on her shoulders and her stomach, on her whole brown bony small body, and the daughter hides inside the cow's body and screams, *stop, stop.*

But do you think he hears, or—if he hears—that he believes what has become of his daughter? What will the farmer tell his wife? What will the daughter tell her mother? Nothing. She will hear nothing about it, for remember, this is a young girl watching her father, and he's beating the cow with a pipe that's long and gray and hollow; he holds it with both his hands. The cow is young like the daughter who's watching. What can she possibly have done to deserve such a beating? Did the young cow kick the girl's father? Being young, she might not have known better, but the girl sees no blood on her father. She looks at his arms and his face and sees nothing but rage—his mouth is clamped shut and his eyes are huge and still swelling in his head. (He has taken off his glasses, and the daughter notices this: that her father isn't wearing his glasses and she can see his eyes.) He looks strange to her. He could be holding back tears, she thinks. He is holding back something, but look at all that is coming out.

The girl looks toward her house, which is across the road from the barn; she searches for her mother in the window to see if she is watching the way she sometimes does. It is too far and too dark to tell. And so the daughter looks back at the barn, at her father in the barn, this man who without his glasses has eyes she hardly knows. This young cow is called, she knows, a heifer. What else should she know?

The Kitchen

We had a chair in our kitchen that was so large I could sit in it doubled up and still have room for my brother and a tub of peas for me to shell. On my right as I sat in the chair, I could see the pasture in front of our house, out the kitchen window, where animals sometimes grazed—cows and horses. The sky was bluer here than anywhere else. Behind the pasture was a semicircle of pine trees, a screen which blocked my view of anything beyond it and formed the limits of my world.

It was on this pasture of grass that phantom men, invaders, conquerors, arose from the earth one day, riding on dusty brown horses, circling the field, riding toward our house. These horsemen wore dusty red scarfs on their necks and blankets on their backs. Dirt from deep inside the earth all about them was kicked up by their horses' feet as we sat, my mother and I, inside the kitchen, waiting for them to surround us, to terrify us, to tell us what they wanted, what crimes they were going to commit. Of course, I opened the door; this was long before I began, in later dreams, to slam and lock all doors and windows against strange men. Tribesmen from deep inside the earth—what could be better? What had they come for? For me, of course. They had come to take me away, or to tell me the secrets of life—whichever, I was ready. I am sure my mother knew, could see that I was ready.

I looked at my mother and wondered what she thought about and if she loved cows the way I loved them. I am the one who watched her, and watching her was all in the world I did for years. Like her I became a cow and I became a mother. I became the barn and the hill behind the barn, the lake and the water cows drink from the lake, the salt and saliva in their mouths. I became, for a while, entirely these things—nothing more. And this is not enough.

———————

Nancy Krusoe lives in Santa Monica, California, and is a graduate student in the creative writing program at California State University, Northridge (CSUN). She was born and raised in Georgia. Her work has appeared in *Magazine, The Santa Monica Review, American Writing,* and *The Georgia Review.* She is currently working on a collaborative novel about Death Valley and the 1994 Northridge earthquake.

I wrote this story while I was a student in Katharine Haake's theory of fiction class at CSUN. The exercise she designed is called the "Burrowing Exercise." The idea is to take a word or sentence and burrow into it, following wherever it takes you until it stops. Then add another piece of language and repeat the process. I began with "A barn is a beautiful place . . ." and worked it from one word to the next. At the same time, we were reading French feminist theory, specifically Julia Kristeva's notion of the chora, the semiotic rhythms of language primarily associated with women's writing, writing in which you work more closely with sound than narrative. Each word became significant because the distance was reduced between me and the sound of the sentence, although Kate Haake says the story is loaded with narrative and it is.

Ethan Canin

THE PALACE THIEF

(from *The Paris Review*)

I tell this story not for my own honor, for there is little of that here, and not as a warning, for a man of my calling learns quickly that all warnings are in vain. Nor do I tell it in apology for St. Benedict's School, for St. Benedict's School needs no apologies. I tell it only to record certain foretellable incidents in the life of a well-known man, in the event that the brief candle of his days may sometime come under the scrutiny of another student of history. That is all. This is a story without surprises.

There are those, in fact, who say I should have known what would happen between St. Benedict's and me, and I suppose that they are right; but I loved that school. I gave service there to the minds of three generations of boys and always left upon them, if I was successful, the delicate imprint of their culture. I battled their indolence with discipline, their boorishness with philosophy, and the arrogance of their stations with the history of great men before them. I taught the sons of nineteen senators. I taught a boy who, if not for the vengeful recriminations of the tabloids, would today have been President of the United States. That school was my life.

This is why, I suppose, I accepted the invitation sent to me by Mr. Sedgewick Bell at the end of last year, although I should have known better. I suppose I should have recalled what kind of boy

he had been at St. Benedict's forty-two years before instead of post-
ing my response so promptly in the mail and beginning that
evening to prepare my test. He, of course, was the son of Senator
Sedgewick Hyram Bell, the West Virginia demagogue who kept
horses at his residence in Washington, D.C., and had swung several southern states for Wendell Wilkie. The younger Sedgewick
was a dull boy.

I first met him when I had been teaching history at St. Benedict's for only five years, in the autumn after his father had been
delivered to office on the shoulders of southern patricians frightened by the unionization of steel and mines. Sedgewick appeared
in my classroom in November of 1945, in a short-pants suit. It was
midway through the fall term, that term in which I brought the
boys forth from the philosophical idealism of the Greeks into the
realm of commerce, military might, and the law, which had given
Julius Caesar his prerogative from Macedonia to Seville. My students, of course, were agitated. It is a sad distinction of that age
group, the exuberance with which the boys abandon the moral
endeavor of Plato and embrace the powerful, pragmatic hand of
Augustus. The more sensitive ones had grown silent, and for several weeks our class discussions had been dominated by the mar-
tial instincts of the coarser boys. Of course I was sorry for this, but
I was well aware of the import of what I taught at St. Benedict's.
Our headmaster, Mr. Woodbridge, made us continually aware of
the role our students would eventually play in the affairs of our
country.

My classroom was in fact a tribute to the lofty ideals of man,
which I hoped would inspire my boys, and at the same time to the
fleeting nature of human accomplishment, which I hoped would
temper their ambition with humility. It was a dual tactic, with
which Mr. Woodbridge heartily agreed. Above the door frame
hung a tablet, made as a term project by Henry L. Stimson when
he was a boy here, that I hoped would teach my students of the
irony that history bestows upon ambition. In clay relief, it said:

I am Shutruk-Nahhunte, King of Anshan and Susa,
sovereign of the land of Elam.
By the command of Inshushinak,
I destroyed Sippar, took the stele of Naram-Sin,
and brought it back to Elam,
where I erected it as an offering to my god,
Inshushinak.

—Shutruk-Nahhunte, 1158 B.C.

I always noted this tablet to the boys on their first day in my classroom, partly to inform them of their predecessors at St. Benedict's,
and partly to remind them of the great ambition and conquest that
had been utterly forgotten centuries before they were born. Afterwards I had one of them recite, from the wall where it hung above
my desk, Shelley's *Ozymandias*. It is critical for any man of import
to understand his own insignificance before the sands of time, and
this is what my classroom always showed my boys.

As young Sedgewick Bell stood in the doorway of that classroom his first day at St. Benedict's, however, it was apparent that
such efforts would be lost on him. I could see that not only was he
a dullard but a roustabout. The boys happened to be wearing the
togas they had made from sheets and safety pins the day before,
spreading their knees like magistrates in the wooden desk chairs,
and I was taking them through the recitation of the emperors
when Mr. Woodbridge entered alongside the stout, red-faced
Sedgewick and introduced him to the class. I had taught for five
years, as I have said, and I knew the frightened, desperate bravura
of a new boy. Sedgewick Bell did not wear this look.

Rather, he wore one of disdain. The boys, fifteen in all, were
instantly intimidated into sensing the foolishness of their impro-
vised cloaks, and one of them, Clay Walter, the leader of the
dullards—though far from a dullard himself—said, to mild laughter, "Where's your toga, kid?"

Sedgewick Bell answered, "Your mother must be wearing your
pants today."

It took me a moment to regain the attention of the class, and when Sedgewick was seated I had him go to the board and copy out the Emperors. Of course, he did not know the names of any of them, and my boys had to call them out, repeatedly correcting his spelling as he wrote out in a sloppy hand.

Augustus
Tiberius
Caligula
Claudius
Nero
Galba
Otho

all the while lifting and resettling the legs of his short pants in mockery of what his new classmates were wearing. "Young man," I said, "this is a serious class, and I expect that you will take it seriously."

"If it's such a serious class, then why're they all wearing dresses?" he responded, again to laughter, although by now Clay Walter had loosened the rope belt at his waist, and the boys around him were shifting uncomfortably in their togas.

From that first day, Sedgewick Bell became a boor and a bully, a damper to the illumination of the eager minds of my boys and a purveyor of the mean-spirited humor that is like kerosene in a school such as ours. What I asked of my boys that semester was simple, that they learn the facts I presented to them in an "Outline of Ancient Roman History," which I had whittled, through my years of teaching, to exactly four closely typed pages; yet Sedgewick Bell was unwilling to do so. He was a poor student, and on his first exam could not even tell me who it was that Mark Antony and Octavian had routed at Philippi, nor who Octavian later became, although an average wood beetle in the floor of my classroom could have done so with ease.

Furthermore, as soon as he arrived he began a stream of capers using spitballs, wads of gum, and thumbtacks. Of course it was common for a new boy to engage his comrades thusly, but Sedgewick Bell then began to add the dangerous element of natural leadership—which was based on the physical strength of his features—to his otherwise puerile antics. He organized the boys. At exactly fifteen minutes to the hour, they would all drop their pencils at once or cough or slap closed their books so that writing at the blackboard my hands would jump in the air.

At a boys' school, of course, punishment is a cultivated art. Whenever one of these antics occurred I simply made a point of calling on Sedgewick Bell to answer a question. General laughter usually followed his stabs at answers, and although Sedgewick himself usually laughed along with everyone else, it did not require a great deal of insight to know that the tactic would work. The organized events began to occur less frequently.

In retrospect, however, perhaps my strategy was a mistake, for to convince a boy of his own stupidity is to shoot a poisonous arrow indeed. Perhaps Sedgewick Bell's life would have turned out more nobly if I had understood his motivations right away and treated him differently at the start. But such are the pointless speculations of a teacher. What was irrefutably true was that he was performing poorly on his quizzes, even if his behavior had improved somewhat, and therefore I called him to my office.

In those days, I lived in small quarters off the rear of the main hall, in what had been a slave's room when the grounds of St. Benedict's had been the estate of the philanthropist and horse breeder, Cyrus Beck. Having been at school as long as I had, I no longer lived in the first-form dormitory that stood behind my room, but supervised it, so that I saw most of the boys only in matters of urgency. They came sheepishly before me.

With my bed folded into the wall, the room became my office, and shortly after supper one day that winter of his first-form year, Sedgewick Bell knocked and entered. Immediately he began to inspect the premises, casting his eyes, which had the patrician set of his father's, from the desk, to the shelves, to the bed folded into the wall.

"Sit down, boy."

"You're not married, are you, Sir?"

"No, Sedgewick, I am not. However, we are here to talk about *you*."

"That's why you like puttin' us in togas, right?"

I had, frankly, never encountered a boy like him before, who at the age of thirteen would affront his schoolmaster without other boys in audience. He gazed at me flatly, his chin in his hand.

"Young man," I said, sensing his motivations with sudden clarity, "we are concerned about your performance here, and I have made an appointment to see your father."

In fact, I had made no appointment with Senator Bell, but at that moment I understood that I would have to. "What would you like me to tell the senator?" I said.

His gaze faltered. "I'm going to try harder, Sir, from now on."

"Good, Sedgewick. Good."

Indeed, that week the boys reenacted the pivotal scenes from *Julius Caesar*, and Sedgewick read his lines quite passably and contributed little that I could see to the occasional fits of giggles that circulated among the slower boys. The next week, I gave a quiz on the Triumvirate of Crassus, Pompey, and Caesar, and he passed for the first time yet, with a C +.

Nonetheless, I had told him that I was going to speak with his father, and this is what I was determined to do. At the time, Senator Sedgewick Hyram Bell was appearing regularly in the newspapers and on the radio in his stand against Truman's plan for national health insurance, and I was loathe to call upon such a well-known man concerning the behavior of his son. On the radio his voice was a tobacco drawl that had won him populist appeal throughout West Virginia, although his policies alone would certainly not have done so. I was at the time in my late twenties, and although I was armed with scruples and an education, my hands trembled as I dialed his office. To my surprise, I was put through, and the senator, in the drawl I recognized instantly, agreed to meet me one afternoon the following week. The man already enjoyed national stature, of course, and although any other father would no doubt have made the journey to St. Benedict's himself, I admit that the prospect of seeing the man in his own office intrigued me. Thus I journeyed to the capital.

St. Benedict's lies in the bucolic, equine expanse of rural Virginia, nearer in spirit to the Carolinas than to Maryland, although the drive to Washington requires little more than an hour. The bus followed the misty, serpentine course of the Passamic, then entered the marshlands that are now the false-brick suburbs of Washington and at last left me downtown in the capital, where I proceeded the rest of the way on foot. I arrived at the Senate office building as the sun moved low against the bare-limbed cherries among the grounds. I was frightened but determined, and I reminded myself that Sedgewick Hyram Bell was a senator but also a father, and I was here on business that concerned his son. The office was as grand as a duke's.

I had not waited long in the anteroom when the man himself appeared, feisty as a game hen, bursting through a side door and clapping me on the shoulder as he urged me before him into his office. Of course I was a novice then in the world of politics and had not yet realized that such men are, above all, likable. He put me in a leather seat, offered a cigar, which I refused, and then with real or contrived wonder—perhaps he did something like this with all of his visitors—he proceeded to show me an antique sidearm that had been sent to him that morning by a constituent and that had once belonged, he said, to the coachman of Robert E. Lee. "You're a history buff," he said, "right?"

"Yes, Sir."

"Then take it. It's yours."

"No, Sir. I couldn't."

"Take the damn thing."

"All right, I will."

"Now, what brings you to this dreary little office?"

"Your son, Sir."

"What the devil has he done now?"

"Very little, Sir. We're concerned that he isn't learning the material."

"What material is that?"

"We're studying the Romans now, Sir. We've left the Republic and entered the Empire."

"Ah," he said. "Be careful with that, by the way. It still fires."

"Your son seems not to be paying attention, Sir."

He again offered me the box of cigars across the desk and then bit off the end of his own. "Tell me," he said, puffing the thing until it flamed suddenly, "What's the good of what you're teaching them boys?"

This was a question for which I was well prepared, fortunately, having recently written a short piece in *The St. Benedict's Crier* answering the same challenge put forth there by an anonymous boy. "When they read of the reign of Augustus Caesar," I said without hesitation, "when they learn that his rule was bolstered by commerce, a postal system, and the arts, by the reformation of the senate and by the righting of an inequitable system of taxation, when they see the effect of scientific progress through the census and the enviable network of Roman roads, how these advances led mankind away from the brutish rivalries of potentates into the two centuries of *pax romana*, then they understand the importance of character and high ideals."

He puffed at his cigar. "Now, that's a horse who can talk." he said. "And you're telling me my son Sedgewick has his head in the clouds."

"It's my job, Sir, to mold your son's character."

He thought for a moment, idly fingering a match. Then his look turned stern. "I'm sorry, young man," he said slowly, "but you will not mold him. I will mold him. You will merely teach him."

That was the end of my interview, and I was politely shown the door. I was bewildered, naturally, and found myself in the elevator before I could even take account of what had happened. Senator Bell was quite likable, as I have noted, but he had without doubt cut me, and as I made my way back to the bus station, the gun stowed deep in my briefcase, I considered what it must have been like to have been raised under such a tyrant. My heart warmed somewhat toward young Sedgewick.

Back at St. Benedict's, furthermore, I saw that my words had evidently had some effect on the boy, for in the weeks that followed he continued on his struggling, uphill course. He passed two more quizzes, receiving an A- on one of them. For his midterm project he produced an adequate papier-mâché rendering of Hadrian's gate, and in class he was less disruptive to the group of do-nothings among whom he sat, if indeed he was not in fact attentive.

Such, of course, are the honeyed morsels of a teacher's existence, those students who come, under one's own direction, from darkness into the light, and I admit that I might have taken a special interest that term in Sedgewick Bell. If I gave him the benefit of the doubt on his quizzes when he straddled two grades, if I began to call on him in class only for those questions I had reason to believe he could answer, then I was merely trying to encourage the nascent curiosity of a boy who, to all appearances, was struggling gamely from beneath the formidable umbra of his father.

The fall term was by then drawing to a close, and the boys had begun the frenzy of preliminary quizzes for the annual Mister Julius Caesar competition. Here again, I suppose I was in my own way rooting for Sedgewick. Mister Julius Caesar is a St. Benedict's tradition, held in reverence among the boys, the kind of mythic ritual that is the currency of a school like ours. It is a contest, held in two phases. The first is a narrowing maneuver, by means of a dozen written quizzes, from which three boys from the first form emerge victorious. The second is a public tournament, in which these three take the stage before the assembled student body and answer questions about ancient Rome until one alone emerges triumphant, as had Caesar himself from among Crassus and Pompey. Parents and graduates fill out the audience. Out front of Mr. Woodbridge's office, a plaque attests to the Misters Julius Caesar of the previous half-century—a list that begins with John F. Dulles in 1901—and although the ritual might seem quaint to those who have not attended St. Benedict's, I can only say that, in a school like ours, one cannot overstate the importance of a public joust.

That year I had three obvious contenders: Clay Walter, who, as I intimated, was a somewhat gifted boy; Martin Blythe, a studious type; and Deepak Mehta, the son of a Bombay mathematician, who was dreadfully quiet but clearly my best student. It was Deepak, in fact, who on his own and entirely separate from the class had studied the disparate peoples, from the Carthaginians to the Egyptians, whom the Romans had conquered.

By the end of the narrowing quizzes, however, a surprising configuration had emerged: Sedgewick Bell had pulled himself to within a few points of third place in my class. This was when I made my first mistake. Although I should certainly have known better, I was impressed enough by his efforts that I broke one of the cardinal rules of teaching: I gave him an A on a quiz on which he had earned only a B, and in so doing, I leap-frogged him over Martin Blythe. On March 15th, when the three finalists took their seats on stage in front of the assembled population of the school, Sedgewick Bell was among them, and his father was among the audience.

The three boys had donned their togas for the event and were arranged around the dais on which a pewter platter held the green, silk garland that, at the end of the morning, I would place upon the brow of the winner. As the interrogator, I stood front row, center, next to Mr. Woodbridge.

"Which language was spoken by the Sabines?"

"Oscan," answered Clay Walter without hesitation.

"Who composed the Second Triumvirate?"

"Mark Antony, Octavian, and Marcus Aemilius Lepidus, Sir," answered Deepak Mehta.

"Who was routed at Phillipi?"

Sedgewick Bell's eyes showed no recognition. He lowered his head in his hands as though pushing himself to the limit of his intellect, and in the front row my heart dropped. Several boys in the audience began to twitter. Sedgewick's own leg began to shake inside his toga. When he looked up again I felt that it was I who had put him in this untenable position, I who had brought a tender bud too soon into the heat, and I wondered if he would ever forgive me; but then, without warning, he smiled slightly, folded his hands and said, "Brutus and Cassius."

"Good," I said, instinctively. Then I gathered my poise. "Who deposed Romulus Augustulus, the last Emperor of the Western Empire?"

"Odoacer," Clay Walter answered, then added, "in 476 A.D."

"Who introduced the professional army to Rome?"

"Gaius Marius, Sir," answered Deepak Mehta, then himself added, "in 104 B.C."

When I asked Sedgewick his next question—Who was the leading Carthaginian General of the Second Punic War?—I felt some unease because the boys in the audience seemed to sense that I was favoring him with an easier examination. Nonetheless, his head sank into his hands, and he appeared once again to be straining the limits of his memory before he looked up and produced the obvious answer, "Hannibal."

I was delighted. Not only was he proving my gamble worthwhile but he was showing the twittering boys in the audience that, under fire, discipline produces accurate thought. By now they had quieted, and I had the sudden, heartening premonition that Sedgewick Bell was going to surprise us after all, that his tortoiselike deliberation would win him, by morning's end, the garland of laurel.

The next several rounds of questions proceeded much in the same manner as had the previous two. Deepak Mehta and Clay Walter answered without hesitation, and Sedgewick Bell did so only after a tedious and deliberate period of thought. What I realized, in fact, was that his style made for excellent theater. The parents, I could see, were impressed, and Mr. Woodbridge next to me, no doubt thinking about the next annual drive, was smiling broadly.

After a second-form boy had brought a glass of water to each of the contestants, I moved on to the next level of questions. These had been chosen for their difficulty, and on the first round Clay Walter fell out, not knowing the names of Augustus's children. He left the stage and moved back among his dim-witted pals in the audience. By the rule of clockwise progression the same question then went to Deepak Mehta, who answered it correctly, followed by the next one, which concerned King Jugurtha of Numidia. Then, because I had no choice, I had to ask Sedgewick Bell something difficult: "Which General had the support of the aristocrats in the civil war of 88 B.C.?"

To the side, I could see several parents pursing their lips and furrowing their brows, but Sedgewick Bell appeared to not even notice the greater difficulty of the query. Again he dropped his head into his hands. By now the audience expected his period of deliberation, and they sat quietly. One could hear the hum of the ventilation system and the dripping of the icicles outside. Sedgewick Bell cast his eyes downward, and it was at this moment that I realized he was cheating.

I had come to this job straight from my degree at Carleton College, at the age of twenty-one, having missed enlistment due to myopia, and carrying with me the hope that I could give to my boys the more important vision that my classical studies had given to me. I knew that they responded best to challenge. I knew that a teacher who coddled them at that age would only hold them back, would keep them in the bosoms of their mothers so long that they would remain weak-minded through preparatory school and inevitably then through college. The best of my own teachers had been tyrants. I well remembered this. Yet at that moment I felt an inexplicable pity for the boy. Was it simply the humiliation we had both suffered at the hands of his father? I peered through my glasses at the stage and knew at once that he had attached "The Outline of Ancient Roman History" to the inside of his toga.

I don't know how long I stood there, between the school assembled behind me and the two boys seated in front, but after a period of internal deliberation, during which time I could hear the rising murmurs of the audience, I decided that in the long run it was best for Sedgewick Bell to be caught. Oh, how the battle is lost for want of a horse! I leaned to Mr. Woodbridge next to me and whispered, "I believe Sedgewick Bell is cheating."

"Ignore it," he whispered back.

"What?"

Of course, I have great respect for what Mr. Woodbridge did for St. Benedict's in the years he was among us. A headmaster's world is a far more complex one than a teacher's, and it is historically inopportune to blame a life gone afoul on a single incident in childhood. However, I myself would have stood up for our principles had Mr. Woodbridge not at that point said, "Ignore it, Hundert, or look for another job."

Naturally, my headmaster's words startled me for a moment; but being familiar with the necessities of a boys' school, and having recently entertained my first thoughts about one day becoming a headmaster myself, I simply nodded when Sedgewick Bell produced the correct answer, Lucius Cornelius Sulla. Then I went on to the next question, which concerned Scipio Africanus Major. Deepak Mehta answered it correctly, and I turned once again to Sedgewick Bell.

In a position of moral leadership, of course, compromise begets only more compromise, and although I know this now from my own experience, at the time I did so only from my study of history. Perhaps that is why I again found an untenable compassion muddying my thoughts. What kind of desperation would lead a boy to cheat on a public stage? His father and mother were well back in the crowded theater, but when I glanced behind me my eye went instantly to them, as though they were indeed my own parents, out from Kansas City. "Who were the first emperors to reign over the divided Empire?" I asked Sedgewick Bell.

When one knows the magician's trick, the only wonder is in its obviousness, and as Sedgewick Bell lowered his head this time I clearly saw the nervous flutter of his gaze directed into the toga.

Indeed I imagined him scanning the entire "Outline," from Augustus to Jovian, pasted inside the twill, before coming to the answer, which, pretending to ponder, he then spoke aloud: "Valentinian the First, and Valens."

Suddenly Senator Bell called out, "That's my boy!"

The crowd thundered, and I had the sudden, indefensible urge to steer the contest in young Sedgewick Bell's direction. In a few moments, however, from within the subsiding din, I heard the thin, accented voice of a woman speaking Deepak Mehta's name; and it was the presence of his mother, I suppose, that finally brought me to my senses. Deepak answered the next question correctly, about Diocletian, and then I turned to Sedgewick Bell and asked him, "Who was Hamilcar Barca?"

Of course, it was only Deepak who knew that this answer was not on the "Outline," because Hamilcar Barca was a Phoenician general eventually routed by the Romans; it was only Deepak, as I have noted, who had bothered to study the conquered peoples. He briefly widened his eyes at me—in recognition? in gratitude? in disapproval?—while, beside him, Sedgewick Bell again lowered his head into his hands. After a long pause, Sedgewick asked me to repeat the question.

I did so, and after another, long pause, he scratched his head. Finally, he said, "Jeez."

The boys in the audience laughed, but I turned and silenced them. Then I put the same question to Deepak Mehta, who answered it correctly, of course, and then received a round of applause that was polite but not sustained.

It was only as I mounted the stage to present Deepak with the garland of laurel, however, that I glanced at Mr. Woodbridge and realized that he too had wanted me to steer the contest toward Sedgewick Bell. At the same moment, I saw Senator Bell making his way toward the rear door of the hall. Young Sedgewick stood limply to the side of me, and I believe I had my first inkling then of the mighty forces that would twist the life of that boy. I could only imagine his thoughts as he stood there on stage while his mother, struggling to catch up with the senator, vanished through the fire door at the back. The next morning, our calligraphers would add Deepak Mehta's name to the plaque outside Mr. Woodbridge's office, and young Sedgewick Bell would begin his lifelong pursuit of missed glory.

Yet perhaps because of the disappointment I could see in Mr. Woodbridge's eyes, it somehow seemed that I was the one who had failed the boy, and as soon as the auditorium was empty I left for his room. There I found him seated on the bed, still in his toga, gazing out the small window to the lacrosse fields. I could see the sheets of my "Outline" pressed against the inside of his garment.

"Well, young man," I said, knocking on the door frame, "that certainly was an interesting performance."

He turned around from the window and looked at me coldly. What he did next I have thought about many times over the years, the labyrinthine wiliness of it, and I can only attribute the precociousness of his maneuvering to the bitter education he must have received at home. As I stood before him in the doorway, Sedgewick Bell reached inside his cloak and one at a time lifted out the pages of my "Outline."

I stepped inside and closed the door. Every teacher knows a score of boys who do their best to be expelled; this is a cliché in a school like ours, but as soon as I closed the door to his room and he acknowledged the act with a feline smile, I knew that this was not Sedgewick Bell's intention at all.

"I knew you saw," he said.

"Yes, you are correct."

"How come you didn't say anything, eh, Mr. Hundert?"

"It's a complicated matter, Sedgewick."

"It's because my pop was there."

"It had nothing to do with your father."

"Sure, Mr. Hundert."

Frankly, I was at my wits' end, first from what Mr. Woodbridge had said to me in the theater and now from the audacity of the boy's accusation. I myself went to the window then and let my eyes wander over the campus so that they would not have to engage the dark, accusatory gaze of Sedgewick Bell. What transpires in an act of omission like the one I had committed? I do not blame Mr. Woodbridge, of course, any more than a soldier can blame his captain. What had happened was that instead of enforcing my own code of morals, I had allowed Sedgewick Bell to sweep me summarily into his. I did not know at the time what an act of corruption I had committed, although what is especially chilling to me is that I believe that Sedgewick Bell, even at the age of thirteen, did.

He knew also, of course, that I would not pursue the matter, although I spent the ensuing several days contemplating a disciplinary action. Each time I summoned my resolve to submit the boy's name to the honor committee, however, my conviction waned, for at these times I seemed to myself to be nothing more than one criminal turning in another. I fought this battle constantly, in my simple rooms, at the long, chipped table I governed in the dining hall and at the dusty chalkboard before my classes. I felt like an exhausted swimmer trying to climb a slippery wall out of the sea.

Furthermore, I was alone in my predicament, for among a boarding school faculty, which is as perilous as a medieval court, one does not publicly discuss a boy's misdeeds. This is true even if the boy is not the son of a senator. In fact, the only teacher I decided to trust with my situation was Charles Ellerby, our new Latin instructor and a kindred lover of antiquity. I had liked Charles Ellerby as soon as we had met because he was a moralist of no uncertain terms, and indeed when I confided in him about Sedgewick Bell's behavior and Mr. Woodbridge's response, he suggested that it was my duty to circumvent our headmaster and speak to Senator Bell again.

Less than a week after I had begun to marshall my resolve, however, the senator himself called *me*. He proffered a few moments of small talk, asked after the gun he had given me, and then said gruffly, "Young man, my son tells me the Hannibal Barca question was not on the list he had to know."

Now, indeed, I was shocked. Even from young Sedgewick Bell I had not expected this audacity. "How deeply the viper is a viper," I said, before I could help myself.

"Excuse me?"

"The Phoenician General was *Hamilcar* Barca, Sir, not Hannibal."

The Senator paused. "My son tells me you asked him a question that was not on the list, which the Oriental fellow knew the answer to in advance. He feels you've been unfair, is all."

"It's a complex situation, Sir," I said. I marshalled my will again by imagining what Charles Ellerby would do in the situation. However, no sooner had I resolved to confront the senator than it became perfectly clear to me that I lacked the character to do so. I believe this had long been clear to Sedgewick Bell.

"I'm sure it is complex," Senator Bell said, "But I assure you, there are situations more complex. Now, I'm not asking you to correct anything this time, you understand. My son has told me a great deal about you, Mr. Hundert. If I were you, I'd remember that."

"Yes, Sir," I said, although by then I realized he had hung up.

And thus young Sedgewick Bell and I began an uneasy compact that lasted out his days at St. Benedict's. He was a dismal student from that day forward, scratching at the very bottom of a class that was itself a far cry from the glorious, yesteryear classes of John Dulles and Henry Stimson. His quizzes were abominations, and his essays were pathetic digestions of those of the boys sitting next to him. He chatted amiably in study hall, smoked cigarettes in the third-form linen room, and when called upon in class could be counted on to blink and stutter as if called upon from sleep.

But perhaps the glory days of St. Benedict's had already begun their wane, for even then, well before the large problems that beset us, no action was taken against the boy. He became a symbol for Charles Ellerby and me, evidence of the first tendrils of moral rot that seemed to be twining among the posts and timbers of our school. Although we told nobody else of his secret, the boy's dim-witted recalcitrance soon succeeded in alienating all but the other students. His second- and third-form years passed as ingloriously as his first, and by the outset of his last with us he had grown to mythic infamy among the faculty members who had known the school in its days of glory.

He had grown physically larger as well, and now when I chanced upon him on the campus he held his ground against my disapproving stare with a dark one of his own. To complicate matters, he had cultivated, despite his boorish character, an impressive popularity among his schoolmates, and it was only through the subtle intervention of several of his teachers that he had failed on two occasions to win the presidency of the student body. His stride had become a strut. His favor among the other boys, of course, had its origin in the strength of his physical features, in the precocious evil of his manner, and in the bellowing timbre of his voice, but unfortunately such crudities are all the more impressive to a group of boys living out of sight of their parents.

That is not to say that the faculty of St. Benedict's had given up hope for Sedgewick Bell. Indeed, a teacher's career is punctuated with difficult students like him, and despite the odds one could not help but hope for his eventual rehabilitation. As did all the other teachers, I held out promise for Sedgewick Bell. In his fits of depravity and intellectual feebleness I continued to look for glimpses of discipline and progress.

By his fourth-form year, however, when I had become dean of seniors, it was clear that Sedgewick Bell would not change, at least not while he was at St. Benedict's. Even with his powerful station, he had not even managed to gain admission to the state university, and it was with a sense of failure then, finally, that I handed him his diploma in the spring of 1949, on an erected stage at the north end of the great field, on which he came forward, met my disapproving gaze with his own flat one, and trundled off to sit among his friends.

It was with some surprise then that I learned in *The Richmond Gazette*, thirty-seven years later, of Sedgewick Bell's ascension to the chairmanship of EastAmerica Steel, at that time the second largest corporation in America. I chanced upon the news one morning in the winter of 1987, the year of my great problems with St. Benedict's, while reading the newspaper in the east-lighted breakfast room of the Assistant Headmaster's House. St. Benedict's, as everyone knows, had fallen upon difficult times by then, and an unseemly aspect of my job was that I had to maintain a lookout for possible donors to the school. Forthwith, I sent a letter to Sedgewick Bell.

Apart from the five or six years in which a classmate had written to *The Benedictine* of his whereabouts, I had heard almost nothing about the boy since the year of his graduation. This was unusual, of course, as St. Benedict's makes a point of keeping abreast of its graduates, and I can only assume that his absence in the yearly alumni notes was due to an act of will on his own part. One wonders how much of the boy remained in the man. It is indeed a rare vantage that a St. Benedict's teacher holds, to have known our statesmen, our policy-makers, and our captains of industry in their days of short pants and classroom pranks, and I admit that it was with some nostalgia that I composed the letter.

Since his graduation, of course, my career had proceeded with the steady ascension that the great schools have always afforded their dedicated teachers. Ten years after Sedgewick Bell's departure, I had moved from dean of seniors to dean of the upper school, and after a decade there to dean of academics, a post that some would consider a demotion but that I seized with reverence because it afforded me the chance to make inroads on the minds of a generation. At the time, of course, the country was in the throes of a violent, peristaltic rejection of tradition, and I felt a particular urgency to my mission of staying a course that had led a century of boys through the rise and fall of ancient civilizations.

In those days, our meetings of the faculty and trustees were rancorous affairs in which great pressure was exerted in attempts to alter the time-tested curriculum of the school. Planning a course was like going into battle, and hiring a new teacher was like crowning a king. Whenever one of our ranks retired or left for another school, the different factions fought tooth-and-nail to influence the appointment. I was the dean of academics, as I have noted, and these skirmishes naturally waged around my foxhole. For the lesser appointments I often feinted to gather leverage for the greater ones, whose campaigns I fought with abandon.

At one point especially, midway through that decade in which our country had lost its way, St. Benedict's arrived at a crossroads. The chair of humanities had retired, and a pitched battle over his replacement developed between Charles Ellerby and a candidate from outside. A meeting ensued in which my friend and this other man spoke to the assembled faculty and trustees, and though I will not go into detail, I will say that the outside candidate felt that, because of the advances in our society, history had become little more than a relic.

Oh, what dim-sighted times those were! The two camps sat on opposite sides of the chapel as speakers took the podium one after another to wage war. The controversy quickly became a forum concerning the relevance of the past. Teacher after teacher debated the import of what we in history had taught for generations, and assertion after assertion was met with boos and applause. Tempers blazed. One powerful member of the board had come to the meeting in blue jeans and a tie-dyed shirt, and after we had been arguing for several hours and all of us were exhausted he took the podium and challenged me personally, right then and there, to debate with him the merits of Roman history.

He was not an ineloquent man, and he chose to speak his plea first, so that by the time he had finished his attack against antiquity I sensed that my battle on behalf of Charles Ellerby, and of history itself, was near to lost. My heart was gravely burdened, for if we could not win our point here among teachers, then among whom indeed could we win it? The room was silent, and on the other side of the chapel our opponents were gathering nearer to one another in the pews.

When I rose to defend my calling, however, I also sensed that victory was not beyond my reach. I am not a particularly eloquent orator, but as I took my place at the chancel rail in the amber glow of the small rose window above us, I was braced by the sudden conviction that the great men of history had sent me forward to preserve their deeds. Charles Ellerby looked up at me biting his lip, and suddenly I remembered the answer I had written long ago in *The Crier*. Its words flowed as though unbidden from my tongue, and when I had finished I knew that we had won. It was my proudest moment at St. Benedict's.

Although the resultant split among the faculty was an egregious one, Charles Ellerby secured the appointment, and together we were able to do what I had always dreamed of doing: we redoubled our commitment to classical education. In times of upheaval, of course, adherence to tradition is all the more important, and perhaps this was why St. Benedict's was brought intact through that decade and the one that followed. Our fortunes lifted and dipped with the gentle rhythm to which I had long ago grown accustomed. Our boys won sporting events and prizes, endured minor scandals and occasional tragedies, and then passed on to good colleges. Our endowment rose when the government was in the hands of Republicans, as did the caliber of our boys when it was in the hands of Democrats. Senator Bell declined from prominence, and within a few years I read that he had passed away. In time, I was made assistant headmaster. Indeed it was not until a few years ago that anything out of the ordinary happened at all, for it was then, in the late 1980s, that some ill-advised investments were made and our endowment suffered a decline.

Mr. Woodbridge had by this time reached the age of seventy-four, and although he was a vigorous man, one Sunday morning in May while the school waited for him in Chapel he died open-eyed in his bed. Immediately there occurred a Byzantine struggle for succession. There is nothing wrong with admitting that by then I myself coveted the job of Headmaster, for one does not remain four decades at a school without becoming deeply attached to its fate; but Mr. Woodbridge's death had come suddenly and I had not yet begun the preparations for my bid. I was, of course, no longer a young man. I suppose, in fact, that I lost my advantage here by underestimating my opponents who indeed were younger, as Caesar had done with Brutus and Cassius.

I should not have been surprised, then, when after several days of maneuvering, my principal rival turned out to be Charles Ellerby. For several years, I discovered, he had been conducting his own, internecine campaign for the position, and although I had always counted him as my ally and my friend, in the first meeting of the board he rose and spoke accusations against me. He said that I was too old, that I had failed to change with the times, that my method of pedagogy might have been relevant forty years ago but that it was not today. He stood and said that a headmaster needed vigor and that I did not have it. Although I watched him the entire time he spoke, he did not once look back at me.

I was wounded, of course, both professionally and in the hidden part of my heart in which I had always counted Charles Ellerby as a companion in my lifelong search for the magnificence of the past. When several of the older teachers booed him, I felt cheered. At this point I saw that I was not alone in my bid, merely behind, and so I left the meeting without coming to my own defense. Evening had come, and I walked to the dining commons in the company of allies.

How it is, when fighting for one's life, to eat among children! As the boys in their school blazers passed around the platters of fishsticks and the bowls of sliced bread, my heart was pierced with their guileless grace. How soon, I wondered, would they see the truth of the world? How long before they would understand that it was not dates and names that I had always meant to teach them? Not one of them seemed to notice what had descended like thunderheads above their faculty. Not one of them seemed unable to eat.

After dinner, I returned to the Assistant Headmaster's House in order to plot my course and confer with those I still considered allies, but before I could begin my preparations there was a knock at the door. Charles Ellerby stood there, red in the cheeks. "May I ask you some questions?" he said breathlessly.

"It is I who ought to ask them of you," was my answer.

He came in without being asked and took a seat at my table. "You've never been married, am I correct, Hundert?"

"Look, Ellerby, I've been at St. Benedict's since you were in prep school yourself."

"Yes, yes," he said, in an exaggeration of boredom. Of course, he knew as well as I that I had never married, nor started a family, because history itself had always been enough for me. He rubbed his head and appeared to be thinking. To this day, I wonder how he knew about what he said next, unless Sedgewick Bell had somehow told him the story of my visit to the senator. "Look," he said. "There's a rumor you keep a pistol in your desk drawer."

"Hogwash."

"Will you open it for me," he said, pointing there.

"No, I will not. I have been a dean here for twenty years."

"Are you telling me there is no pistol in this house?"

He then attempted to stare me down. He was a man with little character, however, and the bid withered. At that point, in fact, as his eyes fell in submission to my determined gaze, I believe the headmastership became mine. It is a largely unexplored element of history, of course, and one that has long fascinated me, that a great deal of political power and thus a great deal of the arc of nations arises not from intellectual advancements or social imperatives but from the simple battle of wills among men at tables, such as had just occurred between Charles Ellerby and me.

Instead of opening the desk and brandishing the weapon, however, which of course meant nothing to me but no doubt would have seized the initiative from Ellerby, I denied to him its existence. Why, I do not know; for I was a teacher of history, and was not the firearm its greatest engine? Ellerby, on the other hand, was simply a gadfly to the passing morals of the time. He gathered his things and left my house.

That evening I took the pistol from my drawer. A margin of rust had appeared along the filigreed handle, and despite the ornate workmanship I saw clearly now that in its essence the weapon was ill-proportioned and blunt, the crude instrument of a violent, historically meager man. I had not even wanted it when the irascible demagogue Bell had foisted it upon me, and I had only taken it out of some vague sentiment that a pistol might eventually prove decisive. I suppose I had always imagined firing it someday in a moment of drama. Yet now, here it stood before me in a moment of torpor. I turned it over and cursed it.

That night I took it from the drawer again, hid it in the pocket of my overcoat and walked to the far end of the campus, where I crossed the marsh a good mile from my house, removed my shoes and stepped into the babbling shallows of the Passamic. *The die is cast*, I said, and I threw it twenty yards out into the water. The last impediment to my headmastership had been hurdled, and by the time I came ashore, walked back whistling to my front door, and changed for bed, I was ecstatic.

Yet that night I slept poorly, and in the morning when I rose and went to our faculty meeting, I felt that the mantle of my fortitude had slipped somehow from my shoulders. How hushed is demise! In the hall outside the faculty room, most of the teachers filed by without speaking to me, and once inside I became obsessed with the idea that I had missed this most basic lesson of the past, that conviction is the alpha and the omega of authority. Now I see that I was doomed the moment I threw that pistol in the water, for that is when I lost my conviction. It was as though Sedgewick Bell had risen, all these years later, to drag me down again. Indeed, once the meeting had begun, the older faculty members shrunk back from their previous support of my bid, and the younger ones encircled me as though I were a limping animal. There might as well have been a dagger among the cloaks. By four o'clock that afternoon, Charles Ellerby, a fellow antiquarian whose job I had once helped secure, had been named headmaster, and by the end of that month he had asked me to retire.

* * *

And so I was preparing to end my days at St. Benedict's when I received Sedgewick Bell's response to my letter. It was well-written, which I noted with pleasure, and contained no trace of rancor, which is what every teacher hopes to see in the maturation of his disagreeable students. In closing he asked me to call him at EastAmerica Steel, and I did so that afternoon. When I gave my name first to one secretary and then to a second, and after that, moments later, heard Sedgewick's artfully guileless greeting, I instantly recalled speaking to his father forty years before.

After small talk, including my condolences about his father, he told me that the reason he had returned my letter was that he had often dreamed of holding a rematch of Mister Julius Caesar, and that he was now willing to donate a large sum of money to St. Benedict's if I would agree to administer the event. Naturally, I assumed he was joking and passed off the idea with a comment about how funny it was, but Sedgewick Bell repeated the invitation. He wanted very much to be on stage again with Deepak Mehta and Clay Walter. I suppose I should not have been surprised, for it is precisely this sort of childhood slight that will drive a great figure. I told him that I was about to retire. He expressed sympathy but then suggested that the arrangement could be ideal, as now I would no doubt have time to prepare. Then he said that at this station in his life he could afford whatever he wanted materially—with all that this implied, of course, concerning his donation to the Annual Fund—but that more than anything else, he desired the chance to reclaim his intellectual honor. I suppose I was flattered.

Of course, he also offered a good sum of money to me personally. Although I had until then led a life in which finances were never more than a distant concern, I was keenly aware that my time in the school's houses and dining halls was coming to an end. On the one hand, it was not my burning aspiration to secure an endowment for the reign of Charles Ellerby; on the other hand, I needed the money, and I felt a deep loyalty to the school regarding the Annual Fund. That evening, I began to prepare my test.

As assistant headmaster, I had not taught my beloved Roman history in many years, so that poring through my reams of notes was like returning at last to my childhood home. I stopped here and there among the files. I reread the term paper of young Derek Bok on "The Search of Diogenes," and the scrawled one of James Watson on "Archimedes's Method." Among the art projects, I found John Updike's reproduction of the Obelisk of Cleopatra, and a charcoal drawing of the baths of Caracalla by the abstract expressionist, Robert Motherwell, unfortunately torn in two and no longer worth anything.

I had always been a diligent notetaker, furthermore, and I believe that what I came up with was a surprisingly accurate reproduction of the subjects on which I had once quizzed Clay Walter, Deepak Mehta, and Sedgewick Bell, nearly half a century before. It took me only two evenings to gather enough material for the task, although in order not to appear eager I waited several days before sending off another letter to Sedgewick Bell. He called me soon after.

It is indeed a surprise to one who toils for his own keep to see the formidable strokes with which our captains of industry demolish the tasks before them. The morning after talking to Sedgewick Bell I received calls from two of his secretaries, a social assistant and a woman at a New York travel agency, who confirmed the arrangements for late July, two months hence. The event was to take place on an island off the Outer Banks of Carolina that belonged to EastAmerica Steel, and I sent along a list from the St. Benedict's archives so that everyone in Sedgewick Bell's class would be invited.

I was not prepared, however, for the days of retirement that intervened. What little remained of that school year passed speedily in my preoccupation, and before I knew it the boys were taking their final exams. I tried not to think about my future. At the commencement exercises in June, a small section of the ceremony was spent in my honor, but it was presided over by Charles Ellerby and gave rise to a taste of copper in my throat. "And thus we bid adieu," he began, "to our beloved Mr. Hundert." He gazed out over the lectern, extended his arm in my direction, and proceeded to give a nostalgic rendering of my years at the school to the audience of jacketed businessmen, parasoled ladies, students in St. Benedict's blazers, and children in church suits, who, like me, were squirming at the meretriciousness of the man.

Yet how quickly it was over! Awards were presented, "Hail Fair Benedict's" was sung, and as the birches began to lean their narrow shadows against the distant edge of the marsh, the seniors came forward to receive their diplomas. The mothers wept, the alumni stood misty-eyed, and the graduates threw their hats into the air. Afterward, everyone dispersed for the headmaster's reception.

I wish now that I had made an appearance there, for to have missed it, the very last one of my career, was a far more grievous blow to me than to Charles Ellerby. Furthermore, the handful of senior boys who over their tenure had been pierced by the beesting of history no doubt missed my presence or at least wondered at its lack. I spent the remnants of the afternoon in my house, and the evening walking out along the marsh, where the smell of woodsmoke from a farmer's bonfire and the distant sounds of the gathered celebrants filled me with the great, sad pride of teaching. My boys were passing once again into the world without me.

The next day, of course, parents began arriving to claim their children; jitney buses ferried students to airports and train stations; the groundsman went around pulling up lacrosse goals and baseball bleachers, hauling the long black sprinkler hoses behind his tractor into the fields. I spent most of that day and the next one sitting at the desk in my study, watching through the window as the school wound down like a clockspring toward the strange, bird-filled calm of that second afternoon of my retirement, when all the boys had left and I was alone, once again, in the eerie quiet of summer. I own few things besides my files and books; I packed them, and the next day the groundsman drove me into Wood-mere.

There I found lodging in a splendid Victorian rooming house run by a descendant of Nat Turner who joked, when I told her that I was a newly retired teacher, about how the house had always welcomed escaped slaves. I was surprised at how heartily I laughed at this, which had the benefit of putting me instantly on good terms with the landlady. We negotiated a monthly rent, and I went upstairs to set about charting a new life for myself. I was seventy-one years old—yes, perhaps, too old to be headmaster—but I could still walk three miles before dinner and did so the first afternoon of my freedom. However, by evening my spirits had taken a beating.

Fortunately, there was the event to prepare for, as I fear that without it, those first days and nights would have been unbearable. I pored again and again over my old notes, extracting devilish questions from the material. But this only occupied a few hours of the day, and by late morning my eyes would grow weary. Objectively speaking, the start of that summer should have been no different from the start of any other; yet it was. Passing my reflection in the hallway mirror at the head of the stairs on my way down to dinner I would think to myself, *is that you?* and on the way back up to my room, *what now?* I wrote letters to my brothers and sister, and to several of my former boys. The days crawled by. I introduced myself to the town librarian. I made the acquaintance of a retired railroad man who liked as much as I did to sit on the grand, screened porch of that house. I took the bus into Washington a few times to spend the day in museums.

But as the summer progressed, a certain dread began to form in my mind, which I tried through the diligence of walking, museum-going, and reading, to ignore; that is, I began to fear that Sedgewick Bell had forgotten about the event. The thought would occur to me in the midst of the long path along the outskirts of town; and as I reached the Passamic, took my break, and then started back again toward home, I would battle with my urge to contact the man. Several times I went to the telephone downstairs in the rooming house and twice I wrote out letters that I did not send. *Why would he go through all the trouble just to mock me?* I thought; but then I would recall the circumstances of his tenure at St. Benedict's and a darker gloom would descend upon me. I began to have second thoughts about events that had occurred half a century before: should I have confronted him in the midst of the original contest ? Should I never even have leap-frogged another boy to get him there? Should I have spoken up to the senator?

In early July, however, Sedgewick Bell's secretary finally did call, and I felt that I had been given a reprieve. She apologized for her tardiness, asked me more questions about my taste in food and lodging, and then informed me of the date, three weeks later, when a car would call to take me to the airport in Williamsburg. An EastAmerica jet would fly me from there to Charlotte, from whence I was to be picked up by helicopter.

Helicopter! Less than a month later I stood before the craft, which was painted head to tail in EastAmerica's green and gold insignia, polished to a shine, with a six-man passenger bay and red white and blue sponsons over the wheels. One does not remain at St. Benedict's for five decades without gaining a certain familiarity with privilege, yet as it lifted me off the pad in Charlotte, hovered for a moment, then lowered its nose and turned eastward over the gentle hills and then the chopping slate of the sea channel, I felt a headiness that I had never known before; it was what Augustus Caesar must have felt millennia ago, carried head-high on a litter past the Tiber. I clutched my notes to my chest. Indeed I wondered what my life might have been like if I had felt this just once in my youth. The rotors buzzed like a beehive. On the island I was shown to a suite of rooms in a high corner of the lodge, with windows and balconies overlooking the sea.

For a conference on the future of childhood education or the plight of America's elderly, of course, you could not get one tenth of these men to attend, but for a privileged romp on a private island it had merely been a matter of making the arrangements. I stood at the window of my room and watched the helicopter ferry back and forth across the channel, disgorging on the island a *Who's Who* of America's largest corporations, universities, and organs of policy.

Oh, but what it was to see the boys! After a time, I made my way back out to the airstrip, and whenever the craft touched down on the landing platform and one or another of my old students ducked out, clutching his suit lapel as he ran clear of the snapping rotors, I was struck anew with how great a privilege my profession had been.

That evening all of us ate together in the lodge, and the boys toasted me and took turns coming to my table, where several times one or another of them had to remind me to continue eating my food. Sedgewick Bell ambled over and with a charming air of modesty showed me the flashcards of Roman history that he'd been keeping in his desk at EastAmerica. Then, shedding his modesty, he went to the podium and produced a long and raucous toast referring to any number of pranks and misdeeds at St. Benedict's that I had never even heard of but that the chorus of boys greeted with stamps and whistles. At a quarter to nine, they all dropped their forks onto the floor, and I fear that tears came to my eyes.

The most poignant part of all, however, was how plainly the faces of the men still showed the eager expressiveness of the first-form boys of forty years ago. Martin Blythe had lost half his leg as an officer in Korea, and now, among his classmates, he tried to hide his lurching stride, but he wore the same knitted brow that he used to wear in my classroom; Deepak Mehta, who had become a professor of Asian history, walked with a slight stoop, yet he still turned his eyes downward when spoken to; Clay Walter seemed to have fared physically better than his mates, bouncing about in the Italian suit and alligator shoes of the advertising industry, yet he was still drawn immediately to the other do-nothings from his class.

But of course it was Sedgewick Bell who commanded everyone's attention. He had grown stout across the middle and bald over the crown of his head, and I saw in his ear, although it was artfully concealed, the flesh-colored bulb of a hearing aid; yet he walked among the men like a prophet. Their faces grew animated when he approached, and at the tables I could see them competing for his attention. He patted one on the back, whispered in the ear of another, gripped hands and grasped shoulders and kissed the wives on the lips. His walk was firm and imbued not with the seriousness of his post, it seemed to me, but with the ease of it, so that his stride among the tables was jocular. He was the host and clearly in his element. His laugh was voluble.

I went to sleep early that evening so that the boys could enjoy themselves downstairs in the saloon, and as I lay in bed I listened to their songs and revelry. It had not escaped my attention, of course, that they no doubt spent some time mocking me, but this is what one grows to expect in my post, and indeed it was part of the reason I left them alone. Although I was tempted to walk down and listen from outside the theater, I did not.

The next day was spent walking the island's serpentine spread of coves and beaches, playing tennis on the grass court, and paddling in wooden boats on the small, inland lake behind the lodge. How quickly one grows accustomed to luxury! Men and women lounged on the decks and beaches and patios, sunning like seals, gorging themselves on the largess of their host.

As for me, I barely had a moment to myself, for the boys took turns at my entertainment. I walked with Deepak Mehta along the beach and succeeded in getting him to tell me the tale of his rise through academia to a post at Columbia University. Evidently his rise had taken a toll, for although he looked healthy enough to me he told me that he had recently had a small heart attack. It was not the type of thing one talked about with a student, however, so I let this revelation pass without comment. Later, Clay Walter brought me onto the tennis court and tried to teach me to hit a ball, an activity that drew a crowd of boisterous guests to the stands. They roared at Clay's theatrical antics and cheered and stomped their feet whenever I sent one back across the net. In the afternoon, Martin Blythe took me out in a rowboat.

St. Benedict's, of course, has always had a more profound effect than most schools on the lives of its students, yet nonetheless it was strange that once in the center of the pond, where he had rowed us with his lurching stroke, Martin Blythe set down the oars in their locks and told me he had something he'd always meant to ask me.

"Yes," I said.

He brushed back his hair with his hand. "*I* was supposed to be the one up there with Deepak and Clay, wasn't I, Sir?"

"Don't tell me you're still thinking about that."

"It's just that I've sometimes wondered what happened."

"Yes, you should have been," I said.

Oh, how little we understand of men if we think that their childhood slights are forgotten! He smiled. He did not press the subject further, and while I myself debated the merits of explaining why I had passed him over for Sedgewick Bell four decades before, he pivoted the boat around and brought us back to shore. The confirmation of his suspicions was enough to satisfy him, it seemed, so I said nothing more. He had been an Air Force major in our country's endeavors on the Korean peninsula, yet as he pulled the boat onto the beach I had the clear feeling of having saved him from some torment.

Indeed, that evening when the guests had gathered in the lodge's small theater, and Deepak Mehta, Clay Walter, and Sedgewick Bell had taken their seats for the reenactment of Mister Julius Caesar, I noticed an ease in Martin Blythe's face that I believe I had never seen in it before. His brow was not knit, and he had crossed his legs so that above one sock we could clearly see the painted wooden calf.

It was then that I noticed that the boys who had paid the most attention to me that day were in fact the ones sitting before me on the stage. How dreadful a thought this was—that they had indulged me to gain advantage—but I put it from my mind and stepped to the microphone. I had spent the late afternoon reviewing my notes, and the first rounds of questions were called from memory.

The crowd did not fail to notice the feat. There were whistles and stomps when I named fifteen of the first sixteen emperors in order and asked Clay Walter to produce the one I had left out. There was applause when I spoke Caesar's words, "*Il Iacta alea esto,*" and then, continuing in carefully pronounced Latin, asked Sedgewick Bell to recall the circumstances of their utterance. He had told me that afternoon of the months he had spent preparing, and as I was asking the question, he smiled. The boys had not worn togas, of course—although I personally feel they might have—yet the situation was familiar enough that I felt a rush of unease as Sedgewick Bell's smile then waned and he hesitated several moments before answering. But this time, all these years later, he looked straight out into the audience and spoke his answers with the air of a scholar.

It was not long before Clay Walter had dropped out, of course, but then, as it had before, the contest proceeded neck and neck between Sedgewick Bell and Deepak Mehta. I asked Sedgewick Bell about Caesar's battles at Pharsalus and Thapsus, about the shift of power to Constantinople and about the war between the patricians and the plebeians; I asked Deepak Mehta about the Punic Wars, the conquest of Italy and the fall of the republic. Deepak, of course, had an advantage, for certainly he had studied this material at university, but I must say that the straightforward determination of Sedgewick Bell had begun to win my heart. I recalled the bashful manner in which he had shown me his flashcards at dinner the night before, and as I stood now before the microphone I seemed to be in the throes of an affection for him that had long been under wraps.

"What year were the Romans routed at Lake Trasimene?" I asked him.

He paused. "217 B.C., I believe."

"Which general later became Scipio Africanus Major?"

"Publius Cornelius Scipio, Sir," Deepak Mehta answered softly.

It does not happen as often as one might think that an unintelligent boy becomes an intelligent man, for in my own experience the love of thought is rooted in an age long before adolescence; yet Sedgewick Bell now seemed to have done just that. His answers were spoken with the composed demeanor of a scholar. There is no one I like more, of course, than the man who is moved by the mere fact of history, and as I contemplated the next question to him I wondered if I had indeed exaggerated the indolence of his boyhood. Was it true, perhaps, that he had simply not come into his element yet, while at St. Benedict's? He peered intently at me from the stage, his elbows on his knees. I decided to ask him a difficult question. "Chairman Bell," I said, "which tribes invaded Rome in 102 B.C.?"

His eyes went blank and he curled his shoulders in his suit. Although he was by then one of the most powerful men in America, and although moments before that I had been rejoicing in his discipline, suddenly I saw him on that stage once again as a frightened boy. How powerful is memory! And once again, I feared that it was I who had betrayed him. He brought his hand to his head to think.

"Take your time, Sir," I offered.

There were murmurs in the audience. He distractedly touched the side of his head. A man's character is his fate, says Heraclitus, and at that moment, as he brushed his hand down over his temple, I realized that the flesh-colored device in his ear was not a hearing aid but a transmitter through which he was receiving the answers to my questions. Nausea rose in me. Of course I had no proof, but was it not exactly what I should have expected? He touched his head once again and appeared to be deep in thought, and I knew it as certainly as if he had shown me. "The Teutons," he said, haltingly, "and—I'll take a stab here—the Cimbri?"

I looked for a long time at him. Did he know at that point what I was thinking? I cannot say, but after I had paused as long as I could bear to in front of that crowd, I cleared my throat and granted that he was right. Applause erupted. He shook it off with a wave of his hand. I knew that it was my duty to speak up. I knew it was my duty as a teacher to bring him clear of the moral dereliction in which I myself had been his partner, yet at the same time I felt myself adrift in the tide of my own vacillation and failure. The boy had somehow got hold of me again. He tried to quiet the applause with a wave of his hand, but this gesture only caused the clapping to increase, and I am afraid to say that it was merely the sound of a throng of boisterous men that finally prevented me from making my stand. Quite suddenly I was aware that this was not the situation I had known at St. Benedict's School. We were guests now of a significant man on his splendid estate, and to expose him would be a serious act indeed. I turned and quieted the crowd.

From the chair next to Sedgewick Bell, Deepak Mehta merely looked at me, his eyes dark and resigned. Perhaps he too had just realized, or perhaps in fact he had long known, but in any case I simply asked him the next question; after he answered it, I could do nothing but put another before Sedgewick Bell. Then Deepak again, then Sedgewick, and again to Deepak, and it was only then, on the third round after I had discovered the ploy, that an idea came to me. When I returned to Sedgewick Bell I asked him, "Who was Shutruk-Nahhunte?"

A few boys in the crowd began to laugh, and when Sedgewick Bell took his time thinking about the answer, more in the audience joined in. Whoever was the mercenary professor talking in his ear, it was clear to me that he would not know the answer to this one, for if he had not gone to St. Benedict's School he would never have heard of Shutruk-Nahhunte; and in a few moments, sure enough, I saw Sedgewick Bell begin to grow uncomfortable. He lifted his pant leg and scratched at his sock. The laughter increased, and then I heard the wives, who had obviously never lived in a predatory pack, trying to stifle their husbands. "Come on, Bell!" someone shouted, "Look at the damn door!" Laughter erupted again.

How can it be that for a moment my heart bled for him? He, too, tried to laugh, but only half-heartedly. He shifted in his seat, shook his arms loose in his suit, looked uncomprehendingly out at the snickering crowd, then braced his chin and said, "Well, I guess if Deepak knows the answer to this one, then it's *his* ball-game."

Deepak's response was nearly lost in the boisterous stamps and whistles that followed, for I am sure that every boy but Sedgewick recalled Henry Stimson's tablet above the door of my classroom. Yet what was strange was that I felt disappointment. As Deepak Mehta smiled, spoke the answer, and stood from his chair, I watched confusion and then a flicker of panic cross the face of Sedgewick Bell. He stood haltingly. How clear it was to me then that the corruption in his character had always arisen from fear, and I could not help remembering that as his teacher I had once tried to convince him of his stupidity. I cursed that day. But then in a moment he summoned a smile, called me up to the stage, and crossed theatrically to congratulate the victor.

How can I describe the scene that took place next? I suppose I was naïve to think that this was the end of the evening—or even the point of it—for after Sedgewick Bell had brought forth a trophy for Deepak Mehta, and then one for me as well, an entirely different cast came across his features. He strode once again to the podium and asked for the attention of the guests. He tapped sharply on the microphone. Then he leaned his head forward, and in a voice that I recognized from long ago on the radio, a voice in whose deft leaps from boom to whisper I heard the willow-tree drawl of his father, he launched into an address about the problems of our country. He had the orator's gift of dropping his volume at the moment when a less gifted man would have raised it. *We have opened our doors to all the world,* he said, his voice thundering, then pausing, then plunging nearly to a murmur, *and now the world has stripped us bare.* He gestured with his hands. The men in the audience, first laughing, now turned serious. *We have given away too much for too long,* he said. *We have handed our fiscal leader-*

ship to men who don't care about the taxpayers of our country, and our moral course to those who no longer understand our role in history. Although he gestured to me there, I could not return his gaze. *We have abandoned the moral education of our families.* Scattered applause drifted up from his classmates, and here, of course, I almost spoke. *We have left our country adrift on dangerous seas.* Now the applause was more hearty. Then he quieted his voice again, dropped his head as though in supplication and announced that he was running for the United States Senate.

Why was I surprised? I should not have been, for since childhood the boy had stood so near to the mantle of power that its shadow must have been as familiar to him as his boyhood home. Virtue had no place in the palaces he had known. I was ashamed when I realized he had contrived the entire rematch of Mister Julius Caesar for no reason other than to gather his classmates for donations, yet still I chastened myself for not realizing his ambition before. In his oratory, in his physical presence, in his conviction, he had always possessed the gifts of a leader, and now he was using them. I should have expected this from the first day he stood in his short-pants suit in the doorway of my classroom and silenced my students. He already wielded a potent role in the affairs of our country; he enjoyed the presumption of his family name; he was blindly ignorant of history and therefore did not fear his role in it. Of course it was exactly the culmination I should long ago have seen. The crowd stood cheering.

As soon as the clapping abated a curtain was lifted behind him, and a band struck up "Dixie." Waiters appeared at the side doors, a dance platform was unfolded in the orchestra pit, and Sedgewick Bell jumped down from the stage into the crowd of his friends. They clamored around him. He patted shoulders, kissed wives, whispered and laughed and nodded his head. I saw checkbooks come out. The waiters carried champagne on trays at their shoulders, and at the edge of the dance floor the women set down their purses and stepped into the arms of their husbands. When I saw this I ducked out a side door and returned to the lodge, for the abandon with which the guests were dancing was an unbearable counterpart to the truth I knew. One can imagine my feelings. I heard the din late into the night.

Needless to say, I resolved to avoid Sedgewick Bell for the remainder of my stay. How my mind raced that night through humanity's endless history of injustice, depravity, and betrayal! I could not sleep, and several times I rose and went to the window to listen to the revelry. Standing at the glass I felt like the spurned sovereign in the castle tower, looking down from his balcony onto the procession of the false potentate.

Yet, sure enough, my conviction soon began to wane. No sooner had I resolved to avoid my host than I began to doubt the veracity of my secret knowledge about him. Other thoughts came to me. How, in fact, had I been so sure of what he'd done? What proof had I at all? Amid the distant celebrations of the night, my conclusion began to seem farfetched, and by the quiet of the morning I was muddled. I did not go to breakfast. As boy after boy stopped by my rooms to wish me well, I assiduously avoided commenting on either Sedgewick Bell's performance or on his announcement for the Senate. On the beach that day I endeavored to walk by myself, for by then I trusted neither my judgment of the incident nor my discretion with the boys. I spent the afternoon alone in a cove across the island.

I did not speak to Sedgewick Bell that entire day. I managed to avoid him, in fact, until the next evening, by which time all but a few of the guests had left, when he came to bid farewell as I stood on the tarmac awaiting the helicopter for the mainland. He walked out and motioned for me to stand back from the platform, but I pretended not to hear him and kept my eyes up to the sky. Suddenly, the shining craft swooped in from beyond the wave break, churning the channel into a boil, pulled up in a hover and then touched down on its flag-colored sponsons before us. The wind and noise could have thrown a man to the ground, and Sedgewick Bell seemed to pull at me like a magnet, but I did not retreat. It was he, finally, who ran out to me. He gripped his lapels, ducked his head and offered me his hand. I took it tentatively, the rotors whipping our jacket sleeves. I had been expecting this moment and had decided the night before what I was going to say. I leaned toward him. "How long have you been hard of hearing?" I asked.

His smile dropped. I cannot imagine what I had become in the mind of that boy. "Very good, Hundert," he said. "Very good. I thought you might have known."

My vindication was sweet, although now I see that it meant little. By then I was on the ladder of the helicopter, but he pulled me toward him again and looked darkly into my eyes. "And I see that *you* have not changed either," he said.

Well, had I? As the craft lifted off and turned westward toward the bank of clouds that hid the distant shoreline, I analyzed the situation with some care. The wooden turrets of the lodge grew smaller and then were lost in the trees, and I found it easier to think then, for everything on that island had been imbued with the sheer power of the man. I relaxed a bit in my seat. One could say that in this case I indeed had acted properly, for is it not the glory of our legal system that acquitting a guilty man is less heinous than convicting an innocent one? At the time of the contest, I certainly had no proof of Sedgewick Bell's behavior.

Yet back in Woodmere, as I have intimated, I found myself with a great deal of time on my hands, and it was not long before the incident began to replay itself in my mind. Following the wooded trail toward the river or sitting in the breeze at dusk on the porch, I began to see that a different ending would have better served us all. Conviction had failed me again. I was well aware of the foolish consolation of my thoughts, yet I vividly imagined what I should have done. I heard myself speaking up; I saw my resolute steps to his chair on the stage, then the insidious, flesh-colored device in my palm, held up to the crowd; I heard him stammering.

As if to mock my inaction, however, stories of his electoral effort soon began to appear in the papers. It was a year of spite and rancor in our country's politics, and the race in West Virginia was less a campaign than a brawl between gladiators. The incumbent was as versed in treachery as Sedgewick Bell, and over my morning tea I followed their battles. Sedgewick Bell called him "a liar when he speaks and a crook when he acts," and he called Sedgewick Bell worse. A fist fight erupted when their campaigns crossed at an airport.

I was revolted by the spectacle, but of course I was also intrigued, and I cannot deny that although I was rooting for the incumbent, a part of me was also cheered at each bit of news chronicling Sedgewick Bell's assault on his lead. Oh, why was this so? Are we all, at base, creatures without virtue? Is fervor the only thing we follow?

Needless to say, that fall had been a difficult one in my life, especially those afternoons when the St. Benedict's bus roared by the guest house in Woodmere taking the boys to track meets, and perhaps the Senate race was nothing more than a healthy distraction for me. Indeed I needed distractions. To witness the turning of the leaves and to smell the apples in their barrels without hearing the sound of a hundred boys in the fields, after all, was almost more than I could bear. My walks had grown longer, and several times I had crossed the river and ventured to the far end of the marsh, from where in the distance I could make out the blurred figures of St. Benedict's. I knew this was not good for me, and perhaps that is why, in late October of that year when I read that Sedgewick Bell would be making a campaign stop at a coal-miners' union hall near the Virginia border, I decided to go hear him speak.

Perhaps by then the boy had become an obsession for me—I will admit this, for I am as aware as anyone that time is but the thinnest bandage for our wounds—but on the other hand, the race had grown quite close and would have been of natural interest to anyone. Sedgewick Bell had drawn himself up from an underdog to a challenger. Now it was clear that the election hinged on the votes of labor, and Sedgewick Bell, though he was the son of aristocrats and the chairman of a formidable corporation, began to cast himself as a champion of the working man. From newspaper reports I gleaned that he was helped along by the power of his voice and bearing, and I could easily imagine these men turning to him. I well knew the charisma of the boy.

The day arrived, and I packed a lunch and made the trip. As the bus wound west along the river valley, I envisioned the scene ahead and wondered whether Sedgewick Bell would at this point care to see me. Certainly I represented some sort of truth to him about himself, yet at the same time I also seemed to have become a part of the very delusion that he had foisted on those around him. How far my boys would always stride upon the world's stage, yet how dearly I would always hope to change them! The bus arrived early, and I went inside the union hall to wait.

Shortly before noon the miners began to come in. I don't know what I had expected, but I was surprised to see them looking as though they had indeed just come out of the mines. They wore hard hats, their faces were stained with dust, and their gloves and tool belts hung at their waists. For some reason I had worn my St. Benedict's blazer, which I now removed. Reporters began to filter in as well, and by the time the noon whistle blew, the crowd was overflowing from the hall.

As the whistle subsided I heard the thump-thump of his helicopter, and through the door in a moment I saw the twisters of dust as it hovered into view from above. How clever was the man I had known as a boy! The craft had been repainted the colors of military camouflage but he had left the sponsons the red-white-and-blue of their previous incarnation. He jumped from the side door when the craft was still a foot above the ground, entered the hall at a jog, and was greeted with an explosion of applause. His aides lined the stairs to the high platform on which the microphone stood under a banner and a flag, and as he crossed the crowd toward them the miners jostled to be near him, knocking their knuckles against his hard hat, reaching for his hands and his shoulders, cheering like Romans at a chariot race.

I do not need to report on his eloquence, for I have dwelled enough upon it. When he reached the staircase and ascended to the podium, stopping first at the landing to wave and then at the top to salute the flag above him, jubilation swept among the throng. I knew then that he had succeeded in his efforts, that these miners counted him somehow as their own, so that when he actually spoke and they interrupted him with cheers it was no more unexpected than the promises he made then to carry their interests with him to the Senate. He was masterful. I found my own arm upraised.

Certainly there were five hundred men in that hall, but there was only one with a St. Benedict's blazer over his shoulder and no hard hat on his head, so of course I should not have been surprised when within a few minutes one of his aides appeared beside me and told me that the candidate had asked for me at the podium. At that moment I saw Sedgewick Bell's glance pause for a moment on my face. There was a flicker of a smile on his lips, but then he looked away.

Is there no battle other than the personal one? Was Sedgewick Bell at that point willing to risk the future of his political ideas for whatever childhood demon I still remained to him? The next time he turned toward me, he gestured down at the floor, and in a moment the aide had pulled my arm and was escorting me toward the platform. The crowd opened as we passed, and the miners in their ignorance and jubilation were reaching to shake my hand. This was indeed a heady feeling. I climbed the steps and stood beside Sedgewick Bell at the smaller microphone. How it was to stand above the mass of men like that! He raised his hand and they cheered; he lowered it and they fell silent.

"There is a man here today who has been immeasurably important in my life," he whispered into his microphone.

There was applause, and a few of the men whistled. "Thank you," I said into my own. I could see the blue underbrims of five hundred hard hats turned up toward me. My heart was nearly bursting.

"My history teacher," he said, as the crowd began to cheer again. Flashbulbs popped and I moved instinctively toward the front of the platform. "Mr. Hundert," he boomed, "from forty-five years ago at Richmond Central High School."

It took me a moment to realize what he had said. By then he too was clapping and at the same time lowering his head in what must have appeared to the men below to be respect for me. The blood engorged my veins. "Just a minute," I said, stepping back to my own microphone. "I taught you at St. Benedict's School in Tally-wood, Virginia. Here is the blazer."

Of course, it makes no difference in the course of history that as I tried to hold up the coat, Sedgewick Bell moved swiftly across the podium, took it from my grip and raised my arm high in his own and that this pose, of all things, sent the miners into jubilation; it makes no difference that by the time I spoke, he had gestured with this hand so that one of his aides had already shut off my microphone. For one does not alter history without conviction. It is enough to know that I *did* speak, and certainly a consolation that Sedgewick Bell realized, finally, that I would.

He won that election not in small part because he managed to convince those miners that he was one of them. They were ignorant people, and I cannot blame them for taking to the shrewdly populist rhetoric of the man. I saved the picture that appeared the following morning in the *Gazette*: Senator Bell radiating all the populist magnetism of his father, holding high the arm of an old man who has on his face the remnants of a proud and foolish smile.

I still live in Woodmere, and I have found a route that I take now and then to the single high hill from which I can see the St. Benedict's steeple across the Passamic. I take two walks every day and have grown used to this life. I have even come to like it. I am reading of the ancient Japanese civilizations now, which I had somehow neglected before, and every so often one of my boys visits me.

One afternoon recently, Deepak Mehta did so, and we shared some brandy. This was in the fall of last year. He was still the quiet boy he had always been, and not long after he had taken a seat on my couch I had to turn on the television to ease for him the burden of conversation. As it happened, the Senate Judiciary Committee was holding its famous hearings then, and the two of us sat there watching, nodding our heads or chuckling whenever the camera showed Sedgewick Bell sitting alongside the chairman. I had poured the brandy liberally, and whenever Sedgewick Bell leaned into the microphone and asked a question of the witness, Deepak would mimic his affected southern drawl. Naturally, I could not exactly encourage this behavior, but I did nothing to stop it. When he finished his drink I poured him another. This, of course, is perhaps the greatest pleasure of a teacher's life, to have a drink one day with a man he has known as a boy.

Nonetheless, I only wish we could have talked more than we actually did. But I am afraid that there must always be a reticence between a teacher and his student. Deepak had had another small heart attack, he told me, but I felt it would have been improper of me to inquire more. I tried to bring myself to broach the subject of Sedgewick Bell's history, but here again I was aware that a teacher does not discuss one boy with another. Certainly Deepak must have known about Sedgewick Bell as well, but probably out of his own set of St. Benedict's morals he did not bring it up with me. We watched Sedgewick Bell question the witness and then whisper into the ear of the chairman. Neither of us was surprised at his ascendance, I believe, because both of us were students of history. Yet we did not discuss this either. Still, I wanted desperately for him to ask me something more, and perhaps this was why I kept refilling his glass. I wanted him to ask, "How is it to be alone, Sir, at this age," or perhaps to say, "You have made a difference in my life, Mr. Hundert." But of course these were not things Deepak Mehta would ever say. A man's character is his character. Nonetheless it was startling, every now and then when I looked over at the sunlight falling across his bowed head, to see that Deepak Mehta, the quietest of my boys, was now an old man.

———————

Ethan Canin is the author of three books, *Emperor of the Air, Blue River,* and *The Palace Thief.* He is currently doing a medical residency in California.

*T*he idea for "The Palace Thief" occurred to me when, twenty years after he'd taught us, I ran into my old history teacher on the street. He'd been my grade-school teacher, not high-school, and I never went to a school like the one in the story, but he was an impassioned lover of history and culture and old-world etiquette who might have been at home at St. Benedict's. He was a brilliant teacher, perhaps the best I ever had. He made us memorize the great paintings of the Renaissance, sit straight in our chairs, and sneeze into handkerchiefs. He was from another time. He never owned a car and never, I believe, had a telephone in his apartment. This story was a tribute to him.

Leon Rooke

THE HEART MUST FROM ITS BREAKING

(from *North Carolina Literary Review*)

The Postman

This is how it happened that morning at the church. The doors burst open and there in the sunlight was someone or something. The Prince of Darkness, I thought. Hold on to your hat. Two children got up and marched out to him—to him or it—and that was the last ever seen of them.

The Dead Woman's Sister

That was the day Sister died. The very minute. Agnes and Cluey go out to this thing some say is their daddy come back from the dead, they disappear, and that very same second Sister dies. And blood on her window you can't get up with wire brush or blowtorch. Those helpless children. No one wanted them. Their mother on her deathbed. Their daddy not seen in nine years and split-hoof mean to begin with. When Sister wakes me calling in the night I sit up in bed and answer back and we go on talking until her spirit quietens. "Are they dead, Sister?" I ask.

"Noooo, nooooo," she says. "Nooooo . . ." she says. Like the wind.

The Preacher

Sure they're dead. I don't know how or how come, or why, not having the divine intervention on the matter, but you can't tell me two snot-rag children are going to get out of this town without anyone seeing them. There's just the two ways of entering or leaving and that's by the one street going one way and the other going the other. So someone saw them.

Dust to dust and the Lord's will abideth! Hallelujah!

Knowing what I know about what goes on in this town, it can't abide soon enough. What I think? They are buried this minute in someone's backyard. Get in a back hoe, we'd find the bodies. I've preached till I'm blue in the face, but who listens? What's salvation to them only wants to lick ice cream of a Sunday? You can't stamp out the devil's work for he's like a mad dog once he gets going—or she—the scriptures don't discount she's a she, you know. Which is maybe why the devil's work is so cunning. It got baleful dark that morning, I know that. Like a twister's struck. Ask Minnie, my organist, she'll say the same.

Minnie, the Organist

I will not. I was at the organ; I didn't want to be, having a killer-cold. Don't need an organist anyhow. No one ever bothers to keep up. I've heard cows mooing in a meadow had more rhythm than that bunch. I saw nothing. Heard nothing. Well, this whine in my ears, these shivers—but that was my cold. Once, through the window, I see a white galloping horse. But it takes a lot in that church to make me turn around. I keep my back to that bunch and that's how I like it.

One time a man's pants caught fire, when Orson Johnson, the cross-eyed one, was playing with matches. I looked around then. That's the only time.

Orson

I'm the one she's talking about.

I strike a match and boom!—I'm a sheet of flames. The wife screeching and suddenly I'm bare-buttock naked in front of the whole congregation, because she's pulled down everything.

I saw the children go out. Saw this black creature at the door. I thought it was Death. Death calling, and he was going to lay his hand over us all. End of the world, is what I thought. I tried to move but couldn't. My hair standing up on my head. "Don't go, children! Run!" The wife tells me that's what I was trying to say— but too scared to get it out. She's got her hand pinching my thigh, shooshing me.

Delilah Orson

"Shoosh, Orson, shoosh!" That's what I'm saying. He's gone pale. He's got sweat beads on his brow an inch deep. So I put my hand up over his man parts and I squeeze. "Stop it! Stay put!" I say. When I see this white horse galloping past the window, and this woman on it with streaming robe.

The children's mother, with this frantic face. She's crying, "Children, children! Run!" All in a blap of light. That's when I dig my nails into Orson's thing. Later on, we get the doctor in, he's got to have a tetanus shot. Infection lasts a month . . . And the children gone. Just gone. Their mother expiring the identical hour.

The Nurse's Tale

Yessss. That poor woman's heart was like water sloshing around in a bowl. Been that way for years on her sick bed, and me nursing her through the worst of it. I was there in her sick room, my head down on her chest listening to the slosh, when all at once she bolts up—her who hasn't moved a stitch in nearly a year! Bolts up out of stark fear! With her gown straps slid to her elbows so her little bosom is exposed to the full eyes of the world.

Yessss. Stark fear. "My children need me!" she cries. "I'm coming, children!"

Next thing I know she's out of the bed and running. Her whose legs the doctor claims are paralyzed.

"You'll not get my children!" she's saying. "You'll not get them! Fiend! Devil-fiend!"

Yessss.

And I'm nurse to her, so I streak after her. Three blocks to the church. Where I witness the most hellacious sight.

She's grappling with this ogre figure. The sky's gone pitch-black. "You'll not have my children! No! You will not have them!"

Just a hellacious fight.

Yessss. My eyes spinning in my head.

This ghost-devil caterwauling his hatred of every living thing. Her biting and clawing the ogre's face.

I've seen pictures. This ogre-monster, it's her husband for sure.

Yessss. The children's daddy, come to make his claim.

When this white horse comes galloping by.

"Run, children. The horse! Run!" Her screaming that.

Then this whirlwind scattering everything.

Me at that point blacking out. Next I know I'm flat on the grass, my dress up to my thighs, and some sex fiend is breathing on my face.

The Sex Fiend

Me. I'm the sex fiend. Fanning her with my hat. I kept saying to her, "Nellie, you're covered. Nothing's showing, Nellie. Calm yourself, Nellie." But she's up and hustling away.

The Nurse

Yessss. Isn't my sworn duty to my patient? Faint on your own time, that's what I tell myself. So I hustle back to the patient's house. And when I walk in, there she is too. Sliding up over the sill, her little breasties bare-naked again. That gown slit and slithers. She's bloody, head to toe. Cut up and bruised. Leaving a trail of blood each inch she comes.

"Help me, Nellie," she says.

Well, that's why I'm there for. I get her back in bed. Get those breasties covered neat and trim.

"They're safe," she says. "My children. It was quite the battle."

I'm making comforting sounds. Washing her face.

"I can expire in peace now," she says. "You got the pennies ready?" And off she goes, poor thing. I root out two pennies from my purse. I wash them off. Dry them on my dress. Place them pennies over her eyes, heads up, just the way they're supposed to do. But the blood, my, my, yessss—that window streaked with blood.

The House Painter

I done the job. I give the old gal a good price and me and my apprentice went at it. White. That's the color. And she wanted two coats, one put on vertical and one crosswise. I said, "Why? Vertical?"

And she says that's how her daddy told her you do it, you want that paint job to stand up to the test of time.

Me, I say, "I never heard that. Have you, Tom Earl? Vertical? Cost you extra." She says, "Extra! Then you go out and stick somebody else."

So I get the message. We smack on the paint, two coats, vertical and crosswise. Then we come to that window. You slap on the paint, that blood soak it right up. "Hit it again, Tom Earl," I say. And again it soaks it right up. That blood still there. Well you know she ain't going to pay. I go out to my truck, haul in hammer and chisels, my blowtorch: one way or another I mean to git that blood hid.

Well, she comes running. "What are you doing, what are you doing?—burning down my house? You call this a paint job?"

"Now look," I say. So I smack on the paint; that blood pops up. "See?" I say. "Your sister's blood. It keeps popping up."

She says, "Leave my sister out of this. I've known you Sparrows all my life and never one of you didn't try to weasel out of work or lie with every breath. Give me that brush." And she goes at it. Nothing doing. "Damn. Drat. Give me that blowtorch!" she says. And before you know it she's all but burnt down the house.

Finally, I say, "Ma'am? That there is demon blood, which is why it won't come out. It's Satan's own blood, which is why."

And she says, "Fine. Fine by me. Let it stay there. But I'm holding back 10 percent your pay till I count this a finished job." Uh-huh. Owes me that 10 percent to this day.

That night me and my apprentice go out drinking. Spooky business done give me a mean thirst.

The Painter's Apprentice

He drank. I didn't because I won't but thirteen and the law wouldn't have it.

The Law

Here's the one reliable eyewitness report we got. Woman at her clothesline. Quote: The creature was dragging the children along, them kicking and screaming, while the bath-gowny woman was up on the thing's back, her legs wrapping its legs, biting into the thing's neck, pulling hair, punching and clawing, and all the while shouting. "Run! Run! Oh children, run!" Finally they break free. They scamper onto this magnificent white horse, and that horse flees with them like the wind. The ghoulish figure lets out a mighty howl; you'd think it meant breaking every bone in her body: "Fiend! Demon!" she's saying.

"You won't have my children. No! No! No!"

A Farmer's Husband

The horse comes by my place, going lickety-split. Plain flying. The horse phantomish, but the riders real enough. Children, they were. I said to my wife, Mary, "Mary, what you make of that?" My dog was down between my legs; it got up whimpering, and hid under the porch. Took two days to lure that dog out.

Mary, the Farmer

"See that yonder?" he said. And pointed off. I went on shelling my peas.

"Don't you have one iota of sense," I told him. "That there is the supernatural."

The Doctor

You are all looking at me. Keep looking, then. I've told you my end before. This woman had been slipping a long time. All of us expecting her to die, but her holding on. "Tory," I said, "I know you are in terrible pain. Let me give you something to ease the ride."

"That's nice, doctor," she said. "I'd like to go off in a nice swoony dream. But I can't die yet, for my children's sake. Their father will be coming back, whatever form it takes. Vowed he would. I've got to stay on and try saving them from him, if I can. No one else will care enough. I'm the only one can."

I don't read anything special into these remarks. It tells us something of her spirit, I suppose, and confirms her love for that pair. Anything else, I'd discount. All this ghostly stuff. She died a natural death, that's what my certificate says. But, yet, she was black and blue. Some bones broken. Someone's skin under her fingernails. Blood you couldn't remove from window and floor, and not her own blood either, as the lab tests showed. And not a blood we could type. But there are reasonable, logical explanations. There always are. Let this woman and her children rest in peace, I say. Let these stories stop right here.

———————

Leon Rooke is a native of North Carolina, now living in Eden Mills, Ontario. He has been writer-in-residence at numerous Canadian and U.S. universities. His novels include *A Good Baby, Shakespeare's Dog, Fat Woman,* and the forthcoming *Kiss.* He has published thirteen short story collections and his work appears in a number of major anthologies.

I f one is born in the rural South, one is born aswim in stories such as that one told in "The Heart Must from Its Breaking." And versions of these stories come at you from all over the place.

I wrote this one more than a decade ago, and for the whole of that decade the manuscript slumbered in a drawer. Kersplat! Nothing doing. Forget this one. But eventually I took another look at the thing. The writing didn't look so bad. Although, at that time, the story went on (boringly, too: I'm telling you) several thousand words beyond its current length. An editor looked at the piece. Then looked at me. "You poor, dumb, bungling fool," he said. "Right here, on page such and such, you've got this character saying, 'Let the story stop right here.' Isn't it obvious?" Well, it was obvious, then! So I instantly chopped off the profusion of extra pages and allowed the story to end where this character in the story said the story was supposed to end.

Reynolds Price

DEEDS OF LIGHT

(from *TriQuarterly*)

I n the summer of 1942, no town in that whole end of the state was far from one of the big new camps, training soldiers for Europe and Asia. Tens of thousands of strong men, most of them boys, answered roll call Saturday and were then cut loose till Monday dawn. Long on strength and curiosity, short on cash, they hitched in pairs to the nearest towns. And since that time and place were guileless, there were no saloons, few theaters, and a grave shortage of dim dance halls with willing girls. So the soldiers tended to take slow walks down leafy streets or lie in the sun on downtown benches and laugh with ladies that stopped to talk or vets from the First War with boring tales of body lice and mustard gas. At dark the boys might band into fours and rent a room in a widow's house and smuggle in some cards and beer, not to speak of occasional risky girls and the first stunned round of young war-widows.

But in the town we're watching now—that whole long summer of wondrous nights—boys would sleep by droves in the warm grass of Whitlow Park under ancient elms and clean black skies with amazing stars. Their chosen spot was a gentle hill above the lake, topped by a road. And full-moon nights, townspeople would sometimes drive past slowly to see that broad encampment sleeping or talking in clumps, all silvered and still. It was years before civilians used flashbulbs, or I'd have pictures to back my claim—a broad hill planted in shining ghosts, waiting to rise at the angel trump to tell their secret sins and hopes.

Sunday mornings my mother and I would drive to the park with friends from our church and furnish steamy urns of coffee, homemade biscuits, country butter, and bacon—eggs were scarce. We'd go so early, the boys would wake up raw and stunned and wouldn't say much but "Yes" and "Fine." We were normal Methodists, not Holy Rollers; so we barely mentioned that our main service would be at eleven and they were invited. That hour was common for the entire Protestant country then; and numbers of the soldiers would turn up anyhow, wrinkled and grass-stained but shaved and, by then, wider awake than hunted creatures bayed in the woods.

Two weeks running I'd watched one boy above the rest. I'd somehow forgot the fact till lately when I ran across two pictures of him beside some older pictures of my father (Father had died when I was five, and pictures are mainly how I recall him); but comparing them now, I see how much the two men shared—clipped sandy hair, eyes so light gray that the pupils fade almost to dots when you step back, and powerful jaws with wide mouths about to grin. They were like a matched pair of young lords packed with life and hope, unquestioned by any god or man; and they still are that, so long as I have working eyes and a mind to watch their fading traces.

Though I dream about my father still, I have to grant that the face on the boy Deke Patrick makes a stronger call on my grown mind, even now with what I finally watched Deke need and take. But after our first Sunday meeting in the park, I knew only one peculiar thing—Deke guessed my name on sight with no clue. He met my eyes dead-level, smiling, and said "Oh Marcus, wake a sad boy up."

I was too young to wonder why he was sad. I took his knowledge of me as a miracle—Marcus is not that common a name—

and I blushed ferociously but managed the coffee and watched him butter two biscuits and leave.

He went twenty yards and sat on a swing that he kept still while he ate his first round. I thought he'd surely come back for more; they mostly did. Deke finished the last morsel, though, wiped his mouth with the back of his hand, and suddenly started to pump the swing till it flung him out parallel to the ground. From the highest peak he let it die, then rose and walked through a howling bunch of his fellow soldiers to the rim of the lake and stood a long time. Nothing strange happened—the ducks and lilies went about their business—but some stubborn mystery in the picture he cut, upright in weeds at the absolute verge of swimming or drowning, made me need to know him more than anything I remembered needing.

The other soldiers seemed to agree in a loud way. For several minutes they yelled and whistled to call him back—it was in their calls I learned his name—but Deke stood his ground. And when they started a football cheer on "Deekey, *Deke*," he turned his back, rounded the lake and vanished in woods on the far side.

By then my brief acquaintance with his face may well have settled far enough down to find the buried face of my father. Whyever, I left the coffee urn and asked our pastor to estimate Deke's age and height (I'd seen him talk to Deke after me).

He said "Six foot, maybe twenty years old—a righteous face. Bet you a dime we'll see that boy in church this morning." He laughed but meant it.

I was already edgy around the word *righteous*; so I said "No, sir, I won't bet against him."

I'd have won the dime. In church I sat near the door and watched. Ten identical soldiers walked in, thirty seconds before the sermon, but no sign of Deke. They sat on the front row, neat as if they'd slept at home—the park had a bathhouse with plentiful showers. Mother and I were twenty feet off, and I spent a while not hearing the pastor but searching the necks for a usable substitute to Deke. Nothing—no instant burn of the kind I'd felt when he said my personal name and walked away like Adam naming the beasts in Eden but finding no mate.

As everybody rose for the last hymn, Mother asked if I'd like to invite a soldier home for dinner, as the midday meal was called back then. Around town lately the idea of bringing soldiers home for Sunday dinner was a growing fad, though we had yet to do our part on our slim budget and everything rationed.

So one more time I scanned the necks. To me, in the merciless-ness of my age, they might have been dead meat. I faced Mother, shook my head, and tore on into "Princely Blood, Our Sovereign Cure," all four verses and a low "Amen."

I was left for at least a week—maybe forever—to wonder how he knew my name when all the locals called me "Snake" because I could swim that fast and clean. Mainly though I wondered why so much of my mind went out to a stranger that I owed nothing but needed to watch, at close quarters soon and the rest of my days. I'd got to fourteen with no romances, no wolfish fix on another face; so this fresh hunger was hard to bear. And by the time I finally managed to sleep that Sunday, my mind had locked its teeth on a plan. It was new for me then but has stayed in use for the rest of my life and caused me tall waves of joy and pain, my kindest gifts and my devastations.

For me the plan amounted to one of those gleaming cries that humans die for—*Liberty or death!* or *God and my right!* My aim was too red-hot to think of failure—*Take what you need and hold on hard.* Young as I was and new to passion, I understood that if I saw Deke Patrick again—next Sunday or fifty years ahead—I'd find a way to learn him, know him, right to the quick of his adult soul. And if you don't think a fourteen-year-old can reason like that, then you don't know sufficient boys. Or you didn't know me.

And whatever else I did all week, I'd see that fervent demanding face that knew my name and a direct way to the place I kept my secret life. The face was what I focused on, the uncanny eyes; no

other part of his ample body came back to call me, not that early.
Despite the hot riptides of puberty, I could sometimes float back
and see the world with the cool unblinking eyes of pure childhood,
that fair and true; and I knew my prey, this single boy that somehow shared my father's face (at supper later on in the week, even
Mother remarked the likeness).

Next Sunday morning Deke's face was not in the biscuit line,
and there was no sign of him down by the lake. I almost asked a
red-haired boy where Deke might be. But that would have meant
exposing my quick, and I was still green for a show of courage. All
the next week, though, I kept my inner eye fixed on Deke, drawing him toward me; and that third Sunday, there he stood awake
near dawn and saying again "Oh Marcus, save me." I guessed he
thought I could save him from hunger.

At one that afternoon, when Mother had got us seated for dinner, she asked Deke please to say the blessing. She and I shut our
eyes and bowed, but a silence followed and stretched so long I had
to look.

Deke was there, head up, watching the food. His eyes were dry
and his lips were parted but still as wood. Finally his eyes came
round to me.

I nodded hard and mouthed "Say 'Thank you.'"

He waited another few seconds, then gave a deep chuckle.
Mother still hadn't looked, but I was watching and saw Deke
spread both hands before him in the air palms-down above the
food—he was still grinning wide. Then he just said "*Blessing*" and
reached for his napkin.

For years it didn't occur to me that Deke may well not have
come from a home where blessings were said and that he was
merely balked in the gate. But then I knew he'd stumbled on the
only appropriate way to bless, as those old Bible pictures with
Abraham raising long arms up through the smoke of a burning
lamb. I also took the moment as one more confirmation that Deke
Patrick was what I hoped for, not for these past two bated weeks

but all my life—a thorough man to learn and copy in every trait and skill I lacked.

By three that hot day, in our cool house at the round oak table, we'd eaten enough for a squad of boys—a brimming platter of Swiss steak, our own fresh vegetables, and strawberry shortcake. Mother had quickly cleared the dishes and readied herself for the weekly drive to see her own mother, twenty miles off. Though she was my one live grandmother, she gave me the fairly serious creeps with her white mustache and spidery hands; so Mother mostly let me use whatever excuses came to mind to spare the strain. Deke Patrick seemed my best excuse yet.

Even in that more tranquil time, few parents would drive off, leaving their only child in the hands of a stranger with training in the arts of death. So apparently Mother shared my sense of trust and expectation in this one soldier. She shook Deke's hand, gave him a standing invitation to be with us whenever he could—maybe spend a night this next weekend. She smoothed my hair, told me to show Deke some of my hobbies, then said she'd be back well before dark and left us clean as a streaking bird.

Since the clammy heat was stacking up in our dim rooms, Deke might rather sit outside in the breezy shade or even borrow Mother's bicycle, ride with me to the city pool, and swim awhile. I couldn't imagine he'd care to see a boy's collections of stamps and rocks or the model submarine I was building. An even stronger fact now was, I'd started feeling strange in his company. Not from fear—I thought his steady eyes were sane—but more because his private presence, in my home with no other people, was so near to being the perfect answer to years of hope that it spooked me mightily, waiting an arm's reach from him at the table.

I could feel a ringing charge in the air, but I couldn't tell if it drew me on or pushed me back. And since Deke kept on talking and laughing about the miseries of basic training, I couldn't tell if he understood how much force his body threw off in the normal room. I thought I could ask what time he'd leave and maybe break the spell that way. But then I knew I liked the mystery. Something crucial to my whole future might happen here, in a minute or never. So I tried to turn loose and take what came, though I braced myself by thinking *He's a lonesome human that'll leave here soon.* Then I said "We could bike ourselves to the pool; it opens at three."

Deke thought and said "We could also wash that world of dishes we just messed up."

It almost shocked me to think Deke had noticed the plates at all. I said "Mother says dishwashing calms her nerves."

Deke said "Same here. Then you got a bathing suit my size?"

The darkest shadow I'd ever known passed over my sight. I thought it came from a cloud outside. Now I can guess that it came from within me; whatever, it brought up a wave of gladness. *Everything's moving my way now.* I said "Sit tight," then trotted to find my father's trunks in the cedar chest.

The trunks were the old kind, burgundy wool with a white belt and a moth hole or two. At first they seemed to cheer Deke up. He laughed and said all he needed now was to part his hair in the middle and grow a handlebar mustache. But once we'd parked our bikes at the pool and entered the bathhouse, he sat on a bench, unrolled his towel, and shook the trunks in the air before us. Two boys a grade ahead of me nearly fell out laughing.

I suddenly thought I'd shamed Deke. So without meeting his eyes, I said, "We don't really have to—"

He groaned a low note, then leapt to his feet and vanished through the restroom door.

I didn't know whether to put on my own trunks or wait to see what he'd do next. But I could feel the lingering charge of where he'd sat. Nothing he'd done yet, nothing he'd said, had stemmed my appetite for help. I'd brought us this far, there were too few hours till he had to leave, I'd take the next step till he said *Quit.* And before I tied my drawstring, Deke was back in the antique suit. At once I was glad, but then I felt wing-shot and falling. So far I hadn't realized how much I needed to see Deke's body, the secret zones; and his shyness had foiled me. I even said "You sure are modest."

He smiled and moved toward the sunny door. "I just don't like to terrify people."

I tried but couldn't begin to guess if he was joking about his size or somehow telling me he had a scar too bad to show.

We swam around in the deep end awhile. Deke swam a lot better than I expected from the coal miner's son he said he was. When I told him that, at first I thought he'd taken offense.

He didn't smile but wiped the chlorine out of his eyes and said "We learned in the old mine shafts that flooded—pretty good swimming but dark and cold, and then sometimes you'd bump a dead miner they never rescued."

I nodded as if I truly believed him.

He shivered and said "Let's rent us some sun."

I said it was free and led him out. We spread our towels on sloping ground above the bathhouse, and Deke may have napped. He lay a good while with both eyes shut, his chest barely breathing and all of him roamed across by sun that was surely bad for skin light as mine. I ignored the risk since there unquestionably he was, a strong man condoning my nearness, my dumb requests for facts about his life and the world. I won't even try to repeat them here— they were so mundane: his favorite sport and movie actor, his shoe-size and weight. I only need to set down clearly the declaration that I'd have stayed beside Deke Patrick in broiling sun till nothing was left of Marcus Black but a handful of ashes.

I was that ready for big news to break. Meanwhile Deke lapsed out again; so I tried to match his power to rest in the yelling midst of children trying to drown each other. I'd nearly snoozed when a girl from the tough side of town walked up to Deke's head and fell to her knees. They cracked like shots.

Deke never looked.

And I pretended my eyes were clamped; but I studied her slyly (old as I was, I was waiting for girls to matter). As long as I watched her two-piece suit and her prominent parts, she seemed like a serious threat to the day.

But again Deke ignored her or was he asleep?

Finally she leaned halfway to his ear, snorted like a skittish mare and said, "Aren't you in the Forty-first?"

No word or look.

She bent farther and breathed cigarette smoke over his eyes. "If you're Deke Patrick, my sister knows you."

His eyes stayed shut but he said "You've got the wrong man, lady. I'm Marcus Black and I was in heaven till just this minute."

She didn't know me from Moses' dog, but she said a quick "Foo" and walked on off.

I thought Deke would look up and wink.

He didn't, not even a nod my way.

So grabbing the end of his lie to the girl—that he was Marc—I told myself Deke was maybe my father, back for this one afternoon to show me useful facts and secrets he'd failed to show when he left so young. I also told myself to wait and not so much as mention what I knew. I'd let his secret purpose pour toward me in its own time.

For now I only knew how he'd answered Mother's questions at the table—he was from Kentucky "more or less" and one of such a crowd of poor children that even his father "barely knew our names at noon, not to speak of midnight." But when half a quiet hour passed, and shadows were starting to cool the ground, I thought I'd better say something at least—Deke hadn't really moved again or talked. I stretched back flat, to look nonchalant, and faced the sky. Then I figured I knew the first question. "Will this war last till I can join?"

Deke took so long I almost thought he was back asleep, but then he rose to an elbow and faced me. His eyes were slow but they looked down my whole lean frame, that had never felt more childish than now. And whatever he thought, he said "Old Marc, you a God-fearing man?"

I said "Some nights."

"Then promise me, every night of your life, you'll ask Friend God to stop this mess before it kills me."

I saw he still hadn't mentioned my chances, but I somehow said "That's already settled" and found myself smiling.

That woke him fully. His eyes spread wide; he started to laugh but pulled up short. "You got some inside dope on me?"

What I wanted to say, I knew I shouldn't—*You mean you're scared?* I let the next sentence in line roll out. "You're the strongest soul I know on Earth." I even believed the outsized claim, and I shut my eyes to certify it—I was in calm charge here, I knew the future, my elders could rest.

Deke let me stay like that a whole minute, but then I heard him standing up. When I looked, he was halfway down the green hill in an excellent rolling chain of cartwheels till he hit water and backstroked a length of that long pool in what felt like world-record time.

He showered with his suit on and dressed in the men's restroom again. So when he came out, combing his hair, I was mad enough to say "You don't have to go with me home."

Deke said "You plan to ride two bikes at once?"

"I can ride mine and hold onto Mother's—done it plenty of times."

He thought about that. "It's a first-rate trick; but if you say Yes, I got my eyes on one last dish of those ripe strawberries."

I seldom ate even homemade desserts (I craved them too much and had sworn off a year ago), but I said "You're welcome to whatever's left. I got to get back to the model I'm building." The whole slow day, I'd kept myself from asking Deke a hard question, hard for me—when would he have to leave for camp? I guessed he'd start out trying to hitch sometime before dusk while cars were frequent. Now though with both of us dressed—and Deke not trusting me with even the sight of his body—I made myself say "You get yourself on back before night."

By then we were out by the cycle rack. Deke said "You forecasting harm if I don't?"

"No, sir, I just—" It shocked me to see a grown man take any words of mine that earnestly; no other man had and few have since.

Deke said "Goddammit, son, don't call me *sir*. You're older than me."

That was crazy but it hit even harder; I stopped to look him square in the face. At one and the same time, everything on him looked young and easy to hurt as a child set down by his mother in an open field but also older than my grandfather who'd died last year, half-starved with pain. I said "Get on your bicycle, please. We'll take the shortcut."

The shortcut ran through a railroad yard, and the ground was paved with broken glass from drunks' wine bottles. I rode on slowly to watch my path; but Deke overtook me, rearing up and lifting his front tire off the ground—that eager for something I couldn't see. Or so I figured; I also figured it had to be something involving a person older than me. Maybe a secret message had passed to the girl at the pool and she was waiting. Anyhow he never swerved or slowed till he was back in the shed at home.

I parked behind him and offered my hand to say good-bye.

Deke looked it over, then solemnly shook it. "You won't even spare me a cool drink of water?"

I halfway knew he meant me to laugh, but the other half (the look in his eyes) reminded me of numerous dreams where I had seen my hungry father locked outdoors in pouring night behind a window that I couldn't raise or even break. I said "Come on" and tried to hide what a nameless struggle—brand new to me and bigger than any I'd known till now—was waging itself inside my head each step of the way to the kitchen door.

* * *

Those were times when nobody thought to lock a house, when your neighbors helped themselves to sugar and left the shelves as neat as if they'd never walked in. So Deke and I had drunk two glasses of warm tap water before he spied a note on the counter and passed it to me. It was from Lennie Crumpler, the lady next door.

Marc, your mother just now phoned me and wants you to call her up in Watson soon as you can. She sounded worried so call her, hear? Then come tell me if she's all right.

Deke held out his hand and asked to read it.

Meanwhile I was breaking out ice for more water.

But Deke said "Haul yourself to the phone. Ma needs you bad."

I told him my mother could handle herself in a rattlers' den.

He shook his head. "Don't leave her hanging at the end of your rope."

I'd never seen it that way before, so I went to the phone and placed the first long-distance call of my career (back then children didn't just phone Europe to see how their best friends felt that day).

Mother answered, first ring. "Oh Marcus, thank God."

This saying *Oh Marcus* was catching on; and it lifted my spirit to hear her thanks—she was such a self-sufficient woman, kind but able and hard to serve. I said "Are you OK or what?"

She said she was all right but that her mother was having a spell. "You know the flashes she gets in her head?—an hour ago she and I were wandering out in the garden; and she flopped down between the tomatoes. Just buckled gently in the sandy dirt and waited there. I was deep in the corn and didn't see her; but when I got back, she was still on the ground."

I said "It's too hot. You ought not to—"

"Marc, I well know Mother's limits. She's better now but her left hand is cold and that whole arm, almost to her elbow."

Grandmother's skin was always cold, but I didn't say it. I said "You sure this isn't a stroke?"

There was such a long pause, I thought I'd lost her. Then she whispered "She's calling me Sybil"—that was Grandmother's sister who died far back. "I'm worried, Marc."

"You called the doctor?"

"You think I should?—it'll scare her badly."

"It'll scare her worse to die," I said. I don't know where such words came from, but they chilled my teeth, and I waited for Mother to shame me. She didn't, but paused. And I understood that was why she'd called, hoping I'd tilt her up or down. She'd once been timid but since the evening my father died, while dozing in his chair, Mother feared nothing but threats to me and her own mother's death. So I chose a kinder voice and said "I'll hang up now, you call Dr. Fritz, then call me back if you need me."

"You can't get here—"

I said "I can thumb a ride and be there quick." Then I knew I'd raised a worse chance for her than a stroke in the family—me killed by a drunk or kidnapped six states off by dawn and strangled in some mangy garage (however safe America was, the tragic fate of the Lindbergh baby a decade past was still a nightmare for thoughtful parents).

Mother said "You stay by the phone till I know more." Then she thought to ask when Deke had left.

I said "Maybe fifteen minutes after you." It gave me a pleasure I knew was wrong. And when Mother hung up, I looked toward the kitchen.

Deke was propped in the door, shaking his head at what he already knew was a lie.

I didn't beg pardon though and didn't wait by the phone one minute. Just in the time I talked to Mother, the sun had slipped down farther toward dusk; and whatever light was left in the house was almost gold. For the first time ever, some new thing in me lunged for what I knew I needed. I walked on straight to the hall closet, found the Kodak, and faced Deke again. "Let's take a picture before it's too late."

He was still in the kitchen door, still somber. But when he finally spoke, he smiled. "You said it wouldn't get too late—for me anyhow."

I stepped closer to him and beckoned hard. He seemed to nod and I led us out in the last of the heat, which is why I have two pictures now and these old memories, fresh and true. In the picture I've thought about most through the years, Deke stands on the edge of our Victory garden with staked tomatoes tall behind him. He's cupping a great ripe globe in his hand, but I always think he's facing me. And even now—with hardly a clue to his fine eyes—I can stare on at him and know again what a draw he was in that green place, that day of my life and on through the night. I know, for instance, how he held the bright tomato toward me; and as I clicked he plainly said "Son, never say I never gave you nothing." To this day anyhow I've never said it.

By the time we were back indoors, I saw it was nearly six-thirty; and I guessed Deke would leave in a minute. But before I could put the Kodak away, the telephone rang. Deke was near it, took up the receiver; and for a long moment, I thought he'd answer and then take over the rest of my life. On the spot there, it was not a bad thought. But he held the phone toward me; I could hear Mother's voice as it passed from Deke's long hand to mine—"Marcus? Where are you?"

I begged her pardon. "I dropped the phone."

"Marc, Dr. Fritz says you were right. She may have had a very slight stroke. No reason to go to the clinic yet and scare her to death. But he wants me to sleep down here tonight."

I understood, for the first time, that my last grandparent was leaving; and even if I didn't like her that much, for a while I felt as tall and unsurrounded as the last whole tree on a burned-out hill. I must not have spoken.

So Mother said "You're not mad, are you—me staying here? Just take your pajamas and your toothbrush to Lettie's and sleep in her new attic. I'll see you right after school tomorrow."

I said I would and sent my love to her and her mother, though what I knew—all over my body—was *I'll stay here tonight, come what may*. And when I'd hung up and looked toward Deke, I knew I'd lie to him as well. I said "Things are fine. She'll eat supper there and head on back." From here I can guess that, being a child, I was trying to make the bitter axe fall, not hang on above me. The day had been sweet, though my wild hopes had slid away in the trough of Deke's silence and inwardness. He had to leave here well before night; so sure, *Force him out, have the house to yourself.*

He rolled my false news over in his mind, then said "Don't lie to me. I *know* you." His eyes and jaw were fixed and blank as any threshing machine in grain.

I nodded, clutched my chest as if he'd shot me, moaned in pain, and dropped to one knee.

Deke said "I'm a guard. I've been on guard. I'll see you through."

Fear and happiness both rushed on me. Was this man addled or a crook on the run? Or say he was just an average soldier, wouldn't he land himself in the stockade to miss roll call tomorrow dawn? In a few more seconds, the fear passed; only the stinging hope stayed in me. Somehow tonight I'd learn the big news I'd been starved of. I said "Please. And thank you, sir."

Deke said "I'm a private. Drop the *sir*."

By eleven o'clock we'd made and eaten waffles with syrup. We'd done my English and history homework, listened to the radio, checked the stars in the deep backyard (they seemed to multiply as we watched; and Deke knew more of their names than me, though now I suspect he made them up). We mixed lemonade and drank the whole pitcher, then finally climbed upstairs bone-tired—Deke laughing that we might both wet the bed with that much sour juice in our veins. At the top of the stairs was the guest room door. Mother kept the bed in there made up, and I switched on the light to give Deke his chance at a private room.

He considered the offer, standing on the rug and turning round the whole white space till at last his eyes got back to me. "One ruffle too many. Where do you sleep?"

I pointed two doors down the hall. "Bunk beds in my room."

"Who you expecting?"

I told him the truth. When Mother was pregnant with me far back, my father had been so sure I was male—and so convinced they'd have a second male in short order—that he went out and bought bunk beds at a bankrupt furniture store for eight dollars. I slept in a baby bed of course for the first two years and no brother came. Then two more years and, with Father dead, I took the lower bunk and slept there ever since, except for ten idiotic nights at Boy Scout camp on the Cape Fear River. The top bunk was covered with a Pendleton blanket that had been my father's, a Navajo pattern; and even at fourteen I spent a fair number of afternoon hours lying up there, trawling space and the deeps of my mind in hopes of knowing whether I could make it on through life and be a sturdy reliable man, maybe even the father to my own child—boy or girl, whatever they sent me.

By the time I more or less told Deke that, he'd slid past me and entered my room. It burned me a little, his forging ahead with no permission, and I hung back.

But then he said one word, "Outstanding."

That drew me on. When I walked in, he was on the top bunk— legs under him, Indian-style. He was holding my submarine model.

It was far from finished. I'd already botched the tricky sanding along the hull that meant to be sleek, and now I despaired of coming near the snaky lines of the handsome picture on the box. The longer I watched Deke hold and stroke it, the worse it looked— one more thing I'd helplessly ruined. I said "I'm planning to burn it up."

Deke held it out with both hands before him. "I got another plan—you give it to me." He sounded earnest.

"Help yourself," I said. "Just don't tell anybody who ruined it."

He shut his eyes and rubbed the hull down the edge of his jaw, then held it toward me. "Finish it please by next weekend."

"What happens then?"

"My last furlough; they're moving us on. I'll take it next Sunday." He held the boat out further toward me; he meant what he said.

I took it and, Lord, it looked even worse. That far back I was one mad perfectionist—any flaw and a whole thing was lost. But here for the first time, somebody said he wanted something I'd halfway made. So finally I said "Help me then." Before the words could cross the narrow space between us, I knew I'd never asked a man for help till now—not a grown man who could crush my skull like a walnut shell and walk on free. A chill crept through me as Deke cleared his throat and moved to speak.

By midnight though—spelling each other with the finest sandpaper—we'd nearly repaired my blunders down one side of the hull. In all that time we talked very little, and nothing Deke said came near to sounding like a sermon or blame. I mean him no insult—in fact, I mean it as genuine praise—to say that sitting at work with Deke was like the granting of one more postponed boyhood dream: living beside a majestic dog that understood my every need and could now and then speak a few clear words of patient advice.

And if I learned a useful thing in that late hour, it's bound up deep in the memory I have before me still—the lasting sight of a man's strong hand, polishing slowly with a touch so light it couldn't have marred a baby's skin but gradually mended most of my flaws. From here I know, Deke worked no magic. He was likely a sensible family boy who'd learned the right relation to time for any hand with a hard job to do—building a model or a ten-room house or carving a stately face in granite: *Assume you've got forever to finish, but start today and don't look up till it's truly done.*

At last Deke set the submarine at the back of my table and said

"You knew how all along; you just got rushed. Take a whole slow week and finish by Sunday. Then I'll give you the seal of approval." He knocked the top of my head with a fist. "Old Marc, next thing—you need to sleep."

The job had waked us both up awhile; but now he was right. I also knew there were miles of questions I meant to ask. For instance, we hadn't even started on the mysteries of my new body, this astounding equipment that grew by the day and ached to drive me opposite outlandish ways, all of them leading far from this house and the peaceful life I'd spent till now. But as I stood there watching my rescued submarine, I asked the only question that came. "Why in the world are you here?"

Again he didn't laugh and he finally said "I already told you— normal guard duty."

I nodded. "But this town's safe as a tub. I could sleep on the center line of the road and not get scratched."

Deke shook his head. "Not so. I know. Go brush your teeth."

I wanted to ask for more details—what danger, from whom?— but like a child in the midst of a party, I suddenly felt my strength run out. I might as easily have dropped in place and slept on the rug, but I took my pajamas to the bathroom and undressed there. When I got back Deke had switched on the desk lamp and was lost in reading *The Boy's King Arthur*, a book that had been my favorite for years. Any hour but then, I could have sat on the edge of my bunk and recited him entire pages of the story—finding the Grail in a blaze of light, shown only to men who were pure in heart.

That way I might have bolstered his courage, more anyhow than I'd yet managed with my dumb promise of a healthy return. He seemed so lost in reading though that all I could do was to tell him the upper bunk was clean. He hardly nodded so I said "Good night." I don't believe he even replied. In the final instant I silently said a one-line prayer—*Don't let either one of us hurt the other.* Before I could think how strange that was—how could I hurt Deke?— sleep drowned me out.

*   *   *

My whole life I'm a marathon dreamer, and a good many dreams stay in my mind when I wake up. I can replay dozens of detailed stories that have come to me at crucial times from the age of four or five till today. But hard as I've tried to think what story I told my sleeping self that night, I come up blank. What I'm sure of is what I saw with clear eyes when I woke up near three o'clock, though it feels to this day more like a dream than provable fact.

Understand this first—the lady who owned the house before us had put up mirrors everywhere. No room escaped; she was that concerned to meet the world with all curls screwed. And her daughter hauled most of them off when the lady died, but one was bolted to the outer face of my closet door; and with our permission she left it there directly opposite where my eyes would open each day. In early years it meant little to me. Every week or so I might try out a promising frown or grimace—wiggling my ears or raising my eyebrows curious ways in hopes of winning affectionate laughter from my classmates.

But lately with my fascinating body in progress, around and beneath me, I'd taken to that tall scabby glass as if it amounted to my first love, a living creature lonely as me. I'd started pressing my lips to the surface two years back; and months before I met Deke Patrick, if I got home in the afternoon and Mother was out, I might well wind up stripped before it, longing to press my warm self through that cold glass and meet the needy body beyond me—the body I half-believed was me, though I knew it was just a common deed committed by light.

So what I saw, as I woke up on the night in question, was a young man standing beyond my bunk, completely naked and serious-eyed. You'll have guessed that first I thought *My father is here.* For years I'd silently begged to see him, a long clear glimpse if nothing else; and everybody said that, sooner or later, prayers got answered, Yes or No. Dazed as I was, it took me maybe ten seconds to see that—if this was the answer—then I couldn't say if the answer was Yes. What I faced was not exactly my own father but more like a changed Deke Patrick in the mirror, more of Deke than I'd bargained on.

Was Deke in some mysterious way a younger model of the man who'd helped to make my life and whom I needed more than ever, with time pellmelling down the road and dragging me breathless? Whatever else I might see later, the live Deke's back was turned toward me and was nearer yet. He was thoroughly still, both hands at his sides; and his eyes never blinked but watched the reflected man in the mirror.

For a long time then, I didn't wonder what this could mean to the man or what it meant to do to me and maybe the world. If it wasn't someway my lost father, it was anyhow a soul that banked on me to sleep in reach of whatever this new presence was. And like the average curious child, I rushed to study the news before me—the first bare grown man in this house in the ten years since my father died, standing frankly in my room, as still as a hunting heron or leopard.

I see the sight in my mind clear as then. No point in straining to show it here. Our language sadly lacks the means to summon a well-made human body, much less one as awesome as Deke's. The truest poets fail in the try to convey any part of the simple flesh that makes our first and final claim on the world's love and pity, its craving and rage, because no words can set such a gift before the reader, clean of shame or lure and threat. I'll only say that, fully awake, I looked for minutes at skin and hair, limbs and nails as finely made as any since. And all the while I thought a single furious thing, *Don't let this end. Let it teach me everything I need.*

But Deke moved. Both hands went up and rubbed his eyes. And then I was almost sure I saw the signs of tears. Next his right hand prowled his chest and belly like a careful doctor—probing, searching. What had he lost? From that point on I changed from famished watching to guessing—what again could this sight mean and who was it for? I understood that nobody else was witnessing this but Deke and I (had Deke seen my eyes open behind him?) and likely God.

What I decided at last was easy; and yet these many years on in life, I can say it was my first manly finding. *Deke is memorizing his bones in case he's wounded or loses a part or comes back home a frozen corpse or just a free invisible spirit, recalled by maybe his mother and me for our short lives.* I felt I had him printed deep in memory; but I went on watching, long as he stood there, to guarantee that my mind anyhow would hold his likeness—him at his best—let come what might. I even realized I was standing guard on him, the first of many nights I've guarded other burdened men and the good woman who bore our child, though none has meant an atom more than Deke that night, near as he was in time and place to my father's death and chiming with everything I'd lost, like a tuning fork that rings in perfect harmony with an unheard chord.

Maybe I dozed. For how long though?—when I looked, the window was maybe a whole shade lighter. But suddenly I looked again, and Deke was taking a step toward the mirror, a handspan off. Slowly he leaned and pressed his forehead high on the surface, both eyes shut. I thought *He's telling somebody good-bye*, whatever I meant. Then he came back upright and reached to the chair. From a neat pile he found his drawers and pulled them on. He took a long last stare at the glass and made what seemed a sign of the cross all down himself, from head to thigh. I'd seen movies with nuns and priests and was old enough to think how few Kentucky boys were Catholics; but maybe he just meant something else, some private bet on health and safety. Then he took two backward steps—I might have reached and touched his calves—and I took the chance to turn away silently, facing the wall.

Next I heard him move again. I felt my sheet lift back, and cool air struck my arms. I had the time to run or say no to whatever he planned, unless he held a knife or worse. But nothing in me was scared or mad. I stayed there toward the wall, eyes shut. And then I felt him lay himself down flat beside me, maybe a palm's breadth from my back. I guessed it was Deke—I still hadn't looked—but we lay on awhile, and the clean salt odor of his hair confirmed it. I was much amazed but still not scared.

I understood from other boys' jokes, and from camporees with weird troopleaders, that men could get as strange as women and reach for more than you could give. I also had a new hot sense of what two bodies could give each other or take by force. But I never feared Deke Patrick's hand, his mind, or any other part. And now I can almost swear that, once he had the sheet back on us, he said one sentence in a calm voice—something about excusing him, could I pardon him please?

I'm sure I didn't speak at the time, and I'm well aware that it's late for regrets; but if pardon was something he truly needed, then I never gave it. I was lost in trying to understand, was he asking for help or trying to give it? At least I hope he knew I didn't blame him—far, far from it. And after a while I tried to signal my grateful trust by rolling back a little, still not touching, though both our bodies were in the range of each other's heat. Then I got my next manly thought. I stayed there, honored, and told myself *This boy is lonesome. Stay still now and let him rest.*

It was all I could feel that early in life, but I may have been right. In a minute longer anyhow, I heard the sound of regular breathing—Deke was plowing sleep like a narrow dugout slow through black marsh water in the dark. I took a minute to say my thanks to the bountiful night; and though I meant to stay on guard till first light showed, the weight of what I'd seen and learned began to press me. Soon enough I was also plowing the blackest sleep I'd ever known.

Morning, I woke alone again. Deke had slid out on me—when and how? I lay to listen for steps in the house; I almost prayed I'd hear him cooking, or I'd smell fresh coffee. But what I heard were empty rooms, the old walls shifting in early warmth; and all I smelled were our hedge roses in heavy bloom. Was I shocked or sad? I thought I'd soon be one or the other; but no, I waited and still felt calm. I finally said one fact aloud, *That was no dream.* Then

I stood and rushed to dress in cooler air than I expected. It was Monday and Mother had made me promise to mow the lawn and paint the shed; then she'd be back (I knew if my grandmother had died, I'd have heard by now). I searched my table for some kind of note—nothing, no word.

But the submarine was there in the place where Deke had left it, rescued and waiting for my new skill. With summer on me, I told myself I had the time to finish it right by Sunday morning, if Deke ever showed. Then I told myself another thing—*Deke's long gone.* That seemed to mean that he and I had finished our business well before day, and neither one of us needed more or had more to give. But even before I went downstairs, I knew I'd have to ignore that chance, in the short run at least.

None of our neighbors had seen Deke leave, so Mother was flabbergasted to hear I stayed alone an entire night, but that passed off and all she did was call her mother and tell the news of Marc's big dare. The rest of the week, I worked in happiness, hours each day, patient as any carpenter bee but also hot to finish on time. Late Saturday night I set the final painted boat back where Deke had left it. I stood and watched it a long time till I knew I'd finished a thing I was almost proud of, my first fair job. I felt nearly sure that Deke would approve. And when I finally managed to sleep, I steadily watched Deke walking toward me from those same woods by the lake in the park, where he had vanished the day I met him.

But Sunday came and soon I knew that part of me had guessed correctly. I gave out the coffee and biscuits again but Deke never showed. As the line of boys passed my table, I dreaded one of them joking about me and Deke last week. I thought our day, not to mention the night, had been a thoroughly private truce; but what after all did I know about Deke, and who he was in other places? If he could leave my room and house without a word, then couldn't he tell his friends any number of lies about us or even the truth?

But none of the hungry soldiers said so much as a word or faced me; they loaded their pistols and walked away. I'd known right along that, if Deke didn't show, I'd never mention his name again. So when we got to the end of church, and still no sign, I told myself I had this much—*Since nobody knows the deal but me, I've got nobody but me to explain to.* With the calm I'd gained, I sat down late that Sunday night and made a list of the news I'd learned from knowing Deke.

The list, to be sure, is long since gone. But I know it said a lot about friendship—what two people can give each other. Since I've done better as a friend than a mate, those cooler bonds have been a lifelong study of mine; but my first lesson came from Deke and amounted to this. Friends can give you a guarantee that your poor body is a fit companion; they can teach you the dangerous duties you owe to neighbors and strangers. Friends lead each other across rope bridges with jagged valleys far below; and then they go their separate ways, though not forgetting the pure air and noble view at such fine heights. Friends, I thought—and time has proved— can show you sights like nothing your kin, your lovers, God, or Nature herself will ever show: no purple canyon or the boundless pardon in a saint's bright eyes.

For years I wondered, did Deke live or die? On in my forties, when Mother died three months ago and I went home to clear the house, I found his pictures—the only two—in *The Boy's King Arthur*; and the past rolled back as real as my hand. I vowed I'd write to the Pentagon and see if they had records on a boy named Deacon Patrick from east Kentucky (he mentioned his full name late in the night and made me spell it). But then I didn't. Some cowardice in me, or maybe good sense, made me think that any news I got would be grim—he'd been dead for years and buried in Europe or the South Pacific or he lived on now as a black-lunged miner on welfare and food stamps or many things worse.

I told myself I'd known Deke Patrick the single day that fate intended. Though I'm no staunch believer now, in fate or God, I tend to believe at least this much—*Things happen in their time*. Whether Deke knew it or not, he gave me what I needed then, that urgent summer, which was human hope—a halfway decent way to start the endless trek out of childhood. He showed me I was made to last a normal while in a world as loaded as any shotgun. I could do what I had to, storm or shine, like most men, women and— Lord God—children (Deke's war proved at least that much: children can last through hunger and torment worse than any man will take). Nothing ahead was truly fearsome but bodily harm; and even harm could pass you by and let you sleep beside rank strangers to end your life at age ninety-six with kind descendants round your bed.

I'm several decades short of ninety; but still my skin, give or take a few pounds, is the direct heir of the younger skin that a grown man trusted for the first time when I was a child on the last doorsill of a guarded life. As I stepped forward to the baffling world, other humans came at me with other big gifts and some with weapons; but nobody stayed much longer than Deke, not till now at least. I don't say that in hopes of pity or mountains of mail with outright offers of hearts and lives. I'm the only man I know today who claims and can prove—in the bitter face of heartbreak, pain, and mortal wrong, all caused by me—that he meets most days with sensible hope; that he sleeps most nights, unpunished by blame and is partly healed by silent dreams.

Reynolds Price was born in Macon, North Carolina, in 1933. He graduated first in his class from Duke University, then traveled as a Rhodes Scholar to Merton College, Oxford University, to study English Literature. He now teaches at Duke as James B. Duke Professor of English.

In 1962 his novel *A Long and Happy Life* received the William Faulkner Award for a notable first novel and has never been out of print.

Since, he has published more than two dozen books. In 1986 his novel
Kate Vaiden received the National Book Critics Circle Award; his most
recent novel *Blue Calhoun* appeared in 1992; his *Collected Stories* followed
in 1993. He has also published volumes of poems, plays, essays, transla-
tions from the Bible, and a memoir entitled *Clear Pictures*; and he has
written for the screen, for television, and the texts for songs with music
by James Taylor. A new volume of memoirs, *A Whole New Life*, appeared
in spring 1994.

T*he story is recent but the impulse to write it began forming in me as
long ago as 1942, the early days of America's entrance into the Second
World War. In those years I lived with my parents and younger brother
in the center of North Carolina, in the small town of Asheboro. Though
Asheboro was a hosiery-mill town with no crucial military significance, it
lay within close range of a number of those army encampments that sprang
up overnight throughout the country. As an immediate result of such migra-
tions, many American towns—including Asheboro—soon found themselves
host to numbers of young, baffled, and momentarily idle soldiers on weekend
leave.*

*At the time I was fascinated by what I could see of the situation of these
young men, the paradoxical air of both young-dog readiness and of deep
isolating sadness that hung around them all. Good-willed as my parents
were, somehow they never took the opportunity to invite one of the soldiers
home for a meal. And though I was nine years old in '42, I don't recall my
begging for any such family hospitality. Maybe I was happy to watch from a
distance; maybe I shied from the knowledge that some boys anyhow were
bound to be killed in the next months and years.*

*Some fifty years later, however, the wish rose in me palpably; and I found
myself suddenly writing a story in which a boy a little like me—in a very
different kind of home—dares to award himself the meeting I never
attempted. I wrote the story as quickly as if it had lain finished in me for long
decades; and every aspect of it gave me pleasure, as indeed it still does.*

Kathleen Cushman

LUXURY

(from *Ploughshares*)

When light came enough that the sky was blue, Ivy and Track had been driving for an hour already, the three girls and Tad in the back and Bella-Jean smug between them in the front seat, holding a paper bag to throw up in if she had to. Buzzy, the baby, lolled on Ivy's lap heavily; the car had put him to sleep. Track drove with an abstracted air, his eyes narrowed against the light reflecting back from the highway. His strong left arm was a reddish brown where it rested against the rolled-down window.

"Georgia," he sang with a kind of deep abandon, in his scratchy voice. "Geor-gia . . ." He sang to keep himself awake, half the time with no words at all. They were in Tennessee still, but tonight they would be in Georgia, the next in the string of moves that made up a sergeant's life. Ivy thought of what she had heard about Fort Benning: not too bad, depending on which end of the range of quarters they drew. She had been lucky so far; they could have sent him to Korea.

Track reached across Bella-Jean and squeezed Ivy's shoulder through her thin dress.

"Sleepy?" he said to her, interrupting his song and winking at her. He passed his hand up toward her neck, where her hair was already damp from the heat, but stopped after he had squeezed it once and went back to the wheel. She turned on the seat so she could see the four in the back, each of them sitting on a different color pillowcase packed with their clothes.

From the seat behind her, Tad was kicking her in the spine, little jarring knocks with the new cowboy boots she had bought him at the post thrift store for two seventy-five. As he kicked, the clothes beneath him began to work their way out of the pillowcase onto the seat, headed for the floor. Tad was the oldest boy, named Oscar Traxton after Track; he wore a patch to correct his lazy eye. Ivy put her arm back over the seat and smoothed back his cowlick.

"You leave off kicking me with those fancy boots," she said to him. "You're gon' wear them out."

When she said the word "boots" Track switched his tune again, moving out of a growling, halfway hum. "'There was *blood* upon the risers, there were *brains* upon the chutes,'" he sang loud to the "Battle Hymn of the Republic," hitting the steering wheel.

"Track," Ivy said, wishing he would stop. But he wasn't looking at her, wasn't thinking about anything but the road. She admired the way he could shut out the noise, knew it was what kept him coming home to her all these years.

The kids had joined in. "'The in*tes*tines were a-*dang*ling from his *para*trooper boots!'" They loved it that their father jumped out of airplanes, the silk billowing over his head like he was an angel, the dangerous thump as he hit the ground hard. He had taught them all how to do it; they jumped from the back of the couch and rolled on the floor, curled up so that thigh, butt, arm, and shoulder took the shock. Every time he had a jump they would do it all day long, while Ivy mixed up a cake and waited for the sound of his heavy boots on the steps outside.

"Are you satisfied?" she said mildly to him across the front seat. They would be singing it into her grave, she was sure. But he didn't mind, gave a smile without looking at her.

"When are we going to stop?" Callie asked. She was lying down on the rear-window shelf, which was a tight fit. Her cheek was pressed against its dirty felt and her dress was twisted up around her waist. No one answered.

"Next year—next year," Track sang, syncopated, "somethin's bound to happen . . . This year—this year—" He turned around while the car went too fast down the straight road and he fixed his fierce look on the children. "Someone got to go again?"

"He does," said Annie, pointing at Tad, who was still making jittery bounces on the seat. "I can tell. I have to sit next to him." She held her nose.

The jolt when the car stopped on the shoulder of the road made Callie fall off the window shelf onto the rest of them. "Everybody out!" Track shouted, flinging open the door. They got out into the hot air that seemed suddenly still and queer.

Ivy mixed peanut butter and jelly together in a big jar on the flat trunk lid. She took out hamburger buns from a plastic bag and spread the mixture onto the soft bread, counting out one for everybody except Buzzy. He sat unsteadily on the hot trunk, reaching for the jar and for the knife as it flashed in her hand. The other children were up the road already, scattering into the piney scrub along its edge. Track walked at a slow pace among them, his loose stride breaking now and then as he stretched first one leg and then the other out in a forced airborne kick. He had got a fresh haircut the day before, and she could see the familiar bony shine of his skull.

She did not hear the boy coming up behind her; what made her turn around was Buzzy's fixed, attentive scowl at something past her. The boy looked older than any of hers, about twelve, with black hair and one shoulder that slanted lower than the other. He carried a paper bag, worn thin as cloth where it had been rolled down so he could hold it shut.

"You goin' on down this road?" he said to Ivy. He spoke right up but he looked at Buzzy rather than directly at her. He was not as bold as he seemed. She could feel him watching as she closed up the buns one by one and opened up the plastic Clorox bottle she had washed out four times last night and filled with water. Her own children were returning to her now; they stared at the stranger talking to their mother and waited to see if she would send him off.

Ivy handed out the hamburger buns, leaving out two for her and Track. She held the bleach bottle to the lips of each of the children, steadying it as the warm water sloshed heavily against its sides. All this time the boy watched her sideways. He crooked a dirty finger at Buzzy, moved it back and forth so that the baby stared, fascinated.

Track was back then, his hand steady on her shoulder and sliding quickly down her arm before he reached for his lunch. "Who's this?" he said to the extra boy.

"Sir," the boy said, letting his hand fall from Buzzy's gaze. He started to say more but his voice caught in his throat and he coughed and looked away.

"He wants a ride," Ivy said. She watched Track heft the bottle and drink, the water going down his sunburned throat. Even in his short-sleeved shirt and old work pants he looked like a soldier, and she knew the boy had been suddenly afraid to ask. It would be foolish to give him a ride; there would be five in the back, then.

"We got a full car," Track said. He wiped water from his lip, took one of the buns, and started on it. "Where you going, boy?"

The boy drew himself up. "Litchie," he said. "I'm going to help out my auntie in Litchie."

Ivy could see the other children getting restless, Annie and Helena whispering and pulling at Callie to get her to come with them.

"You all make sure none of you has to go," she said. "Then get on back in the car. Did you hear what I said, Bella-Jean?"

She took out a wet washcloth from a plastic bag and wiped their faces one by one, moving among them with Buzzy holding on at her hip. When she looked back, she saw that the boy was still standing and waiting by the car, though Track had turned away from him and leaned against the hot green fender with his eyes shut against the glare.

While she watched he opened his eyes and barely turned his head in their direction.

"I guess we can swing by Litchie," she heard him say.

*   *   *

In the back seat, the children grabbed their places, pushing their bulging pillowcases into the cracks and under their knees and feet. None of them wanted to sit next to the boy; he ended up jammed against Tad in the middle, with Annie on his other side looking scared, her thumb in her mouth though she was eight years old. Cranston, he had said his name was when Tad asked, and Ivy heard the bravado in his voice.

"See that line?" Tad showed Cranston the roll of vinyl trim that went down the middle of the seat. "You stay on your side." He had to hold his pillowcase in his lap to make room, and he hunched forward over it.

Track counted them aloud and added one. Then he pulled the gearshift toward him and up with a grinding sound. They lurched onto the highway and against each other, Buzzy staring over Ivy's shoulder toward the back, his mouth open on the diaper she'd put over her dress.

"In my solitude—" Track started right up, and Ivy looked at him wondering if he meant the joke, but he was already absent, humming vaguely. He was just as likely to put in anything when he forgot the words, their whole life history coming right out to the tune of an old hit song. "Be *boo*, be-be *boo*," he sang. "I know that I'll soon go mad—" and then he interrupted himself. "Give me a look at that map," he said to Bella-Jean beside him.

All the windows were rolled down in the car, but it was still hot. Ivy could see Callie sweating where she lay on the back shelf, her face humid and flushed. Tad and Cranston began to poke at each other.

"Bet you're eleven," said Tad. "Helena's eleven." Tad was ten and short for his age.

"Thirteen," said the boy. Tad didn't believe him; he started to tickle Cranston. "I can get you down," he teased, linking his arm through the boy's and trying to get him flat on the seat. "Let's play Luxury," he said to the rest of them.

Helena hung her hair out the window and let it blow, ignoring them. She was the oldest and ought to have been in the front by rights, but Bella-Jean had cried and said she was going to be sick again.

"Get his feet, Annie," Tad said. Annie held Cranston's feet, so nervous that she was stronger than usual. "Do you want me to sit on them?" she said, panting. Ivy let them wrestle it out, trying to pay no mind. She thought of how it would be in Georgia, whether the commissary and the schools would be close enough to walk.

As Cranston pinned Tad to the seat, Callie rolled purposely onto both of them from the shelf. She sprawled on the boy's thin back and groaned, her tongue hanging out. "Luxury," she moaned in exaggerated pleasure, Cranston writhing weirdly beneath her. "Lux-ury!"

The commotion broke through Track's song and he thrust his fist behind him without looking around. "I'll show you luxury," he threatened.

Ivy reached back wearily to straighten Callie's dress. "How many times do I have to say," she said.

The boy straightened up, dumping Callie down by the drive-shaft hump on the floor. Ivy heard the rip of comic books as the child tried to right herself, and smelled the stink of sneakers and stale peanut butter. Anything clean on these kids was a lost cause now.

"You wouldn't have won if you played fair," he said.

"You don't even know the rules," said Callie. There was an aggressive pout to her voice, like she was spoiling for a sickness. Ivy's own head began to ache with the heat and the quarrel.

Cranston looked at the child with contempt. "The one on top says luxury," he said. "You think I don't know what that means?" He had a long scrape across his elbow and his teeth were set far apart. Callie twisted away so that she was hanging over the front seat.

"How long until he gets out?" she said, too loud.

Ivy put the back of her hand on the child's cheek and felt it for fever. "Hush up," she whispered. "Not too long, I think."

*   *   *

"I know where Litchie is," Track said conversationally. He flipped the map with one hand; it fell open another fold onto Bella-Jean, who was picking a knee scab till it bled. "I was in Litchie once, a long time ago. Looking for work. Bottling plant there, isn't that so?" he asked the boy over his shoulder.

"Before you joined the army?" Tad said. They all loved to hear Track's stories. Ivy suspected that half of them were made up, anyway, making Track out to be a wild and dangerous boy, not knowing what he was going to do, no work for anybody. In the army he had met up with Ivy, who had a job in the Woolworth's off post. "I met my million-dollar baby," he sang whenever he told them about it.

She took the map when he handed it back to her and saw where Litchie was, another hundred miles at least, and fifty of those out of the way, a deep swing south when they could have gone straight on the main highway. In the back, Annie began to cry; when Callie climbed back on the shelf she had stepped on her leg and ripped the waist of her dress.

"That's enough back there," Ivy said. "Stop the car," she said to Track. "He's going to have to find his own way, I guess."

Track appeared not to hear her, his eyes straight ahead against the sun.

"I didn't do anything," the boy said. He was defiant and cold, on the dangerous edge of youth; he knew more than any of her children did yet. "They was just playing their game."

"Track," Ivy said, reaching across Bella-Jean to put her hand squarely on his driving arm. "We got too many in this car to take this boy along. We need to let him out."

He glanced at her sharply. When he barked back over his shoulder they all stiffened; it was a sergeant's voice. "You men shape up back there," he said. "We got two hours to drive before we're stopping, and I don't care how bad you got to go. Where'd you say you were going in Litchie, anyway, boy?"

"My aunt has a diner," Cranston said, triumphant.

"Track," said Ivy, low and urgent. "We got too many kids back there."

He looked at her then, and she wondered what was spoiling behind his gaze, flat now in a way she knew to leave alone. "I wouldn't mind swinging by Litchie," he said. "Been a long time since I've seen that old place." He was like a stubborn boy himself, she saw, and bit her lip against her anger. He was already singing again, some song she could not even identify.

Ivy shut her eyes against the fields of cotton, dry and poisonous-looking in the heat. They were on the outskirts of Litchie, its business district hunched a mile or two away in a dim brown haze. They would have to stop for the night down here, but she didn't want to go into town—paying good money to listen to street ruckus all night. Better one of those roadside places where for a couple of dollars extra all the kids could stay in the same room, on the floor. She would open the big jars of baby food and stand the children in line, spooning it out with one spoon. On her tongue she could already taste the furry texture of junior lamb, the smooth, watery strained peas, bliss of apricots from the last jar.

The sun was coming straight in the rear window onto the lot of them. Annie was asleep and Helena was reading again, giving herself a headache so she could sit in the front. Since they had passed the big lake an hour before, the boy Cranston had been watching for the turnoff he wanted. Ivy could smell him sweating, keyed up; he had the rough odor of adolescence, not like the clean dirt smell of the younger ones.

"Here it is," said Cranston suddenly.

It was gleaming in the late sun, a silver box of low trailer on the side of the road. Windows went all the way across the front, and there were cement steps up to the door. BITE-N-BIDE, said the plastic sign that faced the road. ENJOY COCA-COLA. A stand of pine out back circled three tar-paper cabins. Track pulled the Plymouth into the dirt parking lot and turned it off. On the back shelf, Callie raised her head up suddenly from sleep, bumping it on the sloping glass.

"Don't mind if I do," said Track, letting a big yawn burst out of him and stretching his arms up over his head. Cranston was teetering anxiously on the floor hump, waiting to be let out. Ivy took her hair and pinned it again at the top of her head. She could feel the small beads of sweat standing out on her neck.

The boy rushed ahead of them into the diner, letting the door slam. "I'll be a minute," Track said to Ivy, nodding across the road to the privacy of some trees.

When she went in with Buzzy over her shoulder, the five children were already sitting at the counter on high stools, swiveling them with the wildness of being let out at last. It wasn't a bad place, the menu in crooked block letters stuck up over the grill. A piano was jammed across one end of the trailer, with brown keys like bad teeth here and there. Cranston spun away from his aunt as soon as he saw Ivy come in, and turned his back to them on the piano stool, fooling around with his left hand. In the moment she saw his face, she wondered what he had told the aunt already.

Without asking, the woman put a glass of cold Coke in front of each of them, six in a row down her empty counter. She had the same black hair as Cranston and his sharp, knowing face.

"Oh," said Ivy doubtfully.

"It's on the house," the aunt said. "Giving the boy a ride all the way!"

Ivy felt the cold, bright shocks of the drink as she swallowed and the stiff tiredness of her neck and back. In the corner she could hear Cranston playing, something she'd heard before, and she thought briefly it must be one of Track's songs. The boy was good; he made the fast notes move, stumbling only a little here and there.

"You driving this family yourself?" the aunt said admiringly. Ivy laughed and settled herself on the seat, giving Buzzy a piece of ice to play with.

"I wouldn't do any of this without my man making me," she said, tossing her hair back from where Buzzy had pulled it out of the pins and inclining her head toward the parking lot. "He's out with the car. We started maybe six this morning from west Tennessee."

"You might could stay here tonight," the aunt said. She jerked a thumb toward the back of the diner. "We got an empty cabin I could let the lot of you stay in for ten dollars."

"Sounds good to me," Ivy said. The aunt was taking blistered pink hot dogs off a spiked rack that turned inside a hot glass case. She put each hot dog in a roll and then onto a thick china plate, and on the side, she put a pile of chips and a pickle. "Dogs included," she said, "for you." Starting with Callie at the end, she served them each a plate, one after another from a stack on her arm.

Ivy was embarrassed. "Now don't you go giving us food," she said. "We got food in the car." She saw the children eating fast without looking her way and thought of the baby food she would have given them, easy and so much cheaper.

From some prickle of attention on the aunt's part, Ivy perceived that Track had come in, had in fact been standing for some while behind her in the door, watching the boy play. "I Got It Bad and That Ain't Good," popped without warning into Ivy's head as he sat down next to her finally; that's what the tune was. She moved herself imperceptibly sideways on the stool so that her leg and arm touched Track's. The day was almost over, anyway.

"This whole crowd of kids belong to you?" the aunt said to Track, giving him a cup of coffee. He put his finger into the saucer and moved it a little to the music, his head cocked. The aunt leaned back against the sink and folded her arms as if she had nothing particular to do. "That one does," she added, nodding at Tad. "Plain as day."

"Every last one," said Ivy for Track, turning her stool around in a quick twirl and putting her hand on his leg. "I can swear that he is responsible." She looked into Buzzy's diaper and shook her head. "Track," she said, brisk and quiet, half turning so she wouldn't be heard. "She's got those cabins out back, all of us for ten dollars."

Track just sat as if he didn't hear her, looking out the windows at the parking lot, his elbow resting on the counter. "She already treated us to those franks," Ivy whispered.

All the children but Cranston had vanished into the lot, their plates littered with pickle and bits of chip. The aunt collected the dishes and began washing them up, her back to them. "I got work to do," she said in the boy's direction. He stopped right in the middle of the tune and pulled back the old stool with a screeching sound. He hesitated for a second, to see if she was going to tell him to do something, and then he gave Ivy a cocky look and darted out the door.

"Plenty of work around here these days?" Track asked. He finished his coffee and the woman poured him some more.

"Some," she said. She shrugged. "Construction, mostly." She looked out the window at the children shrieking in the pink dust. "I got to have me another cabin built, for instance."

Ivy could feel Track's attention fix on the aunt. She looked at her again; she wasn't pretty enough for him to be interested. Two black wings of eyebrows grew too close together in the middle, giving her an odd scowl, like the boy's.

He laughed in a queer, dry way. "I could have used some of that the last time I was here."

The aunt glanced at Ivy. "Y'all didn't say you was here before," she said, with a flicker of the kind of interest Ivy had come to hate in these years of army life. They all thought you had it good, the people who had to live in these towns full time. They wanted to leave and they couldn't, pinned down by mothers and uncles and jobs and places they had saved for years to put a down payment on. When they saw you come into their stores, they knew they needed you but they hated you, anyway, for getting to move on, to see what would always be hidden from their eyes. What did they know about what it was really like, a world with troubles just as hard as theirs, everywhere people trying to ward them off one moment at a time? What would Track care to hide, anyway? Ivy hitched her dress up a little and put Buzzy on her bare knee, bouncing him to a tuneless rhyme under her breath as if she wasn't listening.

"I lived on Genessee Avenue," said Track. "Over the store." He ran a finger over his upper lip, tightened against his teeth. She was aware of the heat of his body making damp patches on his cotton shirt.

"Fay Ann's store?" the aunt said, and Track grunted assent. Ivy could tell the woman was surprised that Track would know someone she knew by name.

He took a couple of sugar cubes from the metal bowl and lowered them very slowly into his coffee. Then he looked at Ivy. She stood up at once and lifted Buzzy away from her. "You are a *mess*," she said, and laid him down on the floor. "I don't know what I am going to do with you!" Before he could object, she had his diaper halfway off.

"Fay Ann still there?" she heard Track say, his back to her again. He held his cup halfway to his mouth and watched the aunt. He wasn't going to drink until she answered, Ivy saw.

"She's there," the woman said. "Her pop died a while back, left her the store. Her and her girl live upstairs from it now." She took another look at Track. "That where you lived?" she asked.

He didn't answer.

"That would have been before my time," she said. "I came up from Macon after the war. I didn't know Fay Ann until her girl was born. I never even met her young man."

Track finished his coffee. "Yeah?" he said.

She shrugged. "He didn't make it back from the war," she said. "I don't know who all."

Track got up from the counter and went over to the old piano, standing in front of it and touching one key with his finger. He sat down, pulling the chair in close, and spread his hands out as if he were going to play, like the boy. Ivy turned from Buzzy and watched him openly now. She half expected him to do it, to make the notes come astoundingly on top of each other, even though as far as she knew he had never touched a piano before in his life. But he just mimed it, gently, on the tops of the keys, and then let his hands go limp on the wood at the end, his shoulders sagging.

"I always did want to learn to play like that," he said. He put his lips together and nodded as if he could hear the tune. Then he looked around, at Ivy for a second and then at the aunt. "Always thinking of them old songs," he said.

The aunt smiled on one side of her face. "Same as that boy," she said. "Stay the night and he'll play you some more." She took a key off a hook under the cash register and held it out to him.

Track got up then, heavily, and went to the open door. He stood there for a minute, his hands braced against the wood on either side, looking out at the parking lot. Ivy could hear the children yelling outside, playing some game and running around in the lot. Then she saw Track reach in his pocket, take out a couple of bills, and put them on the counter for the aunt to take. For just a half second he hesitated, looking at her as if he had forgotten what he was going to say.

"This'll be for the food," he said. "I guess we got to be going on."

When the kids finally settled back into quiet, they had been on the road for an hour at least. Bella-Jean had fallen asleep on the back shelf while the car was being loaded up, and Helena sat up in front, in the middle. Buzzy was snoring lightly, his open mouth against the breast.

With her face turned toward the open window, Ivy could feel the slow cooling of the air as they drove. They were well out of Litchie now on some road without a number, heading northeast to where they could pick up a highway and stop. The sky was already turning dark down by the hills in the distance, and Track sang to himself under his breath, not much louder than the low noise he made when he slept. She was tired through.

"I don't see why we couldn't have stayed there," Tad said from the back. She turned to hush him; he was slumped against his pillowcase in the corner of the seat, his face streaked with the day's dirt, his eyes that were Track's looking sleepily back at her. Across Helena between them, Track reached over his hand in the middle of his song and laid it on Ivy's lap. For a moment she could not think what to say; she was aware only of the weight of the car on the road, its tires moving heavily over the hot macadam, the rough, freckled skin of Track's hand next to Buzzy's baby leg. She shut her eyes and saw it all still in her mind.

"It cost too much, honey," she said at last, thinking to answer Tad. "You go on to sleep." Track lifted his hand to the dash; she saw him open the pocket and take out the map. "When you wake up, we'll be there," Ivy said to her children in the back, making her voice slow like a lullaby, to rock them into the darkness. Out the car window, the light was fading swiftly, and she looked into the expanse of evening, imagining her limbs opening into its space, her arms stretching over her head as far as she could reach them. She better not make any promises she couldn't keep. "When you wake up next time, we'll be almost there."

Kathleen O'Neill Cushman grew up without regional roots, in a military family that moved frequently, but the grandmother she is named for was one of a sprawling Irish family from Charleston, South Carolina. A writer of fiction, essays, and poetry, she now lives in Harvard, Massachusetts, where she is at work on a novel. Her work has appeared in *Grand Street, The New Yorker, The Atlantic Monthly,* and many other publications.

S *omething about the small towns on the fringes of army bases has always drawn my imagination—the pawn shops and cheap transient housing; the furniture rental stores; the bleak landscapes with their hidden, unexploded mortars; the brief, unexplored friendships. This story grew out of the tension between the lax, temporary ethos and the tight, hot intensity of growing up in a big family, so permanent and interdependent you might spend a lifetime dreaming of release. I wanted "Luxury" to play one against the other in an almost unnoticeable way, barely suggesting the other possibilities, the way life tends to do.*

John Sayles

PEELING

(from *The Atlantic Monthly*)

"**M**udbugs coming!" Big Antoine calls, like he always does when he dumps them onto the table. Little Antoine, his father, used to have to step on a box to do it; Big handles a twenty-gallon can like it was a slop bucket. Big sweats a lot, even more since he took over the place, and he tries to be courtly.

"Good to see you ladies working so nice," he'll say, hurrying through, wiping his face with the towel he carries around his neck. "Y'all looking exceptional today."

They don't look up unless it's something special. Even when he dumps, crawfish spilling out red and steaming onto the shiny steel table, a new hill of legs and feelers and black-bead eyes, the women keep their faces in it, peeling. Big Antoine always has two cans on the fire. The one with the corn and onions and potatoes mixed in the boil is for the straight-up orders—two pounds or five on a round metal tray, "peel em yourself." In the other can the women put tail meat for the bisque and the gumbo and the *étouffée* and the po-boys.

"Tour bus just come up," Antoine says, shaking the can out. "Gonna keep you ladies busy."

It is Ophelia and Vinie and the new girl, LaTonya, and Ly and Jasmine and Pearl around the table, Vinie and Jasmine at opposite corners. They reach in and sweep a new little pile from the mound in the center.

"*Écrevisse, exercice*," says Ophelia, who still speaks French at home and likes to rhyme.

"Man make me hot, the way he sweat," Jasmine says.

"Ought to lose him some blubber."

"Nuh-uh." Jasmine raises her eyebrows the way she does when informing them of the latest scientific findings. "Man carry that much weight into his age, worst thing he can do is lose it. Like a drinkin man, past a certain point goin dry will just *kill* you."

"It depend on what the fat is *made* of," Pearl says. "Cajun man like Antoine, it's all butter fat. Everything they make is one stick of butter this, two stick of butter that. He want to lose weight, all it is he got to leave out that butter. It just melt away off his hips. But you take a man like Clarence Toussaint—"

"Butcher-man Clarence?"

"That's him. That man is *wide* and he's *solid*. Boys he grow up with call him Mudslide, cause he open his belt this big black belly come rumblin out—"

"*Mud*slide—"

"—and that is solid pork-chop fat. Man could run the marathon race every morning, eat on bean sprouts and water like them fashion ladies do, but that fat is goin nowhere."

"*Et qu'est-ce que c'est cela?* What this hangin over your chair?" Ophelia says, and the others giggle. Pearl is big, big and thick-armed and strong-coffee colored.

"Beignets," she says, taking no offense. "Which is mostly lard. Got a serious liking for beignets."

"It's not the lard that kills you, it's the sugar," Jasmine says. "You breathe that powdered sugar down your lungs, choke you right to death."

"It's no lie."

The conversation dies there and they are quiet awhile, peeling. Wet tearing sounds, tossing the meat to one side and the carcass to the other. They don't have a radio because Big Antoine says it interferes with his *Greatest Cajun Hits* tape, which they hear playing for the customers whenever the door swings open.

"Chank-a-chank," Ophelia says when the accordion sounds pump in, *"neuf à cinq."*

They are shucking crawfish like this for five minutes before Vinie finally says "Beer."

"What?"

Vinie usually has the last word, reacting after the fact to topics already filed and forgotten, as if she needs the time to consider all the possibilities.

"Beer. That's beer fat the man's luggin around. You ever see him put anything else in his mouth?"

Most of Big Antoine's trips through are to the cooler for another can of Dixie. On a busy day he'll do two six-packs.

"Man drink beer all day, never pees."

"How you know that?"

"Girlene is lookin right at the customer bathroom all day long, tells me she never see him go in." Girlene is the red-faced cashier down from Slidell. "And we know he can't *fit* in the employee bathroom. Man is made of beer."

"Beer and worry," Pearl says.

"He didn't worry," Vinie says, "he wouldn't squeeze through that doorway."

Vinie is small, with wispy gray hair and light brown eyes and wrinkled butterscotch skin. She wears glasses low on her nose and peers over them to the crawfish. She has a delicate way of peeling, quick and light, and is the only one without at least one Band-Aid on her fingers.

The new girl is wearing eight. On her first day Jasmine laid it down to her.

"Antoine got but two rules," she said. "No cursing allowed, and you got a cut, you put a Band-Aid on right away."

By noon the new girl's hands were raw and bleeding.

"You'll get used to it," Pearl said, being nice. "And then your hands will toughen up some."

"I don't want to get used to it," LaTonya said. "I want to get a real job."

The others all smiled then.

"This ain't real enough for you?"

"Girl wants one of those six-figure jobs."

"You find one, girl," Pearl said. "Don't give up on it. Don't be like us old-timers."

"*Sans rêve,*" Ophelia said, shrugging, "*pas de grève.*"

LaTonya had her hair braided African-style, which the others all admired but said they could never do themselves. The new girl was the only one of them under fifty, except maybe Ly, who was some kind of Asian and hard to figure.

"Me and my sisters had braids when we were girls," said Jasmine, who wore makeup to work, and a wig with straight bangs made of plastic that gave off oily rainbow highlights when the sun slanted through the little high window about four o'clock every day.

"You had to have some *length* to do it, but we Cherokee on my mother's side and we all had long black hair."

You can still see how pretty Jasmine was some forty, fifty years ago, with her high cheekbones and hazel eyes.

"She gonna tell us about Pocahontas again," Pearl said.

"That wasn't her name." Jasmine has this way of talking sometimes, like she's dealing with small children. "All I'm sayin is, it run us some *time*, dealin with them braids. I admire a young woman take some care with her appearance."

"I do it while I watch TV," LaTonya said. "It keeps my hands busy."

"You get some babies," Ophelia said, "you forget about your hair. *Zenfants n'arrêtent pour rien.*"

LaTonya looked to Vinie, who usually does the translating.

"She's tellin you enjoy it while you can," Vinie said, "cause them kids will run you to the *bone.*"

Mostly they work in silence, hours at a time, pulling off the head, ripping the body apart and squeezing the tail meat out with thumb and forefinger, stripping the blue-black vein when it's big enough to see. Pearl hums to herself sometimes, pretty, churchlike pieces of songs that make her face crease with feeling. Pearl is the only Baptist among them, and asks the others detailed questions about nuns. Do they get their monthlies, do they take baths together, do they have a special kind of underwear? Pearl is good for hours on the subject of nuns, and Ophelia likes to tell her wild stories. The new girl still gets mixed up and will put the meat on her left and the husk on her right and swear and then apologize to Jasmine. Ly never says anything and peels with seamless intensity, staring at the crawfish as if they might have a story to tell. When the silence is finally broken, they seem to have agreed to speak all at once, their talk like rain held too long in heavy clouds.

Jasmine usually starts it.

"There isn't no manner you can endure gainst the ways of the Devil," she says.

"Speakin for yourself," Pearl says.

"It's envy wakes the Devil up."

"Envy—"

"Got you a house, got a job, got a man—Devil wants a *taste* of that—"

Vinie sighs, shakes her head. "Here it comes," she says quietly.

"We gonna hear about *him* again," Pearl says.

"*La même histoire.*"

"Had me a man name of Lucien Beaucoup," Jasmine continues.

"Don't start." Vinie doesn't look up, but her hands are still.

LaTonya feels the tension and looks around. Older women, church women, women her mother's age, maybe even her grand-mother's. Jasmine pushes on.

"Pretty-lookin, sweet-smellin, church-goin man. Good to his mama. Worked him a job on the shrimp fleet, out of Delc'm—"

"She's bringin him back—"

"He was a young man then, just over with his schooling. Come round the back of my house, three nights out of four, and he *sings*. Wouldn't knock on the door, wouldn't wait up for me on my path to school, wouldn't tell no brags to the other boys. Cause he *shy*, see, and re*spect*ful. Not like what they got today."

"Not at all—"

"Little tiny boys with them big bold eyes. Impertinent."

"Lucien Beaucoup," Ophelia says, into the rhythm of it now.

"That's right, *Lu*cien."

"Singin out back—"

"Out back of my house whilst me and my sisters was helpin our mam with her mending. Three nights out of four."

"My mam took in mending too," Pearl says, coming in strong to head the story off. "Washing, mending, leatherwork. Could sole up some shoes. Learnt it from Papa fore he was kilt in France."

"What's he doing in France?" LaTonya asks.

"He was in the World War. The first one."

Vinie smiles. "You that old, Pearl?"

"This is after. He walked through that war thout a scratch on him. Come back home, five, six years pass, he get a letter from some woman in France."

"White woman," LaTonya says.

"That's what they got there, mostly. She say he's got him a little daughter he left behind, she needs him. He gets his money together, books a ride on a ocean liner. Goin to bring that little girl back."

"Her mama, too?"

"He didn't know bout that. Left my mam on the dock, carryin me inside her. She knew it, but hadn't got to tellin him yet."

"Went off to France."

"Went off to France. Town name of X. That's how you say it, like 'X marks the spot.'"

"Got a ticket to X—"

"Walks down the main street, goes to the address, knocks on the door, door opens—French girl papa standin there, BAM! Put a bullet smack in my papa head. Laid him *out*."

"Lord."

"French girl papa had her write that letter, just to bring him in front of his pistol. So my mam took up with Mr. Lester when she heard. Mr. Lester was behind all my brothers and sisters that come after."

"And you never seen your own."

"Not but a picture. Big handsome man in a uniform. He was a cobbler, and he left my mam with some knowledge of it. She always tell me the story when she workin on some shoes."

"Wonder what happened to that little French girl," LaTonya says.

"With her papa dead on the street and growin up mongst all them white people."

"Little French girl cost me knowin my own blood," Pearl says, flicking tail meat onto the counter. "She can *fry*."

The women are peeling, thinking about the French girl, when Jasmine starts to sing.

> *Jolie fille, jolie fille*
> *Écoutes-toi ma chanson—*

She closes her eyes, pulling their attention back.

> *T'es la reine de la ville*
> *La lumière et le son—*

She looks at them.

"That's a *fais dodo*," Ophelia says to LaTonya. "Bout how pretty this girl is to him. Queen of the world."

"That's what he sing," Jasmine says, "three nights out of four. My sisters look up from the mending, tease me something terrible. My cheeks would take color, my fingers trippin all over each other. Only thing worse was the nights he wouldn't come. Those nights my ears would hurt from listenin for his voice out back."

> *Jolie âme, jolies yeux*
> *Tellement douce et gentille—*

she sings—

> *T'es la reine de mon coeur*
> *La raison de ma vie.*

"Don't hear that kind of song no more," Ophelia says after a moment.

Pearl waves a crawfish in her hand as she talks. "Now they all got they own radio station, carry it up on their shoulder wherever they go, rattle the walls with that noise they put in their ears. Most of em is deaf to a normal voice." She realizes, turns to LaTonya. "No offense, darlin."

LaTonya shrugs. "S'not *my* music."

Jasmine raises her voice a little. "Lucien Beau*coup*. Church-goin, sweet-singin man. He come for *me*."

"It's the same old story—"

"All set to marry us at Mary Star of the Sea Church, down in Terrebonne Parish."

"Same sad story."

"We was *meant* for each other."

"Like beans and rice."

"Only the other one come between—"

"A snake in the garden—"

"With her yellow eyes—"

"Watch it now—"

"And her hot nasty words—"

"Careful—"

"The other one that come and wrecked up my life. Not cause he would have looked at her twice. But cause she worked the Devil on him. Cause she traffic with the dark spirits."

Vinie stands suddenly and walks off into the employees' washroom. Pearl and Ophelia slowly push their chairs away and then Ly and LaTonya join them, standing and stretching. Vinie is the one who asked Antoine for the five-minute break, so she gets to decide when to take it. Jasmine, tight-lipped, keeps peeling.

One by one the women go in to wash and dry their hands. Ly leans against the wall with her arms folded across her chest, eyes unfocused. She never speaks in English, though she seems to understand a little. Pearl mutters about her feet, shifting weight from one to the other, and LaTonya massages her fingers. She worries about the cuts, wondering if they'll ever heal, one scab peeling off and another starting to form. Vinie is serious about the five minutes, watching the second hand on the big clock on the wall, poised over her chair, then sitting back down on the click. She figures they should be honest, since Antoine gave it up without a fight.

"I don't see any problem in it," he'd said. "Long as my mudbugs keep coming."

Jasmine is frosty when they all sit around her again. She holds her chin tilted as if rising above pain or insult. The other women seem to ignore her.

"Might gonna rain pretty soon," Pearl says.

"Be a flood in my yard *s'il pleut*," Ophelia says.

"You livin down by the water these days?"

"*À côte du lac*. Little bitty rain, I got to walk ankle-deep to hang the laundry out, take it two days to drain."

"I'm up on a hill now," LaTonya says.

"Us too."

They work awhile, Pearl humming and rocking as she peels. Vinie breaks the silence.

"I come through the flood of thirty-five," she says.

"That were some high water."

"My mam was workin for a man name Buster Petite," Vinie says. "Lived over in Plaquemine. Had the rheumatism in both his legs, sit up all day in this rocker chair, wavin his cane, yellin out orders. Kept my mam on the run from the minute she set foot in that house till the minute she feed him his hot milk in bed at night."

"*Ma mère ne bouge pour ce bruit*. Always tell her people, 'Case you didn't hear, M'sieur Lincoln freed the slaves.'"

"You got to train em," Pearl says. "Most of your white folks is capable of learnin, long as you got *patience*."

"Like Antoine."

"Big Antoine is *noth*ing. You remember his daddy—"

"Little Antoine a holy terror in his day. We had some *wars* with that man, God rest his soul."

"Amen."

"This was other times," Vinie says. "White people was outa control in them days." She turns to Ly. "You maybe weren't here, Miss Ly, but that's the truth."

"She don't understand you, Vinie."

"Sure she does."

Ly doesn't acknowledge that they're talking about her.

"Woman is from Vietnam. Talk that goulash."

"That's a food, not a *lan*guage."

"I heard her talk it once, sound like goulash to me."

"Yo, Miss Ly, you from Vietnam?"

"She from someplace worse than here, I bet."

"Don't be mean. Where you from, miss?"

Ly just looks at them, not comprehending, or pretending not to.

"See? She don't even know that."

"So what happened to Buster Petite?" LaTonya asks.

The women all look at the new girl.

"These young ones always in a hurry," Jasmine says, breaking her silence. "Got no patience atall."

Vinie sighs. "Mr. Petite see the first rain comin, he says it won't amount to spit in a windstorm. But my mam knows different. She seen the yard animals actin up, yellow dog eatin dirt, chickens walkin backwards, house cats walkin with they tails low. But the old man says his legs tell him no, and that they don't ever lie."

"My knees just fill up, ever it's gonna rain," Ophelia says.

"My ankles start to hurtin," Pearl says.

"Mr. Petite wouldn't let my mam pull him outa there. Water's up to the top of the porch, leakin in under the front door, he still says it's just a shower. He runs that cane under the arms of his rocker and grip hold and says, 'Here I sit, come hell or high water.' The windows bust through then and Mam grab me up and run into the attic, us and Buster Petite fifteen house cats, all of em jumpin on us and diggin in with they claws, tryin to push close."

"Hell or high water," Pearl muses. "Nothin on earth more stubborn than a old white man."

"Man has that many cats," Ophelia says, "you got to *won*der."

"Them cats in Mam's hair," Vinie says, "up my back, yawlin and scratchin, and all the while Buster Petite downstairs yellin like he's in a rumpus with the Devil—'Get back!' he yells. 'Get back, dammit, this *my* house.' There was bangin then, and we look out the little attic window and see it's telephone poles, tore loose and come runnin by in the floodwater. Levee broke under and there's all manner of things afloat and we can't hear no Buster Petite any-more."

"Man sound nasty," Pearl says. "I hate to hear a man yellin out orders in a house."

"*Les blancs de ma mère* had a buzzer for a while. I'd be down in the quarters with the others that worked for them. Sound go right up my spine, every time they push it."

Pearl and Vinie nod. Antoine blasts through and then crosses back out with a cold can of Dixie sweating in his hand. Cajun music pounds in, fades as the door closes behind him.

Jasmine hasn't given up. "You ever hear the sound of a woman had her heart pulled out of her?"

"Uh-oh."

"Listen what come to life," Vinie says.

LaTonya looks around and sees that the others have resigned themselves to whatever is coming next.

"I had me a man name of Lucien Beaucoup," Jasmine says.

"I heard that name before."

"That man was de*vo*ted to me. Promised to hold me up like the night holds the stars."

"You hear violins playin?"

"But another woman laid her greedy eyes on him. Woman that traffic with the dark spirits, woman stoop to *gris-gris* cause she couldn't catch a man no other way."

"Gettin personal now—"

"First she take the egg from a black hen, write my name on it backwards, and throw it clear over my house. Make me burn with a fever. My eyes swole up tight, skin prickle like it's a million ants crawlin on me—" She wiggles her fingers around her neck and makes a face. "Then she take a cock rooster and bury him up to his neck in the yard, so's he can see but he can't move. She let another rooster into the yard, and first he have at all the hens, and that buried rooster comb fill up with angry, and then he peck the buried rooster's eyes out and she cut that comb full to burstin with angry off and hang it in a frog-leather pouch between her titties. Next day she pass Lucien Beaucoup on the lane, says 'Mornin, Mr. Beaucoup' all honey-voiced and cow-eyed, but he pay her no mind cause she's ugly as warts on a dog. After he pass, she write his name in the dirt and spit on it and circle it nine times walkin backwards, holdin on to that cockscomb. Next mornin she see him on the path, she don't say a word, but he fall like a shot bird right down into her arms. Charm had *worked*. That moment I broke from the fever, sweat gone *cold* on my body, and I sensed I'd lost him forever. I set up a wail then—my sisters say it chilled the blood and sent the hound runnin under the house to hide. Done pulled the heart right outa me."

A long silence. LaTonya is unsettled by the passion of Jasmine's telling, her hands frozen over her tiny pile of crawfish .

Pearl notices. "Can't spect you to keep up with the rest of us," she says gently, "but you got to *try*."

"Sorry." LaTonya plunges her hands back into it.

"It's just Antoine, he sees six women in here, he dump six women worth of mudbugs on the table."

Landry, the day cook, comes in then to shovel up the tail meat they've peeled and bring it back to the kitchen. Landry reports on what people are eating.

"Boudin's not movin," he says. "Dirty rice just sittin there. They all went for the blackened fish." He makes a disgusted face. "Must be from out of state."

The women hold to their rhythm when he's gone. LaTonya's heart always sinks a little when she sees her morning work disappear as if it never existed. Fifteen minutes pass before Vinie speaks.

"He just give up on you," she says simply.

Jasmine frowns. "Somebody talkin?"

"He got tired of sittin outside your window all night, waitin for you to decide. He went to find him a live woman."

"I feel a bad wind, like somebody *talk*in—"

The two women keep their eyes on the table, fingers flying. "Got tired of you protectin what didn't nobody else *want*. Give it up for a bad idea."

Jasmine slaps down tail meat. "How you know that?"

"Cause Lucien *told* me, is how! I live with the man fifty years, you don't think he *talk* to me?"

LaTonya has never heard Vinie raise her voice before. The two women lock eyes across the table for a moment and then look away.

Jasmine mutters just loud enough for the others to hear, "My mama's day they'd have hung you for a witch."

Vinie works this in her head a moment, frowning, building an answer. She doesn't get to say it.

The first thing Ly shouts is more like an animal cry than language. The rest, as it comes out, is loud and passionate and singsong, harsh and deep one moment, climbing to an airy whine the next, Ly looking to each of them for confirmation as she rails. LaTonya sits staring next to her, pummeled by the sounds, feeling loss and betrayal and deep anger behind them. Ly's neck is taut, face darkening, her wiry body straining to wrench the words out. She holds a crawfish tight in her fist, crushing it as she pounds the table for emphasis.

She doesn't stop so much as run out of breath. The storm is over as suddenly as it began, and Ly sits looking into the center of the crawfish pile. Big Antoine pokes his head in.

"Something the matter, ladies?"

"Not a thing, Antoine."

He nods at Ly. "She's not peeling."

"She does em faster than us," Pearl says. "Ever little bit she's got to stop and let all us catch up."

Antoine shrugs. "Long as that meat keep coming." He wipes his face with the towel and goes back out.

"She does that sometimes," Pearl tells LaTonya. "No sayin what sets her off."

"She had a hard life, *la pauvre*," Ophelia says. "You can see it in her face."

The older women sigh.

"Gonna rain."

"Feel it in my knees."

"Feel it in my ankles."

LaTonya watches Ly's hands as they slowly come to life, ripping heads, peeling. "What happened to the old man?" she asks.

"Old man?"

"Old man. Buster Petite."

"He *drown*ded, girl," Vinie says. "What you think? That were the flood of thirty-five, couldn't no old man in a rocker chair sit through that."

LaTonya nods. "Your mother must have been relieved."

"*Relieved?* Child, you ever seen someplace after the floodwaters run off? She had to *clean* that house. Only thing made her happy in the whole business was when the water got up under the attic window and she throw Buster Petite cats out, one by one, and watch em float away. I helped her catch em. Cats near clawed my mam to death."

"Some folks say," Jasmine says, "whoever kill a cat gonna hear it wailin every night for the rest of their life."

Vinie glances up at her. "I sleep fine," she says. "Sleep like the *dead*."

Toward quitting time LaTonya's thumb splits open.

"Damn," she says.

"No cursin," Jasmine says.

Pearl puts a Band-Aid on it. "You just sit it out till five, darlin," she says. "We give Antoine plenty crawfish today."

"I'm not pulling my weight."

"You got plenty years to run past us."

"Not if I can help it."

"Might be you *can't* help it," Vinie says. "Don't want you thinkin that way, but it might be an actual fact. I been here some twenty-five years."

"*Vingt-trois, moi.*"

"Me too."

"I went to school," LaTonya protests.

The older women smile.

"Well, child, I guess you got no problem."

When the women get up to wash their hands and gather their things, Ly sits, staring at the remaining crawfish. Ophelia touches her shoulder.

"*Viens avec nous, mon ti,*" she says. "Whatever it is weighin on you, it's all in your head now."

But Ly is still there when the night women come in to take their places, peeling.

———————

John Sayles is the author of three novels, *Pride of the Bimbos, Union Dues,* and *Los Gusanos,* and a story anthology, *The Anarchists' Convention.* He is a screenwriter and the director of several films. He is currently at work on another story collection, *Dillinger in Hollywood.*

"Peeling" *was originally several scenes in a film script for the movie* Passionfish, *set in southwestern Louisiana. The characters were originally women who worked as domestics, who waited at the same bus stop to go out to their jobs in suburban Lafayette. The rhythm of their conversation comes from several jobs I've had where conversation between the employees was not only possible but necessary to break the tedium of the work. When I cut the "bus ladies" from the script for reasons of length, I'd stored them away with the idea of making a short story. On a British travel/cooking show there was a segment on the workers who shell crawfish at a restaurant and I realized that was the perfect setting.*

Richard Bausch

AREN'T YOU HAPPY FOR ME?

(from *Harper's Magazine*)

William Coombs, with two 'O's," Melanie Ballinger told her father over long distance. "Pronounced just like the thing you comb your hair with. Say it."

Ballinger repeated the name.

"Say the whole name."

"I've got it, sweetheart. Why am I saying it?"

"Dad, I'm bringing him home with me. We're getting *married*."

For a moment, he couldn't speak.

"Dad? Did you hear me?"

"I'm here," he said.

"Well?"

Again he couldn't say anything.

"Dad?"

"Yes," he said. "That's—that's some news."

"That's all you can say?"

"Well, I mean—Melanie—this is sort of quick, isn't it?" he said.

"Not that quick. How long did you and Mom wait?"

"I don't remember. Are you measuring yourself by that?"

"You waited six months, and you do too remember. And this is five months. And we're not measuring each other by anything. William and I have known each other longer than five months, but we've been together—you know, as a couple—five months. And

I'm almost twenty-three, which is two years older than Mom was. And don't tell me it was different when *you* guys did it."

"No," he heard himself say. "It's pretty much the same, I imagine."

"Well?" she said.

"Well," Ballinger said. "I'm—I'm very happy for you."

"You don't *sound* happy."

"I'm happy. I can't wait to meet him."

"Really? Promise? You're not just saying that?"

"It's good news, darling. I mean, I'm surprised, of course. It'll take a little getting used to. The—the suddenness of it and everything. I mean, your mother and I didn't even know you were seeing anyone. But no, I'm—I'm glad. I can't wait to meet the young man."

"Well, and now there's something *else* you have to know."

"I'm ready," John Ballinger said. He was standing in the kitchen of the house she hadn't seen yet, and outside the window his wife, Mary, was weeding in the garden, wearing a red scarf and a white muslin blouse and jeans, looking young and even happy, though for a long while now there had been between them very little happiness.

"Well, this one's kind of hard," his daughter said over the thousand miles of wire. "Maybe we should talk about it later."

"No. I'm sure I can take whatever it is," he said.

The truth was that he had news of his own to tell. Almost a week ago now, he and Mary had agreed on a separation. Some time for them both to sort things out. They had decided not to say anything about it to Melanie until she arrived. But now Melanie had said that she was bringing someone with her.

She was hemming and hawing on the other end of the line: "I don't know . . . See, Daddy, I—God. I mean, I can't find the way to say it really."

He waited. She was in Chicago, where they had sent her to school more than four years ago, and where after her graduation she had stayed, having landed a job with an independent newspaper in the city. In March, Ballinger and Mary had moved to this small house in the middle of Charlottesville, Virginia, hoping that a change of scene might help things. It hadn't; they were falling apart after all these years.

"Dad," Melanie said, sounding helpless.

"Honey, I'm listening."

"Okay, look," she said. "Will you promise you won't react?"

"How can I promise a thing like that, Melanie?"

"You're going to react, then. I wish you could just promise me you wouldn't."

"Darling," he said. "I've got something to tell you, too. Promise me *you* won't react."

She said *promise* in that way the young have of being absolutely certain what their feelings will be in some future circumstance.

"So," he said. "Now, tell me whatever it is." And a thought struck him like a shock. "Melanie, you're not—you're not pregnant, are you?"

She said, "How did you *know*?"

He felt something sharp move under his heart. "Oh, Lord—seriously?"

"Jeez," she said. "Wow. That's really amazing."

"You're—*pregnant.*"

"Right. My God. You're positively clairvoyant, Dad."

"I really don't think it's a matter of any clairvoyance, Melanie, from the way you were talking. Are you—is it sure?"

"Of course it's sure. But—I mean, that isn't the really hard thing. Maybe I should just wait."

"Wait," he said. "Wait for what?"

"Until you get used to everything else."

He said nothing. She was fretting on the other end of the line, sighing and starting to speak and then stopping herself.

"I don't know," she said finally, and now he thought she was talking to someone in the room with her.

"Honey, do you want me to put your mother on?"

"No, Daddy. I wanted to talk to you about this first. I mean, I think we should get this over with."

"Get this over with? Melanie, what're we talking about here? I mean, maybe I should put your mother on." He thought he might try a joke. "After all," he added, "I've never been pregnant."

"It's not about being pregnant. You *guessed* that."

He held the phone tight against his ear. Through the window he saw his wife stand up from the flowers and stretch, massaging the small of her back with one gloved hand. *Oh, Mary.*

"Are you ready?" his daughter said.

"Wait," he said. "Wait a minute. Should I be sitting down? I'm sitting down." He pulled a chair from the table and settled into it. He could hear her breathing on the other end of the line, or perhaps now it was the static wind he so often heard when talking on these new phones. "Okay," he said, feeling his throat begin to close. "Tell me."

"William's somewhat older than I am," she said. Now she sounded as though she might hyperventilate. "There."

He left a pause. "That's it?"

"Well, it's how much."

"Okay."

She seemed to be trying to collect herself. She breathed, paused. "This is even tougher than I thought it was going to be."

"You mean you're going to tell me something harder than the fact that you're pregnant?"

She was silent.

"Melanie?"

"I didn't expect you to be this way about it," she said.

"Honey, please just tell me the rest of it."

"Well, what did you mean by that, anyway?"

"Melanie, *you* said this would be hard."

Silence.

"Tell me, sweetie. Please?"

"I'm going to." She took a breath. "Dad, William's sixty—he's—he's sixty—sixty-three years old."

Ballinger stood. Out in the garden his wife had got down to her knees again, pulling crabgrass out of the bed of tulips. It was a sunny near-twilight, and all along the shady street, people were working in their little orderly spaces of grass and flowers.

"Did you hear me, Daddy? It's perfectly all right, too, because he's really a *young* sixty-three, and *very* strong and healthy, and look at George Burns."

"George Burns," Ballinger repeated. "George Burns? Melanie, I don't understand."

"Come on, Daddy, stop it."

"What are you telling me?" he said. His mind was blank.

"I said William is sixty-three."

"William who?"

"Dad. My *fiancé.*"

"Wait, Melanie. You're saying your fiancé—the man you're going to marry—*he's* sixty-three?"

"A young sixty-three," she said.

"Melanie. Sixty-three?"

"Dad."

"You didn't say six *feet* three?"

She was silent.

"Melanie?"

"Yes."

"Honey, this is a joke, right? You're playing a joke on me."

"It is not a—it's not that. God," she said. "I don't believe this."

"You don't believe—" he began. "You don't believe—"

"Dad," she said. "I told you—" Again she seemed to be talking to someone else in the room with her. Her voice trailed off.

"Melanie," he said. "Talk into the phone."

"I know it's hard," she told him. "I know it's asking you to take a lot in."

"Well, no," Ballinger said, feeling something shift inside, a quickening in his blood. "It's—it's a little more than that, Melanie, isn't it? I mean, it's not a weather report, for God's sake."

"I should've known," she said.

"Forgive me for it," he said. "But I have to ask you something . . ."

"It's all right, Daddy," she began, as if reciting it for him. "I really know what I'm doing. I'm not really rushing into anything—"

He interrupted her. "Well, good God, somebody rushed into *something*, right?"

"Daddy!"

"Is that what you call him? No, *I'm* Daddy—you have to call him *Grand*daddy."

"That is *not* funny," she said.

"I wasn't being funny, Melanie, and anyway that wasn't my question." He took a breath. "Please forgive this, but I have to know."

"There's nothing you really *have* to know, Daddy. I'm an adult. I'm telling you out of family courtesy."

"I understand that. Family courtesy exactly. Exactly, Melanie, that's a good phrase. Would you please tell me, out of family courtesy, if the baby is his."

"Yes." Her voice was small now, coming from a long way off.

"I am sorry for the question. I just have to put all this together. I mean, you're asking me to take in a whole lot here, you know?"

"I said I understood how you feel."

"I don't think so. I don't think you quite understand how I feel."

"All right," she said. "I don't understand how you feel. But I think I knew how you'd react."

For a few seconds there was just the low sea-sound of long distance.

"Melanie, have you done any of the math on this?"

"I should've bet money," she said in the tone of a person who has been proven right about something.

"Well, but Jesus," Ballinger said. "I mean, he's older than *I* am, kid. He's—he's a *lot* older than I am." The number of years seemed to dawn on him as he spoke. "Honey, nineteen years. When he was my age I was only two years older than you are now."

"I don't see what that has to do with anything," she said.

"Melanie, I'll be forty-five in December. I'm a *young* forty-four."

"I know when your birthday is, Dad."

"Well, good God—this guy's nineteen years older than your *own father*."

She said, "I've grasped the numbers. Maybe you should go ahead and put Mom on."

"Melanie, you couldn't pick somebody a little closer to my age? Some snot-nosed forty-year-old?"

"Stop it," she said. "Please, Daddy. I know what I'm doing."

"Do you know how old he's going to be when your baby is ten? Do you? Have you given that any thought at all?"

She was silent.

He said, "How many children are you hoping to have?"

"I'm not thinking about that. Any of that. This is now, and I don't care about anything else."

He sat down in his kitchen and tried to think of something else to say. Outside the window his wife, with no notion of what she was about to be hit with, looked through the patterns of shade in the blinds and, seeing him, waved. It was friendly, but even so, all their difficulty was in it. Ballinger waved back. "Melanie," he said, "do you mind telling me just where you happened to meet William? I mean, how do you meet a person forty years older than you are? Was there a senior citizen–student mixer at the college?"

"Stop it, Daddy."

"No, I really want to know. If I'd just picked this up and read it in the newspaper I think I'd want to know. I'd probably call the newspaper and see what I could find out."

"Put Mom on," she said.

"Just tell me how you met. You can do that, can't you?"

"Jesus Christ," she said, then paused.

Ballinger waited.

"He's a teacher, like you and Mom, only college. He was my literature teacher. He's a professor of literature. He knows everything that was ever written, and he's the most brilliant man I've ever known. You have no idea how fascinating it is just to talk with him."

"Yes, and I guess you understand that over the years that's what you're going to be doing a *lot* of with him, Melanie. A lot of *talking*."

"I am carrying the proof that disproves *you*," she said.

He couldn't resist saying, "Did *he* teach you to talk like that?"

"I'm gonna hang up."

"You promised you'd listen to something I had to tell you."

"Okay," she said crisply. "I'm listening."

He could imagine her tapping the toe of one foot on the floor: the impatience of someone awaiting an explanation. He thought a moment. "He's a professor?"

"That's not what you wanted to tell me."

"But you said he's a professor."

"Yes, I said that."

"Don't be mad at me, Melanie. Give me a few minutes to get used to the idea. Jesus. Is he a professor emeritus?"

"If that means distinguished, yes. But I know what you're—"

"No, Melanie. It means *retired*. You went to college."

She said nothing.

"I'm sorry but, for God's sake, it's a legitimate question."

"It's a stupid, mean-spirited thing to ask." He could tell from her voice that she was fighting back tears.

"Is he there with you now?"

"Yes," she said, sniffling.

"Oh, Jesus Christ."

"Daddy, why are you being this way?"

"Do you think maybe we could've had this talk alone? What's he, listening on the other line?"

"No."

"Well, thank God for that."

"I'm going to hang up now."

"No, now please don't hang up. Please let's just be calm and talk about this. We have some things to talk about here."

She sniffled, blew her nose. Someone held the phone for her. There was a muffled something in the line, and then she was there again. "Go ahead," she said.

"Is he still there in the room with you?"

"Yes." Her voice was defiant.

"Where?"

"Oh, for God's sake," she said.

"I'm sorry, I feel the need to know. Is he sitting down?"

"I *want* him here, Daddy. We both want to be here," she said.

"And he wants to marry you."

"Yes," she said impatiently.

"Do you think I could talk to him?"

She said something he couldn't hear, and then there were several seconds of some sort of discussion, in whispers. Finally she said, "Do you promise not to yell at him?"

"Melanie, he wants me to promise not to *yell* at him?"

"Will you promise?"

"Good God, who *is* this guy?"

"Promise," she said. "Or I'll hang up right now."

"All right. I promise. I promise not to yell at him."

There was another small scuffing sound, and a man's voice came through the line. "Hello, sir." It was—as far as Ballinger could tell—an ordinary voice, slightly lower than baritone. He thought of cigarettes. "I realize this is a difficult—"

"Do you smoke?" Ballinger interrupted him.

"No, sir."

"All right. Go on."

"Well, I want you to know I understand how you feel—"

"Melanie says she does, too," Ballinger said. "I mean, I'm certain you both *think* you do."

"It was my idea that Melanie call you about this."

"Oh, really. That speaks well of you. You probably knew I'd find this a little difficult to absorb and that's why you waited until Melanie was pregnant, for Christ's sake."

The other man gave forth a small sigh of exasperation.

"So you're a professor of literature."

"Yes, sir."

"Oh, you needn't 'sir' me. After all, I mean *I* am the goddamn kid here."

"There's no need for sarcasm now, sir."

"Oh, I wasn't being sarcastic. That was a literal statement of this situation that obtains right here as we're speaking. And, really, Mr.—it's Coombs, right?"

"Yes, sir."

"Coombs like the thing you comb your hair with."

The other man was quiet.

"Just how long do you think it'll take me to get used to this? You think you might get into your seventies before I get used to this? And how long do you think it'll take my wife, who's twenty-one years younger than you are, to get used to this?"

Silence.

"You're too old for my *wife,* for Christ's sake."

Nothing.

"What's your first name again?"

The other man spoke through another sigh. "Perhaps we should just ring off."

"Ring off. Jesus. Ring off? Did you actually say 'Ring off'? What're you, a goddamn *limey* or something?"

"I am an *American.* I fought in Korea."

"Not World War II?"

The other man did not answer.

"How many other marriages have you had?" Ballinger asked him.

"That's a valid question. I'm glad you—"

"Thank you for the scholarly observation, sir. But I'm not sitting in a class now. How many did you say?"

"If you'd give me a chance, I'd tell you."

Ballinger said nothing.

"Two, sir. I've had two marriages."

"Divorces?"

"I have been widowed twice."

"And now—oh, I get it. Now you're trying to make sure that never happens to you again."

"This is not going well at all, and I'm afraid I—I—" The other man stammered, then stopped.

"How did you expect it to go?" Ballinger demanded.

"Cruelty is not what I'd expected. I'll tell you that."

"You thought I'd be glad my daughter is going to be collecting social security before I do."

The other was silent.

"Do you have any other children?" Ballinger asked.

"Yes, I happen to have three." There was a stiffness, an overweening tone, in the voice now.

"And how old are they, if I might ask?"

"Yes, you may."

Ballinger waited. His wife walked in from outside, carrying some cuttings. She poured water in a glass vase and stood at the counter, arranging the flowers, her back to him. The other man had stopped talking. "I'm sorry," Ballinger said. "My wife just walked in here and I didn't catch any of what you said. Could you just tell me if any of them are anywhere near my daughter's age?"

"I told you my youngest boy is thirty-eight."

"And you realize that if *he* wanted to marry my daughter I'd be upset—the age difference there being what it is."

Ballinger's wife now moved to his side, drying her hands on a paper towel, her face full of puzzlement and worry.

"I told you, Mr. Ballinger, that I understood how you feel. The point is we have a pregnant woman here and we both love her."

"No," Ballinger said. "That's not the point. The point is that you, sir, are not much more than a goddamn statutory rapist. That's the point." His wife took his shoulder. He looked at her and shook his head.

"What?" she whispered. "Is Melanie all right?"

"Well, this isn't accomplishing anything—" the voice on the other end of the line was saying.

"Just a minute," Ballinger said. "Let me ask you something else. Really now, what's the policy at that goddamn university concerning teachers screwing their students?"

"Oh, my God!" his wife said, as the voice on the line huffed and seemed to gargle.

"I'm serious," Ballinger said.

"Melanie was not my student when we became involved."

"Is that what you call it, 'involved'?"

"Let me talk to Melanie," Ballinger's wife said.

"Listen," he told her. "Be quiet."

And now Melanie was on the line. "Daddy? Daddy?"

"I'm here," Ballinger said, holding the phone from his wife's attempt to take it from him.

"Daddy, we're getting married and there's nothing you can do about it. Do you understand?"

"Melanie," he said, and it seemed that somewhere far inside himself he heard that he had begun shouting at her. "Jee-zus good Christ. Your fiancé was almost *my* age *now* the day you were born. What the hell, kid? Are you crazy? Are you out of your mind?"

Now his wife was actually pushing against him to take the phone, and so he gave it to her. And stood there while she tried to talk.

"Melanie," she said. "Honey, listen—"

"Hang up," Ballinger said. "Christ. Hang it up."

"Please. Will you go in the other room and let me talk to her?"

"Tell her I've got friends. All these nice men in their forties. She can marry any one of my friends—they're babies. Forties—cradle fodder. Jesus, any one of them. Tell her."

"Jack, stop it." Then she put the phone against her chest. "Did you tell her anything about us?"

He paused. "That—no."

She turned from him. "Melanie, honey. What is this? Tell me, please—"

He left her there, walked through the living room to the hall and back around to the kitchen. He was all nervous energy now, crazy with it, pacing. Mary stood very still, listening, nodding slightly, holding the phone tight, with both hands, her shoulders hunched as if she were out in cold weather.

"Mary," he said.

Nothing.

He went into their bedroom and closed the door. The light coming from the windows was soft gold, and the room was deepening with shadows. He moved to the bed and sat down, and in a moment he noticed that he had begun a low sort of murmuring. He took a breath and tried to be still. From the other room his wife's voice came to him. "Yes, I quite agree with you. But I'm just unable to put this—"

The voice trailed off. He waited. A few minutes later she came to the door and knocked lightly, then looked in.

"What?" he said.

"They're serious." She stood there in the doorway.

"Come here," he said.

She took a step to the bed and eased herself down, and he moved slightly to accommodate her. He put his arm around her, and then, because it was awkward, clearly an embarrassment to her, took it away. Neither of them could speak for a time. Everything they had been through during the course of deciding about each other seemed concentrated now. Ballinger breathed his wife's presence, the odor of earth and flowers, the outdoors.

"God," she said now, "I'm numb. I don't know what to think."

"Let's have another baby," he said suddenly. "Melanie's baby will need a younger aunt or uncle."

Mary was silent.

"Did you tell her about us?" he asked.

"No." She sighed. "I didn't get the chance. And I don't know that I could have."

"I don't suppose it's going to matter much to her."

"Oh, don't say that. You can't mean that."

The telephone on the bedstand rang and startled them both. He reached for it, held the handset toward her.

"Hello," she said. Then, "Oh. Hi. Yes, well, here." She gave it back to him.

"Hello," he said.

Melanie's voice, tearful and angry: "You had something you said you had to tell me." She sobbed, then coughed. "Well?"

"It was nothing, honey. I don't even remember what it was."

"Well, I want you to know I would've been *better* than you were, Daddy, no matter how hard it was. I would've kept myself from reacting."

"Yes," he said. "I'm sure you would have."

"I'm going to hang up now. And I guess I'll let you know later if we're coming at all. If it wasn't for Mom we wouldn't be."

"We'll talk," he told her. "We'll work on it. Honey, you've both just got to give us a little time."

"There's nothing to work on as far as William and I are concerned."

"Of course there are things to work on. Every marriage—" His voice had caught. He took a breath. "In every marriage there are things to work on."

"I know what I know," she said.

"Well," said Ballinger. "That's—that's as it should be at your age, darling."

"Good-bye," she said. "I can't say any more right now."

"I understand." When the line clicked, Ballinger held the handset in his lap for a moment. Mary was sitting there at his side, perfectly still.

"Well," he said. "I couldn't tell her." He put the handset back in its cradle. Then he said, "God. A sixty-three-year-old son-in-law."

"It's happened before." She put her hand on his shoulder, then took it away. "I'm so frightened for her. But she says it's what she wants."

"Hell, Mary. You know what this is. The son of a bitch was her goddamn teacher."

"Listen to you—what are you saying about her? Listen to what you're saying about her. That's our daughter you're talking about.

You might at least try to give her the credit of assuming that she's aware of what she's doing."

They sat there for a few moments.

"Who knows," Ballinger's wife said. "Maybe they'll be happy for a time."

He'd heard the note of sorrow in her voice and thought he knew what she was thinking, then he was certain that he knew. He sat there remembering, like Mary, their early happiness, that ease and simplicity—and briefly he was in another house, other rooms, and he saw the toddler that Melanie had been, trailing through slanting light in a brown hallway, draped in gowns she had fashioned from her mother's clothes. He did not know why that particular image should have come to him out of the flow of years, but for a fierce minute it was uncannily near him in the breathing silence; it went over him palpably, like something on his skin, then was gone. He looked at his wife, but she had averted her gaze, her hands running absently over the faded denim cloth of her lap.

Finally she stood. "Well," she sighed, going away. "Work to do."

"Mary?" he said in a low voice, but she hadn't heard him. She was already out of the doorway and into the hall, moving toward the kitchen. He reached over and turned on the lamp by the bed, and then lay down. It was so quiet here now. Dark was coming to the windows. On the wall there were pictures; shadows, shapes silently clamoring for his gaze. He shut his eyes, listened to the small sounds she made in the kitchen, arranging her flowers, running the tap. *Mary*, he had said. But he could not imagine what he might have found to say, if his voice had reached her.

Richard Bausch lives in rural Virginia with his wife, Karen, and their five children. His most recent books are the novels *Violence* and *Rebel Powers* and the collection *Rare and Endangered Species*. His stories have appeared in *The Atlantic Monthly, Esquire, Harper's Magazine, The New Yorker, Redbook, The Southern Review, Glimmer Train,* and other magazines, and he has been widely anthologized, including *The Granta Book of the American Short Story, Best American Short Stories, New Stories from the South,* and *O. Henry Prize Stories.* He is currently on a Lila Wallace–Reader's Digest Writer's Award, which has allowed him to devote full time to his writing. In May 1993, he received an award from The American Academy of Arts and Letters.

M*y memory of composing "Aren't You Happy for Me?" is a bit sketchy—it was written during a period when I was working on several things at the same time. I seemed to hear the conversation on the phone as I began to write, and I let it go where it seemed to want to go from there. It took about a week, I think, to finish. I don't remember that I had any theme in mind, nor any particular idea as to how it would come out, though I did know quite well what the young woman had to tell her father.*

But my most pleasant memory about this story is what it was like telling friends I'd sold it. I had such fun with that:

"I sold a new story."

"Oh, well, that's nice. What's the title of it?"

"Aren't You Happy for Me?"

"I'm very happy. Don't I sound happy? I just said it was nice. What's the story called?"

"Aren't You Happy for Me?"

"I just said I was happy, for God's sake. Tell me the title."

You get the idea.

Pamela Erbe

SWEET TOOTH

(from *The Antioch Review*)

The big topic of conversation at PopPop's viewing was how he died with every tooth God gave him in his head and only two cavities in seventy-two years. Imagine! The fact that there were thirty-six teeth beneath the skin the embalmer had puckered a little around the mouth was considered a significant achievement, as much admired as his years of service as an organizer and officer of the carpenters' union. Fourteen of his fifteen brothers and sisters were still living when he died, and they all came, even Great-Aunt Edna, all the way from Florida, riding with Uncle Rollo in the two-tone. Dressed in Sunday clothes, they took turns clustering coffin-side in groups of two or three. They stood among the funeral wreaths big as Buick tires sent by the AF of L and the CIO and the Carpenters, Teamsters, Lions, and BPOEs, and greeted old friends and third cousins and total strangers.

I remember Great-Aunt Edna, whose figure was the type described in those days as *stout,* standing by a spray of bright orange glads arranged in the shape of a cross, Great-Aunt Edna in a shiny emerald-green and black dress with a little black hat perched jauntily, like a parakeet, on her head and attached to it, a black net veil that covered the top half of her face. In her hand she clutched a perfumed hanky as she talked to a big union man in a fur-collared overcoat who had come to pay the members' respects.

He bent over my grandmother and spoke quietly to her, shook hands with a few men he knew, drifted over to the coffin, checking his watch as he went, and stood next to Edna with his head bowed as if in prayer. My great-aunt leaned his way. "Joe's still got all his teeth," she told him. "Thirty-six, including wisdom, and only two fillings. Pinholes, hardly worth mentioning. Beautiful teeth, white as laundry day. It's a shame they don't show. How many people do you know who can say they died with every tooth God gave them in their heads?"

The union man blinked at Great-Aunt Edna's non sequitur. "Just about none," he said after a moment.

She nodded, satisfied. "I'm Edna Banks, née Woodhouse," she said, "sister of the deceased. He was the only one among the sixteen of us—well, fifteen were living after we lost my oldest brother Cleveland last year—the only one with all his teeth. And you are—?"

"Michael Maltesta," the union man said. "A professional acquaintance."

"Thank you so much for coming," said Great-Aunt Edna. My brother would have been so happy to see you." She lifted the veil with one hand and dabbed at her eye corners with the other.

My grandfather had known a lot of people, and close to three hundred signed the guest book, including Buster Tumbridge. I saw him come in, I saw how he hesitated in the doorway, then eased into the room and pulled the hat off his head with such effort that it looked like the hat was part of his body, as if he were pulling off an arm or a leg. He stood there for a moment, scanning the room. When people noticed him there, their backs stiffened, they stood up straighter and craned to get a better look to be sure, yes, it was Buster. Each time, in response to being recognized, Buster bobbed his head in a gesture half nod, half ducking a blow. Then he made for the coffin and gripped the side of it like a ship's rail, and leaned in and looked the body up and down, as if he had to see for himself that it was really Joe Woodhouse in there, not some impostor.

"He looks good, don't he?" said Buster to Great-Uncle Harvey from Hagerstown, who was on greeting duty at the coffin just then. "Looks like hisself."

Harvey made a face. He had a degree and a house with two bathrooms, and it was clear from across the room that he hadn't much to say to a man who used improper pronouns and who came to a viewing in a pilly cardigan and a hat whose crown was rimmed with ancient sweat stains. "It was an unexpected blow," said Harvey, half turning away from Buster as he spoke. "He was a healthy man, extremely fit, you know."

"That he was," Buster agreed. "Strong as a ox."

"None of us thought Joseph would be next, after my brother Cleveland," said Harvey, who was in his eighties. "Cleveland passed at ninety-six. The Woodhouses are long livers."

"That a fact?" Buster asked, peering into the coffin again. "Must of been a freak thing."

Harvey flinched. "And how were you acquainted with my brother?" he asked. Later on, he said he had been afraid that Buster was a gate-crasher, a bum who had no more known my grandfather than the man in the moon. This was his attempt to smoke Buster out.

"Oh, Joe and I, we went 'way back," said Buster.

"How far, exactly?" Harvey persisted.

Buster chuckled and pulled at his jaw. "*Welllll*," he said slowly, "I believe I met Joe Woodhouse just after the first war. We was both veterans before we went to work for the union."

Harvey relaxed. "Ahhh," he said. "So you're a union man."

"Never wasn't," said Buster, "except in service."

When I came up behind Great-Uncle Harvey, the two of them were still in what looked like pained conversation. It was with relief and something else—mischief? amusement?—that Buster greeted me with a salute and a bow from the waist. "Good evening, Miss," he said. "It's nice to see you after such a long time."

"Catherine," I reminded him. "How are you, Mr. Tumbridge?" And without waiting for an answer, "Thank you for coming." I was surprised at how difficult it was to look in his eyes, at how uneasy I felt, standing right next to him.

"How long's it been now, Miss?" Buster counted on his fingers. "Six years? Seven? You must be in high school. You doing good? Making your grampa proud? Bet you're surprised to see me here, aincha?" he said.

I said, "Do you remember when I used to come with him to visit you when I was a little girl?"

"I do," he said, "I surely do. Been some time since you been by. You come with him when he brung me Christmas dinner or the odd item."

"I wasn't aware you were home again," I said.

"Yes, ma'am," Buster said. "Been home almost a month now, earlier than expected."

"Well. Thank you for coming," I said again. I wished he would just say good night and leave. I could feel people staring at us, I could hear the buzz of their voices whispering over us. But instead, he took a step closer to me and leaned towards my ear.

"I hold no hard feelings, Miss," he said, like a secret. "I want you to know that. Nothing you could've done nohow."

Great-Uncle Harvey was twitching. "Excuse me, sir," he began and stepped between Buster and me and tried to nudge Buster to another part of the room.

Buster stepped nicely around him. He jerked his head towards Harvey. "Fella here was telling me your grampa died with all his teeth in. Did you know tooth enamel is harder than bone? That's something I learned recently from reading a book on for-*enz*-icks." He pronounced the word slowly and carefully. "Know what else? If you was ever to dig him up, even if everything else was gone— skin, hair, everything—you'd know it's Joe from the grin and that big space between his two front teeth."

"Really, this is *most* inappropriate—" Great-Uncle Harvey had one hand on my back and the other on my arm and was herding me away from the region that included Buster. "This is not fit conversation for a young lady, for a funeral!"

Buster yanked his shoulders ear-high and wiped his forehead with the palm of his hand. "Pardon the indelicacy," he said, which made me smile, though I tried not to.

My parents were lost in a boating accident when I was too young to remember, so my grandparents took me on at a time in their lives when they thought they were finally through with all that. As a kid, I ended up doing a lot of old-people things, regular events like trash burning on Friday evening, and Sunday afternoon rides in the country, and hospital visiting. My grandfather kept lists of people from work, and from the organizations he and my grandmother belonged to, and just from the neighborhood, people suffering gallbladders, female problems, broken-down veins, and once a month or so we'd pile in the car and swing by all the hospitals and spend a few minutes in a lot of different sickrooms.

Many of the people we saw had had their teeth extracted, all of them, even the good ones. They'd be propped up in the hospital bed, unable to form words with their sore, puffy mouths, grunting and trying to talk with their hands. Driving home, my grandfather would say to me, "That's what happens when you don't clean your teeth three times a day. Isn't that right, Roselle?"

"Oh yes," my grandmother would say. She had lost her first teeth in her thirties, then had them all out when she was fifty-six. "I wish I had known to take care of my teeth when I had some." Then, unless she was especially tired, she would tell again the story about how the first teeth were pulled with no gas, her wide awake. And as she described how the dentist had to brace himself with his foot against the chair to get enough leverage to pull, PopPop would make the sound effects of molars creaking and cracking away from their bony sockets before they popped out. From the back seat of the Packard, this performance seemed to me like George Burns and Gracie Allen, witty and sophisticated, and I squealed and groaned with horror, then laughed at PopPop's sound effects every time.

My grandfather had a fierce respect for oral hygiene, a new discovery in his lifetime, like the internal combustion engine and the telephone. He would call me into the living room to watch his favorite commercial on the tiny porthole screen that bubbled out the front of our new television. It was a cartoon with Tooth Decay as the villain in black cape and stovepipe hat and handlebar mustache. The fair damsel, a tooth with golden hair, was saved from the onrushing train by a tube of toothpaste, which stuck out its chest and gleamed.

"When I was a boy, we'd never heard of toothpaste," he told me. "We cleaned our teeth just like we took baths—once a week—and you used baking soda or salt on a rag. You went to a dentist to have bad teeth taken out, that's all. No such a thing as prevention. People expected to lose their teeth."

"Lands!" said my grandmother. "I never went near a dentist until I was twenty-five, and by then it was too late. Your grandfather, he was one of the lucky ones. He was born with good teeth."

There was something fascinating about a jaw with nothing in it but bald gums. With her dentures out, the whole bottom half of my grandmother's face was sucked in, and without the balance of a filled-out jaw below, her eyes looked huge. The overall effect was benign and faintly stupid. If she smiled, her mouth stretched incredibly wide and exposed a rubbery pink cavern. She always brought her hand up to cover it.

My grandmother said how lucky she was that my grandfather made a good living. A lot of people lost their teeth and couldn't afford dentures, and they had to go around with gaping holes in their faces, like Buster Tumbridge. My grandfather had known him for years from the union, but he never came to the house. The categories of people in my grandparents' life were relatives, friends, professional or club acquaintances, and folks they grew up with. PopPop called Buster "someone I know."

He lived alone not far from us in a bungalow coated with faded pink shingles. It had a crooked tin chimney and leaned a little to the west. By the time I knew him, he was an old man with knobby red knuckles twisted by arthritis, and long, hard fingernails curved and pointy like dog claws. Winter and summer he wore the same gray felt fedora, gray cardigan sweater, and white shirt aged to a pale yellow. A dark stubble usually sprouted from his chin and jaw, and there was a big, black space where his front teeth, upper and lower, used to be, framed by crooked lines of small, worn-down, gravel-colored molars. Unlike my grandmother, Buster Tumbridge smiled all the time and he never covered his mouth with his hand. Every time PopPop and I went to see him, PopPop said, "Buster, you know my granddaughter, Catherine." But Buster never called me anything but "little sister." Since he had no front teeth, he hissed when he said it.

Buster had fallen on hard times, but the nature of his troubles was a mystery. My grandparents never discussed him in front of me. I knew this was deliberate because more than once I had walked into the kitchen when they were drinking coffee at the table, and I'd heard his name before one of them spied me and said, "Lit-tle pitch-ers" in that sing-song tone that was always followed by throat-clearing and talk about the weather.

On holidays and sometimes on regular days, PopPop and I would drive over to Buster's with packages. Once we took him a garden hose, and once a woolen blanket. Once a couple of watermelons when somebody at the Booth's Corner farm market had let PopPop have them at two for a quarter and he'd bought six. Once we took him a pair of brown and white shoes that my Uncle Rollo had bought and then decided didn't suit him. Buster took one look at the shoes my grandfather held out to him and said, "Two-tones? These belong to the Lollapalooza?"

That's what some called my Uncle Rollo, my mother's brother. He had thickly furred forearms and eyes like a strong suit, and ink-black hair slicked back and sweet with Vitalis. His job was selling costume jewelry wholesale, but he was also a gambler who won. He liked to pull a neat, fat roll of bills from his pants pocket and say it was his tax-free bonus. My grandmother hated that about her son, and also his scorn for any but tailor-made clothes and also his car, a flashy two-tone job—light blue over dark, only he said "powder and midnight"—with white leather seats.

My grandfather said, "Yes, but he never wore them. They aren't used." And he turned them over to reveal the pale leather soles with only the slightest scuff marks on them, no dirt.

Buster brushed something away from his face. "I ain't worried about that," he said, working one foot out of his old cracked black shoe and scooting it into the low-slung elegance of my uncle's spectator wingtip. "I was just curious is all. You know I ain't proud, Joe." Buster didn't bother with the laces, he just turned his foot this way and that, enjoying the view from all angles. The new whiteness of the shoe made his foot look extra large. "I bet he buyed these in Florida," he said.

"Might've done," my grandfather said. Uncle Rollo went to Florida a lot. He drove the powder-and-midnight car down Route 1 to Miami Beach, and brought back photographs of himself taken in nightclubs with women wearing low-cut dresses and rhinestone earrings that burst like sprays of fireworks on either side of their faces. My grandmother was hopeful he might get married, but if she said anything, Uncle Rollo would always respond that there was no need to buy the cow if you were getting the milk free, so after a while she stopped asking.

"They look like Florida shoes, don't they?" Buster asked.

"They're fancy, all right," my grandfather said. "You know Rollo." Miami Beach was the place where everyone we knew who had money went. Miami Beach and Havana, Cuba, where Uncle Rollo had also been and won a lot of money.

"Ain't they fine?" Buster turned to me and wiggled my uncle's shoe in my direction. "What do you think of them, little sister?" he asked.

I wasn't used to being asked for my opinion of clothes. But I had heard my grandmother often enough to know what to say. I said, "They're very becoming. They do something for you," and Buster threw his head back and laughed as if I was Dorothy Kilgallen on *What's My Line*, that clever. I looked up at my grandfather to see if he was laughing too, but his gaze was fixed on Uncle Rollo's two-tone shoe stuck on the end of Buster's leg.

On holidays we loaded up platters and bowls for Buster and covered them with waxed paper and tea towels—turkey, fried chicken, biscuits, succotash, chow chow, and big slabs of pink ham. When we stepped inside the house, I stayed near the door. It was dark inside and faintly damp. The walls were covered with faded floral wallpaper that bulged in places and reeked a sweet, fusty odor I couldn't place. Buster always offered me a Hires root beer and lemon meringue pie and I always said no thank you even though lemon meringue pie, ice cold, was one of my favorite things on earth. There was something not quite clean-feeling about the place, and I imagined Buster's kitchen teeming with polio germs or ringworm, the two infections everyone feared most.

Once, when my grandfather asked why I never took anything Buster offered, I told him how I was afraid I might get polio from Buster's pies. "Stop that silliness," he said roughly. "No such a thing! Poor Buster doesn't need anything more to be sad about in his life. I don't ever want you to be anything but Miss Emily Post herself to Buster Tumbridge, do you hear me?" I said yessir, and he calmed right down and said, "Okay, then. Okay."

Much as I disliked Buster's house, I liked his yard. He had two big holly trees and a dozen rose bushes arranged in two straight lines in the front, and in the back a vegetable garden, hung all around with silver pie pans to keep the birds off his strawberries and tomatoes. The pie pans were stamped BOND, from the Bond Bakery, whose uniformed men came to our door twice a week, lugging heavy trays of bread, donuts, cakes, and pies, and calling, "Bread man!" Buster Tumbridge must have had fifty pie pans strung up. They spun slowly on their fishing line, dazzling your eyes like a flashbulb when they caught the sun and shot it back at you. My grandfather said Buster Tumbridge ate too much pie, and that one look at his toothless smile should tell me all I needed to know about people who indulged a sweet tooth. "Let that be a lesson to you," he told me.

"What's wrong with him?" I asked my grandfather once, out of the blue, on our way home from delivering ham and potato salad, a chunk of homemade coconut cake, and a twenty-pound sack of aphid powder to Buster.

"It's too sad a story for you, honey," PopPop said from behind the wheel.

"Things happen to people sometimes, and they happened to Buster."

As time went on, I began to wonder which of my teeth it was that was the sweet one. I thought maybe I could have it pulled— that one, just that one, to save all the rest. I had fallen in love with penny candy, and I knew it would be the end of me.

I had finally reached an age when I got to run errands for my grandmother by myself. I could be trusted to carry money to the corner store and buy a loaf of bread or some butter or lunch meat and bring home all the change but a nickel, which was mine. The store was one block south and one block east and I didn't have to cross Linwood Avenue, the big street near our house, to get to it. There were just two rules. One: never cross a street without looking both ways. Two: never speak to strangers, especially men. My grandmother and grandfather harped on the second rule like it was the word of God. They took turns reciting the litany of danger until it became as meaningless, and powerful, as the Latin in church.

"Beware of strange men. Strange men are dangerous."

"If a strange man comes by in a car and offers you candy or a soda if you get in, don't do it, no matter what."

"It's a trick. No decent strange man would ever offer you candy."

"Or ask you to get in his car."

"Another trick they play, he might say one of us sent him to pick you up."

"They have a million tricks, these strange men."

"We'll never send a stranger to pick you up, so anybody who ever says that to you, you'll know he's lying. If we ever had to send somebody, it'd be somebody you know, like Nick Kowal."

"Or Mr. Bailey."

"We're saying don't even go near a strange man in a car."

"That's right. A strange man in a car, that's as dangerous as it gets. But also a strange man on the sidewalk."

"A strange man at all. Just walk away."

"Turn and walk away fast the minute the car slows down."

"If he rolls the window down. Or says anything."

"Even if it sounds innocent, like asking directions."

No one ever actually said what would happen to me if I spoke to a strange man. Instead, they told stories. Long before I was born, a little girl who lived two blocks down got into a car with a strange man and they didn't find her body for almost a month. Every child in my neighborhood had heard that story told fifty times at least. It was a cautionary tale that grew a little with each succeeding year, sprouting details no one could have known—how the man had called her "Honey" and enticed her into the car with a Hershey's bar (a double-dip vanilla fudge cone, butterscotch Tastykakes, a kitten), how the man said he was a friend of her daddy's (a teacher from school, a new neighbor), how the little girl climbed right into that car and never thought a thing about it. She was found in a shallow grave (in a ditch, nibbled by wild animals, beneath a melting snowbank). Six years old.

The cash register at Fazio's sat atop a display case whose shelves were filled with white paperboard boxes of penny candies nestled in waxed-paper layers. Sticky red licorice twists, orange slices and spearmint leaves, caramel cremes, Mary Janes, sour cherries, candy pills, Turkish taffy, bacon strips, jawbreakers. My absolute favorites were lemon squashes, yellow hard candies formed into lemon shapes and dusted with yellow sugar. One lemon squash fit just comfortably in your mouth. The hard candy shell was thin, and after you had sucked on it for a while, you'd roll the candy around with your tongue and position it between your upper and lower back teeth, so you could gently crack the shell between the flat surfaces of your molars and make the soft, gooey center with its tart lemon taste ooze out. The trick was to work your teeth so that you cracked the shell just a little, so the center came out slowly, bit by bit. You could make one lemon squash last five minutes if you had the patience and worked on the technique.

I got into the habit of selecting my candy first, leaving the store, and walking two houses down to the church organist's house, where there was a sloping bank shaded by a snowball tree. I would sit in the shade beneath the umbrella of branches and suck lemon squashes and chew on Mary Janes until my mouth burned from sugar, then stuff what I couldn't eat in my pockets, return to the store for whatever my grandmother needed, and head home. If my grandmother said anything about how long I'd been gone, I would just say what a beautiful day it was and how I was enjoying the fresh air. My grandmother believed in fresh air, so this made her happy. The extra candy got squirreled away in my room, to be eaten illegally in bed at night.

If my grandfather had known, he'd have killed me. He could not have imagined such a violation of proper dental hygiene. Just before my bedtime, he would hand me a juice glass with an inch of Listerine in it and time me while I swished it around for one full minute. Then he handed me a toothpick and watched while I excavated all the spaces between my teeth, digging for bits of food. Then I brushed with a paste he mixed in his palm—half Arm and Hammer baking soda and half Colgate toothpaste. He propped his big gold Bulova up on the glass shelf over the wash-basin so we would know when I had brushed three full minutes. Then four complete rinses. Once a week, we brushed our teeth with salt. He had our dentist show me pictures taken through microscopes—little herds of furry rods and speckled blobs. "They're bacteria. They grow on your teeth every day," PopPop told me. "If you don't clean them off, they stick to the teeth and make them rotten."

PopPop said you could tell everything you needed to know about a person by how they cared for their teeth, and I was to avoid children like Danny Pomeroy, a skinny, freckled boy from around the corner, whose teeth were ridged and mossy green. I asked him once how often he brushed, and he shrugged and said once in a while.

"I brush three times a day," I said, hoping to give him ideas.

"Why?" he asked.

"To stop tooth decay in its tracks," I said, repeating the commercial. "Aren't you afraid of losing all your teeth?"

"Nah," he said. It was a relief when his part of the street turned into a polio block and I didn't have to make excuses about why I wasn't playing with him anymore.

My Uncle Rollo was home for a while. Between sales trips, he sometimes stayed with us in his old room. He'd go out at night, come in long after we had all gone to bed, and sleep until noon. And he spoiled me. He'd be getting dressed to go out, shooting his cuffs and splashing on Old Spice, and I'd tell him how nice he looked, and he'd pull quarters from behind my ear and tuck them into my hand.

I was hoping he would stay around, but I was also living in a perpetual spasm of shame and guilt. Stale candy was nestled in among my clean socks and undershirts, white paper bags splotched with grease stains were stuffed in my bookcase behind the Nancy Drews. I could eat only so much candy, and with my added income from Uncle Rollo, I was accumulating such excess that I feared I was about to be found out. I dreamed that all my teeth turned black overnight, and even though these nightmares woke me up sharply and sent me running to the mirror to make sure it wasn't true, still I couldn't help myself, I couldn't stop.

On a hot August afternoon, when my grandmother was busy in the kitchen, canning tomatoes with her next-door neighbor, I made a sweep of my room and left the house with a lunch bag full of all the candy I'd been hoarding. Some, like the licorice sticks I'd packed into my rubber rain boots, was getting tacky from the heat, and some pieces had lint stuck to them. These I planned to throw away. With the rest I was planning to have one last huge candy feast, and then I had promised myself I would never eat sweets in bed after brushing my teeth again.

I walked for a while, avoiding the polio blocks, and ended up in Miss Kitt's front yard, where I settled in, my back against the rough bark of the snowball tree, and opened up the bag of candy. I'd decided to eat the candies like a meal: I'd begin with spearmint leaves for salad, then have bacon strips and Mary Janes, and finally orange slices, sour cherries, and lemon squashes for dessert.

Buster Tumbridge appeared during the entree, when my mouth was packed with coconut and peanut butter toffee. From my snowball tree tent, I could see Uncle Rollo's shoes, then Buster's face appeared. He was bending over to see who it was beneath the low-slung branches. "I thought that might be you, little sister," he said. "Reckanized your shoes. What're you doing up there?"

The temperature must have been over ninety, and the air was so thick that just turning your head made you break into a sweat, but Buster was decked out in full Buster regalia—the felt hat, the wool sweater, formal shirt. My mouth was too full to speak. I chewed fast and held up my hand so he would know I wasn't being rude and ignoring him. Finally I swallowed several times, forcing the big lump of half-chewed goo down my gullet. "Hello, Mr. Tumbridge. I'm having a snack," I said.

"This ain't your yard," he said, as if he had caught me in a lie.

"Just getting some shade," I said, pointing up at the thick-leaved branches.

"It's a hot one, all right," Buster said. He pulled his hat off and wiped a sleeve along his forehead. Then he used the hat as a fan. Then he aimed it my way and fanned me. "Hafta make your own breeze," he said and laughed, exposing his browned back teeth and the expanse of empty gums in front.

I remembered my manners and picked up the bag and held it towards him. "Care for a candy, Mr. Tumbridge?"

He took the bag and peered in. "Well, thank you," he said. "A candy would be nice." He plucked out a sour cherry and popped it between his lips, then handed the bag back to me. He went on waving his hat, first at himself, then in my direction. After a minute he said, "You know what I could do with? An ice cold soda. Could you go for that?"

My mouth was so thick with sugar and heat that I did not hesitate. "Could I ever!" I said.

"I'll just be a minute," he said and he tipped his hat and was gone.

The dangers of men offering sodas had been drummed into me so mercilessly that a slight chill slid over my skin as I sat in the hot shade, and I felt a surge in my chest and a tingling in my legs, as if my body was revving to get me out of there fast. It passed quickly. Buster was no stranger. My grandfather would never have taken me to visit a dangerous man. Things had happened to him and I was to be as nice to him as I could be.

But I felt uneasy when Buster returned from Fazio's with a dripping Pepsi bottle in each hand and came up the slope and bent over and crawled beneath the snowball branches into the little circle where I was sitting. Bent double beneath the low branches, he held a soda out to me, then settled himself on the grass close by me. He placed his hand low on my outstretched leg and patted it, he turned his ruined smile on me and said, "This'll taste good going down."

I fit my lips around the icy glass rim of the bottle and tipped my head back to take a sip of Pepsi, but I never took my eyes off Buster. He was so close that I could almost feel heat coming off his body, I could almost see little wavy lines rising from his sweater, I could smell the faint odor of naphtha and stale tobacco smoke that clung to his clothes. It wasn't anything specific, just a vague sense of trespass, of the natural space I took up being pressed in, collapsed against me. I felt edgy and could not have put words to it if I had tried.

Buster gulped down half his soda at once, then let out a long, "Ahhhhhhh." He leaned back on his elbows, jackknifed one leg, and took off his hat and placed it on his raised knee. He wiped the

cold bottle across his forehead. His hair was matted down in a circle where his hat had been, and the hairs at the back of his neck
were wet. "Hot enough for ya, little sister?" he said.

"Too hot," I said. Then, because he was looking at me and I
couldn't think what else to say, I held the candy bag out to him
again. "Another candy?"

"Nah," he said, waving it off. "Too much sugar make you sick
on a day like this. You be careful not to eat too much."

"Why do you wear a sweater on a day like this?" I asked.

Buster didn't seem to find the question rude. "Habit, I guess,"
he said, fingering the top buttonhole. "It's what I wear. That way,
people'll always know it's me!" He threw his head back and
laughed and I laughed too, though I didn't get the joke. Grownup humor, I thought, beyond me.

He laughed for a long time, and when he finished there were
tears in his eyes. Buster took another long swig of Pepsi and wiped
his eyes with the back of his hand. Trickles of leftover chuckling
kept sliding out of him, but finally he seemed to be done, and he
shook his head a few times and sighed deeply. "Little sister," he
said, like the end of a sentence. "You surely break my heart, do you
know that?"

Break my heart. Words from television shows, Hank Williams
songs, man-and-woman romance words. What was he getting at?

"Your grampa ever tell you about my Alice?" he asked and
sighed again, then sniffed. The laughter had left him with a runny
nose too. "You put me in mind of her," he said. "Not that you look
like her—she was a tiny thing, all bones and eyes. But she was
about your age and she was well behaved and sharp like you, smart
as a whip, I used to say, I used to say, 'Alice, you're gonna set the
world on fire, girl.' And I believe she could have too. She loved it
when I said that." He paused and looked off through the curtain
of leaves, then he took a deep breath in and held it for a second,
then he went, "Huh huh huh" and shook his head as he let it out.

"Who's Alice?" I asked when he didn't say anything more.

Buster gave me a look that seemed to indicate surprise that I was there. "He didn't tell you nothing about that?" I shook my head. "Well," he said. "I wonder if it's my place to say, then."

"Why wouldn't you?" I asked him. "You just told me about her. Why wouldn't you say who she is?"

"Well, maybe your grampa wouldn't like it," he said to me. One of his hands was pulling blades of grass aimlessly out of the dirt, and his face kept changing expression, as if he were having a conversation with someone who wasn't actually there.

"I don't think he'd mind," I said. I had no idea whether he would, but I wanted Buster to tell me.

After a minute, Buster said, "I believe you're right. I don't think there's any harm in it." He turned his face towards me and his old eyes fastened onto my face. "Alice was my little girl," he said.

"Your daughter?" I asked. I could not imagine such a thing, Buster as a father, I could not picture it. Was that what he meant?

He nodded, yes. "My daughter, yes," he said, "my baby girl, my sweet girl." His nodding shifted imperceptibly to head-shaking. His hand went on pulling up grass.

"Where is she?" I asked him. "And where is your wife?"

"Well," said Buster, looking away from me again, "they are gone. They are both gone," he said.

"Gone where?"

"They are not among us no more," he said. "Do you understand what I'm saying?"

I didn't, but I was embarrassed to tell him. Did he mean they had moved away? I decided it was best to say nothing. Finally, after what seemed like a long time, he turned his head my way again. I shook my head.

"Humph," he said and frowned. After a moment, he said, "Well, what I mean is they are dead." He said this like an apology, like he was sorry he had to break the news to me. It made me want to say, *That's all right.*

But instead I said, "What do you mean, 'dead'?"

"I mean just that," he said. "I mean they are dead. They was both killed," said Buster.

"My mother and father were killed," I said, "in a boat."

"This was different," said Buster. "Alice and my wife was killed by someone. A person or persons unknown was what the police decided in the end. But there was some as said I was the one did it. Some still believes it. Not your grampa, though, not Joe Woodhouse. He stood up for me. We was never what you would call close, but he knew me, he knew me for years. He knew me enough to know such a thing was not possible on this earth."

I was having some trouble following, and my comprehension was further impeded by the fact that Buster was muttering, that he kept turning his head away from me as he talked. I asked, "How did it happen?" in the hopes that he would remember I was there and speak clearly, and to me.

Instead, he became more agitated. He started to jiggle the jack-knifed leg, and his hat wobbled on his knee. "It was terrible, terrible," he said, "as terrible as you could imagine if you could imagine such a thing. Like a nightmare so bad," he said, "you would never sleep again. I come home from work, just like always, it was on a Tuesday, I come in the back door like I always done and set my lunchpail down and took off my work boots like my wife liked me to do so as not to get her clean floors dirty. Usually Alice would come running soon as she heard me at the back door, but this time it was a deathly quiet there, not a sound, no sign of anyone, no dinner smells.

"Once I got my boots off, I called out to them. I called, 'Where are you, baby girl?'" He cupped his hand to his mouth as he told this part and called up into the leaves of the snowball tree. "I called to my wife, I said, 'Anybody home?' I said, 'Poppa's here now and wants his supper!' Teasing them, don't you know. And still not a sound. So I figured they wasn't home although I couldn't think where they might be at dinnertime, and I went into the living room to put the paper down before I went to wash up." His Adam's apple hopped up and down like he had swallowed a frog. "And they was there, both of them, in the living room," he said. "Torn to bits, torn to pieces like dogs had got at them, only it wasn't dogs, it was someone, some person done that to them with a knife—"

I guess I screamed. Whatever sound I made, it snapped Buster Tumbridge back to where he was, sitting on the grass next to a little girl he had just frightened out of her wits. He buried his face in his hands for a moment and moaned. "Oh, little sister," he said, "I am sorry. I didn't mean to scare you, I didn't mean to go on so. I forgot myself," he said. "I forgot where I was. You just put this out of your mind, can you do that? This don't have nothing to do with you," he said. "There is nothing in this world for you to be afraid of."

I was shivering, shaking so violently that my teeth chattered, and even though I could see plainly how my reaction upset Buster, there was nothing I could do about it. I hugged myself with both arms and tried to stop, but I felt ice in my bones. And Buster didn't know what to do either. His hands fluttered about me like butterflies, not quite daring to settle or touch, and he kept saying, "Oh God, now look what I've done, look what I've done."

I'd have given anything if I could have told him that I wasn't afraid of him, only of the pictures he had drawn and of his own pain, his helplessness. It frightened me to know that such things could happen in your own house, with your own mother there, with your own father out working, thinking it was just a day like any other day, that the strange men could get out of their cars and come inside.

But I couldn't put any of this into words. I stood up and said, "I'm sorry, Mr. Tumbridge," and I ran out of there and all the way home. When I reached the house, I kept on running into the bathroom, where I slammed the door shut and vomited up half a bag of old candy and a bottle of Pepsi. My grandmother came running in from the kitchen and held my head and put a wet washcloth on the back of my neck. She kept murmuring questions: "What happened? . . . Where have you been? . . . You didn't go near the polio blocks, did you?"

She was a great worrier about meat going bad on hot days, so I told her it was probably some Lebanon bologna I'd eaten, and she made me take milk of magnesia and she sponged me off with cool water and put me to bed. She set a bowl of ice cubes on the night stand and aimed the big floor fan so that it blew over the ice and onto me.

I woke up when I heard the gravel crunching under the Packard's tires. The room was cooler. It must have been around six. After a few minutes, PopPop came tiptoeing into my room. I had my eyes closed, but I could feel his gaze on me like heat. "I'm not asleep," I said.

"I know," he said. "Your eyelids were twitching." He pulled a chair over to the bed and sat down. His face was gray. "What upset your stomach?" he asked. I told him the Lebanon bologna story. He frowned and leaned forward, his elbows on his knees, his hands clasping and unclasping. "Now, listen to me," he said gently. "That's a lie."

I struggled to sit up, started to protest, but he hushed me, told me to lie back down. "I'm not angry," he said. "You are not in trouble. You are not going to be punished. But honey, you have to tell me what happened with Buster Tumbridge, and you must tell the truth."

Miss Kitt had called my grandmother. She had heard me scream and trotted to her front window just in time to see me burst out from beneath her snowball tree and go tearing down the street towards home. And then she saw Buster crawling out, clutching my abandoned candy bag, brushing grass off the seat of his trousers. My grandfather wanted to know what had happened. He explained how serious a matter it was. He said Buster could go to jail.

"What for?" I asked. "He didn't try to kill me."

"Of course not," said my grandfather, "but what did he do? What did he do with you under that tree?"

I was alarmed, distraught. How could they be thinking of sending Buster to jail? What had he done? I couldn't decide what was the right thing to say. I didn't know what they would be most upset about—that he had touched my leg, or bought me a soda, or that he had told me what happened to his wife and daughter. I was paralyzed. I could not say one word. If I said the wrong thing, Buster would be finished.

My grandfather waited a few moments, and finally leaned over very close so that his face was level with mine, and he spoke very softly, he spoke like love, like comfort to the dying. "Did he touch you?" he asked. "Did Buster touch you under that tree?"

So then I knew what it was they were afraid of, but still it seemed like a lifetime passed before I could answer, before I could make up my mind whether to lie. Finally I said, "No."

"He didn't touch you? He didn't touch you anywhere?"

I shook my head. I looked down at the sheets. I remembered Buster's rough hand on my shin, how his palm had patted me. This was what they wanted, and I did not love Buster and didn't want to lie for him, but they couldn't put him in jail for that. "No," I said.

My grandfather nodded and looked thoughtful for a moment. Then he took a deep breath, leaned back slightly, and pointed a finger between his own legs. "He didn't touch you here?" he said, so quiet.

At that I sat straight up. "No!" I said, and then I said it some more. "No! *No!*"

"Then why did you scream? What made you scream?"

"He told me what happened to Alice," I said. "He told me the story, and it scared me, the part where he comes home and finds them all torn to pieces."

My grandfather seemed to go limp. "Oh God," he said. "Is that what it was?" I nodded, relieved to be able to tell the truth about this part at least. "He shouldn't have told you that," my grandfather said.

"But they shouldn't send him to jail for it," I said.

"No," PopPop said. "Nobody's going to jail." And that was the end of it. Except that he never again took me with him to Buster's house. My grandmother continued to put food aside for him and my grandfather kept going there, kept taking Buster things, but he never again asked me to go with him, and I never asked to go.

I overheard them talking about the whole affair once when I had come home from playing down the street and was just about to open the back screen door. They were talking in the kitchen while my grandmother made dinner. I heard water running and the refrigerator door opening and closing. I heard my grandfather say Buster was "simple in the head," and my grandmother said a man like that could get into trouble before he even knew he was in the same county as trouble was.

"He never had much on the ball, and he hasn't been the same since it happened," my grandfather said, and my grandmother said, "Who would be? Who ever could?" They spoke of him tenderly and with sadness and resignation, a man whose life was beyond hope, who had come into the world poorly endowed to begin with and then seen the little life he had made wrecked by a single event so dreadful, so beyond comprehension, that all some people could do to reassure themselves was to say it must have been Buster. What else would you say—that it was random? That the killer, whoever he was, didn't choose the Tumbridge house for a reason, he just happened upon it? And he had never been caught, so was he still around? And if so, was he a madman from somewhere else who had moved on, or was he one of us, a monster, like a werewolf, a normal person until something innocuous happens, the full moon shines, and he goes on a rampage, and you could be next?

My grandparents had steadfastly defended Buster then and they held to their beliefs now, even after Miss Kitt stopped speaking to them and told everyone at church, everyone who would listen, just why. How two foolish old people refused to believe what was plain as the nose on your face, even though it was their own flesh and blood—that was me—who had come so close to ending up just like Alice Tumbridge and her mother.

It was the following summer that they finally sent Buster away. My grandfather said it had the look of inevitability about it. He said what happened to Buster proved two things: that some people are born with bad luck, and that a town that gets an idea in its head is as dangerous a thing as anything on earth.

There were rumors and rumors of rumors, and then there was Buster's story, told to my grandfather when he went to see him in jail. But what it came down to was that they found a little girl who lived down the street from Buster in his kitchen, sitting at his table, eating lemon meringue pie. Her parents said she had been warned again and again never to talk to strangers and not to leave her yard, and she was a good girl and would not have gone willingly with this man. And even though the girl said that Buster had not touched her, had not hurt her in any way, the child's parents demanded that something be done.

Miss Kitt resurrected her version of what had happened to me in her yard. The story she told now was her original story expanded to three times its length and packed with new details. Now, when I ran from beneath the snowball tree, I was screaming for help, and my blouse was flying out loose behind me, and Buster was fiddling with his trousers when he emerged. There were rumors that I would be called to testify in court—first against Buster, then for him. But my grandfather had powerful friends and called in a few favors to make sure that I would never have to go anywhere near the courtroom, would never be part of what was sure to be a sensational trial, that I would never have to hear the lurid descriptions and accusations that would fly back and forth like demons and angels battling for a mortal soul.

In the end, Buster wasn't charged with kidnapping or attempted murder or rape or any of the terrible things the townspeople had first speculated about. The charge was corrupting a minor. In court, a psychiatrist was brought forth to testify about Buster and his affection for little girls. He depicted Buster as a victim of crime, not a criminal, a man with a huge emptiness inside and a simple mind that tried to fill up the ache with other Alices. "He has never been known to treat these children with anything but kindness," said the doctor. "He shows poor judgment, but that is not a crime." The union paid the psychiatrist's fee out of the discretionary fund.

He was convicted anyway and sent off to the prison farm for seven years for being a strange man offering sweets to little girls. He had just finished up his time on the day PopPop died.

He came and said good-bye to me before he left the viewing. "Well, good night now, Miss," he said and smiled at me. "I'll be saying good night now," he said, and widened his grin even more. He seemed to be aiming it into my face like a flashlight.

"Thank you again for coming," I said. I shook his hand. "We appreciate it."

Buster grinned and grinned at me. "It won't be the same without him," he said. "He was such a help to me all my life, your grampa."

I nodded and Buster went on grinning. He stood in the parlor doorway, rocking forward and back on his heels, his hat clutched in front of his chest, and his lips pulled back in a bright, sunny smile.

"Well," I said finally, not knowing what else to say. "Well. Thank you. Again."

Buster reached up and tapped a fingernail against one of his front teeth. I dropped my head back and laughed. The sound caused people around us to stop their talking and turn to stare. The silence pooled out from us as if my laugh had been a stone dropped into a pond. "Buster!" I said. I think it was the first and only time I ever called him by his first name. "You've got teeth!"

Buster stretched his lips even wider and turned his head from side to side, so I could view the dentures from all directions. "Are they something?" he asked.

"They look wonderful," I said.

"You know who got me these teeth? Joe Woodhouse," said Buster. "Once when he come to visit me up at Statesboro he said to me, 'You should take advantage of your situation, Buster. They have to take care of you. It's the law. You ought to get those nasty old teeth of yours pulled and get yourself a decent set, long as you're here? I never would've thought of it on my own."

"That sounds just like something he'd have told you," I said.

"Don't it, though?" Buster agreed. "That was Joe Woodhouse all over, wasn't it? Like prison was a union. Like I was entitled. I thought, well, maybe I am."

I told him that I thought his teeth were very becoming. "They make you look younger," I said.

"You could hardly imagine," said Buster Tumbridge, "what a difference such a thing can make in your life. How much a little thing like teeth can mean."

―――――――――

Pamela Erbe received an M.F.A. from the Iowa Writers' Workshop and taught at the Universities of Iowa and Michigan. She now lives in Chicago, where she works as a medical writer and continues to write fiction. Her stories have appeared in *The Antioch Review, North American Review, Ms.,* and *Columbia Review,* where she won the Carlos Fuentes Award for Fiction. She has received grants from the National Endowment for the Arts, the Michigan Council for the Arts, and the Illinois Arts Council. She is working on a novel set in southern Delaware, the magical place where she spent all her childhood summers.

M*y stories start when a scene pops into my head. If I write it down and the people in the scene have more to say or do, the story develops— maybe right away, maybe months later. "Sweet Tooth" started with the funeral scene that begins and ends the story. I'd been to a funeral and, driving home, was thinking about my grandfather's funeral twenty-five years ago. Into this daydream stepped Buster Tumbridge, a completely imaginary figure, but one who reminded me of the hard-luck men my grandfather knew and whom we sometimes encountered around town. To my grandfather, these men—who had been ruined by the Depression and never recovered—were objects of pity. But to me, they were embodiments of the big terrors of the early 1950s—the Strange Men in Cars; the polio that attacked children every* *summer, and which the grown-ups I knew secretly believed got its foothold in homes that were not quite clean; and the terrible choice offered by dental hygiene in those days before fluoridation—having cavities drilled without Novocain or losing all your teeth. When Buster Tumbridge walked into the funeral parlor, he had something of his own to say. In the first draft, the story took a wrong turn down a topical side road, but it was so easy to revise, as if Buster had been telling me his story all along, and the first time I just wasn't paying attention.*

Tony Earley

THE PROPHET FROM JUPITER

(from *Harper's Magazine*)

My house, the dam keeper's house, sits above the lake on Pierce-Arrow Point. The dam juts out of the end of the point and curves away across the cove into the ridge on the other side of the channel. On this side is the water, 115 feet deep at the base of the dam, and on the other side is air: the gorge, the river starting up again, rocks far down below, a vista. There are houses on 100-foot lots all the way around the lake, and too many real estate brokers. Sometimes at night, the real estate brokers pull up each other's signs and sling them into the lake.

A family on Tryon Bay has a Labrador retriever that swims in circles for hours, chasing ducks. You can buy postcards in town with the dog on the front, swimming, swimming, the ducks always just out of reach. There is a red and white sign on the Tryon Bay bridge that says NO JUMPING OR DIVING FROM BRIDGE, and I could drop the water level down a foot and a half any summer Saturday and paralyze all the teenage boys I wanted. Sometimes rednecks whoop and yell *nigger!* and throw beer bottles at Junie Wilson, who walks up and down Highway 20 with a coat hanger around his neck. Junie drops a dollar bill into the water every time he crosses the bridge. The Prophet from Jupiter brings his five young sons to the bridge to watch the Lab swim. The six of them stand in a line at the guardrail and clap and wave their arms and shout encouragement for the dog. Down in the water, the ducks let the dog get almost to them before they fly away. They fly maybe thirty, forty yards, that's all, and splash back down. The townies call the dog Shithead. You may not believe me, but I swear I have heard ducks laugh. Shithead, as he paddles around the bay, puffs like he is dying. This is where I live and this is what I think: a dam is an unnatural thing, like a diaphragm.

The most important part of my job is to maintain a constant pond level. But the lake rises all night, every night; the river never stops. When I drive below town, coming back toward home, I'm afraid I'll meet the lake coming down through the gorge. When Lake Glen was built, it covered the old town of Uree with eighty-five feet of water. As the dam was raised higher and higher across the river, workmen did not tear down the houses. Fish swim in and out of the open doors. Old Man Bill Burdette left his 1916 chain-drive Reo truck parked beside his house when he moved away.

The diver who inspected the dam in 1961 told the Mayor that he saw a catfish as big as a man swimming by the floodgates. The fish is a local legend. At night I fish for it, from the catwalk connecting the floodgates, using deep-sea tackle and cow guts for bait. The fish hangs in the water facing the dam, just above the lake's muddy bottom, and listens to the faint sound of the river glittering on the other side of the concrete. The Prophet from Jupiter says, *When you pull your giant fish out of the water, it will speak true words.* When they tell history, people will remember me because of the fish, even if I don't catch it.

The Prophet from Jupiter's real name is Archie Simpson. He sold real estate and made a fortune in Jupiter, Florida, until nine years ago when God told him that he was the one true prophet who would lead the Christians in the last days before the Rapture. The Prophet says his first words after God finished talking were, *Jesus Christ, you gotta be kidding.* He is not shy about telling the story, and does not seem crazy. He has a young wife who wears beaded Indian headbands and does not shave under her arms.

Old Man Bill Burdette's four sons hired divers and dragged their father's Reo truck out of the lake fifty years to the day after the water rose. The Burdette boys spent $6,000 restoring the old Reo and then said to anyone who would listen, *I don't know why Daddy left it. It was just like new.* Bill Jr., the eldest son, drives it in the town parade every Fourth of July, the back loaded with waving grandchildren. The oldest ones look embarrassed. In town, in front of the Rogue Mountain Restaurant, there is a plywood cutout of a cross-eyed bear. The bear holds up a red and white sign that says EAT.

Before I start fishing, I pour ripe blood from the bottom of my bait bucket into the water. I use treble hooks sharp as razors. A reel like a winch. Randy, the assistant dam keeper, is an orderly at the hospital in Hendersonville and fishes with me after he gets off work. He does not believe the story about the fish as big as a man. I fish all night. Sometimes small catfish, ripping intestines from the treble hooks, impale themselves and make a small noise like crying when I pull them out of the water. I hold them by the tail and hit their heads against the rail of the catwalk and toss them backward over the edge of the dam.

At dawn, I open the small gate that lets water into the turbine house, throw the generator switches, and go to bed. The Town of Lake Glen makes a million dollars a year selling electricity. Everybody who works for the Town of Lake Glen has a new town truck to drive. The Prophet from Jupiter makes miniature ladder-backed chairs that he sells wholesale to the gift shops on the highway. His young wife braids long bands of cowhide into bullwhips and attaches them to clean pine handles. With a hot tool she burns a small cross and the words LAKE GLEN, NORTH CAROLINA on the sides of the handles. She once said to me, *I know that what my husband says about God is true because every time we make love he fills me with the most incredible light.* The bullwhips she makes hang like snakes in front of the gift shops, and tourists stop and buy them by the dozen. It is inexplicable. Once, during lunch in the Rogue Mountain Restaurant, the Prophet from Jupiter looked down into his bowl of vegetable soup and said, *You know, in the last days Christians won't be able to get corn.* The high-voltage wires leading away from the turbine house, you can actually hear them hum.

Sometime during the afternoon—cartoons are on television, the turbines have spun all day, in the Town Hall they are counting money, the skiers are sunburned in their shining boats, and the fishermen are drunk—the water level drops back down to where I try to keep it and the alarm goes off. I get out of bed and go down the narrow stairs to the turbine house and close the gate. All around Lake Glen it is brilliant summer: the town policemen park beside the beach and look out from under the brims of their Smokey the Bear hats at the college girls glistening in the sun. The night of the Fourth of July, the main channel of the lake fills up with boats, and the running lights on the dark water glitter like stars. The fireworks draw lines on the sky like the ghosts of the veins in your eyes after you have stared into the sun.

People who should know better play jokes on Junie Wilson. If they tell him that hair spray will scare away ghosts, he carries a can with him everywhere he goes, like Mace, until somebody tells him differently. If they tell him that ghosts at night drive ski boats, he will not walk by the marina for days or get within 200 yards of a fast boat. The Prophet from Jupiter says that Junie has the gift of true sight. The Mayor gives Junie rides to keep him out of trouble. This is what it's like to live on Lake Glen: in the spring the sun shines all the way through you and you twist down inside yourself, like a seed, and think about growing. There are red and white signs on the waterside of the dam that say DANGER! MAINTAIN A DISTANCE OF 200 YARDS, but you can't read them from that far away. In April the wind blows down out of the mountains and across the cove toward my house, and the sun and the water smell like my wife's hair. Along the western shore in the summer, in the campgrounds beside the highway, gas lanterns glow like ghosts against the mountains. Boys and girls who will never see each other again, and somehow know it, make desperate promises and rub against each other in the laurel; they wade in their underwear in the cold river. In the summer night bullwhips pop like rifles.

Lake Glen was built between the mountains—Rogue Mountain and Rumbling Caesar in 1927 by the Lake Glen Development Company. They built the dam, the municipal building, and a hotel with 200 rooms before the stock market crashed. My wife's name is Elisabeth. She lives, until I leave Lake Glen, with her mother in Monte Sano, Alabama, and has nothing to say to me. Twice a day the town tour boat stops 200 yards from the dam and I can hear the guide over the tinny loudspeaker explain how it would be dangerous to get any closer. Two summers ago the town made a deal with the family on Tryon Bay to keep Shithead penned until the tour boat came to the bay at ten and two. The ducks, however, proved to be undependable. In his pen Shithead became despondent. The problem was that the ducks swim on Tryon Bay every day, you just never know when. Elisabeth says that for years I had nothing to say to her and that I shouldn't expect her to have much to say to me. There are hurricane-fence gates at each end of the dam, and only Randy and the Mayor and I have keys. When fishermen approach it in boats I stand in the kitchen and ring the alarm bell until they leave. They shout at me perched on top of a cliff of water. This is something they do not consider.

The old people say that when Aunt Plutina Williams left her house for the last time before the lake was flooded, she closed her windows and shut and locked the door. Some of the streets in the Town of Lake Glen still have the old Development Company names: Air Strip Road. Yacht Club Drive. H. L. Mencken Circle. Elisabeth, before she left, taught the church preschool class every other Sunday. One year she brought her class here for an Easter egg hunt, and when she unlatched the gate on the front porch they tumbled in their new clothes down the grassy slope toward the lake. Elisabeth followed me down to the turbine house once and over the roar of the generators screamed into my ear, *Why won't you talk to me? What are you holding back?* The new police chief asked for a key to the hurricane-fence gates, but the Mayor refused to give him one.

The Lake Glen Hotel is sold and renovated about every five years, and banners are hung across the front of it on the days it reopens. A crowd gathers and old men sit and watch from the shade under the arches of the municipal building. A Florida Yankee makes a speech about the coming renaissance in Lake Glen. The Mayor cuts the ribbon and everybody claps. But the Town of Lake Glen doesn't have an air strip or a yacht club: the hotel never stays open longer than a season. Most of the time, the signs of every real estate broker in town are lined up in front of it like stiff flags.

Elisabeth stood in the lake that Easter in a new yellow dress; the water was up over her calves. The children squealed on the bank. Maybe then, watching Elisabeth, I believed for a minute in the risen Christ. This is what has happened: my wife, Elisabeth, is pregnant with the new police chief's child. Randy never mentions my misfortune, unless I mention it first. I am grooming him to be the new dam keeper. From the catwalk at night we see in the distance across the channel the lights of the town. There is no reason to come here and stay in a hotel with 200 rooms. There is no reason to stay here at all.

Randy fishes for crappie with an ultralight rod that is limber as a switch and will some nights pull seventy-five, a hundred out of the dark water, glittering, like nickels. He fishes in his white orderly clothes. He smells disinfected and doesn't stay all night. This is what I have done: I took the passenger-side shoulder harness out of my Town of Lake Glen truck and bolted it with long screw anchors into the side of the dam, behind the catwalk. I buckle up when I fish. I don't want to be pulled into the water.

Randy is twenty years old and already has two children. He is not married. His girlfriend is tall and skinny and mean-looking. Randy says she fucks like a cat. The old people say that the morning of the day the water came up, somebody asked Aunt Plutina why she closed her windows and locked her doors, and she said, *Why you never know. Sometime I just might want to come back.* Junie Wilson has seen her. I am afraid that someday I will see her, too. The last time I slept with Elisabeth, two hearts beat inside her.

Randy will go far in this town. Sometimes I can see Elisabeth bending her back into the new police chief. Randy says don't think about it. He is an ex-redneck who learned the value of cutting his hair and being nice to Floridians. He someday might be mayor. He brought his girlfriend to the town employee barbecue and swim party at the Mayor's glass house, and her nipples were stiff, like buttons. My shoulder harness is a good thing: sometimes late at night I doze, leaning forward against it, and dream of something huge, suspended in the water beneath me, its eyes yellow and open. At the party I saw Randy whisper something into his girl-friend's ear. She looked down at the front of her shirt and said out loud, *Well, Jesus Christ, Randy. What do you want me to do about it?*

During the summers in the Thirties the Lake Glen Hotel was a refuge for people who could not afford to summer in the Catskills anymore. Down the road from the hotel, where the Community Center is now, there was a dance pavilion built on wooden pilings out over the bay. Elisabeth stood in the lake in a new yellow dress, holding a jar. The kids from the Sunday school squatted at the edge of the water and looked for tadpoles. The Mayor was diag-nosed with testicular cancer in the spring and waits to see if he had his operation in time.

From my dam I have caught catfish that weighed eighteen, twenty-four, and thirty-one pounds: just babies. Randy said the thirty-one-pounder was big enough. I think I scare him. I got my picture in the paper in Hendersonville, holding up the fish. My beard is long and significant; the catfish looks wise. I mailed a copy to Elisabeth in Monte Sano. The new police chief drives up to the hurricane-fence gate after Randy goes home, and shines his spot-light on me. I don't even unbuckle my harness anymore. The

Mayor is not running for reelection. I will stay until inauguration day. The new police chief will live with Elisabeth and their child in the dam keeper's house; Randy's girlfriend is pregnant again and the house isn't big enough for three kids.

The dance pavilion orchestra was made up of college boys from Chapel Hill and black musicians who had lost their summer hotel jobs up north. The college boys and the black men played nightly for tips, in their shirtsleeves on the covered bandstand, tunes that had been popular during the Twenties. On the open wooden floor out over the water the refugees danced under paper lanterns and blazing mosquito torches. Bootleggers dressed in overalls and wide brimmed hats drove their Model Ts down out of the laurel and sold moonshine in the parking lot.

The new police chief came here from New York State and is greatly admired by the Florida Yankees for his courtesy and creased trousers. I try to hate him, but it is too much like hating myself for what I have done, for what I have left undone. Florida Yankees have too much money and nothing to do. They bitch about the municipal government and run against each other for Town Council. They drive to Hendersonville wearing sweat suits and walk around and around the mall. Randy will not express a preference for Town Council candidates, not even to me. He will go far. His girlfriend will be the first lady of the Town of Lake Glen.

The Mayor came here on summer break from Chapel Hill in 1931 and never went back. He played second trumpet in the Lake Glen orchestra. He took his trust fund and bought lakefront land for eighteen cents on the dollar. At the end of the night, the Mayor says, after the band had packed up their instruments and walked back to the hotel, the last of the dancers stood at the pavilion rail and looked out at the lake. Fog grew up out of the water. Frogs screeched in the cattails near the river channel. The Mayor says that the last dancers would peel off their clothes and dive white and naked into the foggy lake. He says that when they laughed he could hear it from the road as he walked away, or from his boat as it drifted between the mountains on the black lake before first light. Some nights I think that if I drove over to the Community Center and turned off my lights I could see them dancing on the fog. Junie Wilson has taught me to believe in ghosts. The music I hear comes from a distance: I can never make out the tune. I remember that Elisabeth used to put her heels against the bed and raise herself up—she used to push her breasts together with her hands. *Ghosts is with us everywhere*, Junie Wilson says.

The old people say that the town of Uree held a square dance on the bank of the river the night before the water came up. They say that Jim Skipper, drunk on moonshine, shit in the middle of his kitchen floor and set his house on fire. This is something that happened: Elisabeth and I tried to have a baby for seven years before we went to see a fertility specialist in Asheville. The old people say that the whole town whooped and danced in circles in front of Jim Skipper's burning house, and that boys and girls desperate for each other sneaked off and humped urgently in the deserted buildings, that last night before the town began to sink. All the trees around the town of Uree had been cut. They lay tangled where they fell.

During the Second World War the government ran the Lake Glen Hotel as a retreat for Army Air Corps officers on leave from Europe. The Mayor says that the pilots—the ones who were not joined at the hotel by their wives—lay in still rows on the beach all day, sweating moonshine. At night they went either to the dance pavilion, where they tried to screw summer girls or the girls who walked down out of the laurel in homemade dresses, or they went to the whorehouse on the second floor of the Glen Haven Restaurant, where the whores were from Charleston, some of them exotic and Gullah, and the jukebox thumped with swing. The house specialty was fried catfish and hush puppies made with beer. The Prophet from Jupiter and his young wife live with their five sons in the Glen Haven building because the rent is so cheap. There are ten rooms upstairs, five on each side of a narrow hall. One Sunday morning in the early spring, the Prophet's son Zeke told Elisabeth that he dreamed Jesus came to his house and pulled a big bucket of water out of a well and everybody drank from it.

The fertility specialist, Dr. Suzanne Childress, said that I had lethargic sperm. *I knew it wasn't me,* Elisabeth said, *I knew it wasn't me.*

Dr. Suzanne Childress said, *Your sperm count is normal. They just do not swim well enough to reach and fertilize Elisabeth's ovum.*

They say that Jim Skipper camped out under his wagon for three weeks beside the rising lake. He borrowed a boat from the Lake Glen Development Company and paddled around the sinking houses. He looked in the windows until they disappeared, and then he banged on the tin roofs with his paddle. He said he did not know how to live anywhere else. They say that before Jim Skipper shot himself, he stood in his borrowed boat and pissed down Old Man Bill Burdette's chimney.

Elisabeth said, *You always thought it was me, didn't you?*

Dr. Suzanne Childress said, *I think that perhaps we can correct your problem with dietary supplements. Vitamins. Do you exercise?*

Elisabeth said, *I'm ovulating right now. I can tell.*

Dr. Suzanne Childress said, *I know.*

They closed the dance pavilion for good in 1944 when a moonshiner named Rudy Thomas, in a fight over a Glen Haven whore named Sunshine, stabbed a B-27 pilot from New York eleven times and pushed him into the lake. Rudy Thomas died of tuberculosis in Central Prison in Raleigh in 1951. They say that Jim Skipper was a good man but one crazy son of a bitch.

Several nights a week during his second summer in town the Mayor leaned a chambermaid named Lavonia over the windscreen of his 1928 Chris-Craft and screwed her until his legs got so weak that he almost fell out of the boat. Junie Wilson says that the boxes on the sides of telephone poles—if the ghosts have turned them on—make him so drunk that he is afraid he is going to fall into the lake. The coat hanger around Junie's neck protects him from evil spirits. *Sweet Lavonia,* the Mayor says, *had the kind of body that a young man would paint on the side of his airplane before he flew off to fight in a war.*

The young Mayor took off his clothes as he drove his boat fast across the dark lake. Lavonia waited between two boulders on the shore near Uree Shoals. The Mayor cut the engine and drifted into the cove. Lavonia stepped out from between the rocks, pulled her skirt up around her waist, and waded out to the boat. The white Mayor glowed in the darkness and played gospel songs on his trumpet while she walked through the water. There wasn't a house or a light in sight. Lavonia told him every night while he squeezed her breasts, *You're putting the devil inside of me.* The boat turned in the water, and the Mayor owned everything he could see. Randy in his orderly clothes, jigging for crappie, tells me there is nothing wrong with me, that to make a woman pregnant you have to fuck her in a certain way, that's all, you have to put your seed where it will take.

Junie Wilson woke me up one morning yelling, *Open the gate. Open the gate.* One of the town cops had told him that ghosts wouldn't walk across a dam, that walking across a dam was the way for a man to get rid of his ghosts once and for all. Junie sees three ghosts in his dreams: he sees a man standing in a boat, he sees a woman looking out the window of a house under water, and he sees his mama wading out into the lake. This last dream torments Junie the most, because he doesn't know how to swim. He stands on the bank and yells for her to come back. We walked across the dam, water up close beside Junie, the air falling away beside me. Junie said, *She better get out of that water if she knows what's good for her.* What my wife said is true: I never thought it was me. After we made love Elisabeth kept her legs squeezed tight together, even after she went to sleep. *Ghosts is keeping me awake,* Junie said. *I got to get rid of these ghosts so I can get me some sleep. Ghosts is crucifying me.*

Something's wrong with me, Elisabeth whispered. *I can't have a baby.*

I said, *I still love you. Shhh.*

Before we went to see Dr. Suzanne Childress, I liked to sit astride Elisabeth, hard and slick between her breasts. Lavonia tried to kill the baby inside her by drinking two quarts of moonshine that she bought from a bootlegger named Big Julie Cooper in the pavilion parking lot. Junie didn't speak until he was four. Ghosts began to chase him when he was twelve. The first time Lavonia saw Junie touching himself, she whipped him with a belt and told him that if he ever did that again a white man would come with a big knife and cut it off. Elisabeth, when I was finished, wiped her chest and neck off with a towel.

Bugs fly like angels into the white light of the gas lantern and then spin and fall into the water. Randy jabs the air with his index finger: *It's special pussy, man, way back in the back. It burns like fire.* The Mayor gave Lavonia a little money every month until she died three years ago. He does not give money to Junie because Junie drops dollar bills off the Tryon Bay bridge. He does it so that the ghosts won't turn on their machines when he walks by telephone poles. The Mayor says, *Jesus Christ, if I gave that boy a million dollars, he'd throw every bit of it off that damn bridge.*

Randy says, *Man, women go crazy when you start hitting that baby spot. They'll scratch the hell out of you. You gotta time it right, that's all. You gotta let it go when you hit it.* He slaps the back of one hand into the other. *Bang. You gotta get the pussy they don't want you to have.*

Junie Wilson and I walked back and forth across the dam until the alarm went off and I had to close the gate and shut down the generators. I didn't tell Junie about the machines in the turbine house. Elisabeth said over the phone from Monte Sano, *I know you won't believe it now, but all I ever wanted was for you to pay attention to me.* In a sterile men's room in the doctor's office, I put my hands against the wall and Elisabeth jerked me off into a glass bottle. Junie Wilson said that he did not feel any better, and I said that walking across the dam does not always work.

In August the air over the lake is so thick you can see it, and distances through the haze look impossible to cross. The water is smooth and gray, and the Town of Lake Glen shimmers across the channel like the place it tried to be. At the beach, policemen sit in their station wagons with their air conditioners running. The college girls are tanned the color of baseball gloves. Randy's girlfriend is starting to gain weight and Randy fishes less; the crappie have all but stopped biting. The Prophet from Jupiter winks and says that in hot weather his wife smells like good earth and that God has blessed him in more ways than one. In the hot summer the ghosts keep their machines turned on all the time, and Junie Wilson staggers through town like a drunk. If there is one true thing I know to tell you, it is this: in North Carolina, even in the mountains, it takes more than a month of your life to live through August.

September is no cooler, but the sky begins to brighten, like a promise, and the town begins to pack itself up for leaving. The college girls go first, their tans already fading, and motor homes with bicycles strapped to their backs groan up out of the campgrounds to the shimmering highway. Boys and girls damp with sweat sneak away to say good-bye in the laurel and make promises one last time. Around the lake, family by family, summer people close up their houses and go back to where they came from in June. The Florida Yankees have mercifully decided among themselves who the new mayor will be, but the council candidates drive around town at night and tear down each other's campaign posters. My beard is down to the middle of my chest. Junie Wilson walks through town with his hands held up beside his face like blinders, to keep from seeing the bright faces stapled to the telephone poles. One afternoon I slept in front of a fan and dreamed it was spring: Elisabeth waded in the lake and I sat on the porch and held a baby whose hair smelled like the sun. I dialed a 1-900 phone love number and charged it to the Town of Lake Glen, and a woman named Betty said she wanted me to come in her mouth. In the closed-up summer houses, burglar alarms squeal in frequencies only bats can hear and the lights burn all night, turned on and off by automatic timers, but the rooms are empty and still.

In the fall the wild ducks fly away after the summer people in great, glittering Vs. Weekend tourists drive up from Charlotte and

Greenville to point at the leaves and buy pumpkins. The ducks skim low over the channel in front of my house, their wings whistling like blood, and then cross the dam, suddenly very high in the air. The Floridians burn leaves in their yards and inhale the smoke like Mentholatum. Randy said, *Man, I hope there ain't going to be any hard feelings*, and stopped coming to fish. Early one morning my line stiffened and moved through the water for twenty yards. When I set the hook, the stiff rod bent double against a great weight. And then it was gone. The next night the new police chief sat outside the gate in his Jeep and played an easy-listening radio station over his loudspeaker. In the town of Uree, Aunt Plutina Williams sits and looks out the window of her house. Jim Skipper wanders in and out of the houses. A giant fish moves through the air like a zeppelin. The new police chief said over the loudspeaker, *Look, chief, I just*—and then stopped talking and backed up and drove away.

In November 1928 the Lake Glen dam almost washed away. A flash flood boiled down out of the mountains after a week of rain, and the dam keeper did not open the floodgates in time. The water rose and filled the lake bed like a bowl before it spilled over the top of the dam. Old Man Bill Burdette drove down the mountain in his new truck to warn people downstream: the lake had turned itself back into a river and was cutting a channel through the earth around the side of the dam. They say that the men of the Lake Glen Development Company construction crews hauled six heavy freight wagons of red roofing slate from the hotel site and threw it over the side of the gorge. Local men came down out of the laurel and worked in the rain filling sandbags and tossing them into the hole. But still the water ran muddy around the side of the dam and over the tops of the sandbags and the roofing. The workers rolled the six empty wagons in on top of the pile. They carried all of the furniture and both stoves out of the dam keeper's house and threw it in. They pushed three Model T Fords belonging to the company, as well as the superintendent's personal Pierce-Arrow, into the channel the river cut around the side of the dam. But the water still snaked its way through the wreckage, downhill toward the riverbed.

This October, Town of Lake Glen workmen hung huge red and yellow banners shaped like leaves from wires stretched between the telephone poles. They built cider stands and arts and crafts booths and a small plywood stage in the parking lot in front of the Lake Glen Hotel. The Chamber of Commerce called the whole thing ColorFest! and promoted it on the Asheville TV station. Hundreds of tourists showed up, wearing bright sweaters, even though it was warm. I saw townies look at me when they thought I wasn't looking, and their eyes said: I wonder what he's going to do. My beard is a torrent of hair. A high school clogging team from Hendersonville stomped on the wooden stage. Little boys stood at the edge of the stage and looked up through the swirling white petticoats of the girl dancers. Shithead's owners walked him through the crowd on a leash. The Prophet from Jupiter and his wife sold miniature ladder-backed chairs and bullwhips from a booth, and gave away spiritual tracts about the coming Rapture. Junie Wilson, crying for somebody to help him before the white man came to get him, showed his erection to three of Old Man Bill Burdette's great-granddaughters, who were sitting in the back of the 1916 Reo truck.

In 1928 the workers at the collapsing dam looked at each other in the rain. Everything seemed lost. The superintendent of the Lake Glen Development Company produced a Colt revolver and a box of cartridges. Big Julie Cooper took the superintendent's gun when nobody else would and one at a time shot twenty-four Development Company mules right between the eyes. The workers threw the dead and dying mules in on top of the cars and the wagons and the red roofing slate and the furniture and the stoves, before the rain slacked and the water retreated back to the lakeside of the dam. Then the superintendent threw his hat into the gorge and danced a jig and said, *Boys, you don't miss your water until your dam starts to go.* When the roads dried out, the Development Com-

pany brought a steam shovel to cover the debris and the mules
with dirt and rock blasted from the sides of the mountains, but not
before the weather cleared and the mules swelled and rotted in the
late autumn sun. They say that you could smell the mules for
miles—some of them even exploded—and that workmen putting
the roof on the hotel, at the other end of the channel, wore ker-
chiefs dipped in camphor tied around their faces. They say that a
black funnel cloud of buzzards and crows spun in the air over the
gorge and that you could see it a long way away. At night bears
came down off of Rumbling Caesar and ate the rotting mules. Big
Julie Cooper said, *By God, now let me tell you something. That son of
a bitch liked to of went.*

When Old Man Bill Burdette's three great-granddaughters
screamed, the new police chief twisted Junie Wilson's arm behind
his back. Junie screamed, *Jesus. Jesus. Oh God. Please don't cut me*,
and tried to get away. The whole ColorFest! crowd ran up close
and silently watched while Junie and the new police chief spun
around and around. *I'm not going to hurt you, Junie*, the new police
chief said. Two other town cops showed up and held Junie down
while the new police chief very efficiently handcuffed Junie and
tied his legs together with three bullwhips the Mayor brought
from the Prophet from Jupiter's booth. The new police chief covered Junie's erection with a red ColorFest! banner shaped like a
leaf. Junie's coat hanger was bent and twisted around his face. The
new police chief pulled it off and handed it to the Mayor. Junie
screamed for his mother over and over until his eyes rolled back in
his head and his body began to jerk. Shithead howled. The high
school clogging team from Hendersonville the whole time
stomped and spun, wild-eyed, on the flimsy plywood stage.

The first Monday after Thanksgiving, I raised one of the
floodgates halfway and lowered the lake eight feet. Randy will fill
the lake back up the first Monday in February. It will be his job to
maintain a constant pond level. Every day I try to piss off the river-
side of the dam in a stream that will reach from me to the bottom

of the gorge, but it is impossible to do. When the lake level is down, the exposed pilings of the boathouses are spindly like the legs of old men. Randy's girlfriend has started to show and her breasts are heavy. The new police chief spends three days in Monte Sano with my wife every other week. The hotel is dark and for sale and locked up tight.

When the water is down the people who live here year round replace the rotten boards on their docks and the rotten rungs on their uncovered ladders. All around the lake circular saws squeal. The water over the town of Uree seems darker somehow than the rest of the lake, and I've always wanted to drop the lake down far enough to see what is down there. At the end of that last night, when Jim Skipper's house had burned down to a glowing pile of ashes, the people of the town of Uree sang "Shall We Gather at the River" and then stood around, just looking at their houses and barns and sheds, wishing they had done more, until the sun came over the dam at the head of the gorge. The Mayor stays mostly in his house now. His successor has been elected. Randy wore a necktie and a sport coat and met with the mayor-elect to discuss ways to generate electricity more efficiently. The Mayor keeps his thermostat set on eighty-five and still cannot get warm. The word from the state hospital in Morganton is that Junie Wilson has no idea where he is or what has happened and screams every time he sees a white doctor.

The lake began to freeze during a cold snap the week before Christmas. There were circles of whiter ice where part of the lake thawed in the sun and then refroze again at night. The temperature dropped fast all day Christmas Eve, and the ice closed in and trapped a tame duck on Tryon Bay. Shithead, going out after the duck, broke through a soft spot in the ice and could not get back out.

In fifteen minutes most of the town of Lake Glen was on the Tryon Bay bridge screaming, *Come on, Shithead. Come on, boy, you can do it*. Nobody could remember who had a canoe or think of how to rescue the dog. The Prophet from Jupiter, before anyone could stop him, ran across the frozen mud and slid headfirst out onto the ice. The duck frozen to the lake in the middle of the bay flailed its wings. I stood beside the new police chief on the bank and screamed for the Prophet to *Lie still! Lie still!* that we would find a way to save him.

The Prophet from Jupiter moved his lips and began to inch his way forward across the ice. It groaned under his weight. Cracks in the ice shot away from his body like frozen lightning. The Prophet kept going, an inch at a time, none of us breathing until he reached forward into the hole and grabbed Shithead by the collar and pulled him up onto the ice. It held. The dog quivered for a second and skittered back toward shore, its belly low to the frozen lake.

We opened our mouths to cheer, but there was a crack like a gunshot, and the Prophet from Jupiter disappeared. He came up, once—he looked surprised more than anything else, his face deathly white, his mouth a black O—and then disappeared again and did not come back up. On the bridge the Prophet's five sons ran in place and screamed and held their arms toward the water. Randy's girlfriend kept her arms wrapped tight around the Prophet's wife, who shouted, *Oh Jesus! Oh Jesus!* and tried to jump off of the bridge. By the time we got boats on the lake, and broke the ice with sledgehammers, and pulled grappling hooks on the ends of ropes through the dark water and hooked the Prophet and dragged him up, there was nothing even God could do. The duck frozen to the lake had beaten itself to death against the ice. The new police chief sat down on the bank and cried like a baby.

Elisabeth's water broke that night. The new police chief called the Mayor and left for Monte Sano, and the Mayor called me. I walked back and forth and back and forth across the dam until all the ghosts of Lake Glen buzzed in my ears like electricity: I saw the Prophet from Jupiter riding with Old Man Bill Burdette, down the streets of Uree in a 1916 Reo truck, toward the light in Aunt Plutina Williams's window, I saw catfish as big as men, with whiskers like bullwhips, lie down at the feet of the Prophet and speak in a thousand strange tongues; I saw dancers moving

against each other in the air to music I had never heard; I saw
Lavonia, naked and beautiful bathing and healing Junie in a
moonlit cove; I saw Elisabeth standing in the edge of the lake in
the spring, nursing a child who smelled like the sun; I saw the
new police chief in a boat watching over his family; I saw the
Mayor on his knees praying in Gullah with Charleston whores; I
saw Jim Skipper and Rudy Thomas and Big Julie Cooper driving
a bleeding pilot beside the river in a wagon pulled by twenty-four
mules; I saw the Prophet from Jupiter and his five sons shoot out
of the lake like Fourth of July rockets and shout with incredible
light and tongues of fire, *Rise, children of the water. Rise and be
whole in the kingdom of God.*

Tony Earley grew up in Rutherford County, North Carolina, and graduated from Warren Wilson College and The University of Alabama. His
stories have appeared in *Harper's Magazine*, *TriQuarterly*, *New Stories from
the South: The Year's Best, 1993*, and *Best American Short Stories*. His first
book, *Here We Are in Paradise*, a short story collection, was published in
February by Little, Brown and Company. He lives outside Pittsburgh,
where his wife attends seminary.

I'*m still not sure where stories, this story or any other, come from—nor do
I think I want to know—but I do remember the precise moment when
"The Prophet from Jupiter" first began to percolate. I had just eaten lunch
with a friend at a small restaurant in Sunny View, California, and on the
drive back, my friend, who is a very religious man, turned to me and said:
"You know, in the last days Christians won't be able to get corn." I could have
kissed him on the spot; I knew he had just given me a story. Four years later,
I'm still not sure where most of it came from, although parts of it, such as the
line quoted above, are stolen outright. For the record, in answer to the
question people have most often asked me about the story: I made up the part
about the mules.*

APPENDIX

A list of the magazines consulted for *New Stories from the South: The Year's Best, 1994,* with current addresses, subscription rates, and editors.

Agni
Boston State University
236 Bay State Road
Boston, MA 02215
Semiannually, $12
Askold Melnyczak

Alabama Literary Review
253 Smith Hall
Troy State University
Troy, AL 36082
Semiannually, $9
Theron Montgomery, Editor-in-
    Chief; James G. Davis, Fiction
    Editor

American Short Fiction
Parlin 14
Department of English
University of Austin
Austin, TX 78712-1164
Quarterly, $24
Laura Furman, Editor

The American Voice
The Kentucky Foundation for
    Women, Inc.

332 West Broadway, Suite 1215
Louisville, KY 40202
Quarterly, $15
Frederick Smock, Sallie Bingham

Antaeus
The Ecco Press
100 West Broad Street
Hopewell, NJ 08525
Semiannually, $30 for 4 issues
Daniel Halpern

Antietam Review
7 West Franklin
Hagerstown, MD 21740
Once or twice a year, $5 each
Susanne Kass

The Antioch Review
P.O. Box 148
Yellow Springs, OH 45387
Quarterly, $25
Robert S. Fogarty

Apalachee Quarterly
P.O. Box 20106
Tallahassee, FL 32316

Three times a year, $15
Barbara Hamby and Bruce Boehrer

The Atlantic Monthly
745 Boylston Street
Boston, MA 02116
Monthly, $15.94
William Whitworth

Black Warrior Review
The University of Alabama
P.O. Box 2936
Tuscaloosa, AL 35486-2936
Semiannually, $11
Glenn Mort

Blue Mesa Review
Creative Writing Center
University of New Mexico
Albuquerque, NM 87131

Carolina Quarterly
Greenlaw Hall CB# 3520
University of North Carolina
Chapel Hill, NC 27599-3520
Quarterly, $10
Amber Vogel, Editor

The Chariton Review
Northeast Missouri State University
Kirksville, MO 63501
Semiannually, $9
Jim Barnes

The Chattahoochee Review
DeKalb College
2101 Womack Road
Dunwoody, GA 30338-4497
Quarterly, $15
Lamar York, Editor; Anna
    Schachner, Fiction

Cimarron Review
205 Morrill Hall

Oklahoma State University
Stillwater, OK 74078-0135
Quarterly, $12
Gordon Weaver

Concho River Review
c/o English Department
Angelo State University
San Angelo, TX 76909
Semiannually, $12
Terence A. Dalrymple

Confrontation
Department of English
C. W. Post of L.I.U.
Brookville, NY 11548
Semiannually, $10
Martin Tucker, Editor-in-Chief

Crazyhorse
Department of English
University of Arkansas at
    Little Rock
2801 South University
Little Rock, AR 72204
Semiannually, $10
Judy Troy

The Crescent Review
1445 Old Town Road
Winston-Salem, NC 27106-3143
Semiannually, $10
Guy Nancekeville

Crosscurrents
2200 Glastonbury Road
Westlake Village, CA 91361
Quarterly, $18
Linda Brown Michelson

CutBank
Department of English
University of Montana
Missoula, MT 59812

Semiannually, $12
Judy Blunt and Bob Hackett,
    Co-editors

Epoch
251 Goldwin Smith Hall
Cornell University
Ithaca, NY 14853-3201
Three times a year, $11
Michael Koch

Esquire
1790 Broadway
New York, NY 10019
Monthly, $15.97
Rust Hills, Fiction Editor;
    Will Blythe, Literary Editor

Fiction
c/o English Department
The City College of New York
New York, NY 10031
Three times a year, $20
Mark J. Mirsky

The Florida Review
Department of English
University of Central Florida
Orlando, FL 32816
Semiannually, $7
Russ Kesler

The Georgia Review
The University of Georgia
Athens, GA 30602
Quarterly, $18
Stanley W. Lindberg

The Gettysburg Review
Gettysburg College
Gettysburg, PA 17325-1491
Quarterly, $15
Peter Stitt

Glimmer Train
812 SW Washington Street,
    Suite 1205
Portland, OR 97205-3216
Quarterly, $29
Susan Burmeister and Linda Davies,
    Editors

Granta
2-3 Hanover Yard
Noel Road
Islington
London
N1 8BE
England
Quarterly, $29.95
Bill Buford

The Greensboro Review
Department of English
University of North Carolina
Greensboro, NC 27412
Semiannually, $8
Jim Clark

Gulf Coast
Department of English
University of Houston
4800 Calhoun Road
Houston, TX 77204-3012
Semiannually, $22 for two years
A. Quinlan and Amy Storrow

Habersham Review
Piedmont College
Demorest, GA 30535
Semiannually, $8
The Editors

Harper's Magazine
666 Broadway
New York, NY 10012
Monthly, $18
Lewis H. Lapham

High Plains Literary Review
180 Adams Street, Suite 250
Denver, CO 80206
Three times a year, $20
Robert O. Greer, Jr.

Indiana Review
316 North Jordan Avenue
Bloomington, IN 47405
Semiannually, $12
Allison Joseph

The Iowa Review
308 EPB
The University of Iowa
Iowa City, IA 52242
Three times a year, $18
David Hamilton

Iris
P.O. Box 7263
Atlanta, GA 30357
Quarterly, $12
Dennis Adams

The Journal
The Ohio State University
Department of English
164 West 17th Avenue
Columbus, OH 43210
Biannually, $8
Michelle Herman, Fiction Editor

Karamu
English Department
East Illinois University
Charleston, IL 61920
Subscription info not listed
Peggy Brayfield, Editor

The Kenyon Review
Kenyon College
Gambier, OH 43022
Quarterly, $24
Marilyn Hacker

The Literary Review
285 Madison Avenue
Madison, NJ 07940
Quarterly, $18
Walter Cummins

The Long Story
11 Kingston Street
North Andover, MA 01845
Annually, $5
R. P. Burnham

Louisiana Literature
P.O. Box 792
Southeast Louisiana University
Hammond, LA 70402
Semiannually, $10
David Hanson, Editor

Mid-American Review
106 Hanna Hall
Department of English
Bowling Green State University
Bowling Green, OH 43403
Serniannually, $8
Robert Early, Senior Editor; Ellen
   Behrens, Fiction

Mississippi Quarterly
Box 5272
Mississippi State, MS 39762
Quarterly, $12
Robert L. Phillips, Jr., Editor

Mississippi Review
Center for Writers
The University of Southern
   Mississippi
Box 5144
Hattiesburg, MS 39406-5144
Semiannually, $15
Frederick Barthelme

The Missouri Review
1507 Hillcrest Hall

University of Missouri
Columbia, MO 65211
Three times a year, $15
Speer Morgan

Negative Capability
62 Ridgelawn Drive East
Mobile, AL 36608
Three times a year, $12
Sue Walker

New Delta Review
English Department
Louisiana State University
Baton Rouge, LA 70803
Semiannually, $7
Catherine Williamson, Editor

New England Review
Middlebury College
Middlebury, VT 05753
Quarterly, $20
T. R. Hummer

The New Yorker
20 West 43rd Street
New York, NY 10036
Weekly, $32
Tina Brown

Nimrod
Arts and Humanities Council of
  Tulsa
2210 South Main Street
Tulsa, OK 74114
Semiannually, $10
Francine Ringold, Editor; Geraldine
  McLoud, Fiction Editor

The North American Review
University of Northern Iowa
Cedar Falls, IA 50614
Six times a year, $18
Robley Wilson

North Carolina Literary Review
English Department
East Carolina University
Greenville, NC 27858
Semiannually, $15
Alex Albright

Northwest Review
369 PLC
University of Oregon
Eugene, OR 97403
Three times a year, $14
John White

Ohioana Quarterly
Ohioana Library Association
1105 Ohio Departments Building
65 South Front Street
Columbus, OH 43215
Quarterly, $20
Barbara Maslekoff

The Ohio Review
290-c Ellis Hall
Ohio University
Athens, OH 45701-2979
Three times a year, $16
Wayne Dodd

Old Hickory Review
P.O. Box 1178
Jackson, TN 38302
Semiannually, $12
Dorothy Stanfill and Bill Nance

Ontario Review
9 Honey Brook Drive
Princeton, NJ 08540
Semiannually, $10
Raymond J. Smith and Joyce Carol
  Oates

Oxford American
115 ½ South Lamar

Oxford, MS 38655
Bimonthly, $16
Marc Smirnoff

Other Voices
Department of English
UNIL Box 4348
Chicago, IL 60680
Semiannually, $16
Lois Hauselman and Sharon
   Fiffer

The Paris Review
Box S
541 East 72nd Street
New York, NY 10021
Quarterly, $24
George Plimpton

Parting Gifts
March Street Press
3006 Stonecutter Terrace
Greensboro, NC 27405
Subscription info not listed
Robert Bixby, Editor

Pembroke Magazine
Box 60
Pembroke State University
Pembroke, NC 28372
Annually, $5
Shelby Stephenson, Editor;
   Stephen E. Smith, Fiction Editor

Playboy
680 N. Lake Shore Drive
Chicago, IL 60611
Monthly, $29
Alice K. Turner, Fiction Editor

Ploughshares
Emerson College
100 Beacon Street
Boston, MA 02116
Three times a year, $19

DeWitt Henry, Editor; Don Lee,
   Fiction Editor

Prairie Schooner
201 Andrews Hall
University of Nebraska
Lincoln, NE 68588-0334
Quarterly, $20
Hilda Raz, Editor-in-Chief

Puerto del Sol
Box 3E
New Mexico State University
Las Cruces, NM 88003
Semiannually, $10
Antonya Nelson, Editor-in-chief

Quarterly West
317 Olpin Union
University of Utah
Salt Lake City, UT 84112
Semiannually, $9
Bernard Wood and Tom Hazuka

Redbook
The Hearst Corporation
959 Eighth Avenue
New York, NY 10019
Monthly, $14.97
Ellen Levine, Editor-in-Chief;
   Dawn Raffel, Fiction and Books

River Styx
14 South Euclid
St. Louis, MO 63108
Three times a year, $20
Lee Fournier

Santa Monica Review
Santa Monica College
1900 Pico Blvd.
Santa Monica, CA 90405
Semiannually, $14
Jim Krusoe

Sewanee Review
University of the South
Sewanee, TN 37375-4009
Quarterly, $15
George Core

Shenandoah
Washington and Lee University
Box 722
Lexington, VA 24450
Quarterly, $11
Dabney Stuart

Snake Nation Review
110 #2 West Force Street
Valdosta, GA 31601
Semiannually, $15
Roberta George, Pat Miller, and
  Janice Daugharty

The South Carolina Review
Department of English
Clemson University
Clemson, SC 29634-1503
Semiannually, $7
Richard J. Calhoun

South Dakota Review
Box 111
University Exchange
Vermillion, SD 57069
Quarterly, $15
John R. Milton

Southern Exposure
P.O. Box 531
Durham, NC 27702
Quarterly, $24
Eric Bates, Editor; Susan Ketchin,
  Fiction

Southern Humanities Review
9088 Haley Center
Auburn University

Auburn, AL 36849
Quarterly, $15
Dan R. Latimer and R. T. Smith

The Southern Review
43 Allen Hall
Louisiana State University
Baton Rouge, LA 70803-5605
Quarterly, $18
James Olney and Dave Smith

Sou'wester
Southern Illinois University at
  Edwardsville
Edwardsville, IL 62026-1438
Three times a year, $10
Fred W. Robbins

Southwest Review
6410 Airline Road
Southern Methodist University
Dallas, TX 75275
Quarterly, $20
Willard Spiegelman

Stories
Box Number 1467
East Arlington, MA 02174-0022
Quarterly, $18
Amy R. Kaufman

Story
1507 Dana Avenue
Cincinnati, OH 45207
Quarterly, $22
Lois Rosenthal

StoryQuarterly
P.O. Box 1416
Northbrook, IL 60065
Quarterly, $12
Anne Brashler, Diane Williams, and
  Margaret Barrett

Tampa Review
Box 135F
401 W. Kennedy Blvd.
Tampa, FL 33606-1490
Semiannually, $10
Richard Mathews, Editor; Andy
    Solomon, Fiction

The Threepenny Review
P.O. Box 9131
Berkeley, CA 94709
Quarterly, $12
Wendy Lesser

TriQuarterly
Northwestern University
2020 Ridge Avenue
Evanston, IL 60208
Three times a year, $20
Reginald Gibbons

Turnstile
Suite 2348
175 Fifth Avenue
New York, NY 10010
Semiannually, $12
Mitchell Nauffts

The Virginia Quarterly Review
One West Range
Charlottesville, VA 22903
Quarterly, $15
Staige D. Blackford

Voice Literary Supplement
VV Publishing Corp.
36 Cooper Square
New York, NY 10003
Monthly, except the combined
    issues of Dec./Jan. and July/Aug.,
    $17
M. Mark

Weber Studies
Weber State College
Ogden, UT 84408-1214
Three times a year, $10
Neila C. Seshachari

West Branch
Bucknell Hall
Bucknell University
Lewisburg, PA 17837
Semiannually, $7
Karl Patten and Robert Taylor

Wind Magazine
RFD Route 1
Box 809K
Pikeville, KY 41501
Semiannually, $7
Quentin Howard

ZYZZYVA
41 Sutter Street
Suite 1400
San Francisco, CA 94104
Quarterly, $28
Howard Junker

PREVIOUS VOLUMES

Copies of previous volumes of *New Stories from the South* can be ordered through your local bookstore or by calling the Sales Department at Algonquin Books of Chapel Hill. Multiple copies for classroom adoptions are available at a special discount. For information, please call 919-967-0108.

NEW STORIES FROM THE SOUTH: THE YEAR'S BEST, 1986

Max Apple, BRIDGING

Madison Smartt Bell, TRIPTYCH 2

Mary Ward Brown, TONGUES OF FLAME

Suzanne Brown, COMMUNION

James Lee Burke, THE CONVICT

Ron Carlson, AIR

Doug Crowell, SAYS VELMA

Leon V. Driskell, MARTHA JEAN

Elizabeth Harris, THE WORLD RECORD HOLDER

Mary Hood, SOMETHING GOOD FOR GINNY

David Huddle, SUMMER OF THE MAGIC SHOW

Gloria Norris, HOLDING ON

Kurt Rheinheimer, UMPIRE

W. A. Smith, DELIVERY

Wallace Whatley, SOMETHING TO LOSE

Luke Whisnant, WALLWORK

Sylvia Wilkinson, CHICKEN SIMON

NEW STORIES FROM THE SOUTH: THE YEAR'S BEST, 1987

James Gordon Bennett, DEPENDENTS

Robert Boswell, EDWARD AND JILL

Rosanne Coggeshall, PETER THE ROCK

John William Corrington, HEROIC MEASURES/VITAL SIGNS

Vicki Covington, MAGNOLIA

Andre Dubus, DRESSED LIKE SUMMER LEAVES

Mary Hood, AFTER MOORE

Trudy Lewis, VINCRISTINE

Lewis Nordan, SUGAR, THE EUNUCHS, AND BIG G.B.

Peggy Payne, THE PURE IN HEART

Bob Shacochis, WHERE PELHAM FELL

Lee Smith, LIFE ON THE MOON

Marly Swick, HEART

Robert Taylor, Jr., LADY OF SPAIN

Luke Whisnant, ACROSS FROM THE MOTOHEADS

NEW STORIES FROM THE SOUTH: THE YEAR'S BEST, 1988

Ellen Akins, GEORGE BAILEY FISHING

Rick Bass, THE WATCH

Richard Bausch, THE MAN WHO KNEW BELLE STAR

Larry Brown, FACING THE MUSIC

Pam Durban, BELONGING

John Rolfe Gardiner, GAME FARM

Jim Hall, GAS

Charlotte Holmes, METROPOLITAN

Nanci Kincaid, LIKE THE OLD WOLF IN ALL THOSE WOLF STORIES

Barbara Kingsolver, ROSE-JOHNNY

Trudy Lewis, HALF-MEASURES

Jill McCorkle, FIRST UNION BLUES

Mark Richard, HAPPINESS OF THE GARDEN VARIETY

Sunny Rogers, THE CRUMB

Annette Sanford, LIMITED ACCESS

Eve Shelnutt, VOICE

New Stories from the South: The Year's Best, 1989

Rick Bass, WILD HORSES

James Gordon Bennett, PACIFIC THEATER

Madison Smartt Bell, CUSTOMS OF THE COUNTRY

Larry Brown, SAMARITANS

Mary Ward Brown, IT WASN'T ALL DANCING

Kelly Cherry, WHERE SHE WAS

David Huddle, PLAYING

Sandy Huss, COUPON FOR BLOOD

Frank Manley, THE RAIN OF TERROR

Bobbie Ann Mason, WISH

Lewis Nordan, A HANK OF HAIR, A PIECE OF BONE

Kurt Rheinheimer, HOMES

Mark Richard, STRAYS

Annette Sanford, SIX WHITE HORSES

Paula Sharp, HOT SPRINGS

NEW STORIES FROM THE SOUTH: THE YEAR'S BEST, 1990

Tom Baily, CROW MAN

Rick Bass, THE HISTORY OF RODNEY

Richard Bausch, LETTER TO THE LADY OF THE HOUSE

Larry Brown, SLEEP

Moira Crone, JUST OUTSIDE THE B.T.

Clyde Edgerton, CHANGING NAMES

Greg Johnson, THE BOARDER

Nanci Kincaid, SPITTIN' IMAGE OF A BAPTIST BOY

Reginald McNight, THE KIND OF LIGHT THAT SHINES ON TEXAS

Lewis Nordan, THE CELLAR OF RUNT CONROY

Lance Olsen, FAMILY

Mark Richard, FEAST OF THE EARTH, RANSOM OF THE CLAY

Ron Robinson, WHERE WE LAND

Bob Shacochis, LES FEMMES CREOLE

Mollie Best Tinsley, ZOE

Donna Trussell, FISHBONE

NEW STORIES FROM THE SOUTH: THE YEAR'S BEST, 1991

Rick Bass, IN THE LOYAL MOUNTAINS

Larry Brown, BIG BAD LOVE

Thomas Phillips Brewer, BLACK CAT BONE

Robert Olen Butler, RELIC

Barbara Hudson, THE ARABESQUE

Elizabeth Hunnewell, A LIFE OR DEATH MATTER

Hilding Johnson, SOUTH OF KITTATINNY

Nanci Kincaid, THIS IS NOT THE PICTURE SHOW

Bobbie Ann Mason, WITH JAZZ

Jill McCorkle, WAITING FOR THE HARD TIMES TO END

Robert Morgan, POINSETT'S BRIDGE

Reynolds Price, HIS FINAL MOTHER

Mark Richard, THE BIRDS FOR CHRISTMAS

Susan Starr Richards, THE SCREENED PORCH

Lee Smith, INTENSIVE CARE

Peter Taylor, COUSIN AUBREY

NEW STORIES FROM THE SOUTH: THE YEAR'S BEST, 1992

Alison Baker, CLEARWATER AND LATISSIMUS

Larry Brown, A ROADSIDE RESURRECTION

Mary Ward Brown, A NEW LIFE

Robert Olen Butler, A GOOD SCENT FROM A STRANGE MOUNTAIN

James Lee Burke, TEXAS CITY, 1947

Nanci Kincaid, A STURDY PAIR OF SHOES THAT FIT GOOD

Patricia Lear, AFTER MEMPHIS

Dan Leone, YOU HAVE CHOSEN CAKE

Karen Minton, LIKE HANDS ON A CAVE WALL

Reginald McNight, QUITTING SMOKING

Robert Morgan, DEATH CROWN

Elizabeth Seydel Morgan, ECONOMICS

Susan Perabo, EXPLAINING DEATH TO THE DOG

Padgett Powell, THE WINNOWING OF MRS. SCHUPING

Lee Smith, THE BUBBA STORIES

Abraham Verghese, LILACS

NEW STORIES FROM THE SOUTH: THE YEAR'S BEST, 1993

Richard Bausch, EVENING

Pinckney Benedict, BOUNTY

Wendell Berry, A JONQUIL FOR MARY PENN

Robert Olen Butler, PREPARATION

Lee Merrill Byrd, MAJOR SIX POCKETS

Kevin Calder, NAME ME THIS RIVER

Tony Early, CHARLOTTE

Paula K. Gover, WHITE BOYS AND RIVER GIRLS

David Huddle, TROUBLE AT THE HOME OFFICE

Barbara Hudson, SELLING WHISKERS

Elizabeth Hunnewell, FAMILY PLANNING

Dennis Loy Johnson, RESCUING ED

Edward Jones, MARIE

Wayne Karlin, PRISONERS

Dan Leone, SPINACH

Jill McCorkle, MAN WATCHER

Annette Sanford, HELENS AND ROSES

Peter Taylor, THE WAITING ROOM